FIRE AND FAE

Duet

By

J.E. Taylor

Fire and Fae Duet © 2025 J.E. Taylor

FIRE & FAE DUET

BOOK 1

WHISPERS OF FIRE AND FAE

Welcome to Solstice City, a place where floating markets shimmer under the glow of rune-powered streetlights and where fate pulls sworn enemies into an electrifying dance of magic and mystery.

Lanae, a fearsome fae warrior whose blade is as sharp as her wit, fights for the honor of her realm. And Draven, the last of the mighty dragons, hides in human guise, haunted by betrayals that nearly annihilated his kind. When an ancient tether cruelly binds their destinies together, they must forge an uneasy alliance.

In a city bursting with secrets, shifting allegiances and forbidden romances spark against a backdrop of political intrigue stretching its deadly threads across fae and magical realms alike. Yet, a darker danger looms in the shadows of Solstice City. As realms collide and mythical creatures flood the streets, Lanae and Draven, alongside a playful baby griffin named Nero, must unravel the sinister force threatening to shatter the world's fragile balance.

Dive into this thrilling fantasy romance where fire meets fae, magic intertwines with love, and redemption hangs in the balance. Every whisper holds a secret, and every shadow could be an ally—or a foe.

CHAPTER ONE
Fateful Collision

BLOOD DRIPPED FROM LANAE Nightshade's blade as she surveyed the carnage surrounding her. Her muscles protested when she crouched to wipe her sword on the tunic of the last dark fae she had cut down. She stood, taking stock of herself, glancing at the blood covering her armor, making sure none of it was hers. Now that the adrenaline of battle had faded, the weight of combat clung to her, creating a deep ache in all her overexerted muscles. The stench of blood and death filled her nostrils as she gazed over the once-vibrant field, now a graveyard.

Their most vicious enemies had attacked Solstice City.

Again.

She cringed at the bloody carcasses dotting the surrounding fields, the grotesque sight a brutal display of the cost of war. Both comrade and foe had succumbed to death in this latest magical attack, but the kingdom's warriors had stopped their attempted invasion.

Although they had spared the city, they lost another few acres of plowing fields to the tainted blood of the dark fae. Their poison was already leaching into the ground and withering the crops, turning the rich earth into a blackened wasteland. The view of the once fertile land now defiled and lifeless made her chest burn with a sense of loss.

Lanae swore this was their purpose. This was why the dark fae leaders sent their men and women to their deaths at the hands of the Solstice warriors: to poison the land and render the kingdom unlivable. Even with their elemental powers at play, the Solstice City guards couldn't push these dark fae off the fields. It was as if they were building a wall against her powers over nature. Once dark fae blood spilled, she couldn't manipulate the plant life to grow in the desolate fields. The thought of her power being rendered useless filled her with a deep, simmering anger.

Lanae's gaze darted around at the remaining soldiers stabbing the enemy survivors too far gone for questioning. Her heart sank with each scene of violence. She searched desperately for her friends' faces amidst the chaos. Rorik's silver-white hair stood out in the darkened landscape.

He was frantically trying to save one of the injured soldiers, his hands stained with blood.

As if he sensed her stare, Rorik looked up, meeting Lanae's gaze. His stoic expression, which was so opposite of his usual exuberance, shot a sobering twinge to her heart. His eyes held the pain of loss, and his head swung back and forth in a slow arc. The guard he was patching up would not make it back to his family tonight.

She looked away, scanning the other soldiers until her gaze fell on one of the handful of females in the Solstice guard. Elara's golden mane was splattered with blood and gore, but she still had a smile of triumph on her lips and that insane sparkle in her eyes that she usually got during battle. The sight of her friend's unyielding spirit brought a small measure of comfort.

Lanae's shoulders fell with relief. Although she had trained with other soldiers and had a certain superficial camaraderie with them, Rorik and Elara had been the only two she had truly clicked with.

Her relief was short-lived as Elara sent a finger wave and a nod toward the city. Lanae closed her eyes and pinched the bridge of her nose. The reminder that it was her turn to report on the battle made her shoulders sag even more. There would be no rest tonight—not when she had to recount the devastation of yet more crops to the demanding members of the Fae Council.

The council ruled over Solstice City, commanding the army and the citizens alike. Other realms had kings and queens, but they had the council of elders and the members were intolerable where any failure was concerned. And they would see this skirmish as another failure.

Lanae couldn't blame her friend for gloating. If she didn't have to spend the next few hours being grilled, she would gloat, too. She rolled her eyes and gave Elara a nod before she sheathed her swords and abandoned the battleground.

The city gleamed in the distance under the late afternoon sunshine, its towers a beacon of hope amidst the desolation. Although the sight lifted Lanae's spirits, she knew by the time she arrived at the gates, the sun would have set and night would have tossed her blanket over the kingdom.

And tonight was a new moon, when Lanae's lunar powers were at their weakest. The notion gave her goose bumps. She would need to be extra vigilant as she navigated the treacherous road back to the city gates. Her powers might be diminished, but her capability with a sword was as sharp as ever.

LANAE APPROACHED THE GATES, her steps heavy with the day's battles. She put her hand on the hidden pad in the middle of the ancient iron that only those within Solstice City knew about. If a fae touched anywhere else on the door, the iron would scald their skin. It was how the city kept their enemies out. The pad glowed at her touch, cataloging the unique lines and contours of her hand. When the magic in the door identified her, the great gears groaned as they moved into place, unlocking the gate and allowing her entry.

As she moved toward the Citadel in the center of the metropolis, she glanced up at the floating markets teeming with fae and other creatures granted asylum in Solstice City. The rune-powered streetlights glowed, casting a variety of colors on the streets below, transforming the cobblestones into a canvas of shifting hues. The hum of bartering filled the air. It was a comforting token of life's persistence, which was more welcomed than the throes of death she had left behind on the battlefield.

Solstice City shimmered with magic, a vibrant testament to what they were fighting for. Magic that the dark fae wanted for their own nefarious purpose.

She remembered her father, a council member and a diplomat, negotiating the peace talks years ago. Every time they were on the cusp of a deal, another attack would occur, and citizens would die at the hands of the dark fae. Eight years ago, they were close enough to a deal to schedule the signing of the peace treaty. Then everything fell apart. She still remembered that night vividly. She and her brother arrived home from a late evening of school activities to find their home ransacked, and no sign of their parents.

That night, the war bloomed in earnest and all dark fae within the city walls were hunted down and slaughtered. Any portals within the city walls were destroyed, cutting off access to the city. And she was saddled with the burden of raising her brother and finding her place in the world. The Solstice City guard offered her a chance to find herself and earn a living fighting the very creatures who had stolen her innocence.

Every battle since reminded her of what she had lost, pummeling pain through her center.

The wind swirled, whipping the loose strands of her pink and white hair into her face and bringing her back to the present. She wiped her hair out of her eyes just as her shoulder slammed into a stranger, sending a jolt of energy through her and making her sidestep to keep her balance.

Irritation burned through her, along with a lingering tingle of power. But just as her gaze landed on the stranger's emerald eyes, she lost the scathing response poised on her lips. She blinked at the intensity of the stare aimed at her and the crop of fiery auburn hair framing his rugged face. His presence was commanding, his aura exuding a raw, untamed energy that resonated with something deep within her.

His cross expression pulled a muttered apology from her lips, but she could not tear her eyes away from him. There was something disconcerting about his presence, something that both drew her in and set her on edge.

His green eyes scanned her and then returned to hers. "Watch where you're going, soldier."

His tone narrowed her gaze as ire burned through her blood in a zip line of aggravation. *Who does he think he is, speaking to me in such a manner?*

"I could say the same to you, sir." Lanae's hand dropped to her sword, the cold steel a reassuring presence at her side, and she skirted by him. Her knuckles brushed his, and another jolt of power filled her, sparking a curiosity she couldn't quite quell. She continued toward the Citadel, but the encounter had rattled her enough for her to glance over her shoulder.

The man still stood where she had left him, his emerald gaze pinned straight through the center of her being. His open-lipped expression was enough to set her heart pitter-pattering against her rib cage. There was something undeniably magnetic about him, and as much as she tried to shake it off, she knew their paths were destined to cross again.

DRAVEN EMBERWING STARED AFTER the gorgeous, pink-haired fae warrior who had stunned him stupid. Her image lingered in his mind: fierce eyes, a determined stride, and that striking hair cascading down her back in a tight braid woven of white and pink silk, like a wave of dawn and dusk. He had been so thrown from the power surge of knocking into her that all his mouth could come out with was a harsh reprimand. His hand still tingled from where her skin had connected and his pulse continued to gallop inside him, thumping in his ears so loud that the din of the market faded to background noise. The world seemed to shrink to the space between them, her presence overwhelming his senses.

"How much of an idiot can you be, Draven," he muttered to himself as she slipped out of sight. Her departure left an unsettling emptiness. The regret of not even asking her name gnawed at him, a missed opportunity that felt uncharacteristically significant.

He had been looking up at the market, contemplating his route, when he slammed into her. But if he had seen her coming, his brain might have worked well enough to at least get her name. Instead, he was left with the lingering impression of her intense gaze and the electric connection that had sparked between them.

He shook the encounter out of his head and focused back on the market, where he had been summoned, and he also hoped to find a drink to soothe his erratic powers. The bustling market was alive with the vibrant energy of fae and other magical creatures, their voices blending into a symphony of bartering and conversation. With no other dragons left, the responsibility to reclaim the Dragon's Heart crystal fell on his shoulders, a burden that weighed heavier each day.

The Dragon's Heart, an ancient crystal of immeasurable power, had been under the protection of the Emberwing bloodline for millenniums. Its loss had been a devastating blow, one that Draven felt acutely. He had been too young to fight in the war where the Dragon's Heart had been lost. But he still remembered the utter betrayal that befell his kin. It burned as if the fire within him would someday consume him and everyone around him in a blinding explosion of light and flame.

That fateful day, his father had been overcome by black smoke and he handed over the Dragon's Heart, dooming all of them. His mother shooed him into a hiding place and ordered him to stay put until she came to retrieve him. He stayed, even when the buildings surrounding him were nothing but ashes. Ashes that blanketed over him, hiding him from the enemy. He stayed even after the last dragon fell from the sky and was slaughtered with swords and arrows. He stayed after the last of the enemies left and nothing remained but smoke and the dead. The memory of his mother's desperate final command haunted him, a memento of the innocence lost that day.

But even today, Draven could still see that wicked, white-haired fae gloating as he held the Dragon's Heart and fed off its powers, killing all those around him he deemed an enemy, including the dragons. The fae's laughter, twisted with malevolence, echoed in Draven's nightmares, a constant sign of the vengeance he had yet to claim.

That fae had been in his home, plotting war strategies with his father, pretending to be an ally. Time only deepened the wound inflicted by that betrayal.

That fae had cursed his father and led an army against the dragons, destroying his family, his actions searing into Draven's soul.

That fae had forever tainted Draven's view of fae as a species, turning what might have been respect into seething hatred.

Draven would much rather deal with an ogre than a fae any day, and twice on Tuesdays. Especially considering he had tried for centuries to find that white-haired traitor and turn him to dust. But that fae was as elusive as the wind. The hunt for the traitor had consumed him, driven him to the brink of madness, and yet, it had also given him a purpose.

As he continued through the market, the encounter with the pink-haired warrior lingered in the back of his mind, a puzzling enigma he couldn't quite shake. Despite his loathing for fae, there was something different about her, something that called to a part of him he thought long dead. But for now, his focus had to remain on the Dragon's Heart and the vengeance he had sworn to deliver.

CHAPTER TWO
Dragon in Disguise

INSTEAD OF CONTINUING TO the Citadel, Lanae diverted to her home. It would be in poor taste to step inside that pristine building with the blood splattering her uniform and boots. The thought of tracking dirt and battle grime into the hallowed halls made her cringe. As she approached her childhood home, she sighed. The building still shined with its pristine marble walls, broken by thriving vines that crawled all the way to the roof. In the spring, they bloomed the most beautiful moonflowers of white with accents of red and blue on the edges of the petals, their fragrance a hint of better days. Her gaze drew to the door and her family crest, a moonflower enveloped by thorns, which announced their status as diplomats.

However, she did not have a diplomatic bone in her body, even though the council expected her to. She was too caught up with raising her brother and trying to unravel the mystery behind her parents' disappearance. It had been eight years since she and her brother had come home to find the house in disarray and no sign of their mother or father. No one in Solstice City had information regarding what had happened. It was as if they had just snapped out of existence, leaving a void that nothing could fill.

With all their connections, neither the council nor the guard were any closer to solving the secrets of her missing parents. The frustration of hitting dead end after dead end gnawed at her, leaving an ever-present ache in her heart.

She inhaled deeply and let it out as she cracked the entry open. Before she could even close the door, her younger brother, Caelum, bounded down the hall. Although Lanae looked more like their mother with her silver-blue eyes and pink and white hair, Caelum was the spitting image of their father, with his jet-black hair and liquid blue eyes. Someday, he would make some woman happy. But for now, she pushed him to excel in his studies and not let his attentions wander.

She braced herself for impact, and he slammed into her, wrapping her in a tight hug. His embrace stole her breath.

"I saw the battle," he whispered against her ear, his breath tender and comforting. "But I did not see how you fared, and I couldn't reach you with my mind."

He trembled in her arms, and she squeezed a fraction tighter before pushing him gently away.

"I'll always return home." She tried to ease the fear in his eyes, but she knew better. Their insecurity flared when not in each other's sight. The bond they shared was a lifeline, a tether that kept them grounded.

His eyes narrowed at her. "You shut me out again."

Lanae raised her eyebrows at Caelum. "If I don't, it could be distracting." Any time she battled, she shut down the connections to reach her telepathically. Distractions in the middle of a fight could be fatal, and Caelum knew it.

He sulked. "Usually, I can sense you. But this time there was nothing, and I thought the worst."

She sighed. "It's a new moon."

"Yeah, well, I didn't even feel you when you were within the city walls."

Guilt pressed down on her. "I'm sorry. I didn't think to open my mind back up. I was focused on what to say to the council." She glanced down at his shirt, which now held traces of grime from her armor. The sight of blood on him twisted something deep inside her. "It looks like we both need to change before I head off to report on the battle." She closed her eyes and erased the barrier in her soul that she had put up prior to combat.

Warmth flooded into her mind, followed by Caelum's relief. With the connection between them reestablished, the comforting presence soothed her frayed nerves.

Thanks, sis. Caelum's voice filled her senses, bringing a small smile to her lips.

"I need to get changed." She squeezed his hand and then headed through the entry and down a short hall to her quarters. The familiarity of her home comforted her weary soul.

Green and violet shades greeted her as she opened her door. The softness of her room took the edge off. By the time she had cleaned the blood off her skin, patched the various scratches from combat, and changed out of her armor, she felt more like herself than the fierce warrior persona she adopted in the fields beyond the gates. The transformation back to her everyday self was always a jarring, yet necessary ritual.

As she unbraided her hair, the day's events crawled under her skin, a persistent itch she couldn't scratch. The dark fae fought without emotion, as if they were only going through the motions and not waging war.

None of it made a lick of sense.

Lanae decided she needed a detour before she recounted the death and destruction of the day to the council.

One that would give her the steel spine she needed in front of those critical fae.

And she knew exactly where to go to get that resolve. Mystic Spirits. Home of some wildly psychedelic cocktails. The thought of their potent drinks brought a hint of a smile to her lips at the promise of a temporary escape from her responsibilities.

DRAVEN CLIMBED THE FLOATING stairs to the market. The air was thick with the aroma of spices and magic, a heady mix that made his senses tingle. He slipped into the tent advertising mind-bending cocktails. The fabric entrance fluttered shut behind him. Inside was dark enough for his eyes to shift, allowing him to see clearly in the dim light. Shadows danced across the walls, creating an atmosphere of mystery and intrigue. He wasn't sure who he was meeting, but he had a feeling whoever had sent him the note hinting at a secret he'd want to know would recognize him in a flash.

He sauntered to the bar and leaned against it, waiting for the chipper bartender with the million-dollar rack to notice him. Her bluish skin radiated under the dull lights, and he blinked his eyes back to his human persona. He didn't want the djinn to see any part of his true form. The last thing he needed was to attract unwanted attention.

Draven caught her eye, and she grinned, flashing blinding teeth. She sidled up to him, nearly salivating, as her gaze raked over him. Her eyes sparkled with a predatory gleam, and he could almost feel her hunger.

He tried not to scowl. All he needed was a djinn to latch onto him with empty promises just so they could sink their teeth into his flesh. Djinn fed off the essence of others, like a metaphysical vampire. Once a wish was granted, the benefactor became just a feed bag for the djinn.

"What can I get for you?"

Even the purr of her seductive voice prickled his skin, tempting him to make a wish. He just shook his head and surveyed the crowd, trying to ignore the pull of her magic.

"How about I get you the house special?" Her voice dripped with allure.

He nodded without meeting her gaze. A moment later, a stein of liquid slid to the spot in front of him. He flipped a gold coin onto the bar as payment.

The clicking of a tongue from behind the counter drew his gaze. "Gold may mean something on the streets below, but up here we trade in magic or favor." The bartender licked her lips as her eyes grazed down his body, her interest unmistakable.

It had been years since he had been back to Solstice City, and he only returned because his contacts tracked that fucking fae to the one place he swore he'd never set foot in again. His former home. The city responsible for all his nightmares.

"Unless you'd like your neck snapped, I suggest you take that as payment." His voice broadcast a warning that brooked no argument.

The bartender paled at his growling voice, and then she reached out, taking his coin before scuttling away in a rush to busy herself with the other patrons. Draven's presence had a way of unsettling people, and he used it to his advantage.

Draven sniffed the drink. A fruity whiff overtook him, along with undertones of whiskey. His first sip gave way to an explosion of citrus, followed by the sweet bite of alcohol. Smooth. And it wasn't as unpleasant as he imagined. He took a heftier sip and indulged in the sensations on his tongue before he swallowed. Warmth spread through his chest.

"Dragon."

The whisper lifted his gaze from his drink. He scanned the bar, but he could not locate the source of the hushed word. His skin prickled, and he ground his teeth together to stave off his annoyance.

Draven hated playing games.

He turned his back on the crowd and focused on his drink. Out of the corner of his eye, a smoke form solidified on the seat next to him. *Great. A frickin' yôkai.* He pivoted toward the smoke-based being next to him, taking stock of him with a suspicious eye.

"Dragon." The yôkai tilted his head in a sign of respect.

He did not want his ancestry announced here, of all places. "It's Draven. And who the hell told you what I am?" He sent a searing glare at the yôkai.

"Marcel mentioned you and your quest." The yôkai's voice was smooth, almost too smooth, and it set Draven on edge.

Marcel, a sprite he had befriended and ultimately employed as a spy, was one of the few beings alive who knew what Draven was. He also was the one who informed him that his nemesis had been seen in Solstice City. "Why would he divulge that information to you?"

"I am an avid historian, and Marcel came to me for information, and here in Solstice City we deal in magic and secrets." Smoke settled around the yôkai as he shrugged. "I am Varkir. It is nice to meet your acquaintance." He offered another respectful tilt of his head.

Draven studied the gray-skinned man, from his sallow cheeks to his near-white eyes and then the rags hanging off him as if he remained in some ethereal wind that Draven couldn't feel. He fished in his pocket and produced the note that had been on his pillow when he returned from the baths this morning. "I assume this was you?"

A smile formed in the smoke surrounding Varkir and then settled onto his face. "Indeed."

"What secret would I be interested in?" He pocketed the note and took another sip of his drink. He just wanted to get back to his room, take off his boots, and stretch out in bed with a good book. Being out amongst the fae made him itch to let his fire loose.

"I see there's no foreplay with you," Varkir sneered at him.

Draven's lips tilted into a smirk. "I'm not interested in foreplay. I'm just here for information." He sucked in another sip of the drink and let the flavors soothe the burning in his veins.

Smoke puffed out of Varkir's mouth, along with an audible sigh. "You are no fun."

"You want to have fun? Engage with the bartender." Draven nodded toward the pretty djinn. "After you tell me what you dragged me to this godforsaken tavern for." Draven sliced a warning glance at Varkir.

"I've heard rumblings that a very dangerous stone has fallen into the wrong hands."

Draven's heart rate picked up. "What stone?" he asked with genuine curiosity, his interest piqued.

Varkir's mouth widened into a strange smoke smirk. "I see that sparkle in your eyes. But no, it is not the Dragon's Heart. The gauntlet stone is much more dangerous than that gem."

A commotion at the door pulled Draven's gaze away. He caught sight of pink hair, and whatever Varkir was droning on about faded into background noise. By the time he looked back at the seat next to him, Varkir had disappeared again.

For the second time today, that pink-haired fae caused aggravation to flow through his form like a vibrating piece of metal.

LANAE STEPPED INSIDE MYSTIC Spirits. The familiar hum of conversation and clinking glasses washed over her. A couple of her fellow warriors made catcalls at her, their voices a mix of camaraderie and teasing. They still had their blood-soaked armor on, whereas she was all cleaned up enough to face the council. She shushed them with a wave of her hand. A small smile played on her lips as she headed toward the only free seat at the bar.

A head of striking red hair slowed her approach until he had the audacity to shoot a dagger-filled glare over his shoulder at her. That one look brought the ire to the surface, but she would not shy away from a drink because of an overbearing dickhead.

She slid into the seat next to him, aware his gaze still tracked her movements. Lanae gave a wave to Nicoli, the bartender who she also played dice with once a week in the city's women's group. She started to attend after her parents vanished to distract herself from the constant urge to uncover the truth. It also gave her insight into the different species that lived in Solstice City apart from the fae.

Nicoli approached with a scowl aimed at the man sitting next to her. Instead of chatting, she put the house special in front of Lanae. "Heading to the council?"

"How'd you guess?" Lanae replied, trying to keep her tone light.

"News travels fast. It's on the house." Nicoli nodded toward the drink and then dipped her head in respect before returning to the rowdier crowd at the other end of the bar.

The man next to her snorted as he tipped his drink to his lips. The sound grated on her nerves.

She finally speared her gaze at him, and her breath locked in her chest. Fiery-red hair, emerald-green eyes, not a freckle to be found on his tanned skin. His strong, chiseled chin jutted out with arrogance at her study of him. This close, he was the most attractive man she had ever seen. Too bad his personality did not match his stunning physique.

She took a breath and sipped her drink, savoring the flavor and the way the alcohol slid down to her stomach, heating everything it touched. "You have something to say?" Lanae's voice carried the edge of irritation.

"Nope." Hostility radiated off him in waves. He tilted his glass as if draining the cup and then slammed it down on the counter. He side-eyed her as he wiped his lips with the back of his hand, the gesture dismissive.

"What did I ever do to you?" she demanded, her patience wearing thin.

He swiveled the seat toward her, and his knees brushed hers. A jolt of energy rushed through her like a lightning strike, leaving her breathless.

He jerked back and stared at where their knees had touched. He blinked and then met her gaze, his eyes narrowing.

The rush of energy petered out into a tingling sensation, but it didn't go away like it had on the street below. It sizzled like a lit candlewick hitting the last of the wax.

His eyes shifted to reptilian citrine with an elongated pupil before snapping back to the bright-green eyes they had been moments ago. Although she had seen many differing species here in Solstice City, she had never seen eyes shift like his just had.

"What are you?" The din of the bar almost drowned out her voice.

"I could ask you the same." He rubbed his knee absently.

The deep timbre of his voice layered over her like a cozy blanket. "I am fae." She straightened her back and flipped her hair over her shoulder, ignoring the gooeyness inside her triggered by his spoken word. She had never had cause to swoon before, but this man's voice nearly undid her.

His lips pinched into a tight line, and he slid off the chair as if he were going to leave. He hesitated, and his head shook back and forth as if he were reprimanding himself. Then he spun on his heel and faced her. "I'm sorry. I've had a pretty trying day today. I'm Draven Emberwing." He bowed in salutation, the gesture surprisingly formal.

She stared at him, and her brain stalled. "I'm not royalty," she sputtered, feeling foolish.

A dimple appeared in his cheek and then his face transformed as his lips curved into a smile she could stare at for hours. "You're a warrior, are you not?"

Heat flushed her cheeks, and she focused on her drink, taking a sip to gather her wits. "Yes. Lanae Nightshade." She dipped her head before her gaze found his again. "I have not seen you around before."

His grin slipped off his face. "Solstice City does not carry pleasant memories for me. It's been years since I've graced these walls."

"Well, I hope this time your view of our city changes." She finished her drink because she had delayed the inevitable long enough. "Maybe I will see you again," she added as she slid off her stool, the words tinged with a hint of hope.

"May I escort you to where you're headed? These streets can be dangerous at night." He waved toward the door with a genuine offer.

"I'm a fae warrior." She raised an eyebrow, challenging his chivalrous offer.

"Yes. But a woman walking the streets alone at night...that's an invitation for trouble."

It was her turn to shine a smile at him. His pupils devoured his irises, and he stepped back as if her pearly whites were too bright for him to deal with. "Trouble avoids me like the plague."

He chewed on the edge of his lower lip, the gesture almost endearing.

"As much as that sounds divine, I need time to formulate my thoughts. I'm heading into what will probably be a grueling few hours of being drilled regarding battle tactics by fae who have never once picked up a sword and stepped into a combat situation." She offered a conciliatory smile. "And I need to have my wits about me."

Confusion marred his brow. "And my walking with you..."

"You're distracting," she blurted, and then covered her mouth with her hand. Her eyes widened and her cheeks burned with embarrassment.

He bowed at her again. "Then perhaps our paths will cross again at a less distracting time for both of us."

Lanae forced her legs to move away from him, even though she would rather have had another few hours getting to know the sexy man who made her heart skip beats with just a smile. But she was sure that would wear thin, especially if the cockiness he oozed kept hitting her like a blunt-edged sword.

Instead of heading down the stairs and approaching the Citadel from the streets below, she cut through the market. Just before the stairs leading to the ground level, something in the alley to her right caught her eye. She stopped and retraced her steps, curiosity piqued.

She squinted into the murky darkness, trying to make out what she thought she saw.

Movement had her striding into the darkness of the alley. She halted, her eyebrows shooting up in surprise.

Lanae crouched, her eyes narrowing as she peered into the shadows of the alley. "Hey there." She held her hand out, her voice soft and soothing. When the small creature hopped out of the shadows, she almost pulled her hand back in surprise. The shock of seeing a miniature griffin pumped a shot of adrenaline through her, melting every inch of her skin and making her heart race.

The little griffin's cuteness rivaled anything she had ever seen, with its small lion-like body and eagle head. One wing differed from the other, as if it had been damaged. The little guy must have fallen out of a nest somewhere because he was only as big as her palm. Despite its condition, the griffin's eyes were bright and intelligent, and full of curiosity.

Lanae kept her hand still, her heart aching at the vision of the injured creature. The baby griffin hopped closer, cocking its eagle head to the side, studying her with an unblinking gaze. Its big, bright eyes stared at her, and it took her finger in its beak, testing it. The touch was light, almost like a tickle, and when it released her and squawked, she couldn't help but chuckle.

"Come on, little one. I can't just leave you out here for the cats to eat." Her voice filled with affection, as if she had already made up her mind to protect the tiny creature.

The little beast tilted its head the other way, as if considering her offer.

"I've got a nice warm pocket here in my coat that you can relax in while I recount my day to the council." She opened her coat, showing the griffin the inviting space.

The griffin pounced into her hand, its little razor-like claws retracting so they wouldn't tear her flesh. It was as if the baby was protecting her from any damage. The movement was quick and sure, a leap of faith from the tiny creature.

Lanae stood and ran a finger over the griffin's soft head, feeling the delicate feathers under her touch. The griffin purred, a soft, rumbling sound that sent a wave of tenderness through her. "I shall call you Nero." The name felt right, a powerful name for the little survivor.

She slipped the baby griffin into her pocket and glanced inside to be sure the creature settled. It turned around three times, its movements deliberate and careful, before tucking its good wing in. Lanae carefully tucked the other wing into place, hoping it would heal, and petted the beast's head once again, her fingers lingering on the soft feathers.

A content purring came from her pocket. She smiled as her heart melted. She continued her journey toward a very uncomfortable grilling by the council.

CHAPTER THREE
Echoes of Hatred

DRAVEN'S NERVES PRICKLED LIKE a thousand tiny needles as he watched Lanae leave the bar, her flowing pink hair casy to discern in the low light. The clamor of the crowded room faded into the background, his senses narrowing to her every move. He rarely acted on his impulses, but one glance at his empty drink clinched it. He had no reason to stay in this overly crowded bar, suffocating beneath the noise and heat. He cast one last glance before melting into the shadows hugging the walls.

He spotted Lanae in the sparse crowd outside, her vivid hair standing out against the sea of muted tones. He kept pace with her, darting from shadow to shadow, the cool night air doing little to calm the tempest brewing within him.

Why am I doing this?

The question relentlessly echoed with every step. Even though he kept reassuring himself that he was just making sure she arrived at her destination safely, he knew it was a load of bull.

The woman had some sort of spell over him, a magnetic pull he couldn't resist. His heart dropped to his stomach when she stopped and backtracked to the opening of a dark alley. Draven stilled where he was, blinking in exasperation as she was swallowed by the darkness. His heart thundered in his ears, each beat reverberating through his entire being. He tilted his head, trying to catch any sound, but the pounding of his pulse made it impossible.

When she stepped out of the alley, she had a griffin perched delicately on her palm. He gawked at her with slack-jawed amazement. The tiny creature's wings fluttered before it nestled into her pocket, a surreal sight that made his eyelids flap just as fast as his heart. Lanae resumed her stride, heading toward the towering structure in the middle of the kingdom—the Citadel. The grandest and most unique building he had ever seen, with woven trees as part of the structure, it blended nature with architectural marvel, rising higher than all other buildings in the city.

When he finally tore his gaze away from the Citadel, Lanae was looking at him with narrowed eyes, and his heart stuttered. He hadn't realized she had stopped and turned, catching him off guard. His stalking skills were certainly rusty these days.

"Are you following me?" Her voice cut through the night like a blade.

His cheeks heated, and he glanced at the ground, searching for a viable answer that wouldn't anger her. He opted for honesty. "I didn't feel right letting you traverse this market alone." He forced himself to meet her cutting glare. "And you should never step into a dark alley like that," he scolded, his voice laced with annoyance at her lack of self-preservation.

"I am perfectly capable of defending myself." Her hand dropped to her sword's hilt in a clear warning.

He arched an eyebrow at her as he approached. "And yet you befriended a griffin. A notoriously unstable animal." He folded his arms and gazed down at her, trying to mask his concern with a stern expression.

She bristled and swept her hair over her shoulder. "He's just a baby, and he's injured." She swiveled and resumed walking, her steps brisk and determined.

This time, he kept pace by her side, even when she gave him a warning glance.

"I told you I needed to be poised tonight."

A smile toyed on his lips. He liked that he distracted her, because she certainly distracted the hell out of him. He hadn't even thought twice about what Varkir had told him before she walked in.

"Yes. You did. But I find I am going in the same direction, so instead of stalking behind you like some sort of creep, I'll just walk with you, so I won't be distracted by wondering if you arrived safe at your destination."

"Ah. So, you admit to being a creep?"

Draven snapped in air, checking his flare of irritation as he gazed at her profile, searching for a smart comeback. But nothing came to mind. "No. And I need my wits about me in the Undercity," he muttered.

Lanae recoiled, stepping away from him as if his words were poison. Her pouty lips turned down even more, a frown deepening on her face. She picked up her walking pace, putting distance between them.

"What?" Draven grumbled, his irritation rising.

Lanae spun toward him, her eyes blazing. "Only criminals frequent the Undercity." She marched faster.

"Or those trying to find what a criminal has stolen." He snarled at his loosened tongue, cursing his inability to keep his emotions in check. He clamped his lips together and matched her stride, his aggravation blooming and pulling fire close to the surface. Smoke snorted out of his nostrils as he tucked his chin to his chest, trying to maintain control. Losing his cool within the city proper would be disastrous. Draven collected himself and chanced a sideways glance at Lanae.

She matched the hurried gait he was setting. Her brows furrowed as she stared straight ahead. Her presence was like fuel to his inner fire. "What was stolen?" Her voice exploded with tension.

"A family heirloom." He shot a glare at her. The words tumbled out of his mouth unbidden, making him wonder what the hell that djinn had put in his drink.

"Oh, crap."

Draven's gaze followed Lanae's stare to the door of the Citadel, which stood open with a tall fae holding it in place. The fae's face was scrunched in disgust as he inspected Draven, his contempt unmistakable.

Draven knew when he had overstayed his welcome. "It has been a pleasure, Lanae. Perhaps we will meet again." His voice was tight with tension. He peeled away from her, heading down the nearest alley to avoid whatever unpleasantries were sure to come based on how the fae had set his glare upon them.

A longing scraped his skin, a desperate urge to turn back and be near Lanae. But he couldn't afford to be under the scrutiny of the Fae Council. It was bad enough he had a compulsion to be near her, almost as if she were a shiny treasure that belonged in his care.

Draven shook his head with a growl. "What the fuck is wrong with you?" he muttered to himself, his frustration boiling over. He stalked off toward the black market, determined to find out as much as he could about the mysterious stone Varkir had mentioned.

LANAE DIDN'T DARE LOOK away from Faide Frostvale, the head of the Fae Council. His usually stoic features were marred with barely concealed anger, his violet eyes blazing with such force that her skin prickled. She reached into her pocket, her fingers trembling as they brushed over the griffin's soft feathers, trying to calm her mounting nerves. The tiny creature's warmth provided a slight comfort amidst the storm brewing around her.

"We are in for an awful couple of hours, Nero." Lanae forced a smile onto her lips as she neared the grand doors of the Citadel.

"Who was that?" Faide's voice dripped with disdain. His gaze slashed to the alley Draven had disappeared into, his pale lips curving downward in a scowl as a breeze ruffled his silver hair.

She did not dignify him with an answer, instead asking, "Why?"

His glare pinned her down, his eyes narrowing. "If you hadn't noticed, we are at war, Captain Nightshade. Fraternizing with strangers could put you in a situation where you are charged with treason."

"Excuse me?" Lanae gave him an incredulous look, her hands popping onto her hips in defiance.

"Why were you talking with him?" He crossed his arms, his icy stare demanding an answer.

"I was being polite," Lanae retorted, slashing a side-eye at him as she crossed the threshold into the interior court of the Citadel.

"Did you get the stranger's name?" Faide pressed, his persistence wearing on her nerves.

He would not let this go, and Lanae sighed. "Yes. Draven Emberwing."

Faide's brows scrunched together, and he closed the door with a definitive thud. "Emberwing?" he muttered under his breath, the name cutting through his foul mood and sending him into a moment of introspection. He strutted away without further admonishment, leaving Lanae to follow.

She was grateful for his faraway look instead of that hawk's eye glare he had fixated on her the moment they came within sight of the Citadel. She hurried to keep up with him as he led her through the atrium into the belly of the building, where an enormous tree sprouted from the ground, its branches reaching all the way to the top of the Citadel's tower. The air inside was thick with the aroma of wood and ancient magic.

A winding staircase carved into the bark spiraled upward, and Faide led the charge up the stairs. Halfway up the dizzying climb sat an arched doorway leading to the council court, carved within the great tree. The council seats were masterpieces in the wood surrounding the council floor, where guests and dignitaries voiced their grievances or where Lanae would submit to all their questions.

Even the guest seats were meticulously carved to match the elevated council seats. Every one of them looked like they were woven from tree limbs, even down to the carved leaves. Lanae slipped out of her coat and laid it across the table where witnesses usually sat. But tonight the gallery was empty, and Nero would be safe from being crushed. Only the council graced this hall, and all their eyes were on Lanae.

Faide took his seat, and his vision cleared enough for that annoying pinched expression to return. He leaned forward with narrowed eyes, and Lanae knew her small reprieve had ended.

"What delayed you from reporting to the council, Captain Nightshade?" His voice was a biting blade, cutting through the silence.

Lanae took a breath, steadying herself. "First, I did not wish to grace this pristine hall with my enemy's blood staining my uniform. And second, I stopped for a drink on the way here to help clear my head of the destruction so I could relay the details of the battle to you."

"And in doing so, you engaged with a stranger." His words fell over the council, and now all eyes homed in on her, the weight of their scrutiny pressing down.

Lanae kept his gaze and nodded. Anything other than honesty might bite her and words would only make things worse.

"An Emberwing, no less," Faide added with a sneer.

But it was the council's reaction to that name that made Lanae pause. At least half the council flinched, their eyes widening in shock.

"I thought the Emberwing bloodline died?" Caitan Windysprite, the eldest of the council, leaned forward. Her gaze locked onto Lanae, as if she could shed some wisdom on the situation.

"He was next to the only available seat at the bar." Lanae lifted her shoulders in a shrug. "And he offered to escort me through the market. He apparently mistook me for a helpless maiden."

A few of the council members smirked, a ripple of amusement breaking the tension in the room, and Lanae allowed herself a small smile.

"And yet you allowed him to accompany you." Faide leaned back in his seat and crossed his arms. His narrowed eyes relayed his suspicion.

She clenched her jaw and straightened her back. "No. He followed me."

"Why?" Faide's voice lashed in a piercing command rather than a question.

"Misplaced chivalry." Frustration laced her words. "Are you more interested in my interactions with this man than the battle losses we incurred?" Irritation snaked into her voice. She knew this would not be a pleasant grilling, but she would have preferred to focus on the battle rather than Draven Emberwing.

"Considering the increased attacks on our realm, we are interested in any stranger to Solstice City when it coincides with an attack." Faide's words struck like a whip.

"He was inside the city when I returned from the battle. None of the attackers made it through our defenses."

"None that you were aware of."

"No. My defenses around the city are solid." Her voice was firm, but doubt gnawed at her mind.

"Tonight is the new moon. Are you certain your abilities to secure the city didn't have any weaknesses at this point in the lunar cycle?" Faide's question was a dagger aimed at piercing her confidence.

"Yes." Lanae answered without hesitation, though his question dug under her skin like a parasite, fanning the flames of her frustration.

Faide relented and nodded, but the disappointment pinching his lips was unmistakable. "Please refrain from engaging with strangers," he instructed. His tone left no room for argument.

"Yes, sir."

He rolled his hand at her, a silent command to continue. "Tell us about the breach today."

"Fifty dark fae crossed through the barrier. Less than the last attack, but they seemed concentrated on our grain crop this time. We lost a good ten acres to their poison blood, along with a half dozen of our soldiers." Although Lanae's voice was steady, their losses pressed heavy on her heart.

"And you cannot heal the land?" Caitan asked.

"No, ma'am. Their blood seems to render the land barren. My magic cannot penetrate it." Heat rose in Lanae's cheeks. She abhorred failure. And not being able to resurrect the crops after battling with the dark fae was a stain on her abilities.

"How many acres have these attacks devastated so far?" one of the mousier council members in the back asked.

"We've lost close to a quarter of our farmlands to the dark fae." What Lanae did not add was if this continued, the people of Solstice City would start to feel the impact. And a starving population could not defend the city for long.

CHAPTER FOUR
The Market of Shadows

DRAVEN STALKED THE STREETS of the Undercity, his senses on high alert. The bustling vendor stalls were a riot of color and noise, selling everything from bottled dreams to enchanted weapons that were illegal in most cities he had visited. Solstice City's magical black market was far more flamboyant and in-your-face than the Undercity he remembered. The scent of exotic spices tickled his nose and the faint hum of dark magic clung to the air.

He had no recollection of such blatant displays of debauchery from his youth in Solstice City. His memories painted this area in shadows, with clandestine meetings held in dark, hidden corners. Now, the black marketers had become bold without the oversight of dragons keeping them in line. His chest squeezed with a pang of regret. If his kin had not lost the Dragon's Heart, these streets of wickedness would not exist, let alone flourish.

Centaurs pranced around, announcing the various magical weapons they forged. Knives that could cut through bone and sinew as easily as butter. Swords that would paralyze the enemy with the first draw of blood. Axes that could render trees into wood piles with a single swing.

Draven hesitated at a centaur's stall, his eyes lingering on the shimmering weapons. The magical axe would make winters so much easier, and the other blades glistened, tickling his dragon's fancy. The urge to purchase all the shiny banned weapons was strong, but he forced himself to offer a polite nod before moving on. Besides, a dwarf was already bartering for the axe.

The next few stalls were manned by a group of kobolds selling various deadly potions. Draven almost missed the small sprites buzzing about the bottles with different labels. One potion boasted it could kill with just a drop. Another announced it created the most painful, prolonged death known to all the realms. A third painted a nasty picture of a trap that slowly ate away at the victim's skin. Although every potion could be helpful, the user faced an equal risk of experiencing the same outcome as their target. Draven shivered and moved beyond the kobold's wares.

He blinked at the next section of the black market. Djinn lounged on soft chairs, selling wishes attached to sexual favors for any passerby. Draven caught an eyeful of bare skin and his body responded.

How long had it been since he had been with a woman?

He shook his head, snarling at the fact that their magical caress almost made him forget his purpose here. He stalked away from the lewd display, smoke drifting from his nostrils. The temptation to cleanse this den of debauchery clawed at his skin, but he couldn't reveal his true nature to this city. Not without death coming to claim him.

The next section of the market reminded Draven of any fae market he had ever been to, except for the magical wares they were peddling. The soft colors calmed him, but the proximity to fae breaking the law made his palms itch to strike out. Perhaps this was where Alestain Firetwill, the fae enemy his contacts had tracked to Solstice City, was hiding.

A jolt of adrenaline surged through Draven's body at the thought. He would happily destroy this entire place to kill that bastard. He moved through the growing crowds, shuffling through the fae section of the shadow market. Beyond the fae, the market dimmed enough to hide the hideous goblins, but he saw them clearly in the gloom. This was more representative of what Draven expected from a black market, and the goblins did not disappoint. Within their stalls sat an array of crystals and stones, each one glowing with a magical signature.

"I'd love to get my hands on the gauntlet stone," a goblin within the stall said.

Hadn't that been what Varkir had mentioned in the bar? Draven stopped outside the shop and glanced at the two goblins leaning against the back table. He stepped inside the dark space, eyeing the one who spoke. His diminutive size belied his viciousness. The gleam of his sharp nails in the ambient light hinted at the harm a goblin could do if they attacked.

He picked up a smooth black cylinder from the nearest table, its surface cool and almost silky to the touch. He inspected it, his eyes flicking over the intricate runes etched along its length while his ears strained to catch more of the goblins' conversation. His heart burst into a gallop, each beat a thunderous drum that threatened to drown out any useful snippet of information.

When nothing more was said, he risked a glance at the two goblins. Their conversation had ceased, and their attention was now fixed on him. The same goblin who had mentioned the gauntlet stone stepped forward, his gray eyes gleaming with greed. "Are you interested in the obelisk?" He motioned to the cylinder in Draven's hands.

Draven placed the cylinder back on the stand with a deliberate slowness, his mind racing. "Not really," he replied, his voice even despite the surge of adrenaline coursing through him. "I'm more interested in what you know about the gauntlet stone."

The goblin's gray eyes widened in shock, the reaction making his green face even more grotesque. His mouth opened and closed a few times, as if he were a fish out of water, before he collected himself. The hesitation spoke volumes, and Draven felt a flicker of triumph. He had touched a nerve.

LANAE ROLLED HER SHOULDERS as she headed toward home, trying to shake the tension from the council's grueling interrogation. All she wanted was to take Nero home and get him a bowl of milk or whatever the little griffin ate to keep himself strong. But her feet had a totally different agenda.

She wanted to corner the man who had gotten her into such trouble and find out what the hell he did to this city to drive the council into such a frenzy. And she wanted assurances he had nothing to do with today's attacks. Draven Emberwing was in for the battle of his life if he had any part of the assault.

Lanae marched down to the Undercity, her steps determined. Vendors shied away from her as she strode through the alleyways, her hand resting on her sword, leaving a trail of silence in her wake.

It had been ages since she graced these unscrupulous pathways. As a ranking member of the Solstice City guard, frequenting the Undercity was frowned upon. On her one and only trip to this haven of immorality, she had accompanied her father on a mission to find a cure for their sick neighbor. One that wasn't available in the floating market, where the city inspectors roamed freely to ensure only items deemed legal were sold.

But here in the black market, anyone who upheld the law was at risk. That's what her father had said, and from the glares she received all around her, she wondered whether she should have changed into something more subtle. Her skin prickled with danger the deeper into the Undercity she went.

She reached out with her magic, but it was weak with the new moon, even with the amount of earth underfoot. A glamour or illusion at this point would be a waste of her power. The eyes following her would see the trickery, and their hostile stances might bloom into something she couldn't control or defend.

She hurried along, sweeping her gaze over the crowd to pick out the largest beings in attendance. But none of them was Draven. She passed the djinn's tent, and her footsteps slowed at the lewd scenery on display. Heat engulfed her, and her thighs pressed together before she could tear her eyes away from the enticements surrounding her. She licked her lips. Her mind momentarily clouded from the seductive atmosphere.

Lanae?

Caelum's voice whispered in her mind, jolting her back to reality. She blinked, focusing on the path in front of her.

What is it, Caelum?

When will you be home? His hushed voice spoke of his insecurities about being left alone for too long.

She had the same issues when he was out of sight for so long. *I won't be much longer. When I get home, I have a surprise for you.* She smiled and ran her fingers over Nero, receiving a purr in response.

Okay. Be safe.

Lanae's gaze drifted around her. She was not being safe at all. *See you soon.* She sent the thought to him, blocking out the angst filling her as she entered the goblin section of the black market. Her hand tightened on the hilt of her sword as her senses tripped on high alert.

A growling demand came from her right, and her gaze darted in that direction. A redheaded giant had a goblin pinned to the wall with a death grip on the goblin's throat. Another goblin lay on the ground, dazed, his chest heaving up and down. The air crackled with tension, and Lanae's heart pounded.

"What the hell are you doing?" Lanae stepped into the booth, her sword forgotten in the heat of the moment.

Draven snapped his head in her direction, his blazing eyes glaring at her before they surveyed the area behind her. "Fuck." He dropped the goblin and reached for Lanae, his movements urgent and desperate.

She tried to pull the sword out of the scabbard, but his hand clasped her wrist with a vise-like grip and yanked her toward him. An explosion of electrical heat hit her, sending tingles through her skin. Before she collided with his chest, he turned and practically dragged her through a sheet blocking a back passage.

Lanae resisted, her muscles tensing despite the tingling sensation his hand produced. She glanced behind her at an angry mob surrounding the shop, carrying weapons meant to kill. Every one of their gazes was pinned on her, their eyes filled with murderous intent.

The sheet dropped, blocking the view, and she stopped fighting his grip. She turned on the speed, almost passing Draven in the tight alley. He kept pace with her, his hand still holding her arm in a punishing grip.

The light grew dimmer and dimmer the farther they ran, until she couldn't discern the shadows from the buildings. Draven skidded to a stop, pulling her with him before they both slammed into the brick wall in front of them.

"Damn it." He let her go and twirled toward the opening they had just flown out of. His gaze darted from side to side, searching for an exit, but the only exit was the alley they had come from, now lit by the approaching horde. They were cornered.

"I thought you knew where you were going." Lanae pulled out her sword and readied herself for another battle.

"There used to be a pathway out from the back of the stalls." He swept his hand through his hair, frustration etched into his handsome profile. Even in the low light, his eyes glowed like fiery embers, sending her heart into a frantic beat.

"Focus." His voice was so soft that Lanae didn't know whether he was talking to himself or to her.

She turned her attention to the alley just as mercenaries armed to kill entered the dead end, fanning around them.

"Well, well, well."

The crowd parted at those words, letting a man holding a double-headed battle axe enter the half circle surrounding them. His presence was menacing, his eyes filled with a violence that eclipsed even Draven's and her own, creating a chill of doubt along her skin.

"What have we here? A Solstice City guard?" He grinned, revealing a blackened tooth on the right side of his mouth surrounded by yellowing teeth that weren't far behind the decayed one.

Even at this distance, the stench from his mouth reached her, sending a shiver of revulsion up her spine. The dark fae in the fields smelled better than this man's breath.

"Did you get lost?" he prodded. "Or did you envision this night on your knees, sucking my cock?" His smile widened in a grotesque display of arrogance.

Draven's chest rumbled with a low, dangerous growl.

The man twirled his sword, missing one of the others standing too close to him by mere inches. "As soon as I'm done filleting this beast, I'll expect you to be a good whore and surrender."

Lanae let out a laugh, her defiance cutting through the tension. "You have no idea who you're dealing with."

He narrowed his gaze and tossed a small vial toward them.

Lanae yanked her powers to the surface, and vines shot from the earth, catching the glass before it could smash. They receded into the ground with the man's potion, neutralizing the threat.

His sneer turned feral, and the group charged as one. Their weapons gleamed in the shadowy light.

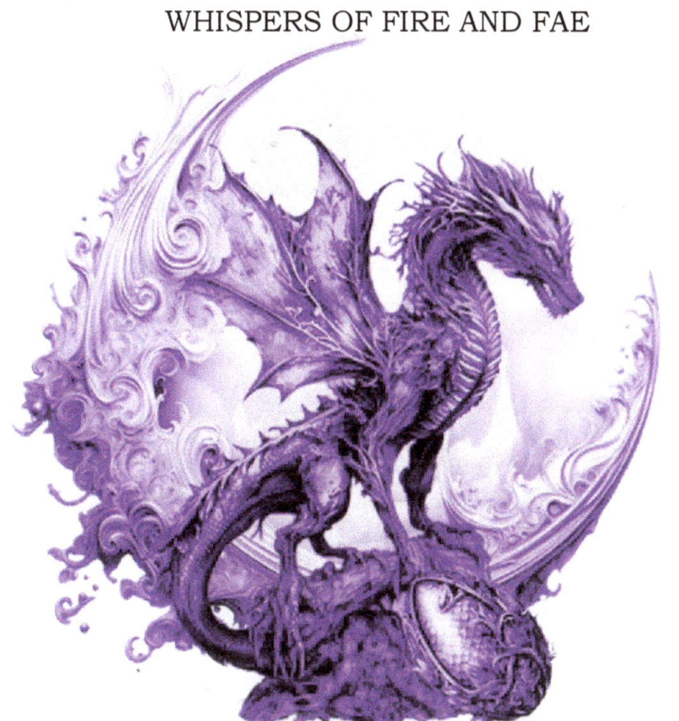

CHAPTER FIVE
The Fate Bond Revealed

LANAE CUT THROUGH THE first wave of mercenaries with a fierce precision, her blade moving as if it were an extension of herself. They fell before her just like the dark fae sent to attack Solstice City, each strike fueled by her determination. Amidst the chaos, she caught sight of Draven, swinging his sword with a deadly grace that momentarily distracted her.

Pain lanced through her shoulder, snapping her focus back to the fight. She parried, catching the steel of a sword and blocking a hit aimed at her neck. Twirling out of the way of another deadly strike, her back collided with Draven's, sending a jolt of electrical energy buzzing through her and stealing her breath away.

The mercenaries tightened their perimeter, closing in for the kill. But before the next strike could land, a wall of fast-moving mist engulfed them, curling up into the sky like the eye of a hurricane, leaving Lanae and Draven untouched at its center. The mist swirled and shifted, creating an eerie, protective barrier around them.

When the smoke cleared, the ground was littered with unconscious mercenaries. A hag with a walking stick emerged from the haze, picking her way through the downed attackers, her eyes fixed on Lanae and Draven.

Lanae pressed closer to Draven, taking strength from his solid back and the rumbling growl vibrating through him. Neither of them lowered their swords, their tension radiating through the small space between them.

The woman's wrinkled skin reminded Lanae of the elders on the council she had just left, but her eyes were entirely white, lacking iris or pupil, as she floated closer to them. An unsettling aura of ancient power surrounded her.

"Who are you?" Lanae demanded, her voice steady despite the adrenaline coursing through her veins.

At the same time, Draven snarled, "What are you?"

"I am Azula of the Bloodworth clan." She bowed to Lanae, a gesture that seemed more mocking than respectful. "I am a powerful witch." She nodded at Draven. "And the two of you caught my attention."

Her grin made Lanae shift uneasily.

Draven glanced at Lanae over his shoulder, their eyes meeting in a shared moment of distrust.

"Why?" Draven's voice rumbled against the buildings surrounding them as he returned his steel gaze to the witch.

"Because it has been a very long time since I've seen a fate bond like you two have." The witch looked between them, her gaze falling to Lanae's pocket before bouncing back to Lanae's face.

"What did you do to them?" Lanae pointed at the men on the ground, ignoring the disturbing words the witch had just thrown out. She did not believe in fate bonds, and it was better to dismiss that information for now.

"Mist of forgetfulness. When they wake, they will be sufficiently confused and will never associate you with this farce." With each step closer, her inspection of them caused her lips to twitch into something resembling a smile. "I have never seen one so bright."

"What are you talking about?" Draven snapped.

"A fate bond," Azula said.

"I heard you. Explain." Draven moved his sword toward the witch, halting her progress.

"Fate bonds don't exist," Lanae said. But instead of pointing her sword at Azula, she sheathed the metal and reached into her pocket to make sure Nero was okay. He nuzzled her palm and purred, bringing a momentary sense of relief. Lanae let out a breath and refocused on the witch.

"On the contrary, fae warrior. You have a unique fate bond to this man, and the fact that the tether is bright with reds, greens, and yellows, like fire wrapped around an ivy vine, shows the strength of that bond."

Draven tensed, his gaze narrowing with suspicion. "Fate bound to a fae?" He shook his head. The way he pronounced "fae" sounded more like a slur. "No."

The witch cackled, the sound echoing off the alley walls. "Yes. And you must accept the bond and work together to strike down the ancient malevolence that is stirring now that the gauntlet stone has been located."

Draven's hand shot out, snatching the witch by her throat and bringing her close to his face. "What do you know of the gauntlet stone?" His eyes blazed with anger.

"Put her down." Lanae drew her sword and pointed it at Draven. "This is exactly how we got into this mess." She nodded toward the fallen mercenaries, her voice calm even with the tense atmosphere.

Draven growled but complied, placing the witch back on her feet.

She stepped away from him, clearing her throat, and offered Lanae a nod of thanks. "The gauntlet stone can create or destroy realms, and it seems the person seeking it right now wants to destroy realms. If they merge the realms into a single instance, everyone who survives is bound to the holder of the stone. We become slaves who can never be freed."

Lanae's jaw slackened as the witch's words sank in. "I am no one's slave." Her voice filled with a dark defiance.

"You will be unless you two can stop the merge. The gauntlet stone must be destroyed before the merge is complete," the witch explained, her eyes serious and unwavering.

The only thing that made Lanae believe the witch was the desperation creeping into her voice. "Where is it?" Lanae asked.

"I do not know. I only know that the destruction side will be initiated soon, and we have little time before worlds collide," the witch replied, her tone grave.

"How do we destroy it?" Draven demanded, his voice a throaty growl.

The witch stared at him for a long moment, as if weighing the consequences of her next words. "Only royal dragon fire can destroy the gauntlet stone."

Gooseflesh broke out across Lanae's arms. "Dragons were killed off years ago. Besides, dragons nearly razed Solstice City. If any existed, the council would know, and they would hunt them down until the last of the species were annihilated."

The witch cut her gaze to Draven, raising an eyebrow.

"A fae slaughtered this entire city when he stole the Dragon's Heart." He glared at Lanae, his voice filled with bitter anger. "The fae were responsible for whatever befell this city. Not the dragons. We were needlessly slaughtered, all because of a fae's greed."

Lanae's gaze narrowed, her suspicion mounting. "We?"

Draven's eyes shifted to burning infernos, and smoke drifted from his nostrils. He ground his teeth as a growl formed in his throat. "Yes. We."

Mother of all, he was a damn dragon.

CHAPTER SIX
Mounting Tensions

DRAVEN STARED DOWN AT Lanae's wide eyes and snarled. She reeked of fear, a scent that mingled with the acrid smoke still lingering in the air. The chirping hiss in her pocket diverted his gaze, which was a good thing because he was sorely at a loss in the control factor right now. If he had any more surprises sprung on him, he might toast the entire neighborhood and then the fae would surely know an Emberwing survived.

Before either of them could turn on each other, the witch cleared her throat; the sound sliced through the tension with the precision of a scalpel. "The freedom and survival of this entire realm is at stake. You need each other in this battle. Otherwise, we all will suffer." She crossed her arms and glared at them, her eyes burning with an intensity that matched the fire in Draven's veins.

Draven sheathed his sword with a sharp click and adopted the same closed-off stance that Lanae sported: arms crossed, brows lowered in a glower. Hostility radiated off her, matching his near boiling temper. As much as he was attracted to Lanae, there was no chance in the underworld that he was ever going to put his trust in her.

"Stay close to each other, because I plan to test the strength of that bond. And my simulated threats will do harm if you do not work together against them. You must show the same trust you displayed here against these thugs." She waved at the mercenaries, still unconscious on the ground, their bodies sprawled in unnatural positions.

Lanae sighed, a sound filled with resignation and frustration. "I need to get home."

Azula's lips twitched up at the sides in a knowing smirk. "Then it looks like you are dragging a dragon along with that little griffin home with you." She turned to leave, but paused and glanced back at them. "Oh, and practice your dancing, because there may be some intel on the gauntlet stone at a grand ball on the morrow. I expect to see you there."

And then she was gone, leaving Draven with this infuriating fae whose touch sent tingles through his form straight to his dick. He didn't know whether he wanted to throttle her or fuck her. From the look on her face and the white-knuckle grip on her sword, *she* wanted to kick his ass.

"I would prefer that you did not know where I live."

"I'd prefer that, too. But the witch made it clear we need to stay close." Draven waved for her to lead the way, his hand trembling with the effort to keep his temper in check.

Lanae pointed him forward, her eyes narrowing with suspicion. "You go first."

Draven palmed his face and dragged his hand over, sighing. Now that she knew what he was, having her behind him didn't settle well. "I don't trust you behind me."

Her hands fisted, and her cheeks flushed an angry red. "I trust you just as much. So, side by side. That way, our backs aren't exposed."

Draven gave her a curt nod. He'd actually rather have the view in front of him, but he understood her aversion to being vulnerable. Side by side, they strolled through the cramped alleyways, with shadows enclosing them like a suffocating shroud. This time, Draven took his time to be sure he took a path closer to the exit of the underground market. He didn't want to risk more murderous forces.

"I have no idea how I'm going to explain you to my brother," Lanae mumbled, her voice registering above the echoing footsteps. "He'll be excited about Nero, but you, not so much."

Draven let her carry on her monologue for most of the walk through the maze back to civilization. His attention focused on potential threats. As they got closer to the exit, he rumbled a growl to quiet her down.

She slashed a glare in his direction, her eyes flashing with defiance. "Do not tell me to be quiet. I had the grand inquisition about you in front of the council, so I have had enough of judgment, sarcasm, and killing today. Otherwise, I would put you down in an instant."

Draven stopped walking and stared at her with his heart pumping double time. "The council?"

Lanae stopped a few paces from him and turned, her lips softened from her tight frown. "Yes. The head scrooge who saw you walking with me asked a dozen questions about the stranger I was with and if you had any connection to the attacks today."

"And what did you tell them?"

"That you were concerned for my well-being and walked me from the bar to where we parted."

"Did you say anything else?" He stepped closer, towering over her as agitation burned through his veins.

"Like what?"

"Like my name."

She bit her lip and took a step back before nodding. "He asked."

"Fuck." His growl echoed on the stone walls around them. If the council knew he was alive, it would get to the fae who stole the Dragon's Heart, and it wouldn't be long before he showed himself and this entire city burned to the ground.

Lanae's eyebrows rose, and her mouth popped open in a cute little O that distracted him from his rising panic.

"If I am cut down before we destroy this gauntlet stone, there is no hope. I'm the only dragon royal left." He raked his hands through his hair and started forward, passing her and giving her his back, despite his internal warnings.

LANAE STARED AFTER HIM, her gaze dropping to his nicely formed ass before bounding back up at his words. *If the witch had been truthful with them, this man, this dragon, was the one the witch said could stop this madness?*

The thought sent chills down her spine. On the heels of that thought, she realized she wanted to know his story now that his secret had been revealed. That kick-started her feet forward. She caught up with him as he entered the Undercity near the centaurs, the air heavy with the scent of damp earth and the distant clatter of hooves.

She gripped her sword, ready to attack anyone who came at them. But no one even looked their way as they slipped out of the black market and up into the streets of Solstice City. The transition from the shadowy Undercity to the bustling streets above was jarring. The noise and light assaulted her senses. When Draven went to turn toward the Citadel, she grabbed his arm to point him in the opposite direction and a pleasant rush of tingles gripped her. She lived closer to the city gates and the floating market than she did to the Citadel.

"Huh." His voice rumbled. "You don't live in the fancy houses around the Citadel?"

"No. I live in the home that my parents raised us in before they disappeared." She dug her hand into her pocket and cradled the baby griffin. The little creature calmed her nerves, and she would need a clear head to explain Draven to her brother without telling him everything.

With a deep breath, she led him through the maze of modest homes, the narrow streets lined with weathered stone and ivy-covered walls. The scent of blooming flowers mingled with the distant hum of the floating market. They reached her street, and she spun on him, jabbing her finger into his chest. "Behave."

Draven lifted his hands in surrender, but his expression reminded her of an enemy about to attack. His eyes glinted with a dangerous light, and she could feel the heat radiating off him.

"I will wrap you in thorns if you scare my brother. Understand?"

He grumbled, and his eyes blazed with enough fire to make her step back. "If a plant so much as trembles while we are inside your house, I will burn your entire world down." He stepped closer, encroaching on her space. "I am dragon royalty, and I do not answer to the fae."

"You're sneaking around my city like a terrorist." She narrowed her gaze up at him. "Were you responsible for the attacks today?"

"No. I don't command the dark fae. As a matter of fact, I'd rather see them burn along with the remainder of the traitorous fae here in Solstice City. And now that your precious council knows my name, it won't be long before someone comes to burn this city down again. Because your council cannot be trusted." He turned his back on her, both his fists clenched, smoke drifting around him like a dark aura.

"What do you mean?" Lanae asked as she focused back on him.

"The fact an Emberwing lives will not be kept a secret, especially since your kind wiped out all the dragons and half this city in their bid for power. So not only do we have to find the gauntlet stone, but we need to find the Dragon's Heart to avoid yet another fucking disaster." He turned his flaming eyes in her direction.

His piercing stare made her heart race. "Gauntlet stone first." That seemed to be the priority, especially if the witch could be trusted.

Draven nodded and lowered his head. His hands slowly uncurled, and the tension in his rigid stance eased. After a few beats, he turned back to her, eyes glowing a vivid green. He gave her a curt nod, the light from his eyes casting eerie shadows on his chiseled features.

Lanae spun on her heels and marched to the third house on the block, with Draven following her. Her skin prickled the closer she came to the house. She still did not know how to explain the hulking man trudging after her. His hostility radiated from him in a way that unnerved her. If she could feel it, no doubt Caelum would as well.

Before she got to the door, it swung open and Caelum stepped into the doorway. His smile faded at the sight of Draven, his eyes narrowing with immediate distrust.

"Is that the surprise?" he asked with obvious disdain.

Lanae reached into her pocket and pulled Nero out. The tiny griffin chirped in her palm, drawing his attention. "No. This is."

Caelum's smile returned. The tension in his shoulders eased as he moved to get a closer look at the griffin in her palm. "He's cute, but that still doesn't explain the guy behind you."

Lanae bit her lip and glanced at Draven, whose gaze was fixed on her with a ferocity that made her heart race. "He lost a game of darts at the bar, and this was what he had bet. He wanted to be sure Nero here had a good home and wouldn't get abused."

Draven cocked an eyebrow at her and then nodded, a smirk playing on his lips. "It was a draw, and you distracted me on my tie-breaking throw."

He glanced at her brother and gave him a tilted smile that sent heat through Lanae. She wondered whether the dragon was capable of a full smile and if it would have the same panty-melting effect on her.

"Draven, this is my brother, Caelum. Caelum, this is Draven. And he was just leaving." She corralled Caelum inside and closed the door, but Draven stopped its progress with a firm hand.

"I'd like to see the inside of the house where my pet will live. If it isn't the right atmosphere, I'll have to figure out a different way to pay my debt." He flashed that tilted smile again. "Besides, it will give me a chance to extend an invitation to the ball tomorrow night."

"A ball?" Caelum glanced between Lanae and Draven.

Lanae grumbled and then nodded as her gaze slashed from Draven to her brother. "Yes. There seems to be a grand ball hosted by the magocrats."

"And you got an invitation?" His eyes sparkled with interest as they locked with hers.

Lanae and Caelum had heard about the grand balls, but only those on the council and the inner court ever received invitations. They didn't let people in the doors without one. Lanae faced Draven and raised an eyebrow, suspicion etched on her face.

"I received an invitation." Draven's smile widened from that half smirk, and it certainly had the intended effect she thought it would. Her knees wobbled with the near swoon.

Caelum regarded him with skepticism, looking him up and down as if his clothing did not meet the bill of an elite. Distrust painted his face as he glanced Lanae's way.

I don't trust him. His voice resounded in her head, the telepathic message clear.

Neither do I. Her thought escaped before she could pull it back, but Draven was already inside their house, his presence filling the small space with an almost tangible sense of menace.

DRAVEN GLANCED AROUND THE small house, noting every detail with a warrior's precision. The space was messier than he expected, cluttered with the telltale signs of a lived-in home. Books, trinkets, and various items were haphazardly piled on tables, as if dropped with the intention of putting them away but never quite making it there. Living with a teenager must account for some of the disarray. Plants lined the walls, their vibrant greens and soft petals adding a pleasant scent to the air—lavender and rose, much like what Lanae smelled like.

Ignoring the discomfort radiating from both Lanae and her brother, Draven refocused on Lanae and swallowed the sudden jolt of protectiveness that flared inside him. He kept his smile in place and remembered the bogus reason he stepped into the house. "This looks like a good home for my pet." He nodded toward the griffin in her hands, trying to maintain a casual demeanor.

Lanae glanced at him, her expression a mix of uncertainty and defiance, as she crossed to the front door. The moment she turned the knob and drew it open, a dense fog slipped into her house, separating them from her brother and enveloping them in a thick, suffocating haze. The air grew icy, and an eerie silence fell over them, broken only by the faint, unsettling cackling that echoed in Draven's ears, reminiscent of the witch in the alley.

His senses heightened. Draven's muscles tensed. Every instinct screamed at him to be ready. Their time was up. The first test was already upon them. The impending danger pressed down on him like a physical force. He stepped closer to Lanae, his body a protective barrier between her and the unknown threat lurking in the fog.

Cackling echoed louder, surrounding them, making it hard to pinpoint its source. Shadows shifted and twisted in the mist, creating menacing shapes that danced just out of reach. Draven's eyes flicked to Lanae, meeting her wide gaze. For a moment, their shared dread hung as thick as the surrounding fog, binding them in a reluctant alliance.

He drew his sword. The blade gleamed in the light filtering through the fog. "Stay close." His voice was low and steady, despite the adrenaline surging through his veins.

Lanae nodded, her grip tightened on the griffin as if she could shield the creature from whatever the witch threw at them.

With every step, the tension grew. The oppressive fog closed in around them as if the very air conspired to trap them. Draven's chest throbbed, but he forced himself to stay focused. This was just the beginning, and he would not fail. Not when so much was at stake.

CHAPTER SEVEN
Hell's Maze

DRAVEN WIPED HIS FACE, the dampness mixing with the sweat beading on his brow. He stepped closer to Lanae. She held the griffin to her chest, and a crease of concentration appeared between her eyes as she closed them.

Her brother's muffled cries echoed behind them.

Draven could almost hear her soothing her brother, though no words were spoken. When she opened her eyes, her brother's calls calmed, a quiet demonstration of their kinship.

"Telepathic?" he asked.

"With my brother, yes." She met Draven's gaze with a determined glint in her eyes and placed Nero on her shoulder before drawing her blade.

Tension crackled like an electrical current between them. Although they had each other's backs against the mob in the Undercity, this was different. Trusting a fae was not something he was used to doing, especially one with a sword.

"What do you think she has planned for us?" Lanae's voice carried an undercurrent of unease.

"Who the fuck knows." Draven stepped outside. The door creaked as he closed it behind him. The familiar weight of steel in his hand comforted the anxiety making his skin crawl. He moved next to her, waiting for the witch's twisted game to begin.

The fog that enveloped them cleared, revealing an entrance to a maze made of tall, dense shrubs. The foliage was dark and foreboding, and shadows played tricks on their eyes.

"Together, you must find your way through this maze. But beware. Death awaits on the wrong path." The witch's voice slithered into their minds, chilling them to the core.

"Great," Draven groaned, his frustration tangible. He glanced at the deep frown on Lanae's face, mirroring his own sentiments.

"I've had enough death today, thank you very much," she muttered, her words laced with exhaustion. Yet, despite her weariness, she stepped into the opening.

Draven followed, his blade resting on his shoulder, the metal catching the dim light. At the first intersection, Lanae turned left, but his instincts screamed at him to go right.

"That's the wrong way." He let his frustration bleed into his tone.

She cast a look over her shoulder and raised a single eyebrow, a gesture that ignited his frustration. Yet he remained in place, unwilling to move in her direction despite the witch's warning.

Lanae slowed, her eyes narrowing. "That is the wrong way." She pointed at the path he had chosen and then disappeared around the corner.

"Damn fae," he muttered and walked around the opposite corner. As he took another step, Lanae appeared a few feet before him with her sword at the ready and a sneer on her lips. But it was the pouch crossed over her shoulder that caught his attention. The Dragon's Heart poked out of the bag.

He roared, the sound primal and raw, and swung his blade. Steel met steel with a clang that reverberated through his entire body. She had the audacity to grin and spin out of his reach, taunting him.

A tickle in his mind diminished the hot fury filling him. He blinked as she swung her blade. He blocked the shot, but a burst of pain bit his shoulder. He pushed her back and glanced at the blood running down his trailing arm. He blinked at the crimson staining his shirt. There was no way her blade reached that arm.

When she came at him again, he blocked her blade with his and stepped closer, reaching for her throat.

His hand went through her, breaking up the illusion. Draven's heart lurched. Although the mirage had not landed her blade on him, he was bleeding.

"Fucking hell." He spun and charged in the direction Lanae had gone. When he rounded the corner, her back was to him and he stalled at his own image attacking her. He switched his blade to his left hand and grabbed her around the waist, pulling her away from the fight despite her thrashing in his grip.

On contact, a jolt of electricity ran through him, turning into a pleasant tingle. Before he could evaluate the sensation, his image charged. Draven thrust his blade into the center of the illusion where a heart would be and the image shattered, leaving a dead ogre attached to the end of his sword.

Lanae quieted, staring at the fiend before glancing up at Draven, her back pressed against his chest. Her wide eyes held a mixture of relief and awe.

Draven yanked his blade free and pulled Lanae back around the corner to where they had separated. His gaze fell on the cut on her upper arm, the same one that mirrored his own. A chill gripped him, and his eyes locked with hers. The reality of their connection sank in.

"I think that definitely was the wrong way to go." He nodded to where they had just been, his voice grim. The maze loomed around them, a sentient reminder of the dangers they still faced.

She blinked up at him, and Nero poked his head out from under her hair, his tiny beak clicking. Then she twirled out of Draven's grasp and huffed. Her breath came in short, gasping bursts. "Are you so sure?" She waved at his bleeding arm, the crimson staining his sleeve.

Draven glanced at his wound, the pain a dull throb. "My illusion never landed a hit." He brought his gaze back to hers, his eyes narrowing. "I would wager it happened when yours did."

Her eyes became glaring slits in response, a spark of anger ignited in their depths.

"We need to stay together," Draven said. The urgency of the witch's instructions spurred him on. "Otherwise, we are likely to encounter much more upsetting images than you taunting me with the Dragon's Heart."

She snorted at him, a sound filled with disdain, as if he had done this just to screw with her. "My illusion was you murdering my parents." She jutted her chin defiantly, as if his aggravation meant nothing in comparison.

He stepped closer, a growl rumbling in his throat. "Whoever holds the Dragon's Heart killed every one of my kind, including my parents and my siblings." He towered over her, his presence overwhelming.

Nero chirped and held out his chest, as if mimicking Draven trying to intimidate her. The tiny griffin's bravado was almost comical, a significant departure from the tension crackling between the two of them.

Draven's eyebrows rose at the sight. A flicker of amusement broke through his anger. Lanae hadn't caught the little creature's antics, but instead of irritating him like it normally would, he found some levity in the little fellow. "I think your friend has an affinity for making fun of me." He cocked his head and let a hint of a smile play on his lips. "Does he have a death wish?"

Lanae glanced at Nero, catching him with his puffed-out chest. She looked back at Draven without cracking a smile, her expression hard as stone. "If you think about harming him, I will cut off your hands."

The venom in her voice ignited, sending a rash of irritation over his skin and turning his good humor to ash. "I'd like to see you try," Draven growled low and headed down the row of hedges, back to the area he had fought her illusion. He paused at the entrance, his eyes dark and intense. "Are you coming?"

The air between them was thick with unresolved tension, each step they took a battle of wills. The maze loomed ahead, a labyrinth of danger and uncertainty. One they had no choice but to face together.

LANAE GLANCED AT NERO as she stepped toward the moody dragon. Her arm stung where it had been cut, the pain drowning out any chance of amusement she might have felt. She did not want to be on this wild-goose chase with Draven. She didn't know him, didn't trust him, and she certainly didn't want a bond with the jackass.

However, if what the witch said was true, Draven was this realm's only hope of avoiding slavery to whomever held the gauntlet stone. And as such, she should protect him from harm instead of threatening him. Unfortunately, her annoyance that he had chosen the right path, and she had not, got the best of her.

They stepped around the corner together, their movements cautious and synchronized, following the path without incident until another split in directions appeared before them. This time it wasn't two trails, but three. The looming hedges cast eerie shadows, and a chill ran down Lanae's spine.

The middle row pulled at her midsection like a magnet. "I think we should go straight," she said.

Draven glanced at all three paths, then his fierce gaze drilled into her. "Why?"

"Do you have a better idea?" she retorted, frustration edging her tone.

He grumbled and inspected the openings again, his brow furrowing in concentration. "I want to know why you are choosing that over the other two."

She sighed, rubbing her temples. "Because it's pulling me that way."

"Like before?" His question was quiet... not a challenge, but seeking clarity.

"No. I didn't have any feeling before." She chewed on the inside of her lip, her gaze flicking between the paths. She faced each entrance, and the pull from the middle one was undeniable. "What way are you leaning toward?"

"I'm compelled to go down the same path as you. But that worries me. It feels too easy."

She huffed, waving her hand at all three entrances. "Two of these paths will lead us to harm."

"I am aware. But I do not trust the witch. Especially when both of us are feeling the same thing. For all we know, it's magically enhanced to lead us to our deaths."

She scanned the openings. Doubt gnawed at her insides as she considered whether to listen to him or trust her instincts. She glanced at Nero, her little beacon of clarity. "Where would you go?"

Without hesitation, his wing pointed to the middle option. She stepped toward the path, and Nero squawked, moving his wing to the farthest opening on the right while shaking his head.

"Are you saying no to both paths?" She gestured toward the middle and right routes.

Nero nodded.

Lanae wiped her face. Her hand trembled with the strain of making the wrong decision again. Her troubled gaze swung to Draven.

He raised his eyebrow, a skeptical look crossing his features. "So, we are listening to the baby griffin?"

She sighed, looking at all three paths, her mind racing. "Have you got a more suitable suggestion?"

Draven shook his head, his expression resigned. "As much as the middle path is pulling at me, I honestly believe we shouldn't go that way. Plus, I think your griffin is attached enough to you that he wouldn't send you into the ogre's den."

"As much as that path is calling, I think you might be right. It's almost like they put a siren in there to manipulate us." She turned to the lane that Nero hadn't said no to, a part of her still curious about the other paths.

Draven laughed, the timbre of his chuckle low enough to bring goose bumps to Lanae. It was the kind of sound that crawled under her skin and took root in the most delicious way.

"I'm just as curious," he admitted, facing back toward the middle trail that called to both of them.

She grabbed his arm as he stepped toward it, and that pleasant jolt of electricity zinged through her. "I have a feeling if we follow the call, it won't be so easy to turn back." Lanae pulled him toward the route that Nero hadn't ruled out, her heart pounding with a mix of fear and determination.

Draven followed with his blade out, his steps measured and silent.

She adjusted her grip on the steel in her palm, testing the weight of her sword as they crept around the next corner. The pathway didn't seem to carry any immediate threat until they rounded another corner that connected with a crossroads midway down the path.

Lanae stepped toward the break in the path, and the ground suddenly gave way beneath her feet. She gasped, her body jolting as she sank. Draven reacted instantly, his grip like iron as he grabbed her arm before more than just her lower leg could sink into the ground. She winced at his grip around her cut, but bit down on her whine of pain, her heart racing.

"What the hell?" She stared at her wet, sandy calf and then at what looked like a solid dirt road before them. Her pulse pounded in her ears. Danger heightened her senses.

Draven sheathed his sword and reached down to scoop up some rocks from the road. He tossed them one at a time on the walkway, watching intently. The earth swallowed each one until the path reached the intersection point. Rocks that landed there bounced away, untouched by the treacherous ground.

"Sinking sand." A frown creased his lips as he glanced at her. The dim light caught the severe angles of his face, making his expression even more foreboding.

Lanae stared at him, then looked at the road before them. "So, this was the wrong path?" Her words were edged with frustration.

Draven shrugged, his demeanor calm, but his eyes alert. "It's not something trying to kill us, but if we fall in, that probably will be the result." He raked a hand through his hair, the movement betraying a flicker of anxiety.

She sheathed her sword and propped her hands on her waist, surveying the problem with narrowed eyes. The oppressive silence of the maze enveloped them, making every second feel like an eternity.

"Before you ask, no. I don't think we should go back and try another path," Draven said, his tone final.

"I would not suggest that." She cut a glare in his direction, annoyed that he had shot down her thought before she even voiced it. "You're a dragon. Why don't you shift and carry me over?"

Draven's cheeks reddened, and he glanced away from her, his jaw tightening. "No."

"Why not?" she challenged, her voice rising.

His eyes turned fiery, burning into hers. "Because I haven't fully shifted in over a hundred years."

His growling voice sent a chill zipping up her spine. She blinked at him. He looked damn good for someone four times her age. If he hadn't given her that information, she would have guessed him to only be a year or two older than her twenty-six years. Heat radiated from his body, and it overwhelmed her. "Well, now is as good a time as any." She pointed to the deadly path before them, while her heart pounded at his proximity.

He stepped closer, crowding her with his presence. "I cannot fully shift. What part of that do you not understand?" Smoke curled from his nostrils.

Lanae stepped back into the thick shrubbery lining the walkway, her back prickling against the rough branches. "Well, what about turning that sand to glass?" she shot back at him, pointing at the quicksand.

He narrowed his eyes, the glow in them fierce. "Do you know how hot fire needs to be to turn sand into glass?"

She shook her head, leaning further back into the unforgiving branches. The tension between them crackled, almost tangible in the air.

"Hot enough that you and everything around us would turn to ash within seconds." He focused on the shrubs surrounding them, his mind clearly working through their limited options. "Is that holding you upright?"

Lanae nodded, her breath caught in her throat at the force of his gaze. He stepped away, still studying the shrubs with such focus that her heart raced.

"You have earth magic, right?"

"Yes, why?" she asked.

"Can you make thick branches shoot out far enough for us to use them to cross to safety?"

Lanae's thoughts whirled, and she licked her lips at his question. She had already used a flare of magic earlier to snag whatever the gang had thrown at them and wasn't sure she had enough power to do what he was asking. "It's a new moon."

A quizzical dent appeared between his eyes before he closed them and exhaled deeply. "Your magic feeds off the lunar cycle?"

"Yes," she answered.

"And you depleted your reserves when you captured the potion before it broke." His eyes opened, and his green irises glowed with understanding.

She nodded. The enormity of their situation bore down on her. The maze pressed in on them, every shadow a signal of the danger they faced and the thin thread of magic they had left to rely on.

"Fuck." He put his hands on his hips.

When she went to speak, he put his hand up, silencing her.

"We don't know how long this damn maze is, and I don't know if we will need that small reserve of yours at a more difficult obstacle." He chewed on his lip. "I could try to burn us a path along the hedges."

"And risk setting this whole maze on fire?"

He huffed. "You wanted me to torch the sand. That would have guaranteed an out-of-control blaze."

His question sparked an idea, and she studied the dense bushes. "What if we used the existing hedges to climb across the sinking sand?" Lanae turned and stepped onto the lower branches of the bushes. She gritted her teeth as she slid her hands into the densely packed thicket, trying to get a good grip. The branches cut into her skin, bringing forth a wince, along with a level of trepidation she hadn't felt since the battle this morning.

She closed her eyes and braced herself before reaching for her next hold.

"It will be slow going, but this way, neither of us has to rely on our already exhausted magic." She hung over the slow death trap below and focused on only her next moment. The feel of Draven's hand on her back almost had her sinking into him, but that would only prolong this torture.

His hand remained until she moved out of his reach.

"Will it hold my weight?" Draven's voice was tinged with doubt as he eyed the branches.

The boughs seemed sturdy enough, but Draven clearly weighed more than she did, with all his sculpted muscle. His broad shoulders and muscular frame were a stark contrast to the delicate branches they were about to rely on.

She looked back at him with a single shoulder shrug. "We could always go back."

"There is no going back." He shook out his hands as if he were mentally preparing himself for the trip across. The persistence in his eyes was clear, even as he tried to mask his apprehension. He tentatively stepped onto the branch she had originally started with and stuck his hands in the bushes.

His wince made her lips tilt into a smile before she focused back in front of her. Step by step, they made their way across with careful placement of their feet, the branches creaking under their combined weight. Each progression was a test of balance and endurance as the thorns dug into their flesh with every movement. Lanae's breath came in shallow gasps; a rapid pulse throbbed in her chest.

Finally, she stepped onto the solid ground of the crossroad. Blood dripped from the multiple gouges on her arms from the merciless branch thorns. The relief of solid ground was tempered by the stinging pain in her limbs.

Draven stepped next to her in the same condition, his arms and chest covered in scratches. "You didn't tell me there were thorns," he grumbled, his voice laced with irritation.

"Would you have crossed if I had?" She ripped a couple of strips from the bottom of her shirt and wrapped her arms to slow the bleeding. The makeshift bandages quickly soaked through, but they provided some relief from the constant sting.

Draven rolled his eyes and then stripped his shirt. His skin glistened in the ambient light, the muscles of his torso highlighted by the silvery glow.

Lanae stopped, her eyes glued to his six-pack of abs, before forcing them to his face. Draven's smirk burned more than the open welts on her arms. Her momentary stun at seeing his near-perfect physique disappeared instantly.

The cocky bastard knew he was beautiful. And now she had to be subjected to his bare chest for the remainder of this ordeal. She finished wrapping her arms and studied the only logical way forward while he tore his shirt and did the same. He tucked the remaining fabric into his belt. "In case we need more." His tone was practical, but his eyes glinted with amusement.

Lanae cast a wary eye roll in return. "Let's just hope we don't need it." She turned her attention back to the path ahead. The maze was far from over, and they needed to stay focused if they were going to make it out alive.

DRAVEN GLANCED AT THE crossroad, the pathways illuminated by the faint, eerie glow of the maze. It seemed as if the other two paths led to the same place, and he wondered whether the other avenues were just as daunting as the one they had taken. The oppressive silence of the labyrinth closed in on him, and the distant rustle of leaves only heightened his sense of foreboding.

"Shall we?" Lanae waved toward the only logical direction, her voice calm despite the tension crackling in the air.

He unsheathed his sword, the metallic whisper of steel a comforting sound. "Let's get this over with." All he wanted was a stiff drink and a soft bed, and the sooner he got through this nightmare, the sooner he could get some much-needed rest. The promise of respite seemed like a distant dream, mocking him with its elusiveness.

She pulled her sword out as well, and they stepped into the path together, their eyes darting around, wary of another test. The labyrinth had been relentless, and neither of them trusted the deceptive calm.

Draven's nerves prickled with each step. He glanced at Lanae and sighed. His fae companion's beauty would be his undoing, especially with her fierceness on display. Her determined gaze and the way she held her sword with such confidence stirred feelings that had long been dormant. Hell, he never believed he would entertain bedding a fae, much less having this protective need messing with his mind the way it had since he bumped into her this afternoon.

He shook the thoughts away and focused on the path ahead. As they approached a jog to the right, his senses launched on high alert. The air seemed to thicken, and from Lanae's sudden stiffness, she felt the thrums of danger, too.

They slid around the corner into an open courtyard the size of the entry to Lanae's house. A single path led out of the enclosure. As they stepped into it, the path they had come from closed off in a rustle of leaves and thorns, trapping them in.

Draven's heart pounded, and he squared himself, waiting for danger. Lanae took the same position, with her sword in the lead. They stepped toward the only exit, and a thick mist engulfed them. The air crackled with energy, making the hair on the back of his neck stand on end. The fog swirled, locking them in place, and when it dissipated, an ethereal being blocked their way.

The eerie being's form shifted and flickered like a mirage, standing twice Draven's height. A long golden whip hung from its belt, and eyes the color of the deepest night glowed out of the palest skin he had ever seen. The being trapped them in the labyrinth's heart, surrounded by shadows which the light couldn't pierce.

Next to the being stood a post with leather cuffs hanging from it.

"You've ventured far, but to proceed, you must each answer three riddles," the being said with a voice made of gravel that echoed in the stillness. A mean smile formed on his lips. "If you get any of them wrong, you will pay in blood."

Dread gathered in Draven's stomach, but he exchanged a determined glance with Lanae. She nodded, her eyes steely with grit.

He stepped forward. "I'll take the questions." He wasn't about to let this being harm Lanae.

"That isn't the way it works. Each of you has to answer three riddles to pass." The entity gave Draven a menacing grin.

"It's okay." Lanae put her hand on Draven's arm.

The tingling electricity sparked through him, and he met her gaze. "No. It isn't."

"We don't have a choice." Lanae squeezed his arm.

A low growl of agreement rumbled in his chest, and he turned to the being. "Go ahead."

The ethereal being's eyes gleamed with otherworldly darkness. "What can be cracked, made, told, and played?"

Draven mulled the riddle over for a moment, then smiled despite his underlying unease. "A joke."

The being nodded approvingly and turned toward Lanae. "What is always in front of you, but can't be seen?"

Lanae was slower than he had been as she repeated the words the being said. After a moment, her eyes lit up with the answer. "The future?"

Another nod. He moved his dark eyes to Draven. "What gets broken without being held?"

Draven stared at the being and then drilled his gaze into Lanae. This one wasn't as easy. It could be many things, but the one that matched up to his lifetime of broken vows bounded to the forefront. "A promise."

When the sentinel turned toward Lanae, a chill of dread bit through Draven, almost like a premonition. His muscles tensed.

"What can be touched but can't be seen?"

Lanae hesitated, then answered, "Air?"

The ethereal being's form flickered ominously. "Incorrect." The word echoed as if the shrubs surrounding them were made of marble.

Draven reached for her, but his hands wrenched down at his side and he couldn't budge.

Lanae gasped, and then her sword dropped from her hand. She moved like a puppet and the sentinel grinned as he unhooked his whip. Her arms shook against an unseen force as they rose above her head and the shackles clasped around her wrists.

"Let me—" Draven's words cut off as the being glared his way and hissed a spell, leaving Draven without the ability to finish his plea. His heart slammed against his rib cage in a staccato beat.

"Don't hurt Nero." Lanae's voice strained with fear, and the little creature disappeared under the cascade of hair as it twirled out of the way over her shoulder.

The crack of the whip made him jerk, and her cry of surprised pain filled him with a fury that ignited the fire inside him. But if he let it loose, the end of the whip would be the least of her worries. Still, smoke billowed from his nostrils as he gritted his teeth through two more cracks as shadows of pain echoed in his own back.

Lanae's shirt sported three bloody rips, and as soon as her arms were released, she hugged her chest and moved back by Draven's side.

"Try again."

Draven's chest torqued at the fear on Lanae's face, and he rubbed his palm on the place over his heart. Her gaze dropped to the motion of his hand.

"What can be touched but not seen?" She rephrased the question and met his gaze. "A heart?"

"That's right." The being turned to Draven, and his laughter was like wind chimes in a breeze. He pinned Draven with a look. "I love the smell of fear."

"Do not make the mistake of thinking this is fear," Draven growled. More smoke rolled from his nose, clouding his vision.

He inclined his head. "What comes out at night without being called, and is lost in the day without being stolen?"

Draven hesitated. This one was harder than the first two. There were a couple of viable answers, and he made a guess. "The moon?"

The ethereal being's form flickered again, and it raised its hand. "Wrong."

The same invisible force that had moved Lanae gripped him in an unforgiving grasp, making him drop his sword and move against his will toward those binds. The moment they bit into his wrists, he growled his aggravation.

Like a hundred bees stinging at once, the whip tore through his flesh, leaving him burning both inside and out. After the third strike, he was released.

"Try again," the being said.

Draven glanced at Lanae, and they both spoke with the answer. "Stars." The concern in her voice matched that in her eyes.

The being's eyes narrowed as he sneered and focused on her. "What thrives when you feed it but dies when you water it?"

Lanae whispered the riddle three times before she finally answered. "A fire?"

The being's form seemed to glow with a billowing darkness. He inclined his head. "One final riddle, and either of you may answer. What welcomes the day with a show of light, and stealthily comes in the night and bathes the earthy stuff at dawn, but by noon is gone?"

Draven and Lanae pondered for a moment. Lanae's eyes lit up as she said, "The morning dew."

The being's form diffused into a less tangible shape as it waved toward the exit. "You may proceed."

Draven retrieved the swords and handed Lanae hers. Hot trails itched the skin of his back. He muttered a curse to the gods under his breath. They stepped from the labyrinth's clutches, with little thought as to what dangers lay ahead.

CHAPTER EIGHT
Caught in a Fib

LANAE WINCED AS SHE stalked forward, pissed at herself for getting the question wrong. Now the sting on her back overshadowed the cuts on her arms. The lash marks from the ethereal being's punishment throbbed with every step, a painful token of her failure. And what was worse, she had felt the bite of fear.

Not for herself. That she could handle. There was always a sense of dread when you stepped into battle. But this was different.

When Draven had been dragged to that post, irrational panic for his well-being flashed through her. She had been gripped by a raw need to shield him, and it had burned deeper than her protective instincts for Caelum. Witnessing the whip slicing through the air toward Draven had ignited a fierce, protective rage within her.

She huffed and wished she hadn't followed the damn dragon to the black market. If only she had listened to her instincts instead of letting curiosity lead her into this mess.

"Care to enlighten me as to what has you stomping toward our demise?" Draven's voice penetrated her reverie, laced with a mix of sarcasm and genuine concern. His attempt to mask his pain was evident in the tightness around his eyes and the stiff way he held himself.

"I wish I hadn't gone to the underground market." Her frustration boiled over. She glanced at the dried blood staining her clothing, feeling a fresh wave of anger at the witch who had put them through this ordeal.

He snorted. "I wish you hadn't either." His voice was flat, devoid of warmth.

She spun on him, infuriated by his snide tone, and pointed her sword at him. Although the idea of someone else hurting the dragon bothered her, she had no qualms about casting a bruising blow. When she swung to do just that, her sword hit his in a thunderous clash. The sound echoed through the maze, a physical manifestation of their pent-up tension. His blow overpowered her, pushing her sword to the side.

Draven stepped into her space and grabbed her chin, tilting her face up. "Are you trying to kill me?"

His low growl produced a heat that the tingle of his touch only increased. "Kill, no. But a flesh wound, that's another matter." Her voice carried every ounce of her frustration.

The muscle in his jaw jumped, and he ground his teeth as he stared down at her. "I already have enough flesh wounds because of you. I don't need any more." His words cut deeper than any blade, filling the space between them with animosity.

He stepped back, and the distance was as dizzying as the sudden absence of his touch.

"Now, if you don't mind, I'd like to get the fuck out of this damn maze and get a decent night's sleep before I procure an invitation to that ball." He looked away from her toward the single pathway, but his sword still held hers at bay.

Lanae relaxed her arm and lowered her blade. "Fine." The word was clipped with resignation, a silent truce.

They stalked down the row of fog-shrouded hedges and back into the entry of Lanae's home.

Caelum almost knocked Lanae over with a hug as the door swung closed behind them.

"I thought I lost you." His voice was full of both relief and worry.

His shaking voice chilled her, and she sought Draven's green eyes, wincing in Caelum's grasp.

"Why are you bleeding?" Caelum pulled away, staring at his hands. His eyes narrowed at Draven.

"He didn't hurt me," Lanae said, defusing the budding aggravation she sensed in Caelum. She laid a gentle hand on his arm, though it did little to ease his concern.

"Where the hell did you go?" Caelum's voice was filled with fear.

Lanae didn't know how to explain the witch's twisted test to her brother and just shrugged. "It's a long story."

"You didn't win a bet, did you?" He wiped his hands on his pants and then crossed his arms as his gaze traveled between the two of them.

Lanae closed her eyes against her brother's angry stare, formulating the words in her head. "No. Draven and I are supposed to stop some apocalyptic event that would leave us all slaves." She cracked a lid, and Caelum's skeptical glare met hers.

"And who informed you of this task?" His eyes landed on Draven and slanted with clear suspicion.

"A witch in the Undercity market."

His gaze snapped back to her as his eyebrow rose higher.

Draven cleared his throat. "The same witch who pulled us into that fog." He waved at the closed door, like that explained the entire ordeal.

Disappointment carved through Caelum's features. "Why him?" His voice was low, hurt.

Lanae cringed and glanced at the shirtless and bloody dragon in their home. "According to the witch, we have a fate bond." The words felt heavy on her tongue, laden with implications she wasn't ready to face.

Hardness replaced disappointment. "Why did you lie to me?"

"My intention was to shield you from all this."

"Like Mom and Dad did?" His arms dropped to his side as his anger filled the room. The memories of their parents' secrets were still raw.

"I should be going." Draven backed away, sensing the rising tension. He glanced at Lanae one last time, his expression unreadable. "I'll pick you up at seven tolls for the ball."

"I'll be ready."

CAELUM STARED AT HIS sister, trying to name the emotions pummeling him. He caught the desire in her eyes when she looked at the stranger. He had read about fate bonds in school but that had been long ago, before his parents disappeared. From what he remembered, they were as rare as a unicorn with wings.

Lanae sat on one of the kitchen stools and began to unwind the bloody cloth from her arms. The fabric stuck to her skin, making her wince.

Caelum grabbed their emergency kit and took the seat next to her, his worry slumping his shoulders.

"Start from the beginning," he demanded, his voice as sharp as a whip. Although Lanae was ten turns older than he, it still didn't settle well that she was the one trying to protect him. He was coming of age soon and would need to find his own path. But for now, he was still her ward, and he'd be the one to patch her up again. He unpacked the first-aid container and then reached for her arm.

She sighed as he dipped a cloth in some disinfectant. The biting fragrance filled the room, mixing with the metallic tang of blood.

"I bumped into Draven at Mystic Spirits before I went to the council," she said with a weary voice.

He waited for more as he cleaned and covered the wounds on her arms, his hands steady but his heart racing. "That doesn't tell me how you found your way to the Undercity market," he pressed.

Lanae turned and offered Caelum her back for him to patch. The tension in her muscles was unmistakable. "He mentioned he was going there and after the grilling the council gave me related to him, I went to confront him. I thought maybe he had something to do with the dark fae attack."

He dabbed a wound, and she winced, pulling away. He followed and continued his task of cleaning and patching her. Each touch felt like an expression of her vulnerability and his responsibility.

"I caught him in a goblin's shop, but I guess I didn't think through going down to the black market in my guard uniform and sword. They are not friendly to Solstice City guards." She peered back at him, her eyes reflecting regret. "Well, we had to make a quick exit and got cornered. The witch saved us and then told us we were fate bonded and had to stop a maniac from merging realms and enslaving us all."

Caelum's hand paused mid-motion, the words sinking in. "Fate bonded? You're serious?" The concept was almost too fantastical to believe.

"Yes," Lanae confirmed, her gaze steady. "And whether either of us like it or not, we are in this together."

"According to the witch."

"Yes."

He finished bandaging her wounds, the gravity of the situation settling in the room. Their world was on the brink of chaos, and the bond with Draven, no matter how unwanted, was now a pivotal part of their survival.

"And what of the ball tomorrow?" Caelum gathered the bloody scraps of his cleaning process, the metallic smell of blood mingling with the sterile scent of disinfectant. He dumped everything into the garbage with a finality that made the moment feel even more tense before packing up their emergency kit.

"The witch said we might find out some information about the gauntlet stone," Lanae replied, her voice tinged with both hope and worry.

"The what?" He washed his hands, the hot water doing little to calm his racing thoughts. The reality of their situation crashed over him like a wave.

"The stone that could make us all slaves to whoever wields it." Lanae leaned on the counter, her shoulders slumping. "I have to figure out what to wear tomorrow that will be glamourous enough for a ball and practical enough to cover all this up." She motioned at the cuts on her arms.

"I'm going with you two," Caelum declared. His tone prevented any dissent.

"Oh no. It's too dangerous for you to be there." She turned down his request with a headshake.

"That's a load of dung and you know it." He pointed a finger at her. "I do not want to be here alone when I can help."

"Caelum," she started, her voice softening.

"No. I am going. I can chaperone you two," he insisted, his eyes hardening with determination.

His hands clenched into fists at his sides, the tension between them thick enough to cut.

Lanae met his gaze, the silence stretching as they stared each other down.

LANAE'S EYES SOFTENED AS she looked at her younger brother. The stubbornness in his eyes was undeniable, a fierce boldness that mirrored her own. Pushing him away would only create more friction between them.

She knew where his fears stemmed from. And she couldn't deny him this request.

"All right." She sighed, relenting. "You can come with us." Her voice was tender but firm.

Caelum's shoulders relaxed. "Good."

Lanae nodded, even though she wasn't convinced it was the right thing to do. "But you have to promise me something."

"What?"

"Follow my lead and stay close. If things get messy, no heroics. Understand?"

Caelum's lips twitched in a small smile. "Understood. No heroics."

They shared a moment of silent understanding.

"If I am caught…" Lanae's voice trailed off with a hint of uncertainty.

Caelum lifted his hand, cutting her off. "I know. Guards are not supposed to attend the balls. But Draven asked you to go, so perhaps that's a loophole you can exploit?" His brow rose, and a hint of mischief played in his irises.

"I'm not sure that is excuse enough to break the rules, especially since the council is already suspect of Draven," she replied, her tone laced with doubt.

The cock of Caelum's head was enough to have her continue.

"Faide saw me walking toward the Citadel with him and gave me the grand inquisition on fraternizing with strangers, especially considering the timing of the attack. Which is why I chased the man down in the Undercity."

Dimples appeared on Caelum's cheeks, punctuating his amusement. "Is that the only reason?"

Heat filled her cheeks. "Don't you dare say a damn thing." She pointed at him, wagging her finger back and forth. "I am not attracted to him."

The snort of her brother's laughter caressed her skin, a teasing sound that made heat encompass her entire face.

"You lie badly, Lanae." He spun away from her, heading toward his room, his laughter taunting her.

Before she retired to her room, she set a small bowl of milk in the corner of the kitchen along with a small box that she lined with a fluffy blanket and placed Nero in the comfortable space. He chirped up at her and hopped to the bowl, drinking a small amount before he settled in the box for the night.

She turned toward her room, her mind racing to the sight of Draven without a shirt. His delicious muscles contracted with each movement. He was a sight to behold, and she wondered whether the rest of him was just as appealing.

She shook the thought out of her head, but her skin had heated enough for her to head to the bathroom and splash frigid water on her face. She met her sapphire gaze in the mirror as she patted the water from her skin. "He may be a looker, but he's an asshole," she muttered to her reflection.

The skepticism in her eyes mocked her attempt at the lie. But she didn't have time to explore this growing need. They had a madman to stop, and she had to decide on an outfit to wear to a magocrat's ball.

A KNOCK ON THE door interrupted her thoughts, and she hurried into a long-sleeve shirt and pants before striding to the door to answer it. Part of her hoped the good-looking dragon had come back to address the insane chemistry that seemed to sizzle between them.

Lanae took a breath and opened the door. Her stomach dropped in disappointment, but she blinked it away and plastered a smile on her face as she took in Elara and Rorik and their alcohol-infused grins.

"Nic told us you had stopped in before going to the council. We figured you'd be back after being drilled by those crotchety bastards." Rorik then produced a bottle from behind his back and, with a hand flourish, proudly displayed the Mystic Spirits label. "Since you never showed, we brought the spirits to you!"

Lanae chuckled. If they knew what she had been through tonight, they would have brought a case instead of just a bottle. She waved them inside and ignored the drag of her dead-tired muscles.

"Caelum was getting antsy, so I came home." She headed for the kitchen with them following behind her. "Plus, I found this little guy on my way to the council, and I couldn't just let him fend for himself." She pointed to the corner where she had set up a little bed for Nero. He lifted his head and cast a sleepy gaze in their direction before his eyes closed again.

Rorik and Elara crossed and stared at the little griffin while Lanae poured three glasses of today's special and took a spot at the table.

"Where did you find a griffin?" Rorik swiped a glass and lounged in the chair next to Lanae.

"In one of the alleys in the floating market," Lanae replied.

Elara snorted, her nose crinkling in that way it always did when she was half-judging, half-amused. "Of course you did. Only you would end up rescuing a mythical creature while running errands. Are you planning to start a petting zoo?"

Lanae laughed, rolling her eyes. "I thought it would add to my collection of oddities." She took a sip and sighed. The warmth of the drink spread through her tired limbs.

Rorik grinned mischievously. "Speaking of oddities, are you going to tell us about that mysterious stranger you met at the bar? Nic was very vague, and you know how much I hate mysteries."

Lanae shot him a knowing look. "Trust me, even I haven't figured that one out yet. Just another enigma to add to my growing list."

Elara's eyes sparkled with mischief. "Oh, come on, Lanae! You can't leave us hanging like that. Was he at least as good-looking as Nic alluded to?"

Lanae smirked and heat brushed her cheeks. "Better. And he had this... presence about him. Like he knew he could make the room bend to his will if he wanted."

Rorik raised an eyebrow. "Sounds dangerous. Or exciting. Depends on the day, I suppose." He took a sip of his drink. "Did you sleep with him?"

"No. Not everyone is like you, Rorik." She speared him with a smirk. He bedded almost every female he met and bragged about his conquests endlessly.

"You should try it sometime." He winked at her.

"Did you at least find him interesting enough to see again?" Elara asked.

Lanae shook her head, smiling. "You two are incorrigible. But yeah, I think I'll likely see him around. He was intriguing. And infuriatingly elusive."

Elara raised her glass in mock solemnity. "To Lanae, our fearless friend, and her endless ability to find trouble and mythical creatures alike."

Rorik and Lanae clinked their glasses together with hers, their laughter filling the room. Nero lifted his head at the sound, letting out a tiny chirp that sounded suspiciously like he was joining in on the toast.

"Who knew griffins were such social drinkers?" Rorik chuckled and reached over to give Nero a gentle scratch behind the ears.

Elara leaned back, a twinkle in her eye. "Well, with Lanae's luck, he'll probably turn out to be some kind of mythical prince in disguise. Just you wait."

Little did they know, her stranger *was* royalty.

"If that happens, you two will be the first to know," Lanae promised, her heart lightening with the comfort of their friendship. She didn't have all the answers yet, but with friends like these, she felt ready to face whatever craziness came her way.

As they settled into easy conversation, Lanae couldn't help but feel grateful. Her life might be chaotic, but it was also filled with moments like these—moments that reminded her of what really mattered.

CHAPTER NINE
Gathering Intel

THE NEXT DAY, LANAE stood in front of her open closet, her hands on her hips as she surveyed the rows of everyday tunics and practical trousers. She frowned, rifling through the hangers in a last-ditch effort to find something suitable for the ball. But no matter how many times she looked, the result was the same—nothing that remotely resembled the elegance required for such an event. She sighed in frustration, knowing there was only one place left to look.

With a determined breath, she called out, "Caelum, can you come here for a minute?"

Her brother appeared at the door, a curious look on his face. "What's up?"

"I need your help." Lanae glanced toward the back of the house. "I have nothing suitable for the ball, and I think the only place I might find something is...Mom's wardrobe."

Caelum's expression softened with understanding. "Are you sure you're ready for that?"

Lanae nodded, though her heart clenched in her chest. "I think it's time. Will you come with me?"

"Of course," he replied, placing a comforting hand on her shoulder.

Together, they made their way down the hallway, each step feeling heavier than the last, as they prepared to enter their parents' room for the first time since their disappearance eight years ago.

Lanae hesitated at the threshold of her parents' bedroom, her hand hovering over the doorknob.

Caelum stood beside her, his expression a mix of tenaciousness and trepidation. "Ready?" His voice barely reached a whisper.

Lanae nodded, swallowing the lump in her throat. "As ready as I'll ever be."

With a deep breath, she turned the knob and pushed the door open. The room greeted them with a faint scent of lavender and old books, a combination that instantly transported her back to her childhood. Sunlight filtered through the curtains, casting a yellow glow on the dust-covered furniture.

Caelum stepped in first, his eyes scanning the room. "It's like they never left," he murmured. His voice carried their shared sadness. "Well, except for the dust." He swiped his finger over the top of their father's desk, creating a clear path among the layers of gray powder covering the surface.

Lanae followed, her gaze falling on the enormous wardrobe that dominated one wall. "Let's find something for the ball." She attempted to focus on the task at hand, but her parents' memories kept invading her head. She crossed the room and opened the wardrobe doors, revealing rows of elegant dresses, each one a testament of her mother's impeccable taste.

Caelum joined her, his fingers brushing against the fabric of a deep-blue gown. "This one would look amazing on you." He pulled it out and held it up.

Lanae smiled. Seeing the dress brought back memories of her mother wearing it to a grand gala. "I remember this one. She looked so beautiful in it."

Caelum let out a gentle puff of a laugh. "You have her grace, you know. You'll look just as stunning."

Lanae's heart thawed at his words, but their parents' absence still hung heavy in the air. She reached for another dress, a shimmering silver one that caught the light. "What about this one?"

Caelum nodded approvingly. "Perfection."

As they continued to sift through the dresses, they shared stories and memories of their parents. The laughter and tears blended in a bittersweet symphony. The room, once a place of sorrow, began to feel like a sanctuary, a space where they could honor their parents' legacy while forging their own path forward.

By the time they had chosen the perfect dress, Lanae felt a sense of closure she hadn't realized she needed. She turned to Caelum, her eyes moist with gratitude. "Thank you for doing this with me."

Caelum smiled, pulling her into a hug. "We're in this together, always."

As they left the room, Lanae glanced back one last time, a silent promise to her parents that she would carry their memory with her, no matter where life took her.

DRAVEN STOOD OUTSIDE LANAE'S modest home, the evening air crisp and filled with the scents of blooming flowers. He adjusted the collar of his tailored suit, feeling somewhat out of his element. The fabric was luxurious, in marked opposition to the rough leathers and armor he usually wore. Tonight, however, was different. Tonight, they had to blend in with the elite of Solstice City.

The door creaked open, and Lanae stepped out. For a moment, Draven forgot to breathe. Gone was the hardened warrior he had fought alongside in the dark alleys and mazes. In her place stood a vision of elegance and grace. Her dress was a deep emerald green, shimmering under the rune lights. The fabric hugged her figure, flaring out gently at the hips, and delicate silver embroidery traced intricate patterns along the bodice and hem.

Draven's heart skipped in his chest as he took in every detail: the way the dress accentuated her curves, the soft glow of her skin, and the shimmer in her eyes. She looked like a queen—a fierce, beautiful queen ready to take on the world.

"Lanae," he breathed, stepping closer. "You look...stunning."

A faint blush tinted her cheeks, and she glanced away, clearly flustered by his admiration. "Thank you." Her voice carried a mix of nerves and a shyness he never expected from her. "You clean up well yourself."

Draven gave rise to a laugh. "I'm not sure about that, but I'll take the compliment." He offered her his arm, feeling a strange but pleasant tingle at the contact. "Shall we?"

Before Lanae could respond, Caelum stepped out, adjusting his own outfit—a neatly tailored suit that contrasted with his usual casual attire. His eyes darted between Lanae and Draven, and protective brotherly concern flared in his gaze.

"Don't forget about me," Caelum said, a playful grin on his face but with a serious undertone in his voice.

Draven cocked his head and sent a questioning glance at Lanae. When she nodded, he acknowledged the younger man. "Of course not."

Caelum looped his arm through Lanae's other arm, creating an awkward but united front as they made their way through the streets toward the grand hall where the ball was being held. The city was alive with the glow of lanterns and the murmur of excited voices, but all Draven could focus on was the woman beside him, and the third wheel, who was her brother.

As they approached the entrance, a surge of protectiveness flared. The night ahead seemed charged with danger and uncertainty, but he was determined to keep Lanae—and, by extension, Caelum—safe.

"We need to act like we belong. Understand?" he asked, his voice low.

Lanae met his gaze, her eyes shining under the soft streetlights. "Understood."

"Caelum?" Draven looked over at him with steely resolve.

Caelum nodded, his jaw tense. "I can do it if you can."

Draven's heart thudded against his ribs as he took a breath and closed his eyes, taking on the air of every self-absorbed aristocrat he ever crossed paths with. His chest expanded and his chin raised. When he opened his eyes, he was ready to enact this farce. They approached the grand steps, and he peeled out his forged invitation, handing it over without as much as a glance at the butler manning the door.

"The invitation is for two," the butler said, eyeing the three of them.

"My date's chaperone." He nodded toward Caelum.

The butler pinched his lips together and tossed the invitation into the stack. "Just make sure he stays to the shadows."

"Of course." Draven inclined his head as they walked inside, letting the tightness in his chest relax.

The lavishness of the ballroom almost overwhelmed him, but he kept his gawking to a minimum. With one glance at Lanae and Caelum, he could tell they were just as impressed by the rich decadence surrounding them as he was. His eyes darted around, taking in the extravagant decorations and the elite guests, each a potential wealth of information or an outright threat.

He leaned toward Lanae, his voice low. "Remember, this is just another ball. So, wipe off the awe written on your face and start acting like we're just here to enjoy the night." His words were meant to pull her back from the edge of impropriety, but they also steadied his own nerves.

She schooled her features into something like boredom, and he suppressed a smirk. He enjoyed her bright-eyed wonder to her current expression, but this was more in line with some of the others they passed.

Caelum had shuttered his expression as well, and he gave Draven a nod of understanding before his eyes surveyed the crowd in a shrewd manner that was well beyond most teenagers he had ever seen.

As they moved through the crowd, Draven kept his senses alert. They were here for a reason, and he wouldn't permit himself to be caught off guard. The pulse of magic in the air and the power of the magocrats surrounded them like a tangible force. They had information to gather, and getting sidetracked due to the opulence was not an option.

CAELUM LINGERED NEAR THE entrance, his eyes sweeping over the sea of guests. His role was to keep an eye on Lanae and to watch out for any unexpected developments. And if needed, provide a distraction. He headed toward the shadows, where chaperones lined up to keep their targets within eyesight.

The grand hall was a whirl of opulence, with chandeliers casting a warm glow over the elegantly dressed attendees. The sound of laughter and conversation filled the air, mingling with the soft strains of a string quartet.

As he watched the swirling dance of gowns and tailored suits, his attention was drawn to a single figure standing apart. She wore a simple gown, yet there was an aura about her that piqued his interest. Her dress, though modest, flowed gracefully around her, and her eyes held a depth that drew him in. She seemed almost out of place among the ostentatious displays of wealth, yet perfectly at ease.

Intrigued, Caelum made his way toward her, his curiosity driving him forward. He had never seen her at the market or at school, and that face was memorable enough. Perhaps the magocrats had staff who collected their goods and tutors who schooled their children. Maybe she held a key to the evening's puzzle, or maybe she was just another distraction. Either way, he was compelled to find out. As he approached, he noted the way she seemed to observe the room, her gaze sharp and calculating, much like his own.

"Good evening," Caelum greeted her, his voice smooth but with an undercurrent of suspicion as he glanced around for her chaperone. No one seemed to pay attention to her. "Enjoying the ball?"

The girl turned to him, her lips curving into a faint smile. "As much as one can enjoy such events," she replied, her tone light but her eyes serious. "And you?"

"I find it more interesting to observe," Caelum admitted, his gaze never leaving hers. "You seemed to be doing the same."

Her laughter sprinkled the air. "Observation can be quite revealing. Sometimes more so than conversation."

Caelum nodded while his heart galloped in his chest. He wanted to get to know this mysterious girl. "Caelum," he introduced himself, extending a hand.

"Arsia," she replied, taking his hand. Her touch was cool, and her eyes held secrets he wanted to uncover.

They stood in silence for a moment, watching the dancers glide across the floor. Caelum's mind raced with possibilities. *Was she an ally, an enemy, or something entirely different?*

"So, Arsia," he ventured, "what brings you to this grand event tonight?"

Her eyes flickered with amusement. "The same thing that brings most people here, I suppose. Curiosity, obligation, and perhaps a bit of intrigue."

Caelum raised an eyebrow, fascinated by her elusive answer. "And are you finding what you're looking for?"

Arsia's smile widened. "Perhaps. The night is still young."

As they continued their conversation, Caelum couldn't dispel the feeling that Arsia was more than she seemed. Whether she held answers to their conundrum or was simply another piece in the evening's elaborate puzzle, he wanted to keep her close. The ball was turning out to be more interesting than he had anticipated.

LANAE TOOK IN THE scene, her breath catching at the sheer beauty around her. The grand ballroom shimmered with opulence—an ocean of golden lights and swirling silks, where nobility and whispers mingled in the air. The chandeliers hung like celestial orbs, casting their glow on the marbled floors that mirrored the vibrant whirl of gowns and coats. Her emerald dress cascaded around her like a waterfall, each step reminding her of the delicate balance she had to maintain.

If any council members recognized her, she was in a world of trouble. She did not have enough power to cast an illusion so she wouldn't be recognized, so she kept to the shadows as much as possible. They needed to find out more about this gauntlet stone, and she scanned the crowd.

No witch stood out, but some familiar faces near the magocrats made her turn away. The critical nature of this mission was at odds with the consequences if she got caught. But in that moment, as Draven approached with a soft smile, everything else faded.

"Shall we?" He extended his hand in an invitation, his eyes sparkling with mischief.

She reached for him, and the same spark of electricity ran through her when their hands met. For a heartbeat, Lanae forgot her purpose. Draven, with his ever-poised demeanor, guided her into the dance with a gentle touch. As they moved together, a bubble of enchantment formed around them, isolating them from the intrigue of the grand hall.

Draven inclined his head, his voice a murmur that sent shivers down her spine. "You know, Lanae, if anyone finds out our invitation was forged, we will be in trouble."

Light strains of laughter filled Lanae as they moved together. If he only knew the consequences she'd face if she was caught here, there would be hell to pay. Instead of enlightening him to the level of danger she would be in if caught, she teased him about his dancing skills. "Oh Draven, I think they'll be too enchanted by our dance to even notice."

He smirked. "Enchanted, huh? You really think we're that good?"

"Well, I don't see anyone else being this close to cracking the code of the perfect waltz," she teased, spinning with finesse under his arm.

Draven chuckled, pulling her back in. "You realize we're supposed to be gathering intel, not charm awards, right?"

"Why not do both? If we're going to be stuck here, we might as well make the most of it." Besides, she was enjoying being in his arms, feeling the warmth and strength of his embrace.

He raised an eyebrow. "Does the best of it include almost tripping over my own feet?"

"If it did, you'd be excelling." She playfully squeezed his hand and smiled at the frown that formed. "You dance like you've done it all your life. How many of these things have you been to?"

"Probably as many as you have." His gaze pierced her, and the smile on his lips almost seemed playful.

"This is my first."

His eyebrow rose, and he broke her gaze to survey the room again. "As I said, as many as you."

"Then where did you learn to dance?"

He spun her in a circle and brought her back into the warmth of his arms.

"I guess I picked it up over the years," he whispered in her ear, his breath tickling her skin.

"Why don't I believe that?" She whispered laughter as he glanced down at her, the closeness making her heart race.

"Believe what you want." He didn't entertain her with any more words. Instead, he pulled her closer, and with that same smirk that heated her to the core, he kept in step with the tune, their movements synchronized perfectly.

As they continued to dance, Lanae lost herself in the moment. The music swirled around them, the grand hall dimming in her mind. The world outside their embrace ceased to exist, leaving only the silent conversation of their hearts beating in tandem.

For that brief eternity, there was no danger or pending disaster—only the magic of their connection. And in that grand hall, amidst a tapestry of deception and desires, Lanae and Draven carved out their own fragment of purity—

two souls lost to the feel of being utterly, exquisitely alive.

The last note of the song lingered in the air as Draven held her close, his arms still wrapped around her. Lanae blinked as the reality of their circumstances crashed down upon her. If the gauntlet stone was activated, this moment—this burgeoning connection—would be impossible. They would become slaves, stripped of any chance for whatever this was that was blossoming between them. Her heart raced from their closeness, the thrill of Draven's touch, and their playful banter. But she couldn't afford to let it distract her from their path.

They retreated to a quieter corner, where the grandeur of the ballroom seemed to soften into shadows.

The political scheming around them was intense, and every glance, every whisper, held a potential secret. Lanae's eyes flickered over the sea of faces, each one a potential ally or enemy. She inhaled deeply. The importance of their mission settled on her shoulders, making them ache from the strain.

"We need to get closer to the magocrats," she said. Dread laced her stomach. Her gaze locked onto a group of elaborately dressed figures, who moved with an air of authority and concealed intentions, and the council members mingled with them.

Draven nodded, his expression turning. "Agreed. But we have to be subtle. One wrong move..."

He didn't need to finish the sentence. They couldn't afford any mistakes. The tension between them was profound, a mix of shared responsibility and the remnants of their earlier connection.

Draven leaned in, his voice a breath away from a whisper. "I'll take this side of the room. You work on the other side. Get close and listen. Gather what you can and I'll meet you near the door."

Lanae nodded, her mind already working through the plan. "Be careful."

"Always," he replied, a hint of his earlier smirk returning. "Just watch your back."

As Draven moved away, blending seamlessly into the crowd, Lanae felt a pang of worry. Their playful banter now seemed like a distant memory, replaced by the pressing danger that loomed over her. She watched him for a moment longer, her heart conflicted between their task and the connection they had forged.

Steeling herself, Lanae moved toward the group of magocrats, her steps deliberate. She called on her magic, subtly cloaking her hair in shadows the closer she came to the people likely to identify her. Anticipation permeated the air, heightening every one of her senses. She needed to be close enough to hear, but not so close as to draw attention.

Voices drifted over her, snippets of conversation that hinted at deeper plots. She strained to catch every word, their secrets more fragmented with each passing second.

"The council must not know..."

"Keep the council distracted..."

"Arriving at dawn..."

"The alliance hinges on..."

"Eliminate any threats…"

Each fragment was a piece of a larger puzzle, one that could change the balance of power if only she could put it together. The closer she got to the council members, the more mundane and less politically motivated the conversation became.

Her heart hammered in her chest as she passed them, praying her illusion would stay in place until she moved out of sight. She caught the heated gazes of the magocrats as they aimed visual bullets at the council members.

Across the room, Draven engaged with another group, his charm and ease a clear divergence from the tension in her own chest. She knew they were walking a thin line, but she trusted him—and herself—to see this through.

Lanae's backbone hardened. They had to uncover the truth, no matter the risk. And as she edged closer, the murmur of secrets grew louder, intertwining with the beat of her own determined heart.

A throat cleared behind her, and she jolted, her heart leaping into her throat. She turned to face a man whose leer made her feel dirty, like she needed to scrub her skin raw. His hair was dark and straight, hanging untethered beyond his shoulders, giving his face a shadowy quality. His eyes were the color of onyx, and their intensity made her swallow hard, her mouth suddenly dry.

"May I have this dance?" He offered his hand.

Lanae opened her mouth to refuse, but she didn't know whether that was the proper thing to do at these events. She licked her lips, trying to moisten them, and forced a smile that felt like it might crack her face. "That would be lovely."

He led her to the dance floor, his grip unyielding. When he wrapped his arm around her, she had to stifle a shiver of revulsion, her skin crawling where he touched her. This was the opposite of what being in Draven's arms had been like—warm, safe, and comforting.

"What's your name?" He started to move her around the floor with a jerky, unpracticed rhythm, nothing like the smooth grace of Draven.

"Lanae. And you?" She offered a smile that was as fake as the invitation they used to get in the door, her cheeks aching from the effort.

"Xoltan. It is nice to make your acquaintance." He twirled her around with a flourish that made her dizzy, then pulled her back into his arms with a force that made her gasp.

DRAVEN WOVE HIS WAY through the grand ballroom. His senses heightened as he tuned into the surrounding conversations. The room was a symphony of laughter, clinking glasses, and whispered secrets, each interaction a potential puzzle piece. His vivid perception and keen hearing caught snippets of dialogue filtering through the layers of pleasantries and politics.

He stalled when he overheard a hushed conversation that hinted at a scheme to overthrow the Fae Council. The words lingered in the air, but Draven masked his interest, seamlessly blending back into the crowd before his eavesdropping could be noticed. The grandiosity of the ball was a mere facade; beneath the surface, there was nothing related to the gauntlet stone, but everything to do with political unrest.

His gaze swept across the room, finding Lanae dancing amidst the sea of opulence. Thunderous rage burned over his skin, taking him by surprise. His fists clenched at his sides, knuckles turning white. He breathed in to quiet the storm suddenly raging inside him, his chest rising and falling with the effort. Seeing another man holding Lanae nearly brought his fire out, his vision narrowing to a tunnel focused solely on them.

Calm your ass down, he silently scolded himself. But his feet weren't listening. They led him directly across the dance floor, his steps purposeful and unyielding. He tapped the man's shoulder with a force that made Lanae's eyebrows shoot up.

"May I cut in?" he asked in more of a demand than a question.

The man gave him a narrow-eyed glare that seemed hauntingly familiar, and for a moment, Draven didn't think he'd relinquish his hold on Lanae. But then he nodded and stepped away, leaving Lanae staring up at him with wide eyes.

He took her hand in his, relishing the electrical current between them, his grip firm yet gentle. As they continued the dance, his blood pumped through his veins in a faster beat than the music.

"What was that all about?" Lanae whispered, licking her lips.

The motion of her tongue made him want to close the distance and cover her mouth with his. He swallowed hard, trying to focus. "Can't a man just want to dance with you?" He wasn't about to reveal the sudden rash of jealousy that had overcome his senses.

She smirked up at him, her cheeks turning a rosy pink. "I guess I should thank you."

"Oh?" His lips tilted into a grin, his eyes never leaving hers.

"Yeah. He made me a bit uneasy." She glanced over his shoulder, her body tensing in his arms.

Draven twirled her, his movements smooth and controlled, and caught the man staring at them from the edge of the dance floor. His glare looked as if he wanted to bury Draven alive for the interruption. Draven glanced down at Lanae and then looked in the opposite direction, where Caelum was still talking to the same girl he had been almost the entire evening. He pulled Lanae in, leaning close to her ear, his breath making the loose strands of her hair flutter. "Have you been keeping an eye on your brother? Caelum seems to be...distracted."

Lanae's eyes flickered toward her brother, who was engrossed in an animated conversation with a mysterious girl. The girl's gestures were elegant yet guarded. Lanae's expression tightened, a mixture of frustration and worry etched across her face.

He leaned closer, his voice a whisper that barely reached her ears over the din of the ball. "Do you know her?"

"No. I don't." Lanae's voice crested a whisper. She tore her gaze away from her brother, focusing on Draven. "He's not paying attention at all."

Draven nodded, his jaw set with determination as he twirled her around the dance floor. "If we have to make a quick exit, he needs to be paying attention." His eyes scanned the room, taking in every detail, every potential threat, including the dark-haired fae leering at Lanae.

"I know." Lanae's voice held a note of frustration. "Have you heard anything?"

Their eyes locked, and a foreign fondness spread through him, heating his core. Her eyes, fierce and determined, held a depth of emotion that threatened to distract him from their purpose here. He would much rather be holding her against him on the dance floor for the rest of the evening. Draven blinked the fondness away and shook his head. "Not about the stone. But almost everyone is talking about some sort of coup."

"Do you think they're related?" Lanae's voice was tight with concern.

Draven glanced around, weighing her question. The room was a tapestry of deceit and intrigue, each thread leading back to the gauntlet stone. If the stone merged realms and made slaves of the inhabitants, then it very well could be connected to the political unrest. "It's possible," he said finally. "If the stone is as powerful as they say, it could be the key to control."

Lanae's eyes darkened with resolve. "We need to find out more."

Draven nodded, his mind already formulating a plan as the music wound down. He led her off the dance floor at the farthest point away from the man who she had been dancing with. "Agreed. I'll keep an eye on Caelum and the girl. You see what you can uncover about the coup. Oh, and don't let that idiot con you into another dance."

Lanae hesitated for a moment. "I won't. Be careful, Draven."

A small smile played on Draven's lips, his eyes softening. "Same to you, Lanae. Let's get through this and then maybe we can dance again."

With a final, lingering look, they parted ways. Draven maneuvered through the throngs of guests, his eyes never leaving Caelum and the mysterious girl. He watched their every move, noting the subtle cues and signals that passed between them.

The tension in the air grew as the stranger maneuvered closer to Lanae. Draven pushed forward until a hushed whisper about a particular historian—a sphinx——and a rare stone reached his ears. He knew of the sphinx and now had a direction to follow to find this stone and protect their world from the darkness that sought to consume it.

It was time to go.

A STRANGE SENSE OF comfort blanketed Caelum as he talked with Arsia. Her presence was a soothing balm, a momentary escape from the ever-looming anxiety. The grand ballroom's opulent surroundings faded into the background, replaced by the enthusiasm of her laughter and the sparkle in her eyes. Her face, framed by soft curls, was a portrait of calm and understanding, and Caelum found himself mesmerized by her every word.

"So, tell me," Arsia said, her voice gentle but curious, "what brings *you* to such a grand affair?

I rarely see someone my age with your...intensity here."

Caelum smiled faintly, attempting to cloak the truth behind a casual facade. "I'm supposed to be chaperoning my sister. Where's your chaperone?"

She waved a hand at the crowd. "Somewhere out there, thankfully."

"Well, you seem to be enjoying yourself."

She laughed lightly, a sound that was both enchanting and disarming. "Appearances can be deceiving, Caelum. I find these gatherings...informative, but not necessarily enjoyable. There are too many masks, literal and metaphorical."

He nodded, appreciating her candor. "I suppose you're right."

Arsia's eyes grew thoughtful. "But sometimes, amidst all the deception, you find moments of genuine connection. Moments like this."

Warmth spread through him at her words. "It's a rarity finding someone you can actually talk to, especially in this environment."

"Perhaps it's because we're both a little out of place," she replied, her gaze steady and sincere. "But that's what makes this conversation so...refreshing."

They continued to talk, their conversation flowing effortlessly. Arsia's penetrating insights and fresh humor were a welcome relief from the tension. Caelum found himself more and more drawn to her, the mutual attraction growing with each passing moment.

But as Draven's gaze caught his from across the room, reality crashed back with a force that left him breathless. The urgency in Draven's eyes was unmistakable, as was the tilting of Draven's head, beckoning to him.

"I have to go," Caelum said in a voice tinged with regret. He held Arsia's gaze, their rapport hard to ignore.

Arsia nodded, her expression one of understanding and unspoken emotion. "Be careful." Her hand brushed his in a fleeting touch that sent a shiver through him.

Caelum nodded, even though the words were strange in this setting. A pang of reluctance slithered through him as he turned away. As he rejoined his sister, a mix of anticipation and dread settled in his chest.

"Who was that?" Lanae asked, as they headed toward Draven.

"Arsia." That's all he really knew about the girl he had just spent the last couple of hours with. That and the fact anxiety burned a path to his heart while contemplating never seeing her again.

Amidst the bustling crowd, the murmur of rebellion simmered beneath the surface of the ball's elegant facade.

His thoughts flickered back to Arsia, her warning echoing in his mind. He couldn't afford to let his guard down, not even for a moment. The gauntlet stone's activation would change everything, and they had to prevent it at all costs.

DRAVEN APPROACHED THEM FROM the opposite side of the ballroom. He scanned the sea of elegantly dressed figures and the glittering chandeliers that cast a rich glow over the scene. Each step he took was measured, his gaze fierce and unwavering. As he neared Lanae and Caelum, the proximity of the stranger to where they were pressed hard on his chest. He didn't want that man near Lanae.

They met at a discreet corner close to the entrance door that led to their freedom. The contrast between the opulence of the ballroom and the shadowy recesses of their meeting spot displayed the peril that lay beneath the evening's facade.

"You have something?" Lanae asked, her voice low and urgent as they drew close enough to whisper. Her eyes flickered with a hint of anxiety.

"Yes. It's time to go." Draven's voice was firm, yet a note of regret threaded through his words. He glanced at the dance floor once more. The sight of swirling couples and the haunting strains of the orchestra tugged at his heart. A pang of longing wobbled his knees, an ache for the moment of respite he had shared with Lanae before.

He would have loved to hold her close just once more, to lose himself in the comfort of her presence before their world shattered to bits. But he knew that time wasn't their friend in this war of the realms. The urgency of their task propelled him forward; the impending doom sharpened his tenacity.

Lanae's hand found his, giving it a brief squeeze. "Let's go." Her steady voice calmed him.

Caelum nodded.

Before they could leave the ballroom, a group of guards approached, blocking their path to freedom. Draven tensed as the guards closed in. He would not be relegated to a cell while these magocrats decided his fate. He had been there a time or two in the past, and those always ended with fire and chaos.

He did not want to chance any harm befalling Lanae, either. But the guards had their icy stares pinned on Lanae with unwavering intensity. The head guard, a burly man with a stern expression, pointed a finger at her. His other hand clasped the hilt of his sword with a menacing grip.

"You." His voice was cold and authoritative. "You should not be here."

Draven glanced at her, and her guilt displayed fully on her pretty face. He stepped in front of Lanae, his posture confident and unyielding. "My invitation did not specify who I could and could not bring to this ball," he declared before the guards reached them. "I chose to bring one of the most beautiful fae in the city. Do you not agree?" He waved at Lanae and smiled as if she were a shiny treasure everyone should be so lucky to have by their side.

The lead guard faltered, confusion flickering across his face as the group halted before them. He seemed momentarily disarmed by Draven's boldness.

"Well, do you not agree?" Draven pressed, crossing his arms and glaring with the haughty demeanor of an aristocrat. The longer this standoff took, the more eyes would take notice. Only those at the peripheral of the room could see them, but if they didn't get out of here soon, this would become a spectacle and Solstice City wasn't known for keeping gossip under wraps. His eyes bore into the guard, daring him to challenge his authority.

The guard sputtered, his composure slipping. "Soldiers are not supposed to attend these functions," he stammered, training his gaze on Lanae.

"She did mention that it wasn't encouraged," Draven continued smoothly, although this tiny fact hadn't been disclosed. He lifted his chin a fraction higher. "But I refused to take no for an answer. I wanted her here with me, and here she is."

The guard's stubbornness wavered; his grip on the sword slackened enough that color returned to his knuckles. He glanced at his fellow guards, seeking support, but found only uncertainty mirrored in their eyes.

The hesitation was enough for Draven to seize the advantage. His flight instinct took control of his better judgment. He grabbed Lanae's hand and sprang into action, darting past the distracted guards and racing down the corridor. The guards' shouts echoed behind them, the pursuit beginning in earnest. Draven led the way, his mind racing as he navigated them out of the building and down winding passageways and narrow alleys.

The chase was a blur of adrenaline and fear, the night air cold against their skin. Every shadow threatened to conceal an ambush; every rustle of the wind hinted at danger. Draven's senses sharpened, his every instinct focused on escape.

Lanae's breath came in quick gasps behind him. Caelum followed closely, his face set in grim perseverance.

Rounding a bend, Draven spotted an old, dilapidated building. He pushed the door open, urging them inside. The interior was dark and musty, a significant contrast to the glittering ballroom they had left behind. They huddled in the shadows, hearts pounding as the guards' footsteps echoed outside.

For a tense moment, silence enveloped them, broken only by their ragged breaths. The guards passed by, their shouts fading into the distance. Draven exhaled as relief washed over him.

"We need to keep moving." His voice didn't hint at the lingering adrenaline coursing through his veins. "Your home isn't far. We can regroup and plan our next step there."

Lanae turned to him, her eyes flashing with anger and disbelief. "They are guards. They know where I live." Her voice cut through the quiet night. "Why did you run?"

Draven stared at her, his mouth opening as if to speak, but he hesitated, words failing him for a moment. Their situation settled between them like a bomb about to ignite. His need to escape cast a shadow over their fragile alliance.

"Do you know how much trouble I'm going to get in for this?" Lanae's fists slammed into her waist. The fire in her eyes was undimmed, a blazing inferno of indignation.

Draven took a step closer. "It's better than being locked up for questioning," he argued, his voice low and urgent. "If they had caught us, we wouldn't have had a chance to explain."

Caelum snorted, and Draven shot him a glare.

"You don't understand." Lanae shook her head, the tension crackling between them. "I will have to report all this to the council. This complicates everything." Her voice trembled with contained anger.

Draven closed the distance between them, his chest brushing hers. "Life is complicated." His eyes searched hers for a flicker of acknowledgment. "Staying there would have put us in immediate danger." His annoyance at her questioning him bled through in his tone.

"Take a step back," Caelum warned. His glare held every ounce of sibling protection in his body.

She looked up at him, her eyes piercing into his soul. The tension between them was palpable, a tightrope strung with their frustrations and unspoken emotions.

"I was trying to protect you," Draven added, stepping out of her personal space. The sincerity in his words hung in the air.

"No, you weren't. You were covering your own ass." Lanae's gaze didn't soften in the slightest. Her words were a finely sharpened knife cutting through the thin veil of his argument. "Next time, make sure we're on the same page before making a stupid move." Her voice kept a dangerous edge.

Draven clenched his teeth, a surge of irritation tightening his jaw. "Fine," he replied. "Let's just get to your place and figure out our next steps." His tone was clipped as the simmering pressure between them threatened to explode.

CHAPTER TEN
Shifting Alliances

ONCE INSIDE HER HOUSE, Lanae bolted the door with a reverberating click, her fingers trembling with the release of adrenaline. She turned and crossed to where Nero nested. The small griffin's feathers ruffled as she lifted him, and then she nuzzled him to her cheek, drawing comfort from his warmth. She collected herself before facing Draven and Caelum.

"What did you find out?" Lanae's tone was even, but there was an edge of urgency that belied her calm facade.

"I overheard someone reference the sphinx and a rare stone," Draven replied, his posture stiff as he remained by the door, as if he couldn't bear stepping farther into her house. The flickering firelight cast shadows on his features, accentuating the weariness in his eyes.

Lanae cocked a brow at him. "A sphinx?"

"Yes. And I have a hunch on where this one might be. But it means another labyrinth, if we can even locate the cursed place." He ran his hand through his fiery hair, the gesture disheveling the clean-cut illusion he had sported for the ball. Now he looked more like the rugged man she had bumped into the day before.

Before he could expand, a harsh knock resounded against the door. The sound was like a thunderclap in the quiet room. They traded a glance, friction crackling between them.

The only visitors they had at this time of night were always related to the council, and considering they had just run from guard members, it only made sense.

"Caelum, go to your room." Lanae handed Nero over to her brother. She didn't want him involved with whatever trouble was brewing with the council.

He didn't argue and jogged to the center of the house, his footsteps fading into the silence.

Lanae turned to Draven and sighed. There was no denying his presence or the fact they had been at the ball while still wearing their fine clothing. She crossed to the door, her heart pounding as she swung it open.

Elara stood there, her honey-spun hair braided in tight rows close to her head, dressed in her formal guard uniform. Her bright-gray eyes narrowed at Draven, then pinned back on Lanae, scanning her with a look that could slice through steel. She wiped her face with her hand in a gesture of disbelief.

"I thought they were kidding," Elara said, her voice laced with incredulity.

"Draven wouldn't take no for an answer." Lanae cut off any protest from Draven. "And he was just leaving."

Draven had the decency to nod and slip by Elara without a word. He slid into the shadows and faded into the night.

Elara stepped inside, her eyes sweeping the room as if searching for someone else. "You've been summoned to appear before the council immediately." She glanced over her shoulder at the retreating figure of Draven, swallowed by the darkness.

When she looked back at Lanae, her expression hardened to granite. "You didn't tell me you were dating a magocrat." She crossed her arms.

"We aren't dating." Lanae's words were careful, each one measured because although Elara was her friend, she was also a soldier loyal to the council and what Lanae did was against the rules.

She blinked and tilted her head. "Was that the stranger from the bar?"

Lanae's cheeks heated, and she chewed her lip, lifting a single shoulder.

Elara wiped her face, focusing on Lanae. "Look, it doesn't matter. He's a stranger, and with the attack yesterday and you violating your orders, I have to wonder about your alliance to the guard." Elara's stance became a barrier between them.

"Look, I'm loyal to the guard, and Draven isn't what you think he is." Lanae glanced at the darkness beyond the door, anxiety gnawing at her. *Was Draven safe?*

"I get it. He's good-looking. But seriously, that can't be what made you break protocol. Please tell me what could possibly make you stray this far from the rules?" Her friend's eyes implored her for a logical answer.

"A dragon." The word slipped out before she could stop it.

Elara jolted as if struck, her eyes widening with shock. She glanced up at the sky, trepidation etched into her features. "A dragon? They are our enemies!"

They had all grown up with the stories of dragons almost annihilating the fae. Lanae understood the fear—she had felt it, too. But Draven had proved himself. Had he not fought alongside her, she might have been inclined to turn him in as well.

"Draven is different," Lanae said.

Elara's gaze bore into hers. "*That* man is a dragon?" She pointed in the direction Draven had gone, disbelief and anger mixing in her voice.

Oh crap. Lanae's heart stuttered. She hadn't meant to reveal his identity like that, especially not to someone like Elara, who had always vowed that if there were any dragons left in this world, she would gut them on principle alone.

"Don't lie to me, Lanae. Dragons are dangerous and they destroyed Solstice City once." Elara's grip on Lanae's arm was vise-like, her gaze radiating an intensity that brooked no argument.

"Save your lies for the council. They can see through them just as I can."

"Fine. But he isn't a danger to us. There's something bigger out there. Something that will enslave us all."

"Yeah. A damn dragon," Elara spat, her words filled with contempt.

LANAE STOOD IN THE center of the council chamber once again. But this time, a frenetic beat pounded in her chest. She was the focus of this gathering, especially wearing the formal gown that screamed she had broken the rules.

The Fae Council, a semicircle of stern faces and unforgiving eyes, with a few notably empty seats representing those still at the ball, loomed before her. A palpable tension hung in the air. Their judgmental silence amplified her every breath.

Elara stood off to the side, her expression unreadable, but Lanae knew better what brewed beneath that blank expression. Her so-called friend was livid.

Betrayal hung in the air between them.

"Lanae Nightshade," Faide Frostvale began, his voice echoing in the vast chamber. "Yesterday you were caught fraternizing with a stranger after the attack on our city. And now we find out that stranger is indeed a dragon? Are you in league with a dragon?" He shot the questions out so fast that she didn't have a chance to answer.

Lanae's throat was dry as a desert, and her mind raced for the right words. "I... I do not deny meeting Draven," she admitted, her voice cool in spite of the turmoil within her. "But he is not our enemy. There are far more dangerous plots in play."

A murmur rippled through the council as the elders exchanged skeptical glances.

Caitan Windysprite, a stern fae with piercing eyes, leaned forward. "And what guarantee do we have that this dragon is not deceiving you? Dragons nearly annihilated the fae. They were thought to be extinct, and now we find out one has been among us all this time?"

Lanae didn't bother correcting them. According to what Draven had told her, he hadn't been in Solstice City for years. Still, she had to consider that he might be deceiving her. She lowered her gaze, trying to view the situation from an outsider's perspective. Although it seemed convenient, between his earnestness and the way their bond sang whenever they touched, she had no choice but to believe him.

Lanae's gaze flickered to Elara, who stood with her head bowed. "I believe Draven is fighting for Solstice City's best interests." With each word, her voice gained strength. "He saved my life. He seeks justice and peace, just as we do."

Elara stepped forward, her voice trembling. "Is she the one who you confronted, who took flight instead of facing the consequences of breaking the rules?"

The guard who had stopped them in the ballroom stepped forward. "Yes, she is the one who ran from us at the ball."

"This is a clear breach of protocol and trust," Elara said.

The council's reaction was swift, their disapproval unmistakable.

Faide's expression hardened. "This is a grave matter, Lanae. By speaking with a dragon, you have placed us all at risk."

Lanae clenched her fists at her sides, fighting to keep her composure. "I acted in the best interest of our people. If we are to survive, we must seek allies, even among those we once considered foes."

Faide's eyes narrowed. "Your intentions may have been noble, but your methods were reckless. You will be reprimanded for your actions. You are hereby stripped of your rank and confined to your house until further notice."

The words struck Lanae like a physical blow, drawing a gasp from her lips. She glanced at Elara, who could not meet her eyes.

Faide's tone softened enough to bring her attention back to the council. "Consider this a lesson in the importance of trust and loyalty. You will have the opportunity to prove yourself in time."

"But..." She still had yet to tell them about the rumors of a coup.

"Silence!" Faide's voice shut her down. "Guards, escort Lanae back to her house and make sure she does not leave."

As Lanae was escorted out of the chamber, the consequence of her actions pressed upon her. She would figure out a way to clear her name and prove the value of Draven's alliance. Her future in the guard depended upon it.

Outside the chamber, Elara approached her, her eyes brimming with sorrow. "Lanae, I—"

Lanae held up a hand, stopping her. "Save it, Elara. We both have to live with the consequences of our actions. I just hope you're prepared for yours."

With that, Lanae walked away, her heart heavy with Elara's betrayal.

CHAPTER ELEVEN
Unexpected Allies

THE SLIVER OF THE moon cast a silver glow over the city, its ethereal light creating a tapestry of shadows and highlights. The night air was filled with anticipation, a tangible tension that clung to the cobblestones and ivy-covered walls. Lanae paced on her terrace, the stone floor cool beneath her feet. Her thoughts were tangled in a web of doubts and frustrations. Elara's betrayal stung like an open wound, made worse by the confines of her house arrest. They had a megalomaniac to stop, and here she was, trapped.

"Lanae," Elara's voice called from the street below.

Lanae turned, her gaze meeting Elara's. The torchlight flickered, casting an unsteady glow over Elara's features. There was a fire in her eyes, a plea for another chance.

"Can we talk?"

Lanae folded her arms, taking in the sight of Elara standing alongside Rorik. It seemed those she had once considered her closest friends were now the very ones keeping her prisoner. The irony was not lost on her.

"Why? So you can gloat?" Lanae's clear voice penetrated the night. "I am one of the best soldiers the city has, and I'm now relegated to my home like a criminal."

Elara lowered her chin, her expression shadowed with guilt. "Did you know Rorik's family was saved by a dragon?" She mumbled the question.

Lanae's eyes darted to Rorik, his curt nod confirming Elara's words.

"Not all dragons are dicks," he said with a tilted smile. The rune light caught the glint of amusement in his eyes. "Unlike dark fae."

His disdain for dark fae dripped through his words. A keen edge that brought a reluctant smile to Lanae's lips. For a moment, the tension eased, replaced by a flicker of friendship.

"Fine. I'll be down in a moment," Lanae relented, her tone softening. She turned and made her way downstairs.

As she descended, her thoughts churned. Elara's crack in her rigid belief that all dragons were their enemies was certainly a welcomed revelation. It gave her a glimmer of hope amidst the suffocating darkness of their possible future. When she reached the bottom of the steps, she opened the door, inviting Elara and Rorik inside.

Elara's eyes filled with regret. "I know I screwed things up, Lanae. But I want to make amends."

Lanae's jaw ached from grinding her teeth as she stared down at her so-called friend. Elara held her gaze long enough for her to unclench her muscles and give a curt nod. "Then let's talk. But we don't have a lot of time." She closed the door on the foreboding night with a decisive click and glanced down the hallway, making sure her brother was out of sight before leading them into the living room. The room was cozy, with a fire crackling in the hearth and the scent of pine lingering in the air.

"I didn't think any dragons still existed. At least that's what my grandfather had said." Rorik shifted his weight and met Lanae's gaze before stepping into the living area. "Tell me about your dragon." He slid into a chair, leaning forward with a curious sparkle in his eyes.

Lanae flicked her gaze to Elara and then back to Rorik. "We went to the ball to gather intelligence, and I overheard some talk of overthrowing the council."

"That is normal in Solstice City." Rorik leaned back. "There is always a plot to overthrow those in power. That does not tell me why you would partner with someone other than us." He pointed between himself and Elara and raised a single questioning eyebrow.

Lanae slid lower in her chair, contemplating his words. Her father had said the same thing to her many times over the years, but with the pending doom of the gauntlet stone, the information had seemed more credible. "According to a witch in the Undercity, Draven and I are destined to stop a madman from merging realms and enslaving everyone." She left out the part of being fate bonded to the sexy scoundrel. That was too personal to share, especially with Rorik's propensity to bring every conversation back to sex.

"Why were you in the Undercity?" Elara's voice was tinged with concern.

"Because I had been drilled about Draven by the council for hours after he escorted me from the bar to the Citadel." Lanae leaned back on the couch, running her hands through her hair in frustration. "I sat next to him at the bar by chance and..." She looked at Elara, searching for understanding. "Well, you've seen him." As if that would explain everything.

Elara's cheeks bloomed red. "He is quite a looker."

Rorik leaned forward again, and a smirk formed on his lips. "So, this is the stranger from the bar?"

Lanae nodded, feeling the weight of their scrutiny.

His eyes lit up. "And you are willing to throw your career away for him?"

"No, it's not that." Lanae dropped her hands into her lap, her frustration mounting.

"Oh, he must be very good in bed." Rorik's salacious grin appeared.

And there it is. Rorik's comment made her face heat. "It is not like that." *Well, wasn't that exactly what you had longed for while he was twirling you around the dance floor?* She scoffed at her internal monologue, and her irritation bloomed. She wasn't sure whether it was aimed at herself for not actually taking Draven to bed or at Rorik for the insinuation. "It isn't my choice."

Rorik's good humor faded, replaced by concern. "He forced himself on you?"

"No. They are fate bonded. That's why she's saying it isn't her choice." Caelum stepped from the hallway, Nero perched on his shoulder, his presence a sudden intrusion.

"Caelum," Lanae said, but the damage was done. Both Elara and Rorik snapped their gazes from Caelum to her, their expressions demanding answers.

"Is this true?" Rorik asked, his voice low and serious.

"According to the witch." Lanae was not about to admit to the electricity between her and Draven in front of her brother.

"Bullshit. I felt your connection at the ball when you were dancing." Caelum settled on the far side of the couch, giving her a knowing look. "Hell, I think everyone in that ballroom felt your connection."

"I didn't think fate bonds were real," Elara said.

"You also thought dragons were our enemies," Rorik shot back at her.

"What do dragons have to do with this?" Caelum asked.

"Draven is a dragon," Elara said before Lanae could stop her.

The words hung heavy in the air for a beat before Caelum's eyebrows shot up, arching high above his widened eyes. His mouth fell open, his lips parting in surprise as he stared, unblinking. The lines on his forehead deepened, accentuating the sheer disbelief etched across his features. His head cocked to the side, as if trying to process the unexpected information, and a faint frown tugged at the corners of his mouth, underscoring his incredulity. "He is?"

Lanae closed her eyes. More and more fae were finding out what Draven was, and it did not settle well. "Yes. He's the last of the dragons."

"Why didn't you tell me this?" Caelum pouted as if Lanae had taken away his favorite dessert.

The room fell silent save for the crackling fire. Caelum's disappointment pounded her muscles, and Lanae wished she had another bottle of spirits to drown her remorse in. "It wasn't my secret to tell." She pinned a frustrated look at Elara.

His poison-tipped gaze bore into her as he pointed at her friends. "Then how do they know?"

Before she could say another word, a soft knock sounded on the door.

When the door cracked open, Draven could have sworn he saw a flash of irritation in Lanae's eyes. The rune lights cast a soft glow over her features, highlighting the tension etched across her face.

"It looks like the guards are gone." His low and cautious voice caressed her.

"No. They are in my living room." She swung the door wide and waved for him to come inside, her movements brisk and impatient.

Tentatively, Draven stepped inside. The warmth of the cottage enveloped him, but his mistrust of the fae bloomed the moment he saw the other two guards sitting across from a sulking Caelum. The flickering firelight painted the scene in stark contrasts, shadows dancing on the walls as if whispering secrets of their own.

"Draven, this is Elara and Rorik. My closest friends and fellow guards," Lanae introduced, her tone neutral but laden with unspoken strain.

"We were just talking about you." Rorik stood and held out his hand.

Draven glanced at the offered hand, his gaze shifting to Rorik before he pinned his eyes on Lanae. His jaw clenched, and he could feel his insecurities bubbling to the surface. "More fae?" His disdain bled through his words, a pointed barb that cut through the room's fragile peace.

Rorik lowered his hand, but he held his ground. "We're all on the same side here."

Draven's eyes narrowed, his mistrust flaring. "I'm not so sure about that." He stepped farther into the room with deliberate caution. Every movement was calculated, his senses fully engaged as he assessed the tension rippling in the air.

Caelum shot him a glare. "A fucking dragon?" He stared Draven down.

"Caelum," Lanae scolded.

Draven's chest clenched. His gaze jumped to Lanae. "You told him?" His low, dangerous growl hung on the air between them.

Lanae's eyes widened, her face flushed with guilt. "I didn't mean to, Draven."

Draven took a step closer, his fists clenching at his sides. "You had no right." His voice trembled with barely suppressed rage. "That was my secret to tell, not yours."

Lanae squared her shoulders, meeting his gaze head-on. "I slipped. It was not intentional. Besides, it's better that we all know the truth."

"The truth?" Draven's laugh held the acute bitterness piercing his heart. "You think you're doing them a favor by exposing me? All you've done is put us in more danger."

Rorik stepped forward, his expression placating. "We all share the same objective," he repeated, his voice calm but firm. "Trust me. I don't have the same wariness of dragons that the council has."

Draven's eyes never left Lanae's. His jaw clenched tight as his mistrust of the fae took another hit. "The council?"

Lanae flattened her mouth and nodded. Her gaze slid to Elara and narrowed. "I made a mistake." She looked back at him. "You can hate me for it later, because right now, it really does not matter. We still have to stop the unimaginable from coming to fruition."

Draven's chest heaved with the effort to control his emotions. His hands shook, and he crossed his arms to hide the effects of him unraveling. He knew she was right, but that didn't stop the sting of her betrayal, mistake or not.

Elara cleared her throat. "We want to understand what's going on, Draven."

Draven's anger simmered beneath the surface, his insecurity gnawing at him. The knowledge that more fae were aware of his true nature made his skin crawl. He had spent so long hiding, protecting his identity, and now it felt like the walls were closing in.

"Understanding is one thing." His voice conveyed his misgivings. "Trusting fae is another."

Lanae's brows furrowed, creating faint lines on her forehead, while her eyes narrowed with a steely boldness. "We don't have time for this. We have to work together if we are going to win this war against whoever is posing this threat. Otherwise, we will all be slaves."

Draven's eyes flicked to Lanae, his anger still simmering.

"A dragon saved my grandfather," Rorik blurted, pulling Draven's attention to him. He smiled and shrugged. "So, I'll happily stand with a dragon. Especially one who has my closest friend here tied in knots." He nodded at Lanae.

Draven's eyebrows shot up and his lips tilted in a smirk. "Knots?" The rest of what Rorik said settled, and his anger faded.

Rorik grinned.

"Damnit, Rorik." Lanae wiped her ever reddening face and wouldn't meet Draven's gaze.

If what he said was true, then one of Draven's relatives had once saved this man's grandfather. Against all his reservations of the fae in general, Draven felt a kinship with Rorik.

"You want to tell us what's going on?" Rorik directed his question at Draven.

"How much do you know?" he asked, unsure of what Lanae had already told him.

"That you and Lanae are supposed to stop someone from merging realms. And that you two are fate bound."

So, she had told them everything. He sent a glare at her and then took a cleansing breath, forcing himself to push past his aggravation. "I overheard someone at the ball talking about a sphinx and a rare stone. I believe I know where this sphinx might be, but it means navigating another dangerous maze, if we can even find the damn place."

The room fell silent. Lanae glanced at her friends, her eyes pleading for their cooperation.

"We must work together if we're going to stop this madman," she said.

Elara's gaze softened. "We're with you, Lanae. All of us."

It had been so long since he had worked together with anyone, but Draven's hope was tempered by his family's alliance with the fae. That turned out to be their death, and he couldn't shake the feeling that this could go sideways just as quickly.

He glanced at Lanae, berating himself for the need to protect her despite her mistakes. If he was honest with himself, he'd admit she had him tied up in just as many knots. The feel of her in his arms lingered. And damn her, he wanted more than just a dance.

He shook the thoughts out of his head and glanced around the room at his unlikely allies. "Let's get to work," he said, despite his lingering doubts. They had a mission to complete, and for now, that was all that mattered.

Lanae narrowed her eyes, studying Draven intently. This was the second time he had mentioned doubts about finding the sphinx. Silence layered over the room, the crackling of the fire the only sound.

"You're not convinced we can find the sphinx?" she asked, even though she had heard rumors of this person all her life.

Draven sighed, running a hand through his disheveled hair. "It's tricky. From what I remember, he shifts locations based on the lunar cycles. He has never been easy to find, and I don't believe time is on our side. So, hunting aimlessly for this place may not be our best course of action."

"It's the only lead we overheard. The witch wouldn't have sent us to the ball unless she thought we would get something concrete." The burn of frustration laced Lanae's words.

"And overthrowing the council doesn't count?" Caelum interjected, his tone sarcastic as he leaned against the wall.

"Everyone plots against the council," Rorik said with a dismissive wave of his hand. He sat back, his rugged features illuminated by the flickering flames, casting shadows that danced across his face.

Just as the conversation seemed to spiral into uncertainty, Elara's voice sliced the tension clean. "I may be able to help with the sphinx." Her statement silenced all of them. "If we understand the patterns, we can make educated guesses as to where the next appearance will be."

Lanae's eyes narrowed as she turned to Elara. "How would you know?" Suspicion rang clear in her voice.

Elara met her gaze. "I know I betrayed your trust," she began, her voice low and filled with regret. "But I have family ties to the sphinx. And based on the last few times my family visited, I could map it out."

Lanae had no idea that her friend was related to the sphinx. Rumors of this creature and his famously elusive labyrinth had been around for as long as she could remember. According to the stories she had heard, the labyrinth was a place of power and danger, its shifting nature a well-guarded secret. Yet Elara had never said a word, not even during the spirited debates they had about the sphinx while training at the academy. That dug under her skin, and she wondered what other secrets her comrade-in-arms had kept from her.

"Why should I trust you?" Lanae's voice cracked with skepticism and the sting of past betrayals.

"Because I want to make things right," Elara replied, meeting her gaze without flinching.

Lanae sensed the sincerity in Elara's words, but her lingering doubt gnawed at her. Her thoughts were interrupted by the sound of Draven's growling frustration bubbling to the surface, his insecurities manifesting in a harsh tone.

"You've already betrayed your friend once. Trusting you is dangerous," Draven said to Elara.

Lanae's heart pinched at his words, understanding the turmoil he was feeling because she had the same doubts. She placed a reassuring hand on his arm. "We don't have a choice, Draven. Elara's information could be the key to finding the sphinx and stopping the threat we all face."

The room fell silent and the fire crackled, casting shadows that seemed to whisper of the challenges ahead. Lanae's mind raced, weighing the risks and the potential rewards. But without Elara's help, it could take weeks to find the elusive sphinx.

"All right," she said finally. "We'll use your knowledge to help locate the sphinx. But we need to move on this because time is not on our side."

Draven nodded reluctantly. His anger and mistrust still simmered under the surface enough it pelted Lanae, dancing on every one of her nerve endings.

She turned and addressed Elara. "What do you need?"

"A map of Solstice City and the land surrounding us. The sphinx is never that far away." The edge of Elara's lip lifted in a partial smile.

It took them hours to map out a timeline of where the sphinx would appear next. They meticulously pored over every scrap of information, every fragment of Elara's memories, and every clue from Elara's family visits. In the end, it was Nero who pecked at a spot on the map, his tiny beak landing on what seemed to be a logical pattern.

Lanae glanced out the window at the sky tinged with the first hints of dawn. "When is the shift change?"

Rorik followed her gaze, his eyes widening in realization. "Oh, shit." He grabbed Elara's hand and pulled her toward the door. "We'll be back for tonight's shift." He shut the door behind them, cutting off any further comment. Moments later, fresh guards approached the front of the house. Their presence reminded Lanae of the constant watchfulness they were under.

"Just in the nick of time." She turned to Draven, who was studying the map spread out on her table. Caelum had gone to bed awhile ago, leaving Lanae acutely aware of the silence that now enveloped the house. Nerves bit at her skin, making every sensation more pronounced. Being alone with Draven, a dragon whose very existence was shrouded in mystery and danger, set her on edge.

Draven shook his head, his expression troubled. "This seems too easy."

"What do you mean?" She approached him, forcing herself to stow her nerves and concentrate on the task at hand.

His green eyes, deep and piercing, locked onto hers, seeming to see straight into her soul. "My kin trusted a fae once. And that landed my entire species in the grave."

"You don't trust me?" She placed a hand on her chest, feeling the steady thump of her heart beneath her fingers.

He bit the edge of his lip, a flicker of doubt in his eyes, but he held her gaze. "I don't trust any *other* fae." His voice was tinged with old wounds. He beckoned her closer. "Let me show you why."

Lanae closed the distance, her heart pounding in her chest and her breath catching in her throat. She trusted him, and that trust propelled her forward. The room seemed to grow hotter as she approached, her skin prickling with anticipation.

He reached out and took her hand, his touch sending a tingle coursing through her veins. It was as if his very essence flowed into her, filling her with an electric warmth that made her skin buzz. Her vision went hazy, the world around her dissolving into a swirling mist, taking her through time and space.

When her vision cleared, she stood in an apocalyptic scene. The sky was a turbulent sea of dark clouds, the air thick with the acrid scent of smoke and burning flesh. A white-haired fae stood before her, his eyes glinting with malevolence as he clutched a red heart-shaped stone. The stone pulsed with an eerie glow, casting a sickly red light over the desolate landscape.

Terrifying dragons soared overhead, their scales glinting like obsidian in the dim light. Each one was struck down by bolts of power emanating from the stone, the force of the blast sending them crashing to the earth. The ground shook with each impact and the thunderous noise reverberated through her very bones. The sight of hundreds of dragons falling from the sky took her breath away, and the evil laughter that erupted from the fae chilled her to the bone. It was a sound that seemed to reach into her soul and freeze her very core.

He released her hand, and the apocalyptic vision shattered like glass, leaving her blinking back in her living area. The cozy, familiar surroundings seemed almost surreal after the horrors she had just witnessed. She stared at her hand, the lingering warmth a stark contrast to the icy dread that gripped her heart. Then she looked up at him, her eyes wide with disbelief. "You can share memories?"

He nodded, his expression somber. "So, you understand why I do not trust the fae?"

"But Rorik and Elara have always had my back," she insisted, trying to convey the loyalty she felt toward her friends despite his dark past.

"Precisely. Your back. Not mine."

His words were an icy reminder of the rift between their worlds, a chasm filled with history and betrayal.

A pang of sorrow for the pain he carried went straight through her heart. His loss was deep, and it made her ache for him, even as it strengthened her resolve. "Draven, you can trust them."

He studied her for a moment longer, then nodded, his expression softening just a fraction. "I want to believe that."

"And you can trust me," Lanae said, her voice firm yet gentle, willing him to see the sincerity in her eyes.

His lips tilted into a soft smile, a rare expression that ignited a warmth within her, spreading from her chest to the tips of her fingers. The force of his gaze made her heart flutter, and for a brief moment, the precariousness of their predicament seemed to lighten.

Nero squawked, breaking the new tension that had crept up between them. The baby griffin flapped his tiny wings, his eyes bright and wide.

Lanae chuckled, the sound easing some of the anxiety coiled in her stomach. She wrung her hands together, trying to ground herself. She couldn't remember the last time a man besides her brother was in the house for more than a few minutes. "Since we are stuck here for the day, why don't we get some rest?"

He cocked his head, a quizzical look on his face. "Stuck here?"

"The council put me on house arrest for going to the ball with you," she admitted. A wry smile tugged at the corner of her lips.

Draven's expression shifted, his features tightening as a shadow passed over his face. His jaw clenched, the muscles working beneath his skin. His eyes darkened, narrowing as his brow furrowed, casting a stern and unyielding look. The softness of his previous demeanor was replaced by a steely doggedness, his mouth set in a grim line that hinted at the intensity of his emotions. "I'm sorry, Lanae. I didn't mean to cause you trouble."

"You didn't," she reassured him. "This was my choice. And I'd do it again if it meant protecting our city."

Draven nodded; his features gradually relaxed, the tension melting away from his face. His brows unfurrowed, and the hard lines around his mouth eased. A subtle tenderness returned to his eyes, softening their intensity. The corners of his lips lifted ever so slightly, hinting at a gentle expression that replaced the previous hardness. The transformation was subtle yet profound, as if a layer of armor had been peeled away, revealing a more compassionate side beneath.

He rubbed his face, covering a yawn. "I need some sleep."

She couldn't argue with that. Her limbs were heavy with exhaustion and the constant tension she experienced in his presence. Their house didn't have a guest room and Lanae wasn't about to share her bed with a virtual stranger, even if they were bonded by fate. She gestured toward a comfortable chair by the fire. "You can take that spot. It's the most comfortable place I can offer."

Draven settled into the chair, and Lanae admired the way the dawn danced across his features, highlighting the shades of red in his hair and the green of his eyes. There was a quiet strength in him, a resilience that mirrored her own.

As the room grew silent, with only the fire crackling, their eyes met. He smiled that soft smile that could shatter any willpower if it had been offered under any other circumstances. She gave him a nod and turned to head to her bedroom.

"Sleep well, Lanae." His voice followed her down the hallway.

At that moment, surrounded by the soft glow of the morning light and the reassuring presence of her unlikely ally, Lanae allowed herself to believe that maybe, just maybe, they had a chance.

CHAPTER TWELVE
The Labyrinth's Shadows

"YOU LET HIM SLEEP here?" Caelum's voice blasted through the remnants of Lanae's restless sleep, pulling her abruptly from her dreams.

Groggy and disoriented, Lanae rolled over to see her brother towering over her. The sounds of clattering dishes and sizzling pans drifted in from the kitchen beyond her bedroom. It took her a moment to remember who he was talking about.

"The guards changed shifts before he could leave," she mumbled, sitting up and rubbing the sleep from her eyes. "What time is it?"

"It's nearly sunset," Caelum replied, his tone exasperated.

Lanae blinked in surprise, the realization hitting her that she had slept the entire day away when they should have been planning their next move. The clang of metal echoed through the house, drawing her attention. "What is he doing?"

"Making dinner," Caelum said, his eyes as wide as saucers. "He shooed me out of the kitchen and told me to get your lazy ass out of bed."

Lanae let out a surprised laugh. The idea of a dragon royal cooking in her humble kitchen left her feeling off-kilter. But the fact that Draven had her brother wake her up after the hellish experiences of the past few days was enough to tickle her funny bone.

"Go." She flicked her fingers toward the door. "I'll be out in a few minutes. And don't let him clean out our cabinets, okay?"

Caelum grinned and nodded, leaving her to shake off the last vestiges of sleep.

Lanae stood up, stretching her muscles, and prepared to face the evening.

The warm shower did little to clear her mind; instead, it seemed to intensify the thoughts of the shirtless dragon that swirled through her head. The water cascaded over her, yet all she could picture was the way his muscles moved beneath his skin, along with the intensity of his gaze. Every droplet felt like a sign of his presence, a tantalizing echo of the heat that had radiated off him.

When she finally stepped out of the shower, the steam swirled around her like a soft embrace. She paused for a deep breath and tried to steady her thoughts. She dressed quickly, donning her battle attire with practiced efficiency. But even as she fastened her armor, her mind lingered on Draven.

Emerging into the living area, a flush of heat spread across her cheeks as she met Draven's gaze. He stood there with a tilted smile and raised a single eyebrow in silent inquiry. The sight of him, so calm and collected, only intensified the fluttering in her chest. Her intention to stay focused wavered, and she couldn't help but wonder whether he knew the effect he had on her.

"Good morning, or evening, as it were." Draven grinned as if reading her mind and waved at the table set for three. Succulent breads, sweetmeats, and an array of delicacies were prepared and set on the table, their enticing aromas wafting through the room. The spread was a feast for the senses, each dish meticulously crafted and inviting. "I hope you don't mind."

She shook her head, amazed at the culinary display. "Not at all."

He held the chair out for her and waited until she sat before he joined her. The warmth of the meal contrasted with the cool evening air. The last rays of sunlight filtered through the windows, casting a golden glow over the scene.

"I trust you slept well?" Draven's baritone timbre swept over her.

"Yes. I hope you did as well." Lanae's mouth watered as she reached for a slice of tender meat, savoring the rich, savory scent.

"Surprisingly well, thank you."

They all served themselves to the meal, filling their plates. But before Lanae could take her first bite, a crisp knock sounded at the door. The unexpected interruption caused her to pause, fork in midair.

"I'll get it." Caelum pushed back his chair and crossed the room. His steps echoed in the quiet space as he approached the door. A moment later, it creaked open, and the familiar faces of Rorik and Elara appeared, silhouetted against the dusky sky.

"The changing of the guards," Rorik announced as he stepped inside, his voice charged with anticipation. "It's time."

Elara followed closely behind, her eyes sparkling with spunk. The sight of her friends bolstered Lanae's spirits, reminding her they were in this together.

"Eat." Lanae waved for them to take one of the empty chairs at the table and then slid her fork into her mouth. The symphony of taste danced on her tongue and she moaned. "This is incredible, Draven," Lanae said, her eyes sparkling with gratitude. "We needed this."

Draven nodded, a satisfied smile on his face. "I thought it would be good for us to have a proper meal before we head out. I have a feeling we're going to need all the strength we can get."

The group ate in a comfortable silence, each of them taking a moment to enjoy the food and the brief respite from their worries. Caelum's reminiscing of their earlier days produced occasional laughter, and even Rorik and Elara allowed themselves to relax and share in the conversation.

Caelum leaned back in his chair, a fond smile playing on his lips. "Remember that time I got lost in the forest for two days? I thought I'd never find my way out!"

Rorik guffawed. "How could I forget? Lanae had the entire guard looking for you. She said you swore you knew the way, but you just kept going in circles until we found you."

Elara grinned, shaking her head. "And let's not forget the wild boar incident. I thought we'd have to carry you back to camp, Rorik."

Rorik laughed, a deep, hearty sound that was so like him that Lanae grinned. "I admit, that boar caught me off guard. But it made for quite a story to tell."

Lanae's eyes twinkled with amusement. "Those were good times. We've come a long way since then."

Elara nodded, her gaze thoughtful. "Yes, we have. And we've faced challenges that would have broken many others. But we're still here, together."

Caelum's smile widened as he looked around the table. "You know, when Lanae and I were kids, we got into all sorts of mischief. There was this one time we decided to build a raft and sail down the river. We were convinced we could make it all the way to the sea."

Elara raised an eyebrow. "How did that turn out?"

Caelum laughed, shaking his head. "Not well, as you can imagine. The raft fell apart within the first mile, and we ended up soaking wet, covered in mud, and having to walk all the way back home. Our parents were not pleased."

Amusement rippled Rorik's abdomen. "I can picture it. You two always had grand ideas."

"Oh, absolutely," Caelum continued. "There was also the time we tried to dig a tunnel to escape chores. We got about three feet down before the whole thing collapsed on us. Lanae was convinced we were in serious trouble, but I just couldn't stop laughing."

The table erupted in laughter, the stories painting vivid pictures of youthful escapades and carefree days.

As the meal continued, the conversation ebbed and flowed, a tapestry of laughter, nostalgia, and quiet understanding. They were more than just friends; they were family, bound by their experiences and their unwavering support for one another.

Lanae set down her fork, her appetite satisfied. "Before Caelum embarrasses me any further, I think it's time to head out and find this sphinx."

As Lanae reached to clear the plates, Caelum put a hand on hers. "Don't worry about the dishes. I'll clean all this up while you go hunt down the information you need."

She gave her brother a quick hug. "I'll keep the channels open." She tapped her temple and received a grateful smile in return.

"Go." He shooed her away as he gathered the dishes and headed into the kitchen.

The air hummed with the anxiety pelting her skin. Draven's eyes met Lanae's, a silent promise passing between them. They had faced the witch's challenges together, and this would be no different.

Nero chirped and flapped his wings, taking flight and landing on Lanae's shoulder. As they exited the house, the night enveloped them. The stars above shimmered like distant beacons. The sphinx's labyrinth awaited, with its shifting walls and hidden dangers.

"Stay close," Draven advised, his dragon lending him an aura of formidable strength. "We move as one."

With Elara leading the way, the group set off into the night, their steps guided by the light of the runes and the map in her hand. Shadows danced around them as they headed to the next point where the sphinx and the labyrinth could be.

IT DIDN'T TAKE LONG for the group to find the shimmering doorway in an alleyway near the farthest point of Solstice City. The air around the portal seemed to ripple. The edges of the doorway pulsated with a faint, ethereal glow. It was a hidden entrance, one that could easily be missed by the untrained eye.

Elara led the way, her movements confident and assured. She peeked over her shoulder, meeting Draven's gaze with a smug, *I told you I could find it* expression that made him uneasy.

Her eyes sparkled with a hint of mischief, and Draven couldn't dismiss the feeling that something wasn't right. It dug into his bones and made his intuition spark, along with his fingertips. He fisted his hands, dousing his sputtering flames.

As she stepped aside, gesturing for him to proceed, Draven's gaze narrowed. Suspicion filled his bones, and an icy knot settled in his gut. He had trusted Elara so far, but something about her demeanor now set off alarm bells.

Draven cast a tentative glance at Lanae, who stood beside him with Nero perched gracefully on her shoulder. The little griffin's eyes were intense and alert, as if the little creature sensed the edginess of the atmosphere.

Together, Draven and Lanae stepped through the shimmering doorway, the portal's magic enveloping them in a cool, tingling sensation. The world beyond was cloaked in shadows, the path ahead obscured by a faint mist that seemed to whisper secrets.

Draven's unease deepened when he realized that Elara and Rorik had not followed. He glanced back, but the shimmering doorway framed only emptiness, as if the portal had closed. The absence of their companions added to his growing sense of dread.

"What's going on?" Lanae reached for his hand.

"The portal closed behind us," Draven replied, his voice low. "Hopefully, your friend led us to the sphinx and not into some other dangerously twisted adventure."

"Trust me. If Elara said she'd get us to the sphinx, this is the right place."

He grunted, but didn't voice any more of his doubt.

Nero chirped, his feathers ruffling as he scanned the surroundings. The little griffin's enhanced senses were their best hope of navigating the labyrinth that lay ahead.

As they moved forward, the shadows closed in around them. The air grew frostier with each step.

Draven's heart raced in his chest, his instincts on high alert. He couldn't escape the feeling that they were being watched, that unseen eyes tracked their every move.

The path twisted and turned, leading them deeper within the maze. Draven's mind raced, trying to make sense of Elara's actions and the absence of both her and Rorik on this leg of the journey. Trust was a fragile thing, easily shattered by suspicion and fear.

When they rounded a corner, Draven drew back, and Lanae followed. Before them loomed the imposing sphinx, its golden eyes boring into his soul. The air crackled with ancient magic.

"I recognize that face." The historian's voice was deep and melodic, sending shivers down his spine.

Draven inclined his head. "It has been ages, sphinx."

"It has. What is it you seek?"

It would do no good to be obtuse with this being. "The gauntlet stone." Draven met the sphinx's golden gaze.

"To unveil the past, answer me this: What walks on four legs in the morning, two legs at noon, and three legs in the evening?"

Draven's mind raced. Memories of old tales surfaced. He hated these games, but he knew the stakes. "Man," he answered, his voice steady. "As an infant, he crawls on all fours. As an adult, he walks on two legs. In old age, he uses a cane."

The sphinx's eyes gleamed with approval. "Well done, dragon," he purred, his voice carrying a tone of ancient wisdom and subtle amusement. With a graceful wave of his paw, a pair of straight-backed chairs materialized before them, their wooden frames intricately carved with arcane symbols. "Sit," he commanded with a twinkle of satisfaction in his eyes.

Draven, ever the gentleman, offered Lanae the far seat with a respectful nod. She settled into it gracefully, her eyes never leaving the sphinx. Draven then took his seat beside her, feeling the firm support of the chair beneath him. He focused on the sphinx, though he couldn't help but feel a twinge of irritation at the creature's dramatic flair.

"Now, for the tale you seek..." the sphinx intoned, his voice rich and resonant. As he spoke, the world around them dissolved and the cavernous interior of the sphinx's lair faded away. In its place, an ancient setting materialized, shrouded in mist and glowing with an otherworldly light. Druids, garbed in flowing robes adorned with mystical symbols, moved with deliberate grace. Beside them, beings of various shapes and sizes—some shimmering with ethereal light, others cloaked in shadow—took part in a solemn ritual.

Awe's cool touch fell over Draven as the scene unfolded before them. The druids and mystical beings worked in unison, their movements synchronized as they chanted incantations and wove spells. The ancient beings created a stone that swirled with a blend of black and white magic. A balance of opposing forces captured in a single, pulsating artifact. The sight filled him with a sense of wonder and reverence for the ancient knowledge being revealed.

"The Druids created the stone to awaken lost realms, but the dark powers imbued in it carry the ability to wreak unimaginable destruction. They did not realize the dangers of mixing light and dark magic together, and what resulted was an unintended consequence. The stone became powerful enough to not just reach lost realms, but to create new ones and the dark powers could destroy realms by merging them all into one universe ruled under a dark lord."

A sudden, gentle grip on his hand pulled Draven's attention away from the mesmerizing spectacle. He glanced down to see Lanae's hand squeezing his, her fingers soft and reassuring. When he looked up at her face, she was entirely absorbed in the vision, her eyes wide with amazement. She was so engrossed that she didn't even seem to realize she had reached out to him.

Draven's heart stuttered as if he couldn't quite draw breath with the warmth of her touch. And he realized he never wanted to draw a full breath again in her presence. The dichotomy of the emotions swirled around him like an out-of-control fire. The connection they shared seemed to solidify before his eyes. A weave of fate bound them together, and the power of that connection shivered down his spine and nested right next to his heart.

As the ancient tale continued to unfold around them, he held onto her hand, making a silent promise to keep her safe in the face of the challenges that lay ahead.

The sphinx's eyes grew even more intense as it continued, its voice carrying ancient knowledge and an ominous warning. "Once the Druids discovered their grave mistake by creating this relic, they cursed the stone and hid it away so no being could wield that much power. You see, the stone can twist even the pure of heart."

His words echoed in the cavernous space. "Its magic is not to be taken lightly. This artifact is a double-edged sword, its true nature hidden beneath layers of enchantment."

Draven and Lanae exchanged uneasy glances as the sphinx's words settled, thickening the air with an almost physical tension.

"Beware of its allure," the sphinx intoned, its gaze piercing and unwavering. "The stone can amplify the desires and fears within you. It can bend reality to your will, but in doing so, it can corrupt your intentions, leading you down a path of darkness."

Lanae's grip on Draven's hand tightened.

"While it can create realms," the sphinx went on, "it also can destroy all that you hold sacred. The power it possesses is raw and untamed, capable of unleashing chaos if wielded without wisdom and restraint. Those who seek to harness its power must do so with a heart free of malice and a mind clear of ill intentions. Failure to do so will lead not only to your downfall but to the unraveling of the very world you seek to protect."

The warning hung in the air, a chilling reminder of the stakes involved. The sphinx's eyes seemed to bore into their souls, searching for any sign of weakness or doubt.

The ancient environment around them faded, and Draven stood, mulling over all he had heard and seen. "The stone can create worlds. But can it resurrect them?"

The sphinx's lips pressed together for a moment, glaring at Draven. "No, it cannot resurrect the dead." The sphinx's voice dropped to a solemn whisper. "The Druids were wise enough to include a fail-safe in the gauntlet stone's creation. They chose the power of their enemies as a way to destroy the relic."

Draven shivered. When Druids existed in this realm, his kind were their enemies. Those ancient wars were recorded in the dragons' history books. Books that were reduced to ash when the fae stole the Dragon's Heart.

The sphinx continued, "If the stone is activated, only the fire of a royal dragon can destroy it. But it must be done before realms merge."

"Where do we find it?" Draven asked.

"I can transport you to the labyrinth that holds the relic. And once you have it, you may return through the portal that you found me with." The sphinx stared down at the two of them. "Handle the gauntlet stone wisely, for the fate of all realms depends on your choices."

With a plume of smoke, the sphinx disappeared.

THE ENTRANCE TO THE labyrinth stood before them, a yawning maw of ancient stone, entwined with vines that pulsed with a faint, otherworldly glow. Magic thrummed in the air in an intense force that set Lanae's nerves on edge. She looked at Draven, whose expression was grim, his eyes reflecting a deep-seated unease. Nero, still nestled on Lanae's shoulder, chirped quietly, his bright eyes alert and scanning their surroundings in a continuous sweep.

As they stepped onto the path, the air grew chillier. The light dimmed as shadows stretched and twisted around them. The walls seemed to shift and breathe, alive with the ancient magic that powered the maze. Each step felt heavier than the last. Magic pressed down on them.

The passageways were narrow and winding, filled with deceptive turns and hidden alcoves. Nero, unaffected by the illusions that plagued the labyrinth, chirped occasionally, guiding them with soft nudges and swift pecks in the right direction.

As they ventured deeper, the magic grew stronger, warping the surrounding air. An icy shiver ran down Lanae's spine as the shadows merged into familiar shapes. Before her stood the spectral figures of her parents, their faces etched with sorrow and longing.

"Lanae," her mother's voice echoed, haunting and hollow. "Why didn't you save us?"

Lanae's breath hitched; her heart ravaged her chest at the sight. "I... I don't know what happened to you." Tears welled in her eyes. "I've tried to find you."

Her father's ghostly form reached out, his eyes filled with disappointment. "You must do more, Lanae. The danger is greater than you know."

The illusion was so vivid, so real, that Lanae's commitment to her cause wavered. She reached out, her fingers brushing against cold, intangible figures, but Nero's loud chirp snapped her back to reality. The baby griffin pecked at her arm. His urgent eyes broke the spell of the illusion.

Shaking herself free of the haunting vision, Lanae refocused on the path ahead. She turned to find Draven's expression twisted in anguish. Around him, shadows had formed into the shapes of his lost dragon kin, their eyes burning with a mixture of accusation and despair.

"Draven, why did you fail us?" one of the spectral dragons hissed, its voice like the crackling of flames.

Another ghostly dragon loomed closer, its gaze piercing. "You were supposed to protect us, Draven. How could you let this happen?"

Draven staggered, his eyes wide with guilt. "I was too little to save you... I couldn't." His voice broke.

Lanae moved swiftly to his side. She gripped his shoulder and gave him a little shake. "Draven, look at me. These aren't real. They're illusions, meant to break us. We can't let them win."

Draven's gaze flickered to Lanae, and he blinked rapidly at her. She palmed his cheek, and the anguish carved into his features softened. He took a deep, shuddering breath, shaking off the shadows that sought to ensnare him.

Nero chirped again, his sharp eyes fixed on a path that seemed to shimmer with a faint, golden light. The little griffin guided them away from the deceptive traps, his instincts leading them through the ever-shifting maze.

Lanae and Draven moved through the winding pathways, following Nero's guidance until they finally emerged from the oppressive shadows into a clearing bathed in the soft glow of otherworldly light.

Breathing in the crisp night air, Lanae turned to Draven and raised her arms in triumph. Her grin was wide enough for her cheeks to ache. "We made it!"

Draven nodded, a small smile touching his lips. "Yes, we did."

Nero chirped happily, fluttered to the ground, and pecked at a small flower.

Lanae kneeled beside him, stroking his feathers with gratitude. "We couldn't have done it without you, little one."

As they stood bathed in the calming light of the glen, their focus fell on the gauntlet stone shining on a pedestal before them. And then their gazes dropped to the bones scattered on the ground.

DRAVEN'S GAZE LATCHED ONTO the stone, its luminescence casting an ethereal glow across the hollow. *That was too easy.* The thought invaded his relief and made his muscles tense. His eyes kept being drawn to the stone, but the bones littering the surrounding ground warred for his attention.

This thing that those ancient druids created was dangerous. The sphinx's warnings echoed in his head, but the lure of the stone sang, drawing him to it like a siren song.

"Destroy it." Lanae's voice sliced through the haze that clouded Draven's mind.

Her words shattered whatever hold the stone had on him. But a small part of him coveted the stone. Its power was intoxicating. Draven ran his hand down his face and forced his gaze to hers.

"Destroy it." She pointed at the stone and kept his gaze.

Lanae's steely stare penetrated deeper than the lure of something so destructive, and Draven breathed deeply, concentrating on the fire within him. He had mastered drawing it to him in human form, but a part of him wished he could use the full force of his flame as a dragon.

He shook off his wandering thoughts and focused on that inferno in the center of his being. A core of raw power ready to be unleashed at his command. His chest expanded as he drew in air, his lungs filled with the scorching heat of his dragon fire.

He pushed Lanae behind him, mindful of the power he held. With a mighty exhalation, Draven released a torrent of flames directed at the rock.

Fire erupted from his mouth, blazing a path straight to the gauntlet stone.

Flames licked an invisible barrier surrounding the artifact, igniting it with an intense white illumination. The brilliance of the light forced them to squint, shielding their eyes from the searing glare.

Fire roared through the glen and the air crackled with energy. As the flames engulfed the stone, a high-pitched popping sound pierced their ears. It echoed through the woods, reverberating off the pedestal.

Then, just as suddenly as they had flared, the flames extinguished, leaving behind a wisp of smoke that dissipated into the air.

With a quick intake of breath that hissed through his teeth, Draven stepped back, unable to believe what he was seeing.

The stone remained unscathed. Its surface gave off an ominous glow.

Draven's heart sank. The flames had no effect. He glanced at Lanae, his eyes meeting hers as an icy hand gripped him. His skin broke out in a clammy sweat as if he had just unleashed hell with his fire.

Lanae turned her attention to the stone and stepped toward it.

Draven put out his hand to stop her. "Take a closer look at those bones, Lanae." He pointed at the ground. "The ears."

Lanae's eyes widened. Fae had unique skeletal features where their ears were that other species didn't have. She stared at the swirl patterns on several of the bare craniums, and her gaze jumped to Draven.

"Fae bones." He swiped the sweat off his face and shook his hands by his side. "Let me try."

"But..."

Draven waved at the pedestal. "It's still standing, so perhaps dragon fire isn't what is needed to destroy the damn thing." He moved forward, ignoring that little voice in his head that begged to either leave it or smash it.

The intensity of the situation pressed down on him, sending a trickle of sweat down his back. But he knew he had to try. The fate of their realm depended on not letting this hunk of stone fall into the wrong hands.

The space between him and the stone seemed to stretch infinitely, each step soaked with anticipation. The closer he got, the more he felt a magnetic pull, a tangible force drawing him in. His breath hitched in his throat. His heart pounded with both awe and fear. The brightly lit stone called to him, its allure almost overwhelming. A greedy need to possess it, to harness its power, stole his breath away. He reached out, his fingers trembling, drawn to the artifact like a moth to a flame.

Just before his skin touched the stone, he hesitated. A flicker of sanity broke through the relic's seductive power, reminding him of the grave warnings they had received. His hands shook as he fought the compulsion, his mind a battleground between desire and reason. With a monumental effort, he removed the stone from the pedestal. Its magic sapped the strength from his legs.

The gauntlet stone thrummed in his hands, its energy coursing through his veins like liquid fire. He could feel the immense potential it held, a raw, untamed power that whispered promises of glory and retribution. Visions flashed before his eyes— of using the stone to rebuild his fallen kingdom, to restore the legacy of his ancestors, and to take vengeance on those who had wronged him. The allure was almost irresistible, a tantalizing dream of what could be.

But then he thought of Lanae. Her face, her strength, her unwavering commitment to their cause. The realm's fate hung in the balance, and the responsibility weighed on him. The temptation to use the stone for personal gain clashed violently with his duty to protect the realm. He clenched his fists around the stone. The gauntlet's energy pulsed against his skin.

Could he really forsake his humanity for his desires?

The question gnawed at him, his heart and mind at war. Draven breathed deeply, grounding himself in the present. He had come too far, sacrificed too much, to let the stone corrupt his purpose now.

FROM THE EDGE OF the glen, Lanae watched Draven with a wary eye, especially with his question about resurrection lingering in her mind. The conflict etched on his face was deep, the way his brows furrowed and the edges of his mouth tightened. His hands trembled as he clutched the gauntlet stone. The artifact seemed to pulsate with a life of its own, casting an eerie light that reflected off his skin. The sight made her heart writhe for him.

She could not fathom being the last of her kind. The weight of her parents' disappearance often felt like a stone in her chest, but she knew she wasn't truly alone. Friends, allies, her brother Caelum—all provided a network of support and shared history. But this man before her, this formidable dragon, had borne the burden of isolation for decades, his existence a lonely vigil.

Drawing in a steadying breath, Lanae stepped closer. The ground hummed with the energy of the artifact, making her feel like she had crossed a river full of fish oil. It pushed down on her, making her clench her teeth against the dark magic radiating from the thing.

Every one of Draven's muscles drew taut at her approach. The way he held the stone was as if he coveted the power it held.

"Draven, this isn't just about us. The realm's future depends on what we do with that relic." She spoke with a mild but unwavering voice, each word carefully measured.

Draven turned to look at her. His eyes swirled with a tempest of emotions—grief, hope, fear, want, determination. His clutch tightened.

Lanae's heart clenched with empathy, knowing that he was wrestling with the impossible choice between personal loss and the greater good. If he didn't choose wisely, she would have to put him down. She drew her sword. The whisper of metal being freed from its sheath drew his eyes to her hands.

When his gaze returned to hers, they were wide with despair.

"We may be fate bound, but I cannot let you take the stone. We need to destroy it." She reached her free hand out and ran her fingers over his exposed forearm. Their connection buzzed through her.

Draven blinked, and all the conflicting emotions faded. He glanced at her with mistrust glazing his eyes.

Lanae prayed he would have the strength to do what was right. Their actions in this moment would reverberate through the ages, shaping the fate of their world.

The glen hummed with residual magic, the air thick with the lingering energy of the relic. Draven cradled the stone. Its power thrummed visibly through his veins. The danger of what they had found—and what it meant—pressed heavily on her shoulders.

"Please, Draven. Destroy that thing."

His gaze bounced between her eyes and then dropped to her fingers still caressing his skin. His lips twitched into a tight smile, and he nodded. "Step behind me."

She did as he asked, but still gripped her sword and kept her free hand on his shoulder because her touch seemed to bring him back from whatever darkness had pulled him under for a moment.

Draven dropped his chin to his chest and his eyes closed. Smoke billowed from his nose, drifting around them like a fog.

Heat radiated from Draven, and he took a great inhale, just as he had before. But this time, when he blew out, only a flicker of fire escaped. He tried again and again and let out a growl of frustration.

Each time he tried, the dark magic in the glen flared, stanching Draven's flame. The black magic made Lanae wish for a hot bath to wash away the dirty feeling. She'd gladly scrub her skin raw to get rid of the slimy residue of this place.

He snickered behind closed lips. "It seems this place won't allow it."

"Then we need to move," Lanae said, her voice steady despite the mistrust roiling inside her. She had seen the lust for power in his eyes. She couldn't discount his deepest desires with the stone, but she needed to get out of this place. The magic here was dark and oily, and she needed to feel clean. "We can't stay here."

Draven nodded. He tucked the gauntlet stone safely into his pocket.

Together, they turned and surveyed the glen for a way out. The path they had come in through was no longer there, and only twisted trees surrounded them. Draven pointed at the far side of the enclosure, where a path seemed to materialize out of nowhere.

With trepidation, they crossed and stepped onto a natural route. It seemed darker and more menacing than the trials of entry had been, with each shadow hiding potential danger.

Nero flew ahead, his keen eyes scanning for threats as they navigated the tunnel through the trees.

A constant undercurrent of tension made Lanae hypervigilant. The surrounding air seemed to grow thicker as they approached the exit, an ominous sign that something was amiss.

She glanced back at Draven, and dread pummeled her bones.

As they rounded the last corner, the exit loomed before them, a faint light filtering in from the outside world. Relief surged through Lanae's veins, but it was short-lived. The moment they stepped into the open, her heart sank.

They were no longer within the walls of Solstice City. A legion of dark fae warriors stood waiting, their forms cloaked in shadow. They filled the clearing, a sea of malevolent eyes and gleaming weapons that robbed Lanae's breath.

The lead warrior stepped forward, his presence commanding and sinister. His eyes locked onto Lanae, a cruel smile curving his lips. "You thought you could escape so easily?" he taunted. His voice dripped with malice.

It was a trap all along. Lanae's stomach dropped with the realization.

Draven stepped in front of Lanae, his stance protective. The air around him crackled with energy, his dragon giving him an aura of fierce power. "I suggest you run." He shifted his eyes into the blazing inferno of a dragon.

The dark warriors tightened their grip on their weapons, readying for battle. Lanae drew her sword, the cool metal a comforting weight in her hand.

Just as Draven sucked air into his lungs as if to annihilate the enemy with fire, the sea of dark fae parted. Lanae gasped and Draven snuffed his flame at the sight of Elara and Rorik being dragged forward at sword-point.

The stalemate lasted a fraction of a breath before Elara twisted in the guard's grip, stripping his sword and cutting him down. Rorik spun away from the blade and jumped, landing a kick to the dark soldier's chest, making his bid for freedom with the same viciousness as Elara.

Lanae's heart raged in her chest, her mind racing as she prepared herself for the inevitable clash.

The first wave of warriors charged, and the night erupted into chaos.

CHAPTER THIRTEEN
Betrayal

THE BATTLEFIELD WAS A chaotic symphony of elemental forces clashing and intertwining, each faction vying for control of the battle. The sky above roared with thunder; bolts of lightning tore through the night, illuminating Solstice City in the distance as torrents of rain lashed the ground. The scent of ozone and the sharp tang of magic set Draven's nerves on edge.

Lanae fought beside him, her movements a blur of silver and pink as she wielded her blade with deadly precision. Their bond, forged in the fires of adversity, lent them a seamless synchronicity. Yet, amidst the turmoil, Draven couldn't ignore the hunch that something was very wrong.

Elara moved with an unsettling grace, her eyes alight with a strange, unnatural glow. Draven had noticed the shift in her demeanor after she cut down that first guard—the way she seemed almost mechanical in her actions—but the urgency of the battle left little room for investigation.

The ground beneath them shuddered, and a fissure split the earth, spewing molten lava. Draven leaped back, summoning a barrier of flames to shield Lanae from the searing heat. Elemental magic surged around them, the very terrain shifting as the battle raged.

Amidst the chaos, Draven's gaze locked onto Elara. She was close enough to reach him and she swung in a killing blow; Draven dodged out of the way enough to save his life, but her blade tore through his clothing, nicking his skin. The pocket holding the relic became another casualty of her blade, and the gauntlet stone tumbled to the ground.

Elara darted forward, swiping the stone from the dirt with a maniacal smile.

"Elara!" Draven shouted, his voice barely audible above the pandemonium. "What are you doing?"

Elara's eyes met his, and for a fleeting moment, he saw a flicker of anguish in their depths. "I'm sorry, Draven." Her voice carried her sorrow. "I have no choice."

Before he could react, the air around her shimmered, and a dark, oppressive energy enveloped her, cascading from her pores like he had seen once before when he was a child.

A chilling realization blanketed him.

Elara was cursed, and he knew without a doubt who could have cast this type of darkness. Only a Firetwill could wield this kind of curse.

"No!" Draven roared, his fury igniting a blaze within him. Flames surged from his body, his rage fueling a partial transformation. Pain gripped every cell as scales erupted along his arms and neck. His teeth elongated to points meant to tear flesh from bone, and his eyes burned with the fierce green glow of his dragon.

The sight of Draven's transformation sent shock waves through the battlefield, both ally and foe screaming in awe and terror. But his focus was singular—Elara and the gauntlet stone.

With a burst of speed, Draven lunged at Elara, but the curse had already taken hold. The ground beneath them heaved and shifted, creating a chasm that separated them. Elara clutched the stone and was lifted into the air by a swirling vortex of dark magic.

"Lanae!" Draven called out, desperation lacing his gravelly voice. "We have to stop her!"

Lanae's wide-eyed shock broke, and she nodded, moving to join him. Together, they navigated the treacherous terrain, their elemental powers clashing against the shifting forces of the battlefield.

Elara, now fully enveloped in the dark energy, was almost unreachable. Draven's fury surged, his dragon form lashing against the confines of his human body, making his bones ache. The dragon within him roared for release, but he did not know how to break the barriers keeping his dragon contained without the Dragon's Heart.

"Elara, fight it!" Lanae's voice shot through the storm of magic, a desperate plea. "You can break free!"

For a moment, Elara's eyes cleared, and the anguish in them was heart-wrenching. "I...can't," she choked out, the curse tightening its grip. "I'm sorry."

With a final, despairing cry, Elara vanished into the swirling vortex. The stone slipped from her grasp and disappeared into the darkness.

The battlefield fell silent; the elemental forces dissipated and the dark fae fell as if someone had turned off all automation with the sweep of a switch. Draven's partial transformation receded, the scales retracting as he fell to his knees. The weight of their defeat crushed down.

Lanae kneeled beside him, her hand resting on his shoulder. "We found it once. We'll find it again, Draven." She glanced at the surrounding devastation. "We can't let this break us."

Draven looked at her and nodded, despite the knot in his stomach. The unyielding conviction in her eyes almost made him wince. He did not share Lanae's faith that they could find the stone again before all hell broke loose.

CHAPTER FOURTEEN
Wounded Trust

THE CRESCENT MOON HUNG high in the night sky, casting a silver glow over Solstice City. The ancient structures and winding streets of the city gleamed under its ethereal light, creating a scene both serene and haunting. Lanae stood on her terrace, the cool night air brushing against her skin as she looked out over the city. Her thoughts were a tangled web of emotions, each thread pulling her in a different direction. The events of the past days had left her reeling—torn between her loyalty to the fae and the unfolding situation that threatened their realm. Elara's betrayal stung deeply, like a thorn embedded in her heart, but she was grateful that Rorik had survived the attack.

Inside, Draven paced back and forth, his footsteps echoing like a rhythmic drumbeat in her mind. Each step he took vibrated with frustration and anger. His turmoil scraped across her skin like a legion of thorns. The bond they shared amplified his emotions within her.

She glanced down from her terrace to where Rorik stood guard alone. His gaunt expression spoke volumes, his eyes haunted by recent events. The once-vibrant warrior now looked like a shadow of himself, worn thin by the strain of Elara's duplicity. None of them had spoken more than a handful of words on the way back into the city, the silence laden with unspoken fears and doubts. After Elara disappeared, most of the dark fae had either dropped on the battlefield or melted away into the shadows, their loyalty as fleeting as mist.

Rorik glanced up, meeting her eyes. She gave him a nod, a silent exchange of strength and understanding. She had always fought for her people, but now the lines were blurring. The stakes were higher than ever, and the threat of a bigger betrayal loomed large.

The curse that had been cast on Elara could be cast on anyone. And that was a chilling realization that left her feeling unsettled and vulnerable.

Turning away from the turmoil outside, Lanae stepped back into the room to face Draven. He looked like a wrecked dragon, his broad shoulders slumped and his face etched with lines of worry. The sight of him, so powerful yet so burdened, tugged at her heartstrings.

"It wasn't your fault." Even as the words tumbled from her lips, Draven's piercing glare made her want to shrink back. His stormy eyes were filled with self-recrimination.

"They played us." His voice held the edge of anger. "The witch, the sphinx...this whole damn quest was orchestrated. Those bones were fae. They didn't have that damn stone until I delivered it to them." He raked his hair with both hands; his frustration screamed with his every movement.

Lanae stepped closer. Her heart raced in her chest as she reached out to touch Draven's arm. The same powerful vibration that always occurred when they touched zinged through her, sending a delicious tremor down her spine. It was as if their very souls resonated with each other, a connection that defied explanation.

"Even this damned connection." Draven's voice vibrated with irritation as he pushed her hand away.

The rejection stung, but Lanae held her ground, her eyes searching his face for any sign of the man beneath the turmoil. "I don't think the witch led us astray on that point." Her voice carried a note of gentle insistence. The conflict in his eyes warred between his desire and his fear.

Draven stared at her, his expression unconvinced. Yet there was a flicker of something deeper in his gaze. A vulnerability he rarely showed.

"You do feel what's between us," Lanae pressed, her voice lifting with a hint of hope. She raised her eyebrows, urging him to acknowledge the bond they shared.

He sucked in his lower lip, his nostrils flaring as he struggled with his emotions. "Yes. I do feel it," he finally admitted with a voice as rough as sandpaper. The admission seemed to unleash something within him, and he stalked closer, his movements predatory and intense.

Lanae instinctively backed away. A strangled sound formed in her throat when her back hit the wall behind her. There was nowhere to go, no escape from his unwavering focus. Draven framed her in with his arms, his body a solid barrier that both trapped and protected her. His eyes burned with a hunger she had never seen before—a raw, unfiltered desire that sent a thrill of anticipation through her.

For the first time, there wasn't a cocky smile on his face, but a look of pure need. The air between them crackled with electricity. Lanae's heart raced; her pulse quickened as she met his gaze, her own desire mirrored in his eyes.

In that moment, all else faded away. It was just the two of them, bound by a connection that transcended words. Lanae reached up, her fingers brushing against his cheek; Draven leaned into her touch, his eyes closing briefly as if savoring the sensation.

"Draven." Her voice trembled with emotion.

He opened his eyes, his steely gaze softening as he looked at her. His gaze lowered to her mouth, and he leaned in. The anticipation built. Her heart kicked up a saucy tango as their lips finally met.

The first touch was gentle, a soft brush of lips that sent chills racing down her back. It was as if their souls were reaching out to each other, seeking solace amidst the madness. The warmth of his breath mingled with hers, creating a heady mix that left her dizzy with longing.

Draven's lips were firm yet tender, a perfect balance of strength and gentleness. Each movement was a dance, a give and take that spoke volumes without a single word.

As the kiss deepened, Lanae's emotions surged, a flood of feelings that she had kept bottled up since that first brush on the street. Desire coursed through her veins, leaving her skin flushed with a heat she had never felt before. It engulfed her, and she reached for his shoulders. Her fingers curled into the fabric of his shirt as she pulled him closer. The curves of his body against hers kept her anchored in this moment.

The bond between them sizzled through her body, igniting a feral call to claim him as her own. Lanae's senses heightened with every touch, every caress magnified by the intensity of the moment. Draven's heart drummed against her chest in a rhythm that matched her own.

His kiss overwhelmed her with an impression of completeness, a melding of souls, a promise of something deeper and more profound. The kiss lingered, each second stretching into eternity, until he finally pulled away, leaving her lips tingling and her heart beating with an insatiable desire.

His lips stretched into a glowing smile, one of conquest and possessiveness that she had not seen before. It was a look that drew all the heat right to her core, igniting a fire that she couldn't ignore. The intensity of his gaze, the way his eyes seemed to claim her, sent a shiver down her spine.

"Lanae," Caelum's voice called from the hallway, breaking the spell.

Draven stepped away, the sudden distance creating a chill Lanae couldn't shake. She had momentarily forgotten about her brother. Hell, she had forgotten the world while Draven's lips were on hers. The connection between them had been so powerful, so consuming, that it had swept her away completely.

No kiss had ever affected her that much.

"What?" Her voice came out a bit too harsh, betraying her frustration at the interruption.

Caelum glanced between her and Draven, his eyes narrowing with suspicion before he turned fully toward her. "While I was out at the market, I overheard something odd."

"Just spit it out." Lanae wiped her face, trying to focus on her brother instead of the carnal need flaming over her skin.

"I heard there was a desertion within the guard," Caelum said.

Lanae snorted and a bitter laugh escaped. "You could say that. Elara is in league with whoever is planning to enslave us."

Caelum's eyes widened. "What happened last night?"

"We found the stone, and she stole it and disappeared." Draven summed up the night in one quick sentence, his voice tight, as if fighting the same barrage of emotions that Lanae was feeling. "And I believe a Firetwill is responsible."

The name triggered a memory she couldn't quite reach. "Firetwill?"

Draven gave a quick nod. "Yes. Alestain Firetwill."

A chill gathered in Lanae's stomach. That name itched the back of her mind, but her brother interrupted her thoughts before her memory could form.

"How do you know?" Caelum's brow furrowed.

"Because I've seen that kind of curse before." Draven's eyes darkened with ghosts of painful memories.

Lanae ran over Elara's betrayal for the umpteenth time since they had left the forest on the outskirts of Solstice City. This time she looked at the memory without emotion, and the way Elara fought struck her. She hadn't been striking out at the dark fae unless they got in her path. A path straight to Draven. Her motions were almost as if automated, much the same as the dark fae fought. The same way the fae attacking their lands fought. It was as if they were not in control of their faculties.

Winter's kiss brushed Lanae's face as the realization hit her.

Perhaps the attacks against Solstice City were orchestrated by this Firetwill and not the realm of the dark fae. The thought sent a quiver down her spine.

"Explain," Lanae said with a voice laced with urgency. She needed to grasp the full extent of the threat they faced.

Draven stared at her for a moment, the silence heavy with his unspoken pain. "Alestain Firetwill, the fae I showed you in my memory, the one with hair whiter than Rorik's and eyes the color of a void, used the same magic to betray my father and steal the Dragon's Heart." His voice was tinged with bitterness as he spoke. "Once he had it in his possession, he fed off the powers of our sacred stone and killed everyone he deemed an enemy. Including all the dragons."

The room chilled with his revelation. The image of Alestain Firetwill, a figure cloaked in darkness and treachery, loomed large in her mind. The name itself felt like a curse, a specter from the past that had returned to haunt them, and a sense of déjà vu slipped over her.

"If you saw it happen, how did you survive?" Caelum's tone was more challenging than Lanae would have liked. He crossed his arms and stared at Draven in a way that screamed disbelief.

"Because I was only seven when it happened and my mother hid me." Draven's voice cracked at the mention of his mother, as if just the memory of her incited nightmares. "She was killed mercilessly, and I still hear her screams in my nightmares." The admission hung in the air, a raw wound that had never fully healed.

Caelum blanched and his bravado faltered. "Oh." He traded a glance with Lanae, and through their bond, Caelum's empathy magnified. *I didn't know.*

Lanae's heart hurt for Draven, for the boy who had watched his world crumble, and for the man who now bore the burden of that loss. She stepped closer, her hand finding his, offering silent support.

Caelum glanced at their intertwined hands. "Well, on that note, I'll leave you two to figure out the next step," he said. "If you need anything, I'll be in my bedroom." With that, he turned on his heel and disappeared down the hallway. His footsteps faded into the quiet of the house.

As soon as he was out of range, Lanae turned to Draven, her cheeks flushing with embarrassment and lingering desire.

"That was...awkward," she admitted. Caelum had never walked in on her in a compromising position before.

Draven stared at her and his lips twitched just before his laugh burst through the room, rich and full, cutting through the remnants of tension like a soft summer breeze.

His laugh left her heart fluttering just as much as his kiss had. His eyes sparkled with genuine mirth, the shadows of their past worries momentarily banished by the joy of the present. She found herself smiling in response, the warmth of his laughter rekindling the fire that had ignited between them.

"At least we hadn't started ripping our clothes off." He squeezed her hand.

She huffed a laugh, imagining the look on her brother's face if he indeed had caught them undressed and in each other's arms. She stepped in front of Draven, still holding his hand, and met his gaze. Her smile faded as their situation fell over her like a turbulent storm.

She sobered. "Do you think the council knows of Firetwill?"

Draven's smile faded. "I don't know. I don't trust the fae, so my viewpoint is tainted." He closed the distance, looming over her. "And it would be dangerous to align with Firetwill." He ran his fingers over her cheek and into her hair, pulling her closer, to within a hair's breadth of his lips. "But desperation does strange things to people."

Lanae nodded but conflict brewed within her. She questioned her loyalty to the council, especially if they were party to the impending destruction of the realms. "I've always been loyal to the guard, but now I feel torn. I see the bigger picture, the greater threat. And...our bond compels me to keep you safe."

"Just the bond?" His lips toyed with a smile.

Heat filled her cheeks. "It's more than the bond now."

Draven's gaze softened, and he pressed his forehead against hers. "Lanae, I understand more than you can fathom. The same need lives in my heart." He unthreaded his hand from hers and ran his hands up her arms. "But life has taught me to question everything. Especially things like this burning need between us." He locked his eyes with hers. "Is it real, or a farce manufactured by a maniac?"

She gazed deep into his emerald eyes. "It would be easy to lose myself in this."

Draven's grip tightened. "You're not alone. It's as if I cannot breathe when you are near. My devotion to getting the Dragon's Heart back wanes, and a need to protect you above all else has replaced my lifelong mission for payback."

Lanae's heart swelled with affection. "If this is a farce, so be it." She tilted her head and captured another kiss. One that transcended time and healed a fraction of the brokenness within both of them. But she knew this peace would soon fracture, just like the rest of their world.

DRAVEN PULLED AWAY FROM her sweet lips, his breath ragged and his heart clanging in his chest. Doubt clouded his perception, a dark shadow creeping into the corners of his mind. This couldn't be real. The intensity of his emotions, the overriding need to claim her and keep her as his, was overwhelming. It felt like a dream, too perfect to be true, and he feared waking up to find it all an illusion.

He cupped her face, his eyes searching hers for reassurance. Their bond was undeniable, a magnetic pull that drew them together despite the chaos around them. But the fear of losing her, of this moment slipping through his fingers, gnawed at him.

"Lanae." His voice thickened, each word filled with his fears and doubts. "I don't know if I can do this. The need to protect you, to keep you safe…it's consuming me." His hands trembled as he spoke. A knot of anxiety tightened in his chest, a visceral reaction to the vulnerability he was exposing.

"What are you protecting me from right now?" Lanae asked, her voice gentle yet insistent.

The question cut through the haze of his turmoil, demanding an answer he wasn't sure he could give.

Draven took in her silver-blue eyes. The depth of her trust shined in her irises. It was both a comfort and a burden. His gaze held hers and the connection between them pulsed like a live wire. "I'm protecting you from me," he admitted, the words slipping out before he could stop them.

The confession hung in the air, raw and unfiltered. Confusion and hurt flashed across Lanae's face, replaced by staunch intent.

"I don't need protection from you." She closed the distance between them. Her presence soothed his frayed nerves. "What I do need is you, Draven. All of you. Your darkest thoughts and your humor. Your fierceness and your vulnerability. All of you. Even the parts you're afraid to show."

The walls he had painstakingly built over the years crumbled under her words. The darkness he harbored, the fear of losing control...it all seemed to pale compared to the light she brought into his life. Yet, the fear of hurting her, of failing her like he had his family so long ago, suffocated him.

"Lanae." His voice cracked. "If we fail..."

She reached up and traced the lines of his face with a tenderness that made his heart twist. "If fate chooses to be that cruel, be vengeance personified and turn it all to ash. Understand?"

His lips stretched into a smile. "I would burn the entire universe down for you."

She tugged him to her lips, and his carnal desire flared. This time, he did not tame his kiss or the need racking his body. He let his greed for her take control. And she met his brutal kiss with one of her own. As their tongues tangled for dominance, she maneuvered him down the hallway and ripped at his shirt just as carelessly as he pawed at hers.

Their movements were a synchronized dance of anticipation and desire. A trail of discarded clothing marked their path, each piece a demonstration to the urgency of their need. The soft rustle of fabric hitting the floor was accompanied by the quickening of their breaths.

The moment her bedroom door closed behind him, the atmosphere shifted, becoming charged with physical electricity. His hunger magnified. A primal need surged through him with an intensity that stole his breath. Her touch was like a flame against his skin, each caress igniting a deeper longing. Her earthy scent enveloped him, a heady mix of lavender and green fields that made his pulse race.

He laid her on the bed; the mattress dipped under her weight. He paused to take her in. His breath caught in his lungs as his gaze caressed every inch of her body illuminated by the soft ambient light filtering through the curtains.

Lanae was exquisite in every way, her beauty enhanced by the raw, primal energy of the battle they had just endured. The bloody scrapes on her torso and arms from the earlier fight added a fierce, almost ethereal quality.

"You are perfect." His voice announced his lust in his low, husky timbre.

Her eyes darkened with the same intensity filling him, and her slow smile as she scanned his form just added fuel to his already raging hormones.

He climbed on the bed and kneeled between her legs before running his finger over a scar on her shin. "What happened here?" He brought her leg to his lips and ran his tongue up the scar.

Lanae propped herself up on an elbow and noted the scar he singled out. "Caelum. When he was little, he was a terror, and I got in the way when he was trying to make his flying saucer debut. He barreled down the stairs on his homemade saucer, and I stepped into his path." She raised a shoulder, offering a smile that melted his heart.

Draven let out a deep-chested chuckle and ran his tongue over the faded scar again, pleased at the sudden hitch in her breath. He kissed his way to another blemish on her perfect skin. This one on her thigh. He trailed his tongue over the length of it. "And this?"

Her breath caught again, and her eyes blazed with need. "Battle scar," she said in a breathless quality he could listen to for the rest of his days.

The smoothness of her silky skin ignited a fierce passion within him. Moving higher on her body, he pressed his lips to a scar on her side. She let out a soft purr, and her eyes glazed over with the same want racking his form. "And this?" He teased it with his tongue, enjoying each gasp of hers.

"Childhood illness," she said in a husky voice ladened with the same need throbbing through his entire form.

He cocked an eyebrow at her.

"Appendicitis. And as for the rest, they are from battle, in case you were planning on torturing me for the entire night."

He grinned and kissed each one of her many scars. By the time he reached her lips, his member throbbed for action and his dragon nature rose to the surface. This fae had captured him at a level he couldn't fathom, and now he wanted to claim her as his, despite any lingering doubts.

"This isn't just a one-night stand." He stared down at her. "That is not what I want from you."

"Tell me, dragon, what is it you want?" She licked her lips, and he nearly came undone at her sultry tone.

"I want you as my partner to share my life, until my heart beats no more. And then when I walk the halls of the great beyond, it is you I want by my side for eternity." He shuttered his eyes and sucked in a breath to calm his libido before he continued. Her bright eyes gleamed up at him, and he smiled. "I wish to claim you tonight."

The slow smile that spread over her lips undid him. "Claim away."

Two words in her husky voice destroyed any barrier left around his heart, clawing it into a frenzy. "Mine," growled from his lips, and he captured her mouth in a brutal kiss that she met with the same ferocity.

When the kiss broke, he trailed his tongue down the graceful slope of her neck to each of her perky breasts. She moaned as her nipples hardened in his mouth. He continued lower, tasting her skin as he headed toward the apex of her thighs.

"I need to taste you."

She purred beneath his touch and her fingers laced into his hair, guiding him to the spot she wanted all his attention on. He moved slowly and deliberately, tasting her sweetness before he flicked his tongue over her sensitive bud. Her purr turned into a breathy moan with his name on it.

He put all his focus on that spot until her cries became reckless and loud, and he was rewarded with a rush of wetness that tasted like sweet honey. He moved from her inner thighs, grazing his way up her body, finding every cut and scrape with a kiss before he hovered over her.

He needed to be sure he wasn't the only one invested in this emotional and physical agony. "I need to be sure you understand what being claimed by a dragon means."

She writhed under him, reaching for him, but he captured her wrist and pinned it to the bed.

"I want you, Draven."

He nipped her lip and pulled back. "Once this burning need between us is consummated, there will be no other. You are mine from here to eternity. And anyone who so much as looks at you will be reduced to ash."

She captured his gaze with frenzied eyes. "Anyone who dares lay a finger on you will meet my steel." She yanked her hand out of his grip and threaded her fingers through his hair. "Because this fucking possessiveness works both ways. You, Draven Emberwing, belong to me."

With a dominating growl, she kissed him. The action fanned the flames inside him into a burning inferno. He thrust his hips and plunged inside her, relishing the arch of her back as he seated his entire length in her exquisitely tight warmth. His eyes fluttered shut, and he paused, enjoying the sensations of electricity flowing between them.

"You are so very perfect," he whispered and then moved his hips in a slow rhythm, drawing the sensations out. She matched his pace, and the little noises of contentment coming from her lips along with her sweet floral scent consumed him.

Her moans, soft and breathless, were a symphony that fueled the rising need within him. Each sound she made was a spark, fanning the flames of his desire. It was a need he hadn't believed he could ever feel...a raw, unfiltered craving that destroyed him entirely. Every fiber of his being was attuned to her, the link between them a powerful force that transcended the physical.

As they moved together, the world outside ceased to exist. There was only the two of them, lost in the moment, their bodies and souls entwined in a dance of passion and connection. The intensity of their desire was matched only by the depth of their emotions; each touch, each kiss, a reflection of the bond they shared. And Draven didn't give a damn whether or not the bond was real.

CHAPTER FIFTEEN
The Undercity's Secrets

DRAVEN STUDIED THE CEILING, catching patterns of the waning light outside, dancing in time with his heart. The solace of having Lanae in his arms was fading, replaced with a gnawing sense that time was running out. The shadows lengthened, casting intricate designs that seemed to mirror the turmoil in his mind.

His fingers traced her shoulder, the touch both tender and urgent, as she nuzzled against him with her hair fanned across his chest. The heat of her body was a comforting presence, but it did little to quell the anxiety building within him. "We need to devise a plan to escape from lockdown here." His voice rumbled in the quiet room.

Lanae turned her head, her sleepy eyes meeting his. There was a moment of vulnerability in her gaze.

"We can't fight this trapped in your house," he added as a gentle gesture of the reality they faced.

"That would put me on the fugitive list," Lanae whispered.

"Better a fugitive than a slave," Draven replied, his tone unyielding. The thought of being bound and helpless was unbearable. The need to protect Lanae, to ensure their freedom, overrode any fear of the consequences.

Draven's heart clenched at the thought of putting her in more danger, but they couldn't afford to stay hidden, not when the fate of their realm hung in the balance. He reached up, brushing a lock of hair from her face, his touch lingering. "We'll need to be smart about this," he said. "We can't afford any mistakes."

Lanae nodded. "We'll figure it out together," she promised, her hand resting over his heart.

The warmth of her touch seeped into him, bolstering his courage. They needed to find Firetwill and take back what he stole.

CAELUM LEANED AGAINST THE counter, his arms crossed as he listened to Draven outline their plan. The strong tea he had prepared sat untouched on the table, its honey-scented steam curling lazily into the air.

"If we can get to my rental, then we can figure out our next steps without the council or the guard dissecting every move of ours." Draven took a sip of the tea.

Caelum's mind raced as he considered the implications. The council and the guard were relentless, always watching, always waiting for a misstep. He knew they needed to move quickly and decisively. "What do you need from me?" he asked, despite the turmoil inside.

"You can't come with us," Lanae said. "It's too dangerous."

Caelum pressed his lips together. A flicker of annoyance bloomed inside his stomach, tightening like a vise. He hated when Lanae treated him like a child, as if he couldn't handle himself. "I am not a child, Lanae." His voice was edged with frustration.

"Your sister is right," Draven interjected, his gaze steady and unyielding. "I will have my hands full with her. I don't need another soul's well-being on my conscience."

A wave of prickly heat surged over his skin as anger filled Caelum. It wasn't just about protecting Lanae; he knew Draven wanted to keep her close for other reasons. "Yeah, you just want some time with her alone so you can seduce her again." He straightened his back and jutted out his chin.

"Caelum!" Lanae scolded in her harshest voice. The one she reserved for reprimand.

"These walls are thin, sister." He tapped on the wall to emphasize his point. He had heard more than he wanted to, and it only fueled his determination to be involved. He would do whatever it took to protect his sister, even if it was from heartache instead of a threat to her life.

Draven's expression softened. A hint of understanding shined in his eyes. "We need you to create a diversion." His tone was more conciliatory. "Draw the guards' attention away long enough for us to slip out."

Caelum bit his lip, contemplating arguing, but the stakes were higher than just his sister's honor. "I can do that." He would prove to them he was more than capable, that he could be an asset rather than a liability.

TENSION HUNG THICK IN the air. Lanae exchanged a glance with Draven as she packed a satchel of her clothing and prepared for their escape. With only two guards stationed outside the house, their chances of slipping away unnoticed seemed promising, but they couldn't afford to make any mistakes. Nero, the little griffin, perched on Lanae's shoulder, his eyes alert and ready.

When they stepped into the hallway, Caelum handed her a bag of food. "I can always show my face at the market. You can't." He turned out the lights in the front of the house and moved to the back door that led to their fenced-in garden. He drew a long breath, closing his eyes as if preparing himself to execute whatever diversion he had crafted in his mind. "Give me a few minutes to get over the fence and around the house. When you hear a ruckus out front, count to three and then sneak out. I'll keep the guards' attention long enough for you to get to the alley down the street."

Draven nodded, but kept quiet, letting her have a moment with her brother.

Caelum crossed to Lanae and wrapped her in a hug. "Stay safe, sis." He broke the hug and tapped his temple. "Let me know when you get to his place."

"I will." Lanae couldn't help but be wary of using her brother like this, but his warm smile gave her a much-needed boost. Still, he didn't open his mind to her. Instead, he had created an impenetrable wall between them, yet his head tilted and he side-eyed her, his dimples appearing briefly as if he were suppressing a grin and failing.

"Ready?" Caelum asked in the stillness of the house.

Lanae nodded. Her chest felt like it was about to burst. She drew a long breath, steeling herself for what lay ahead. Draven gave Caelum a firm pat on the shoulder, a silent thanks for his bravery.

With a final nod, Caelum slipped outside, his footsteps light and silent.

Lanae and Draven moved to the front door. She cracked the door and waited for what Caelum had planned.

She caught sight of Caelum at the edge of the yard. When he got to the street, he approached the guards in a zigzag pattern of someone who had had too much spirits. He stumbled, dropping keys and change onto the street, causing a loud ruckus that immediately drew the guards' attention.

"Hey, what's going on here?" a guard barked, moving toward Caelum.

Caelum played his part perfectly, acting confused and disoriented as he patted his pockets. "I'm sorry, I just… I think I lost my keys. Can you help me look?" he babbled, ensuring the guards' focus remained entirely on him.

Go. Caelum's whisper echoed in Lanae's mind.

As the guards moved away from the entrance, focused on Caelum, Lanae gave Draven a nod and he grabbed her hand, pulling her through the door. She closed it quietly and followed Draven into the shadows. They moved as fast as they could away from Caelum and the guards to the alley nearby without making a sound.

Nero flew ahead, his keen senses guiding them through the darkened streets. They stuck close to the walls, avoiding open spaces where they might be seen.

Every creak or rustle of leaves set her nerves on edge, but they pressed on, determined to escape their captivity. The cool night air was filled with the distant sounds of the city, helping to silence their footsteps.

Draven moved swiftly with her at his side. Her heart pounded out a rhythm that matched her footsteps. Behind them, the sound of the guards' voices grew fainter, showing that Caelum's clever diversion was still holding their attention. With each step, they put more distance between themselves and her house, inching closer to safety.

Finally, after many dark alleys and switchbacks, they reached the edge of the city, where Draven's temporary housing awaited in the dim glow of the rune lights.

We made it safely to Draven's. Lanae sent the thought to Caelum.

Be safe. Her brother's thought resounded in her head.

"I'm surprised your brother didn't give those guards the slip and follow us. He seems intent on protecting you," Draven remarked, casting a quick glance over his shoulder before swinging the door open to his rental. "Pardon the mess."

Inside, the little sleeping quarters lay in a state of absolute chaos—papers scattered across a coffee table next to a half-finished cup of something that may have been good at one point but had gone sour, leaving a foul smell behind. His bed was unmade, and a book sat open on the side table. The only thing neat was the outfit he had worn to the ball hanging over the back of the chair.

"Looks like you left in a hurry." She cast a look at Draven, but he was staring at his bed. Gooseflesh spread over his exposed arms as he stepped inside, the door creaking shut behind them.

She followed his gaze to an envelope with his name scribbled on it, propped on the pillow of his rumpled bed.

"Damn yôkai," he muttered under his breath, crossing the room in a few swift strides to snatch the envelope off the bed.

"Excuse me?" She narrowed her gaze.

Draven waved the envelope, his eyes flashing with irritation. "A yôkai was the one who tipped me off about the gauntlet stone. He's the one who set this whole debacle in motion." His jaw ticced with suppressed anger. "And now it looks like he's back to meddle in my affairs."

An artic chill brushed up her spine as the implications of his words sank in. The heat of irritation burned under her skin. If this being meant to harm Draven, then she'd gladly run him through with her sword. "Then we should have a talk with him."

Draven nodded, his mouth curving upward in a grim smile that didn't quite reach his eyes. "I'd rather you bind him in ivy, and I carve him to pieces until he either tells me why he sent me on this path or dies a slow death." His voice rumbled low, filled with a dark promise. His eyes sparkled with malice, a dangerous glint reflecting the depth of his anger and the hint of a sinister satisfaction at the thought of administering pain.

"There's that, too," Lanae replied, her lips curving into a mischievous grin. Instead of shying away from his violent intentions, his casual reference to torture set her blood rushing to parts that he had fully satisfied the night before. Heat scraped her cheeks, and her gaze collided with his head-on.

He peeled open the note and cocked an eyebrow.

"What do you think?" Draven handed Lanae the letter.

Her mouth popped open in surprise and then she focused on the words his initial contact scribed.

Perhaps the yôkai wasn't the enemy. The man admitted he hadn't known about certain players in the mix when he had initially sought him out. He hinted at a portal in the Undercity that might help as long as Draven got there before their shared nemesis.

She lifted her gaze. "It seems this yôkai feels the same way about Firetwill that you do."

He scanned her body as he lifted a shoulder in response. Then he waggled his eyebrows and glanced at the bed and then back at Lanae, his gaze as heated as she felt.

"Did you want to"—he made finger quotes—"rest, or do you want to check this out first?" He flicked the note in her hand.

LANAE LED THE WAY through the twisting alleyways of Solstice City, kicking herself for not taking Draven up on his insinuation, but the rotten drink stunk up the room so badly that she couldn't stomach the thought of being intimate in that space. Instead, they headed toward the Undercity using the directions in the note.

This time, she didn't have her dress sword like she had before. They wanted to blend in. With her hair braided down her back and shielded by the shawl draped over her head, the likelihood of being caught was low. The night air was heavy with the presence of living shadows. The walls themselves seemed to whisper and shift, tendrils of darkness reaching out like curious fingers. The unsettling environment kept her on edge. Her senses heightened as she moved with quiet footsteps through the alleys.

Beside her, Draven sneezed, billowing smoke ahead of them. Sparks of flame flickered on his fingertips, only to sputter out a moment later. He kept shaking his head and sniffling, as if his sinuses were in mutiny. His eyes, normally bright and focused, held a shadow of their own—a vulnerability that Lanae hadn't seen since she met him.

Draven's powers continued to fluctuate wildly, bursts of energy coursing from him unpredictably as they traversed the dark streets. His forehead glistened with perspiration, and Lanae wished she had opted to rest first.

Lanae reached out, her hand brushing his arm. "Are you all right?"

He met her gaze, his eyes reflecting his turmoil. "I don't know. I've never felt this out of control."

"Why now? You haven't shown this affinity for magical outbursts since we met." She stopped them from moving forward and turned to him. Only one thing had truly changed, and a flash of guilt scraped over her skin.

"I partially shifted." He met her gaze. "And I don't have the Dragon's Heart, so this happens whenever I try, especially when I exhaust myself." A slow smile surfaced. "Not that I regret the way I exhausted myself."

Lanae rolled her eyes, glad it hadn't been her that had caused his issues. She continued through the Undercity's back alleys. This time, they came out of the back streets right into the middle of the dream-trader section beyond the goblins.

Much like the djinn, these ethereal beings moved with a fluid grace, their forms shifting like smoke. They bartered in dreams and memories, offering glimpses of hidden truths in exchange for fragments of one's past.

One of the dream-traders approached Lanae, its eyes glowing with an otherworldly light. "Care to trade, fae?" Its voice was a soft, enticing whisper. "A secret for a secret?"

Lanae shook her head, keeping her gaze forward. "Not tonight." She guided Draven away from the enchanting pull of the dream-traders.

Nero, perched on Lanae's shoulder, chirped. The baby griffin's antics had a way of breaking the gloom, and tonight was no different. He fluttered off Lanae's shoulder, darting through the shadows with playful curiosity.

"Nero, stay close!" Lanae called, her heart pounding as the little griffin disappeared around a corner.

They followed Nero's chirps, weaving through the living shadows that seemed to part in the griffin's wake. Lanae's pulse quickened as they turned a corner and found Nero pecking at the ground. His bright eyes focused on a patch of cobblestones that shimmered with a faint, mystical light.

Draven's eyes widened as he kneeled beside Nero. His hand brushed the stones and magic flared, showing the portal the note had mentioned. "Do we trust the yôkai?"

Lanae looked away from him and down at Nero. "I don't know." Unease filtered through her. "But it could give us answers."

Draven picked up Nero and handed the little griffin to her. "Then let's take the gamble." He held his hand out, waiting for her to jump with him.

Hand in hand, they stepped onto the portal, the magic swirling around them like a gentle breeze. The world shifted and blurred; the alleyways faded into a kaleidoscope of colors and light. A strange sense of weightlessness gripped Lanae, her grasp on Draven's hand the only constant as they were transported to a new realm.

CHAPTER SIXTEEN
The Seer's Prophecy

HIS WORLD JARRED AS his feet landed on solid ground. Draven fought the sudden vertigo as he blinked away dizziness from the portal. When the light faded, a vast, ancient forest surrounded them. The air filled with the scent of pine and moss. The portal had led them to a place of forgotten magic, a sanctuary hidden from the chaos of their world.

In the center of the sacred grove stood a being of liquid crystal within a glade bathed in a soft, ethereal glow. The surrounding trees whispered ancient secrets, their leaves shimmering with a luminescent light.

Over the years, he had heard tales of the seer's cryptic visions, but he thought it had been a figment of someone's overactive imagination. And now he paused, recalling all the stories of past and future fortunes told by this...thing. Dread coated his tongue as they stepped into the glade. The seer's form shifted and swirled, a mesmerizing dance of liquid crystal that caught the light in a dazzling display.

"Welcome, seekers of truth," the seer intoned, its voice resonating like the chime of delicate glass. "I have awaited your arrival."

Lanae shivered. "We seek guidance," she said.

Draven squeezed her hand in support as they stepped forward. She returned the gesture but didn't look away from the ethereal being in front of them.

The seer extended a crystalline hand toward Lanae, its surface rippling with light. "Touch my hand, Lanae, and behold your fate."

Taking a deep breath, Lanae reached out and placed her hand on the seer's. The world around them dissolved into a swirl of colors and light, and she was plunged into a vision, dragging Draven with her.

In the vision, Lanae stood atop a desolate hill, wielding the gauntlet stone. She glowed with immense energy. Lightning crackled above in a dark and tumultuous sky. At her feet lay the ruins of a once-great city, now reduced to ashes and rubble. Power coursed through her veins, a force so overwhelming it threatened to consume her.

As she looked around, she saw faces she recognized—Caelum, Rorik, Elara, Faide, guardsmen and women, faces from the bar she frequented and those who played dice with her, council members, and her breath stalled when her gaze landed on Draven—all fallen, victims of the destruction she had wrought.

"No." Tears streamed down her face. "This can't be my fate."

The vision faded, leaving her trembling and breathless. The oracle removed its hand, its crystalline form shimmering with a soft, empathetic light. "The future is not set in stone," it said. "But you must be wary of the paths you choose."

As Lanae stepped back, pale and shaken, a surge of protective instinct struck Draven. Although her vision crawled under his skin like a malignant disease, he could not accept it as fact. The woman he fell in love with would never harm those close to her. She would rather die than harm those who held a place in her heart.

The seer's gaze shifted to him, its liquid form rippling with anticipation. "And you, Draven, of the dragons. Touch me and see what awaits."

Draven hesitated for a moment before he unlaced his fingers from Lanae. If his vision was as horrifying as Lanae's, he did not want her to be even more upset than she seemed. Taking a deep breath, he extended his hand and contacted the seer's crystalline palm. The world around him dissolved into a cascade of light and shadow, pulling him into the depths of a vision.

In his vision, Draven stood on the edge of a great precipice, the landscape below shrouded in mist. Centuries of memories swirled down on him. The ghosts of his kin whispered in his ears.

Ahead, he saw a figure cloaked in darkness, wielding a weapon of pure energy, ready to strike.

This figure represented the ultimate threat to their world. Deep in his heart, Draven knew the only way to stop it was through a great sacrifice. His image stepped forward, embracing his full dragon form. His scales shimmered with fiery light. With a roar that shook the very foundations of the earth, he launched himself at the dark figure.

A chilling reality gripped him. His life very well may be the price for the salvation of the realms.

The vision faded, leaving Draven gasping for breath, his heart choking with what he had seen. The seer withdrew its hand, its voice a soft whisper. "The path to victory is fraught with sacrifice. The choices you make will determine the fate of many."

Lanae reached out to Draven, a worried look in her eyes. "What did you see?"

Draven met her gaze, his expression solemn. "A sacrifice. One that might be necessary to save us all."

Lanae's grip on his hand tightened. "We will do whatever it takes to make sure these visions don't come to fruition."

He nodded, but he had the benefit of seeing both visions and wasn't so sure they could escape what he had been shown. As the seer said, his choice would be the one to seal their world's destiny.

The seer watched them with an inscrutable gaze, its liquid crystal form shimmering in the ambient light. "Your fates are intertwined. The future holds many challenges, but also the potential for great triumph. Trust in your bond, and you may yet overcome the darkness."

215

CHAPTER SEVENTEEN
Heartbeats and Whispers

THE PORTAL FROM THE seer dumped them in a small glen in the woods outside the northernmost wall of the city. The Citadel shined in the distance beyond the fields surrounding Solstice City. Lanae sighed.

"I don't have the energy to get back into the city tonight." Lanae remained at the edge of the clearing, rubbing her arms against the chill.

Draven's hands landed on her shoulders. "Then we should gather some wood for a fire."

She leaned back into him, enjoying the warmth he radiated and the energy buzzing between them. But the seer's vision still dragged her thoughts into the darkness. "You saw."

"I saw the vision the seer showed you, but that is not you. Nor is it your future."

His deep timbre reverberated through to her bones, and she almost believed him. Instead of harping on it, she pulled away and started to gather branches until her arms were full. She followed Draven to a clear spot, and he built a small firepit and layered the sticks before he blew a small stream of fire out of his mouth, igniting the wood.

"That's certainly handy."

He laughed and glanced at her. "With the way my powers have been fluctuating, I had a fifty-fifty chance of turning it to ash instead."

Her smile gained traction at the twinkle in his eyes. He leaned against a log and put his arm out for her to join him. She settled next to him on the ground and leaned her head on his shoulder.

"You really..."

"Let's not talk about what-ifs. The seer showed us possible futures and I, for one, refuse to entertain the one she showed you. It won't happen. So let's just enjoy this peaceful night here by the fire and pretend that our world isn't going to shit. Okay?"

She twisted to look at him. "But—"

He silenced her with a kiss and broke away much too soon for her liking. "Shush. We both need rest." Sparks broke out on his fingertips. "See." He fisted his hands and took a breath.

Nero fluttered up to the branches above them, leaving them to explore more of their intense connection.

"Okay." She pecked his cheek and snuggled into him again, finding a comfortable position in his arms. In the peaceful silence, Lanae's mind wandered to the past. "You know, I've always wondered about the past of dragons. What was it like before...everything?" She glanced up at his emerald eyes shimmering with shadows of the firelight.

Draven's lips relaxed into a smile, a touch of sadness in his eyes. "It was a world of endless skies and hidden realms. Dragons were guardians of ancient secrets, keepers of balance. We lived in harmony with the elements, but it wasn't without conflict. Betrayal, wars...they eventually led to our downfall."

Lanae reached out, her fingers whisking his cheek. "I'm sorry for what happened, Draven. It's not fair that you've had to carry that burden alone."

He half shrugged, almost as if weren't a big deal. "I've found something worth fighting for now." His gaze locked onto hers with an intensity that made her heart flutter. "Someone worth fighting for."

WARMTH SPREAD THROUGH DRAVEN as Lanae's hand rested on his cheek. Her presence was a comfort to his troubled soul, and for the first time in decades, he felt a semblance of hope.

"Tell me about your dreams, Lanae."

Lanae's gaze clouded with a faraway look. "I want to find out what happened to my parents."

"And after that. What do you want for you?"

Lanae cocked her head, resting it on his shoulder. The silence stretched long enough that he wasn't sure she was going to answer.

"I've always dreamed of a world where the fae and other magical beings can coexist peacefully. A place where Caelum can grow up without fear, and where I can build something lasting. And...a life where I don't have to choose between duty and my heart."

Draven's chest ached at her words. "It sounds like utopia. I'm not sure we will ever see a world where there isn't conflict. Power has a way of corrupting even the pure of heart. But if I could, I would gladly give you that kind of peace." He palmed her cheek.

Before his lips brushed hers, he paused and pulled back. She looked around too.

"You..."

He covered her mouth and put his finger over his lips.

Underbrush crunched under soles loud enough to be close. And from the sound of it, whoever was out there was not alone. Adrenaline surged, clearing the tiredness from his mind and muscles. She moved off him, and he reached for his sword before climbing to his feet. Both annoyance at the interruption alongside a lingering sense of dread clawed at his insides.

A squad of fae wearing the Solstice City colors stepped into the clearing. A special insignia that looked like the Citadel graced each one of their chest plates. And they stared at Draven and Lanae with cold, hard eyes.

"LANAE OF THE NIGHTSHADE lineage," one announced, his voice authoritative. "By order of the Fae Council, you are to return with us immediately."

A rapid beat pulsed in Lanae's chest. These were not ordinary guards. These were the elite guards of Solstice City. It was one position they all aspired to, but she did not have enough seasons of service to be considered.

If they were here looking for her, it meant they found out about her escaping from house arrest. "Is my brother all right?"

The lead guard's forehead scrunched and his lips pinched. "I know nothing of your brother. I only have my orders."

"She has done nothing wrong." Draven went to step in front of her, but she put her hand on his arm, stopping him.

The enforcer's glare sharpened. "The council has decreed it. She has no choice."

She put up her finger and turned her back on the guards, facing Draven. He needed to back off. They were outnumbered, and the enforcers weren't untrained fae. If they made a stand, they could lose their lives and then no one could stop Firetwill. "Draven." She put her hands on his chest, capturing his attention. "This isn't your battle," she whispered. "You need to continue what we started."

Draven's eyes flashed in annoyance.

As the tension thickened, a sudden flurry of movement caught Lanae's eye. Nero darted from the trees, his bright eyes alert and determined. He landed on Draven's shoulder with a small, glowing scroll clutched in his beak.

Lanae took the scroll, and her hands trembled as she unrolled it. The message inside was hastily written but clear: *Trust no one. The council's ranks are compromised.*

A chill crawled down her spine, and she pressed the note into his hand and closed his fingers around it. She wondered whether the elite guards were working for her allies or enemies.

The lead enforcer cleared his throat. "Lanae, you broke your house arrest. You must come with us to face charges for your treasonous actions."

Lanae's mouth dried. They didn't throw around a treason charge on a whim.

Draven's hand dropped to the grip of his sword.

She covered his hand with hers. "I can straighten all this out with the council. Please take Nero home and make sure Caelum is okay."

"They threatened a treason charge," he growled and met her gaze.

"It's a scare tactic. Please do as I ask. I will be okay." She straightened her spine and turned toward the enforcers. "I will come without causing any trouble."

AS LANAE FACED THE enforcers, Draven's hand slipped into hers and squeezed before he released his hold. His caged heart thrashed in his chest as he searched for a way out. And a wave of silent fury filled him as the enforcers each took one of her arms and led her away from where they had made camp.

Nero chirped confidently, a small yet powerful note of his presence. Draven ran his hand over the little creature and received a purr in response.

Lanae glanced back at them once with eyes filled with dread just before they disappeared into the shadows.

Draven dragged his fingers through his hair and glanced around their little camp before he unrolled the note she placed in his hand.

Trust no one. The council's ranks are compromised.

He thought he recognized the handwriting, but wasn't sure where Nero could have gotten this outside of the city. With the possibility of a treason charge, the note left an icy grip on his chest.

If any of his contacts were this close, big trouble had to be brewing.

He packed up their belongings and kicked dirt over the fire, dousing the flames to ash. The conflict within him burned. He wanted to charge after the guards and free Lanae, but he knew they were more formidable fighters than they had encountered in the alley and on the battlefield. He did not want to take the chance of her getting seriously wounded.

"Fuck. What do I do now?"

Nero pointed his wing toward where Lanae had disappeared.

"I can't stop them. Not without killing them." He met the griffin's gaze and swore he saw a protective flare there. "Besides, they wouldn't dream of harming her." He looked back at the woods as his heart filled with doubt. "Right?"

CHAPTER EIGHTEEN
War Council

BEING IN FRONT OF the sour-faced council was getting old, even with the breathtaking chamber surrounding her with its heady scent of pine and earth mingled with the faint aroma of burning sage. The domed ceiling sparkled with enchanted lights, mimicking a starlit sky, while the walls were adorned with intricate carvings that told tales of ancient alliances and shared victories.

Lanae stood at the heart of this living sanctuary, her eyes sweeping over the assembled representatives. Anxiety smothered the hall, and the gravity of her situation was crystal clear in the wary glances and hushed murmurs that filled the room.

Faide cleared his throat, breaking the silence. "You have violated your house arrest." His voice echoed off the stone walls. His stern expression directly opposed the beauty of their surroundings, his eyes boring into Lanae with an intensity that demanded a response.

"I am investigating a more sinister threat than the dark fae," Lanae replied, her voice steady despite the tremor shaking her form. She held her chin high, refusing to be intimidated by the council's disapproval. Not when their very survival depended on her finding the fiend who wanted to destroy realms and enslave everyone.

Faide leaned forward, his brows knitting together. "There is no bigger threat. Even your dragon is not a bigger threat than the dark fae." His voice dripped with conviction and a touch of disdain.

Just then, an assembly of creatures marched into the chamber, drawing the attention of everyone present. It looked as if all the leaders of the various species in Solstice City had been summoned for these proceedings. The dwarves entered first, their sturdy forms accompanied by the rhythmic thud of their crafted wooden poles against the stone floor. Following them were the elves, their ethereal glow casting a soft light around them, their movements graceful and otherworldly. The gnomes, with their earthy scent and small statures, appeared next, their eyes wide with curiosity.

Goblins shuffled in, their monstrous features contrasting with the elegance of the chamber.

Trolls followed, their scowls deepening the creases on their faces, while kobolds, with their magical potions clinking on their belts, added an air of mystique. The djinn, their markings on display, entered with an aura of power and ancient wisdom. Finally, ogres towered over all the others, their presence commanding and formidable as they filtered into the room.

The room grew silent, the tension palpable as the diverse assembly awaited the continuation of the proceedings. Lanae swallowed hard at the pressure of their collective gazes upon her, the responsibility of her actions and decisions pressing down like a physical burden.

They only brought in the leaders of all the species in the city when there was a grave sentencing to be decided. And she was in the spotlight.

Faide's eyes narrowed as he observed the other species' leaders. "This is not just about you, Lanae." His tone carried the power of authority. "Your treasonous actions of partnering with a dragon have repercussions for us all."

Lanae met his gaze, her expression unwavering even as her stomach twisted. "I did not betray the realm. I am trying to protect it from a threat that will enslave all of us." Her voice reverberated in the chamber.

Faide leaned back in his chair. "I will give you one chance to explain. But understand this, Lanae—if you are wrong, the consequence of treason is death."

Lanae took a fortifying breath, steeling herself for what was to come. Her role today was not that of a warrior, but of an accused looking for salvation. She stepped forward, her eyes sweeping over the stern faces of the council members, her voice carrying every ounce of her courage. "I broke guard rules and went to that ball to find information related to the gauntlet stone."

An excited murmur filled the chamber. The representatives shifted forward in their seats.

"And did you find this fabled artifact?" Faide crossed his arms, skepticism radiating through the room like a tangible force.

She nodded, her heart pounding. More than a dozen eyebrows rose in response, the atmosphere charged with anticipation.

"It's not real," Faide said. But this time, his tone held doubt.

His denial reminded Lanae of when she was told about fate bonds. "Yes. It is."

"Let us see it," Lirse Wondergust, another Fae Council member, demanded, leaning forward in her seat.

Lanae pressed her lips together and sighed. "It seems Elara has stolen it at the behest of our enemies." Her frustration leaked into her tone, along with regret. Even if they had gotten out of that fight with the stone, Draven would have destroyed the thing by now.

Faide mopped his face with a handkerchief, his composure faltering. "You've consorted with a dragon, broken house arrest, and now lost something that could destroy the realms if the stories are correct?" His voice rose with each accusation.

Her failures pressed onto her shoulders, making them droop. "Yes, sir." The words were bitter on her tongue, a reluctant admission of her shortcomings. But she had something more to say about their adversary. "I think the dark fae are under our enemies' control. I don't think they are truly our enemies."

Half a dozen council members recoiled, their expressions a mix of shock and dismay.

"That is treasonous thinking. Explain yourself." Faide's eyes narrowed with suspicion.

"Elara was cursed and attacked us. She never would have done that unless she was controlled by someone else." Lanae licked her lips, her mind racing to find the right words. "When we lost the stone, we were attacked by a legion of dark fae with the same vacant look as those we have fought in the fields outside the city time and time again."

She pointed toward the gates. "If I hadn't seen it with my own eyes, I wouldn't have believed it either, but they all looked like they were compelled to kill, or steal, in this case. None of the soldiers had a will of their own. And if we don't come together as one against this common enemy who wields the gauntlet stone, we will all be as mindless as the dark fae." She drew a deep breath and scanned the faces in the chamber. "The threat we face requires us to act as one. Our divisions have only made us weaker. Now is the time to stand together."

Her words resounded through the chamber, hanging in the air like a magical force. Representatives from various factions—gnomes, fae, djinn, and even a few goblin envoys—shifted uneasily in their seats. The room was filled with a sense of urgency, as if the very walls understood the critical nature of their meeting.

The ogre elder, with skin the color of aged bark, spoke up, her voice filled with skepticism. "We have been bickering for centuries. How can we trust one another now?"

Lanae met her gaze, praying she had a little of her parents' peacekeeping finesse. "The enemy we face seeks to exploit our divisions. If we continue to fight among ourselves, we will fall. We must learn to trust and support one another."

The chamber fell into a tense silence; the representatives exchanged uncertain glances. Their judgment settled down on her. She knew that some within the council saw her plea for cooperation as a threat to their power, but this fight had to be made. They had to listen to reason.

"The dark fae are targeting our crops," someone in the ranks called out, breaking the silence with a worried tone.

Lanae nodded. "If they wanted to overthrow Solstice City, why kill the very land that would provide them with food once they have conquered us?" Her question rang through the room, bouncing off the stone walls.

"To make us weaker," a troll said with a grumble, his voice rumbling like distant thunder.

Faide raised his hand for silence, his voice commanding attention. "Enough. We know they are targeting our food sources." His gaze landed on Lanae, piercing and unyielding. "This is not what we are here to discuss, and you have not offered a sufficient defense." He pointed a bony finger at Lanae, his knuckles white with tension.

"Lock her in the dungeon while we decide her fate."

Guards converged on her, their expressions stoic as if she were a stranger. They stripped her of her weapons and then dragged her toward the chamber door. The metal of their armor clinked, echoing through the chamber like a final judgment.

"You don't understand. The gauntlet stone is in the hands of a madman," she yelled as they hauled her out of the chamber. The door slammed closed behind her with a resounding thud, and an oppressive silence blanketed the hall.

The rush of footsteps approaching made the guards surrounding her stall. Caelum rounded the corner and slid to a stop, his eyes wide with shock. He glanced at the procession and then met Lanae's gaze. "What the heck?" he balked.

"I've been charged with treason," Lanae said before any of the guards could speak. "They are bringing me to the dungeon until they decide what to do with me."

"You can't do that to her. There's something bigger going on," Caelum pleaded with the guards.

"We have our orders." The guards started to move again, but Caelum blocked their way, his stance defiant.

"Can I at least have a word in private with my sister?" Desperation tinged his voice.

"You may follow us to the dungeon, and as soon as she is locked in a cell, we will give you a minute with her. But that is it," one guard replied sternly.

Caelum met Lanae's gaze as the guards marched her past him. *I didn't believe Draven when he told me you were arrested for treason.* His thoughts echoed in her mind.

I thought I could talk my way out of this. Lanae sent her thought to Caelum. *But I'm not so sure now that I've seen the council's reactions.*

While I was at the market, I overheard a council member talking about aligning with Firetwill. Caelum's urgent thought filled her head.

Who? Lanae sent the thought back.

I didn't see her, but when the name Firetwill was mentioned, I lingered long enough to pick up the fact that they think it's the only way to survive the power play, Caelum replied.

Was it Faide? Lanae's heart pounded.

No. I would have recognized his voice, even in a hushed whisper. It was a woman and a man talking. I'm not sure if they both are council members or if it was one just talking with their significant other, Caelum explained.

A chill gripped Lanae, sending shivers down her spine. If the council was compromised, that wouldn't bode well for her sentence. Especially with what she knew. This whole proceeding could be a farce put in play by the real traitor.

The guards threw her in a dank dungeon cell that smelled of rot and piss. The cold, damp air clung to her skin, dousing her magic the moment the door slammed shut behind her. The cell cast a barrier around her that even her mind reading abilities couldn't breach. She turned to her brother's worried gaze, the flickering torchlight casting shadows on his face.

"I won't let you rot in this cell," Caelum vowed, his lips pressed together in obstinance as he glanced over his shoulder at the retreating guards.

"You don't have a choice," she breathed. "Go home and let Draven know what's happening."

Caelum let out a sarcastic laugh. "I don't think your dragon is going to take this very well. He might just burn down the Citadel out of rage."

Lanae smirked and shrugged, a faint glimmer of humor breaking through her fear.

"Time's up," the lead enforcer snapped from the hallway entrance, his voice harsh and unforgiving.

Caelum reached for Lanae's hand, and she took it, squeezing gently. "We will figure something out," he promised, his eyes burning with determination.

"Don't let Draven do anything stupid." Her concern cast deep in her tone.

"It's not Draven you have to worry about," Caelum said aloud, his eyes flashing in the darkness before he walked away.

CHAPTER NINETEEN
Nero's Origins

DRAVEN PACED THE ROOM in Lanae's house, his footsteps echoing in the empty space as he turned over the new missive in his hands while waiting for Caelum to return. Anxiety gnawed at him, each passing second amplifying his unease. After Caelum had run off to the Citadel to find out what was happening, he had made a quick trip to his rental to gather his things. A new envelope graced his pillow, its unexpected presence adding to his tension. He grabbed it, along with the rest of his belongings. He'd worry about living arrangements later; right

235

now, his instincts screamed he was needed at Lanae's place.

He thought Caelum would be back before him, but the house was just as empty as he had left it, leaving Draven on edge. The stillness was oppressive. He glanced at Nero. "Should I wait for Caelum or open this now?" He waved the envelope in front of the creature, seeking distraction from the growing dread.

Nero pecked the envelope and cocked his head, waiting.

"You want me to open this," Draven mused, a faint smile tugging at his lips despite his anxiety.

The baby griffin nodded, and Draven laughed. The creature understood more than he gave him credit for, and the diversion would take his mind off all the awful speculations dancing in his head.

He ripped open the wrapper and pulled the note out. "It seems the yôkai has another quest for us." His lips pulled down in a frown at the hints of Nero's hidden abilities and additional cryptic references about potions and a daring escape plan. He glanced at Nero. "And it has to do with you, my little friend." He looked at the note as Nero peered down at the scrawling script.

Nero squawked again and fluttered his wings, a spark of excitement in his eyes.

"These tasks seem to always end in disaster," Draven said just as the door opened.

Caelum walked into the house with disheveled hair, as if he had raked his hand through it repeatedly on the way home. When his gaze landed on Draven, Draven's heart sank at the devastation reflected in the boy's eyes.

"They are charging her with treason. She's in the dungeon until sentencing."

Draven glanced at the note. The escape references now made more sense. Potions and Nero's hidden abilities had a great deal to do with the vague plan scrawled on the page. He stretched out his arm, offering the paper to Caelum.

Caelum stripped the paper from his grip and scanned it twice before looking up at Draven with questioning lines furrowing his brow. "What is this?"

"It's from someone who I think is on our side."

"Oh, you think he's on our side?" Caelum challenged. "My sister is imprisoned and will probably be executed for treason, and you want to go on a wild-goose chase?" He waved the letter, his hand trembling.

"If what the letter says is true, it will give us the means to break her out of there so we can get on with stopping Firetwill." Draven snapped the note out of Caelum's grip. He breathed in to calm his racing heart. "How long do we have?"

Caelum rubbed his face, the precariousness of their predicament etched on his features. "Executions are scheduled during a crescent moon when our powers are not at their fullest. Which means if they agree with her sentence, then we are looking at either tomorrow or the next day at the latest. They will make this a public spectacle, considering she's a high-ranking guard." He grimaced and met Draven's gaze, his eyes filled with fear.

"Fucking hell." Draven pocketed the note, his mind racing. "We have to go now if we're going to get back in time to free her." He went to his pile of belongings and dug out his weapons. He clipped on knives and his sword before turning to Caelum. "Are you coming?"

Caelum pointed at his chest, his brows arched.

"Yes, you. I need someone at my back who I trust, and since Lanae isn't here, that's you." He handed Caelum another one of his swords. "You know how to use that, right?" He tossed a scabbard to Caelum as well.

"Are you forgetting who my sister is?" Caelum twirled the sword before slipping it into the holder and cinching it to his belt.

"Point taken." He stormed out of the house with Caelum on his heels and Nero perched on his shoulder. The sun breached the horizon, painting the world in a yellow hue as they navigated their way outside the gates and through the fields to the northern woodlands.

"You really think Nero is related to the first griffin?" Caelum asked as they crossed deeper into the woods, the trees casting long shadows in the early morning light.

"I don't know. Most of what I heard about the first griffin predated the dragons. If he is one of those legendary beasts, he's an ancestor of the first guardian of the realms. The ones tasked with keeping the peace before the dragons." Draven couldn't escape the suspicion that something was about to unfold. He sensed Nero was special, but now that intuition grew stronger.

"According to the legends we were taught at school, griffins had a couple of special traits." Caelum studied Nero and then continued. "Storm magic, for one, and the other was rare. They have healing abilities."

Draven grunted. "Along with the usual griffin traits. Eagle eyes and hearing, and the speed and strength of a lion." He patted the baby griffin's head. "We already know he can fly and damn fast, too."

Nero squawked and ruffled his feathers, his razor-like claws digging into Draven's leathers, scraping the skin underneath.

Their conversation was interrupted by a sudden rustling in the underbrush. A figure emerged, its form shimmering with an otherworldly light. The creature was small, no taller than Draven's knee, with wings that sparkled like dew-kissed leaves.

"Greetings, travelers," the sprite said, his voice a melodious chime. "I have been expecting you."

"I assume you are Jairamon, the magical sprite we were told to seek." Draven unfolded the note and handed it to the sprite.

"Yes. I received a similar correspondence with a directive to help you, along with a hefty payment to ensure my cooperation." He smiled up at Draven, his eyes landing on Nero. Jairamon's wings fluttered. "It seems the baby griffin's presence has impacted the ancient magic of this realm. I am here to guide you on a quest to retrieve a charm that will awaken his ancestral abilities."

Nero chirped excitedly, his bright eyes full of anticipation.

Draven's blood surged with hope. "And what of the potion?"

"As soon as we retrieve the charm, I will provide you a potion that will help you traverse the dungeons of the Citadel and free your fate bound." Jairamon's expression darkened. "That path is treacherous, but you both must survive in order to defeat the descending darkness."

"I hate riddles." Caelum's frustration rang clear.

"Mind your manners, young man," Jairamon warned as he led them deeper into the enchanted forest. The canopy above whispered ancient secrets as they walked until they came to a narrow ravine and a zigzagging path cut into the walls leading to the ground shrouded in fog.

The path was dotted with slippery mud and shifting rock, and the way down was slower than Draven would have liked. But if they didn't proceed with caution, they could easily fall to their deaths.

They reached the bottom of the ravine and the fog cleared, exposing a mossy clearing that glowed with a gentle light. A stream cut through the ground, breaking up the green with a vein of bright blue, as if the river itself came from glaciers in the far north.

The water cut a path around an island of moss, and in the center of that small land mass lay a pendant that pulsed with rhythmic energy. Golden coins lay both in the water and sporadically on the moss, as if people had flicked them for wishes, like this was a wishing well instead of a mystical relic.

"Is this the Isle of Dreams?" Caelum asked, a hint of awe in his voice.

"Yes, my boy. It is where travelers flip a coin and make wishes," Jairamon replied, his tone soft and reverent.

"There's a force that protects the isle." Caelum looked at Draven and then Nero, his eyes wide with concern.

"You are correct. The only being that can reach the island, and the pendant, is one that has the lineage of the first griffin," Jairamon explained.

"And what happens if the being trying to cross does not?" Draven's hand instinctively palmed Nero, unwilling to see any harm come to the creature. His heart relentlessly bounced against his rib cage.

Both Caelum and Jairamon grimaced, their expressions reflecting the seriousness of the situation.

But Nero chirped and fought to get loose, his tiny wings fluttering with fortitude. Finally, Draven relented, his hands trembling as he let Nero fly from his palm. The little griffin circled the island, his movements graceful and assured, and then dove from directly above the pendant.

Draven held his breath, his heart in his throat, until the little griffin landed next to the charm. The tension in his body eased, replaced by a sense of wonder.

The little griffin pecked at the charm, and a brilliant light enveloped him. Awe filled Draven as Nero's form shimmered and the pendant disappeared, reappearing around Nero's neck. Lightning crackled above him in a dazzling display of storm magic. When the light faded, Nero stood tall, with his chest puffed out and his eyes brighter and more intelligent than ever before.

"My friend, can you collect some of those gold coins for me?" Jairamon asked with a hopeful lilt, his eyes twinkling.

Nero scanned the surrounding ground, his keen eyes spotting the coins. He gripped two coins before taking flight and dropped them in Draven's palm. Nero settled back on his shoulder, his posture proud and attentive, and stared at the little sprite.

Draven glanced at the little griffin, a deep respect forming for the creature. He deliberately didn't give the gold to the sprite. Draven's grip tightened around the coins. He needed the potion and had a feeling that if he relinquished the gold now, he'd have to find a different form of payment, and they did not have time to dick around. "I'll take those potions now," he said.

Jairamon held out his hand. "The gold." His eyes narrowed.

Draven was not about to give away his leverage. "Not until you give me what we need to break into the Citadel and free my fate bound."

Caelum smirked and glanced away. Nero ruffled his feathers and settled on his shoulder in a move that screamed approval.

Jairamon stared him down, his expression serious. "The path is treacherous," he warned, "but I will provide you with a potion that will reveal the hidden way inside and another potion to melt away the bars holding her hostage."

With a graceful flourish, Jairamon produced two small vials filled with shimmering liquid. One red and one blue.

"The blue reveals hidden entries and should be dumped on the outer wall of the Citadel opposite the grand entrance. The red will devour the iron holding her prisoner." Jairamon offered them to Draven in his open palm and held his other hand out for the coins.

Draven took the vials, his fingers brushing against the cool glass, and dropped the coins into the sprite's hand. He slid the vials into his breast pocket and gave the sprite a nod.

Jairamon produced a green vial, his eyes gleaming. "For another coin, I will open a portal into Solstice City for you."

Caelum reached into his pocket and retrieved a gold piece. "It will save us time." He offered the coin to the sprite.

Jairamon eyed it and then nodded, taking it from Caelum before tossing the green vial on the ground. A portal appeared, the streets of Solstice City shimmering on the other side.

"Thank you, Jairamon." Draven stepped toward the portal with Caelum by his side, his heart pounding with anticipation.

The sprite smiled, his eyes twinkling with ancient wisdom. "Good luck, brave souls. The future of our realms depends on your success."

CHAPTER TWENTY
The Siege Begins

LANAE SAT ON THE cot in her cell, the hard surface pressing uncomfortably against her back. As she awaited her sentence, her fingers twisted nervously in her lap. The ground rumbled beneath her, sending vibrations through the stone floor and up her spine. Her throat closed in terror, and she swallowed the lump down, her breath quickening. The continuous rumble meant one thing.

Execution.

She had seen this before—the crowds beating the ground with the soles of their shoes as the guillotine was dragged into the town square. Her heart fluttered erratically, panic clawing at her insides. Usually, prisoners got a day's reprieve before their death sentence was carried out. It hadn't even been half a day since she had been in front of the council, and they hadn't bothered to bring her back to announce her sentence.

A wave of panic left her skin hot and clammy; sweat trickled down her temples.

A door at the far end of the cell block creaked open, and a hulking figure shrouded in darkness stepped into the hallway. At the opposite end of the cell block, where she had been led into the dungeons, the jangle of keys scraped the door, echoing eerily in the silence. The whisper of a sword unsheathing came from the darkness, followed by the flash of green eyes that glinted in the dim light.

"Give me your sword." Draven's command settled over her, firm and urgent. He moved by her in a flash, his movements swift and precise, and slid a sword through the door handle and into a space on the wall, effectively locking the dungeons from the inside.

Caelum came from the darkness to her cell door, the sheath on his hip vacant. In his hands, he held a vial that glittered red in the faint light. "Step back," he instructed, his voice steady.

Lanae moved to the rear of the cell, her heart pounding in her chest. Caelum smashed the vial against the lock on the door, and red smoke sizzled. An acrid scent filled her nostrils.

Draven waited a minute, his muscles coiled with tension, then kicked at the bars. They swung open as if no lock had ever existed. He grabbed her arm, his grip firm yet reassuring, and then reached for Caelum, dragging them both into the darkness. They moved quickly, their footsteps silent as they ignored the guards pounding on the door to the dungeons, the sound a distant roar in their ears.

They traversed a switchback, the narrow path winding through slick, forgotten passages lined with empty cells. The ground was uneven beneath their feet, and Lanae stumbled a few times, her breath coming in ragged gasps. They emerged from a door that immediately disappeared from view, blending seamlessly with the stone wall behind them. The evening sky greeted her, the air crisp and cool, along with the distant drumming of feet from the courtyard in front of the Citadel.

"What the hell happened?" Caelum asked, his voice laced with urgency as they ran away from the building toward the sketchier part of Solstice City.

"I don't know," Lanae replied, her breath heaving from the sprinting. Her legs burned with exertion, and her pulse pounded in her temples. "Where are we going?"

"The Undercity," Draven said, his tone grim. "And hope like hell we can find a place to hunker down where the guard won't think to look for you." He led the way, his movements fluid and confident despite the urgency of their flight.

"They were going to execute me." Lanae's voice dripped with bitterness. She couldn't believe they had turned on her so swiftly, the betrayal stinging more than the physical exhaustion.

"If a council member or two are compromised, they could have pushed for an accelerated execution," Caelum explained breathlessly, his words sending a rash of icy gooseflesh across her arms.

Draven led them through the maze of alleys, the narrow passageways twisting and turning. The shadows deepened as night fell, and the sounds of the city seemed distant and muted. He finally found a quiet dead end for them to catch their breath, the walls of the alley offering a temporary refuge.

Lanae glanced at Nero perched on Draven's shoulder, the baby griffin's feathers ruffled from the flight. She blinked at the pendant hanging around his neck, its surface catching the faint light and giving off a soft, otherworldly glow in the darkening night. Her gaze jumped to Draven. "What's with the necklace?"

"Nero is a descendant of the first griffin," Caelum answered.

"The yôkai left another note." Draven dug his hand into his pocket and took out a crumpled piece of paper, his expression serious as he offered it to her.

She took it and squinted to make out the words in the dark, the faint light from the pendant providing just enough illumination. As the contents penetrated her mind, she blinked and then glanced up at Draven, her eyes wide with realization. "Your messenger saved my life."

"It would seem so." He wiped his face and leaned against the brick wall. "If we hadn't gone when we did..." He paled, making the green of his eyes stand out in stark relief.

The ground quaked, knocking Lanae off her feet, but Draven grabbed her, pulling her to his chest as they moved to the center of the alley, away from the buildings. A rumble split through the air as the buildings around them shifted in the earth.

Lanae grabbed Caelum as well, keeping him close.

Terrified screams echoed all around them.

The sky over Solstice City crackled with energy, the air itself charged with powerful magic.

Shock slammed into Lanae as the buildings shifted again, tearing foundations from the earth. Mist hissed from the ground as the nearby river evaporated in a blink. The once-familiar streets of the city twisted and bent, morphing into an otherworldly labyrinth.

"Fuck."

Draven's curse brought her gaze to him. But his focus was on the sky above them.

A frigid certainty scraped the edges of her mind as she witnessed the realms converging. The bastard had engaged the darkness in the gauntlet stone. Now they had to find and destroy that relic or become slaves to a new unforgiving master.

"WE CAN'T HIDE HERE."

Draven dropped his gaze to her as her words pummeled his insides. If he could slip into another realm and keep her safe, he would, but since the stone had been activated, no realm was safe.

"We have to help them." Her eyes darted around for an exit, but Draven kept his tight hold on her, afraid that if he let her go, he would fail her. Her death would break him.

"If we go back to the Citadel, they will kill you," Caelum said before Draven could launch an argument to dissuade her.

"We cannot stay here." She struggled against Draven's grip and broke free.

Both he and Caelum followed her through the maze of alleys to the exit from the Undercity. She skidded to a halt, and her arms fell to her sides. The shock of the chaos had Draven stopping next to her. The Undercity had been just a primer to the devastation.

The confusion and terror among the citizens—both magical and non-magical—echoed in every scream drifting in the air. People scrambled in every direction. Mothers clutched their children, shopkeepers abandoned their stalls, and guards struggled to maintain order.

Lanae's chest heaved, and she raised her arms as if reaching for the floating buildings. Vines shattered from the earth, speeding toward the structures, then enveloping them and returning them to the ground.

Sweat dripped from her brow, and Caelum stepped to her side, putting a hand on her shoulder. The glow of pure power encased the two of them as more vines fought to contain the disaster.

Draven didn't know where to focus. A massive boom ripped his gaze away from the floating buildings to the outer walls of the city, where a great section lay in rubble, as if a bomb had ignited.

A flash of white hair caught his attention, and his gaze landed on Lanae's friend Rorik being dragged away by a dark figure he couldn't quite make out. His allegiance to Lanae and her friends flared, and he turned to her just as Nero flew from his shoulder and landed on Lanae's.

The flare of magic around her increased and where the wall had fallen, branches grew, thatching together in a solid web of defense against the breach.

Lanae's scream yanked his attention back to her. An arrow stuck out of her arm and the magic that had surrounded her was gone. His protective instincts flared, along with a growling rage. He stepped in front of her and let his fire loose, torching the guards with nocked bows running toward them.

He swiveled around and scooped her into his arms, bolting away from the Citadel toward the only place that might give them a moment to regroup and the possibility of information on where the hell that damn stone was so he could destroy the cursed thing.

The portal to the seer.

CHAPTER TWENTY-ONE
Fae and Fire United

LANAE HISSED IN HIS arms, her face contorted in pain. The arrow jolted in her arm with each clap of his feet against the pavement, sending jabbing pangs up her shoulder. Her breath came in ragged gasps, and each step Draven took jostled her wound further. Caelum ran behind them, his wild eyes wide with panic, his fear as palpable as the beast clawing at her insides.

Firetwill had activated the stone, and the countdown to total devastation had been kicked off. Impending doom pressed down on them.

"Where are you going?" she gasped, her voice strained, as Draven rounded another corner, his grip on her tightening to keep her steady.

"The seer," he replied, his breath coming in short, desperate gasps.

His answer sent Nero from her shoulder. The tiny griffin sped ahead of them, leading the way over rubble and the dangers of the levitating buildings. The creature's boldness shone through his swift, agile movements.

This time, when Nero reached the portal, his newly found magic opened it without either her or Draven's touch. The four of them recklessly barreled into the portal, the world around them blurring into a whirlwind of colors and sounds.

The world spun around them, and they tumbled out onto the ground in a tangled mass of arms, legs, and feathers. Lanae cried out as the arrow snapped on contact, the sharp crack echoing in her ears. Pain shot through her arm, and her surroundings wavered before her eyes as a fresh set of tears blurred her vision.

The ancient forest she remembered was now toppled. The once ethereal glow turned hellish, as if this realm was almost completely consumed already. The being they were seeking crawled toward them with a silent scream of her own. Her pearlescent skin cracked as if her crystalline being was shattering from within. Her eyes, filled with desperation, pointed at the portal behind them, imploring them to escape.

Draven turned to Lanae, his eyes meeting hers with a fierce determination. He gripped the end of the arrow, his jaw set. "Hold still." He yanked the arrow out. Pain raced through her, accelerating into excruciating agony. Without hesitation, he stuck his flaming fingers inside both the entry and exit wounds, the intense heat cauterizing them.

Caelum pushed him away, his face a mix of horror and concern.

"It's okay." Lanae huffed the words out, her voice weak. She coaxed her empty stomach not to spew out the acid roiling within. "He cauterized the wound."

Wings fluttered, and Nero rubbed his feathers over her arm. A tingling sensation replaced the pain, and before she could formulate a coherent thought, the wound stitched together until there was nothing but a red blemish on her skin.

"Damn," Caelum said, awe evident in his voice. He ran a finger down her arm, his touch gentle.

The air crackled around them, charged with an evil energy. Their senses heightened, and they turned toward the seer.

A legion of dark fae stood at the ready, their swords gleaming with ethereal power. The sight sent chills down Lanae's spine. But it was the fae with his foot on the seer's throat that froze her blood.

"Oh, crap." The gravity of their circumstances settled over them like a suffocating shroud.

DRAVEN GLARED AT THE vaguely familiar face, his eyes narrowing with recognition. It wasn't Firetwill, but it was a face that had accompanied that bastard to their house many times when he was a young boy. His mind raced, reaching into the recesses of his memory, and a name surfaced.

"Vargus." The name spit out between his clenched teeth, his voice blazing with venom.

"Well, well, if it isn't the last of the Emberwings." Vargus's voice dripped with malice, his lips curling into a sneer.

Flames licked at Draven's fingertips, casting a flickering light on his face. "I should have known you'd be involved in this madness."

Vargus laughed, the sound grating and hollow, echoing in the tense air. "You should have stayed hidden, Draven. Now you'll join the rest of your kind in oblivion."

The air between them crackled with tension, the atmosphere prickling with impending violence. Rage boiled within Draven, his muscles tensing as his dragon instincts urged him to unleash his full power. But if he did, Lanae, Caelum, and even Nero would fall to his fire along with his enemy. He had to stay focused—this was not just a personal vendetta; it was the future of their world.

Vargus pushed the point of his sword through the seer's throat, the blade slicing through flesh with a sickening sound. He yanked it to the side, severing her head in a brutal display. Blood sprayed, and Vargus smiled as he pointed the dripping blade at Draven. "You're next."

LANAE GASPED AS BOTH men charged, their fury filling the air with an electrical current that seemed to shatter the paralysis holding the legions in place. The dark fae darted around the two combatants, their movements swift and menacing, running straight for her and Caelum.

Panic surged within her. Both she and Caelum were unarmed, vulnerable against the oncoming threat.

Caelum grabbed her around the waist, his grip tight and protective, as he backed up toward the portal. "We have to get out of here," he urged, his voice strained with desperation. Nero took flight, his wings beating frantically as the sky erupted into a web of lightning and cracking thunder, the noise deafening.

But they weren't fast enough. A wall of dark fae crashed into them, their bodies solid and unyielding. Lanae felt the impact like a sledgehammer, knocking the wind out of her as they were dragged into the portal. The sensation of being pulled through space twisted her insides, and she struggled to breathe.

The last view she had of Draven was his blood spilling from Vargus's strike, the vivid red staining the ground. Her heart clenched with devastation, a scream trapped in her throat as her world tumbled again. The portal spit them out onto a cold marble floor, the sudden change in surroundings disorienting.

They landed in a heap, their limbs tangled, the hard surface bruising her skin. She struggled to sit up, her breaths coming in ragged gasps. Dozens of armed fae surrounded them. Both dark and light soldiers had their swords pointed menacingly at her and her brother. The metallic sheen of the blades gleamed under the faint illumination.

Fear and perseverance warred within her as she met the gaze of the fae soldiers. Her body trembled with exhaustion, and she reached for

Caelum's hand. He clasped it and squeezed tight. His fear broadcast through their mind link, and she needed to be strong for his sake. She didn't have time to wallow in her shattered heart. They needed to figure out a plan to get back to Draven and save him so he could destroy the damn gauntlet stone.

THE COMMOTION NEAR THE portal drew Draven's gaze away from Vargus, causing him to miss the block. Vargus's blade sliced into his arm, and Draven spun away, dislodging the blade. Blood splattered the ground, but that wasn't what tightened his chest and made his vision turn red. Lanae and Caelum disappeared into a sea of dark fae, devoured by the gateway before it blinked out of existence.

Draven roared, blocking Vargus's counterstrike. With Lanae and Caelum out of harm's way, he had free rein with his fire. He blew a blast of flame at Vargus, but it fizzled as it hit a wall of dark magic. The air thickened with smoke as Vargus's magic slammed into his chest, knocking him off-balance.

Lightning lit up the sky, distracting Vargus enough for Draven to regain his footing. Draven unleashed a torrent of flames, the fire consuming everything in its path except Vargus. The bastard countered with more dark magic, the two forces colliding with explosive intensity.

"You betrayed us, Vargus," Draven spat, his voice saturated with fury. "And for what? Power? Glory?"

Vargus sneered, his eyes glowing with malevolent energy. "I did what I had to do to survive. And now, I'll ensure you don't."

The battle raged, each strike fueled by years of hatred and betrayal. The weight of Draven's ancestors' legacy pressed down on him, but the strength of his bond with Lanae and his need to protect her and her brother gave him the tenacity to keep chipping away at Vargus's barriers.

He was fighting for more than just himself—he was fighting for a future where their world could thrive. With a final, powerful burst of flame, Draven overcame Vargus's defenses. The traitor fell, screaming in agony as he was consumed by the very fire he had sought to extinguish.

CHAPTER TWENTY-TWO
Dark Bonds

THE GUARDS PARTED, AND a familiar face stepped forward, followed by two faces that were even more familiar to both her and Caclum. A gasp escaped their lips as they stared at the vacant expressions of their parents. The lifelessness in their eyes chilled Lanae to the bone. Beyond them, bound in chains, stood both Elara and Rorik. The only one with any expression was Rorik, and the blaze in his eyes conveyed he was spitting mad, his fury like a burning ember refusing to be extinguished.

"What the fuck?" Caelum's voice shook with his shock and disbelief.

Lanae glanced at him, her heart aching, before turning her attention back to their surroundings and the familiar face that made her nearly vomit on the floor. "You." Lanae bared her teeth in a snarl at the fae in charge. The same fae who had danced with her at the ball.

Xoltan grinned at her, and his onyx eyes danced with a menacing glee.

"Where are we?" Caelum's voice trembled.

"In my realm, where I have been plotting the enslavement of all the realms for centuries," he replied, his voice smooth and stony, sending chills down her spine.

Although he hadn't told her his surname at the ball, she made an educated guess. "Firetwill?"

The bastard inclined his head, a disturbing smile playing on his lips.

Lanae climbed to her feet, her legs shaky, but she forced them to hold her weight. She glared at him, and a blaze of defiance lit in her soul. "You didn't stop with the destruction of the dragons?" she spat, her voice laced with contempt.

He gagged on a laugh, the sound devoid of any warmth. "That was my brother's debacle. But his oversight left us access to the gauntlet stone. Unfortunately, your dragon has served his purpose." He tilted his head and stared down at her, his eyes calculating, inspecting her from crown to toe and back.

His study of her made her feel dirty, as if his gaze could strip away her dignity.

"You chose a dragon over an emperor?" he asked.

"I chose my heart over a stranger," she replied and jutted out her chin.

His lips curled into a smile, and he stepped close enough for her to feel his breath. "I am sorry to inform you that your heart has been mercilessly slaughtered today." His gaze lowered to her chest, and he licked his lips.

Caelum moved in front of her, his posture protective. "Don't look at her like that," he growled.

Firetwill nodded at their parents, and they marched forward, their movements mechanical and devoid of any recognition. They took hold of Caelum, their grip unyielding as they pulled him away from Lanae.

"Don't hurt him, Da." A crisp, urgent voice split through the tension, echoing in the charged atmosphere.

CAELUM GAPED AT THE girl who stepped out of the crowd. Arsia from the ball. His heart sank. The girl who had weaseled her way into his heart couldn't be associated with this madman. She had to be under the same spell that his parents were. They held him in an unforgiving grip, their hands like iron shackles, as they marched him away from Lanae.

Arsia met his gaze, and regret filled her eyes. "I'm sorry for deceiving you."

"You knew what his plan was?" He nodded toward Firetwill.

"Of course." She smiled. "I was there for the same reason you were, although we were spying on different sides."

Fury ignited within Caelum, a burning rage that consumed him. He spit at her, the act earning him a cuffed palm to the back of his head from his father. The sting of his reprimand did nothing to quell the bite of betrayal closing down his heart, the pain cutting deeper than any physical blow.

"Don't worry, Arsia. He will be as compliant as you want him to be. Just like she will be." Firetwill gave Lanae a smile that made Caelum's stomach twist with revulsion.

"You are just as monstrous as your father." Caelum's voice dripped with venom. His words were a desperate attempt to lash out, to hurt the girl who had caused him so much pain. But his defiance was short-lived as he was dragged into a glass case, his wrists and ankles bound tightly before the door closed with a resounding thud. "Don't do this!" he cried, his voice cracking with desperation.

Lanae, help me!

GUARDS GRABBED LANAE, THEIR grips like iron shackles, and she fought against them with all her might. Her brother's thoughts barreled through her mind, urgent and desperate. He locked eyes with her as smoke filled the case, forcefully driving into Caelum's nose and mouth.

Her brother screamed in her head, his mental voice filled with agony. The pain and fear in his scream were almost unbearable, and her legs gave out as his screams faded, the mind link numbing to a dull, aching void.

The smoke cleared, revealing Caelum's usually expressive eyes now carrying that vacant, hollow look she had seen time and time again. Her heart broke at the sight. When the door opened, Arsia stepped up, her expression unreadable. She took Caelum's hand, leading him out of the room with her. Arsia sent a chilling grin over her shoulder, a twisted smile that made Lanae's blood turn into an icy sludge before she disappeared around the corner.

"You bastard. I will never become a mindless zombie." Lanae kicked at her captors, her movements wild and frantic, but their grasp was unyielding, like chains forged from iron.

"I will enjoy breaking you." Firetwill winked at Lanae before he gave a nod to the guards holding Rorik. His eyes gleamed with sadistic pleasure.

Elara's gaze moved to Rorik, and a clarity shone through her eyes, breaking through the haze of control. Lanae's heart pounded as Elara stepped forward, placing herself between Rorik and the machine designed to steal his mind. She opened her mouth and let out a hauntingly beautiful melody, her siren song aimed at the guards holding Rorik. The melody drifted through the room, freezing the dark fae in place, their movements halted by the power of her voice.

"Run, Rorik." Her urgent voice filled with love. "Find the dragon and spill your secrets." She resumed her song, the one that Lanae had heard in battle. It rendered the dark fae useless, immobilizing them with its power.

The chains holding Rorik fell away, clattering to the ground, and he bolted from the room. A blast of magic hit Elara, silencing her song abruptly, and she crumpled to the ground in a lifeless heap.

Lanae turned her gaze to the monster in the room, the one who leered at her like she was his next conquest. He strolled forward with an air of arrogance and gripped her chin, his touch cold and invasive. "Her usefulness just ran out." His whisper was as menacing as the darkness in his gaze. He cocked his head, a sinister smirk twisting his mouth. "Yours has just begun."

His gaze moved behind her, commanding and authoritative. "Chain her in my chambers," he ordered.

"Yes, master," her parents replied in unison, their voices devoid of emotion.

Lanae dug her heels in, her shoes skidding helplessly on the polished marble floors. The smooth, unyielding surface offered no traction, and her efforts to resist were futile. She called on her magic, willing her vines to sprout and break through the slick stone surrounding her, but the marble remained impervious, mocking her desperation. A chill turned frigid, seeping into her bones at the sight of the shackles hanging ominously from Firetwill's ceiling and clasped on the floor. The dark metal glinted menacingly in the dim light.

She fought with renewed anguish, her muscles straining as she struggled against her parents' iron grips. A frantic rhythm pulsed in her chest, each beat a desperate plea for freedom. But no matter how fiercely she resisted, she couldn't escape her dark fate. Their hands were like vise grips, unyielding and merciless.

Iron bit into her wrists and ankles, the cold metal burning her skin and nullifying any magic inside her. The pain was excruciating, a searing agony that spread through her limbs like wildfire. She screamed, her voice echoing off the stone walls, a raw and primal sound filled with fear and defiance. She struggled against the bonds, her body writhing in a desperate attempt to break free, but she was at the bastard's mercy now, her strength no match for the cruel restraints.

DRAVEN STEPPED THROUGH THE portal with Nero on his shoulder, emerging into a narrow alley in Solstice City. His heart clanged in his chest, each beat loud and jarring as he surveyed their tilting world. There were no signs of Lanae and Caelum or of dark fae anywhere near the portal entrance. He ventured forward, his gaze sweeping over every nook and cranny, searching desperately for any indication that they had fled this way.

The chaos in Solstice City had reached a fever pitch. The air crackled with energy, buzzing with the presence of mythical creatures like phoenixes and thunderbirds manifesting in the streets. Their powerful forms added to the pandemonium, their cries echoing through the city. The once-familiar cityscape had transformed into a battlefield of magic and myth, buildings shuddering under the destruction of the merging realms, their foundations cracking and groaning.

His desire to find Lanae was overshadowed by his need to find and destroy the stone. He weaved his way through the bedlam, his movements quick and purposeful, aiming for Lanae's house. It was the only logical place they would go. Nero stayed perched on his shoulder, his keen eyes scanning their surroundings. A silent sentry amidst the chaos.

Nero chirped when Lanae's home came into view, untouched by the changing landscape, as if her magic prevented the home from uprooting and toppling over like so many other structures they had maneuvered around. His relief at seeing the home intact was short-lived when Rorik stumbled toward him, his steps unsteady.

"Draven," Rorik gasped, his voice hoarse with exhaustion.

Draven hurried to his side, concern etched on his face, and pulled him into the house.

"He has them." Rorik collapsed on the floor in a wheezing mass of flesh and bone. His breaths came in ragged gasps, each one a struggle.

"Who?" Draven's heart pounded with dread.

"Firetwill," Rorik choked out.

Draven's world spun on its axis, and he sat down hard on the nearest chair, his knees weak. He clenched his eyes and reached out to the bond between them. It still existed. He dug further, and what came through in faint waves was utter panic. His eyes snapped open, a fierce determination replacing his initial shock.

"Where are they?" He picked Rorik up by his shirt, his grip tight and desperate.

"Not in this realm." Rorik shook his head. "But there is a hidden portal in the Citadel. At least that's where I ended up when I jumped through the one in Firetwill's palace."

Draven set Rorik down on his feet, his mind racing.

"They have Caelum under their mind control." Rorik's voice trembled as much as his body.

"And Lanae?" Draven asked, his voice tinged with fear.

"I don't know. Elara created a diversion so I wouldn't receive the same fate." His voice cracked, a deep sorrow filling his eyes. "And she died for helping me escape." He swallowed hard at the painful memory. "But before that happened, Firetwill told Lanae he would enjoy breaking her. He is a twisted bastard."

"Break her?" Draven's mind went to a dark place, where he imagined Lanae bloodied and begging for death. His anger surged, filling every pore with searing heat.

"Firetwill wants to breed with her."

Rorik's words were worse than being tied to a whipping post, each syllable a lash against Draven's soul.

Heat flashed to flame, and Draven's vision tinged with red flares. He roared his anger, a primal, guttural sound. Lanae was his, and he would raze the universe if that bastard so much as laid a finger on her.

CHAPTER TWENTY-THREE
The Final Strategy

RORIK PRESSED HIMSELF AGAINST the wall, his back flattening against the hard stone as he tried to distance himself from the flaming dragon in the small, confined space. "Do you want to burn Lanae's house down?" He cursed the tremble in his voice.

Draven growled, the sound low and menacing, and he glared at Rorik. But his words seemed to break through the fury. He blinked and shook his head. Rorik knew the beast of a man wouldn't want to harm Lanae. The flames licking at his skin retreated before he could do any more damage than the singed floor beneath his feet.

"Take me there." Draven's voice was rough and commanding.

Rorik's eyebrows rose in surprise, and he shook his head, his defiance masking his fear. "I don't want to be reduced to a mindless minion."

Draven stalked toward him with a predatory gait, and then he pinned Rorik to the wall with a fierce grip. "Take me to Lanae, or you will not live to see the end of this war," he threatened, his eyes blazing with unrestrained anger.

Rorik trembled under his threat. The wild rage in Draven's eyes made him clamp his legs against pissing himself. He gulped down a knot of fear and it burned his dry throat. He nodded. Although he didn't want to lose his mind, he also didn't want to die. "But I'm not going unarmed," he insisted, his voice shaky but resolute.

Draven released him, the pressure lifting from his chest, and he pointed to the corner where a small arsenal of weapons sat. "Help yourself."

Rorik didn't second-guess the command, his mind racing. He picked out a dozen knives and killing stars, their cold metal reassuring against his palms, and lined his belt with them, and then chose one of the swords. When he turned back, Draven nodded with approval.

Rorik's stomach grumbled, the noise loud in the tense silence. "I need something to eat before we go," he admitted, his face flushing with embarrassment.

Draven growled but stalked into the kitchen, his footsteps loud as the cracks of a whip. When he returned, he held two rolls stuffed with sweetmeats. He handed one to Rorik and inhaled the other himself. "You can walk and eat," he said through a mouthful, his words clipped and impatient.

Rorik took a bite, the taste a brief comfort amidst the madness, and headed out the door with Draven on his heels.

LANAE'S BODY THROBBED FROM being in the same position for what felt like an eternity, her legs wide and her arms spread over her head. The iron shackles still burned, the metal biting into her skin, but the sting had dulled enough to not want to scream. Her muscles throbbed with a relentless ache, and her joints felt stiff and unyielding. Her eyes drooped, heavy with exhaustion, and her head bounced forward, jerking her awake. She had no idea how long had gone by since she had been left in chains. It seemed like hours, and the stiffness in her joints concurred.

Her tongue stuck to the roof of her mouth, dry and parched. She tried to form some spit, but her mouth and throat were as dry as desert sand, each breath a struggle. The click of the lock wiped the haze from her mind, snapping her back to the present. She straightened her back, locking down any tremble that might betray her unease. Her jaw clenched in anticipation of what Firetwill might attempt. Even chained, she'd do everything she could to stop whatever dark deeds he had in mind.

When he stepped into the room, he grinned at her with an evil smile that sent a shiver of dread through her. Behind him, the door clicked shut, and with a flip of his fingers, he engaged the lock.

Her heart lodged in her ribs, each beat a drum of fear. She sent a silent prayer to the goddess, begging for a way to escape this hideous man and his hungry leer.

Firetwill stalked across the room, his movements predatory, and he stopped before her.

"Do not touch me." Lanae's voice trembled with defiance.

The smile that formed on his lips sent a shiver of revulsion through her, strong enough to rattle the chains holding her in the most vulnerable position.

"I will do whatever I please with you." He ran his finger down the front of her shirt, the touch cold and invasive, until he reached her belt. With nimble fingers, he unhooked the leather and pulled it free. He folded it in half and struck his palm, smiling at the slap of leather against flesh.

He took a step back and grinned as black magic poured out of him, the dark energy swirling around him like a malevolent aura. He directed it at her, and her worst nightmare came to fruition as her clothing shredded and fell to bits around her feet. The freezing air bit at her exposed skin, adding to her humiliation.

"That's much better." He struck his palm again as he walked around her in a circle, studying her naked form with a greedy gaze. He stopped in front of her and slapped her across the face with the belt.

The sting of leather on her cheek made her draw in a quick breath, the pain searing and immediate. The hot drizzle of blood followed, trickling down her skin.

"Do you know what a blood curse is?" His voice dripped with malice.

Lanae didn't trust her voice to not tremble with the fear coursing through her, so she shook her head, her eyes wide with terror.

"It's different from the machine. It doesn't take your mind, but it makes you compliant despite your reservations." He reached out and swiped her cheek, then slipped his fingers in his mouth. "Mmm. Delicious."

Her body betrayed her, shaking the chains with her constant quiver, the fear and pain overwhelming her.

"I want you to suffer for so many sins."

"What did I do?" She tried to keep him talking rather than acting upon whatever dark ideas were in his head.

"You forsook me at the ball." He tilted his head, studying her, and then lashed out with the belt, striking her ribs.

The sting of it drew her breath in. "I wasn't interested. Still aren't." She forced the words out.

"And then there are the sins of your father's." Another slap of the belt. This time on her thigh.

"What did he do?"

"His sins are numerous. First, he failed at brokering a successful peace between Solstice City and the dark kingdom. And my wife at the time was killed in a surprise attack." He slapped her breasts with the belt and stepped closer. "And then when I saw you, I told your father you were payment for his disastrous negotiation skills. I wanted you to breed me magical children. He agreed, but only after some convincing by your mother. When you turned of age and were supposed to be betrothed to me, he denied me the alliance I wanted." He circled behind her and slapped her back with the belt, the pain searing through her.

She arched away from the sting, her body instinctively trying to escape.

"He said a seer told them you were fate bound to a dragon." He slapped her again with the belt. "You were not there the day I used black magic to kidnap your parents. Otherwise, you would have given me a half dozen heirs by now." Another slap of the belt, each one punctuated by a growl. "Your father promised me I would never have you." He hissed a laugh. "I made that bastard watch as I stripped your mother of her mind and showed him all the ways I intended to violate you. And before I took his mind, I promised him you would be on your knees worshiping me until you sired a magical army, and then I would return his mind in time to watch you die at my hands in the most heinous way possible."

The belt connected mercilessly against her thighs, leaving deep, painful welts with each strike. He grinned as he stepped in front of her on his third pass around her, continuing the maddening circle around her.

"He did one useful thing, though. He brought me the dark fae leader, along with his closest advisors, who thought they were entering a peace treaty. Once I had them under my mind control, the rest of the dark fae army succumbed to my will."

He stepped close and wrapped the belt around her throat, yanking it tight enough to make Lanae wheeze. "I waited and gathered key pieces in my chess game. The sphinx, a witch, a yôkai, a few council members, and a warrior close enough to you to manipulate you and the dragon to my whims. Trails of bogus clues were planted to draw the dragon back to Solstice City, and then every move since has all been at my discretion. Every trickle of information, every quest you were subjected to...they were all planned right down to the last detail so your dragon would break through the barriers preventing me from getting the precious gauntlet stone in my hands."

"What?" Lanae glanced over her shoulder at his sadistic grin.

"I was exceedingly angry at my brother when he killed all the dragons, enough to exile him to the other side of this realm for his thoughtlessness. He was supposed to bring me a dragon, and instead he wiped them from existence. You see, only dragon fire could break the protections around the gauntlet stone."

His fingers trailed down her back and pressed into one cut left by the belt. She hissed and arched away from the pain.

"You can imagine the shock that went through me when your father told me what the seer revealed to him." He pressed another welt, chuckling. "Since you were not at the house when I came to exact justice on your parents, I bode my time and put all the pieces in place for a much more satisfying game."

Her breath hitched. They had been played so expertly. She let out a cry of frustration and yanked at the chains holding her in place. "So, everything the witch told us was a lie?"

"Perhaps. Perhaps not." Firetwill chuckled; his breath on her ear was foul enough for her to turn her head away. "Now that I have the stone, I have waited long enough. I want what I was promised. I want you on your knees, worshiping me."

"Never," Lanae breathed out between gasps, her defiance unwavering.

"I want your spirit shattered and your body yielding to my every whim." He ran his free hand over her abdomen suggestively, his touch cold and repulsive.

"No." Her voice filled with obstinance.

He pressed his body against her back, his presence suffocating. "Yes." He held out the hand he had caressed her with and whispered an incantation. When the skin split, he placed his open wound against the one on her cheek, whispering a dark curse in her ear.

Her breath hitched as their blood mixed. The burn of the curse seized her muscles. She screamed, trying to expel the poison from her bloodstream, but it was no use. Black smoke wrapped around her, seeping into her skin, and her stomach roiled with nausea and fear.

When the smoke cleared, Firetwill said, "Stand still."

Her body complied with his command, her muscles locking in place against her will. The chains released and metal clattered to the floor, but she remained in the same position even though her brain screamed to run. Every fiber of her being urged her to flee, but she was trapped in her own body, a prisoner to his dark magic.

"You can put your arms down." He crossed to stand in front of her, a cocky, knowing smile on his lips as her arms dropped to her sides, her movements mechanical and devoid of her own volition. "On your knees."

Her legs buckled, dropping her to her knees with the hard outline of Firetwill's crotch inches from her face. Humiliation and rage warred within her, her mind a storm of emotions. She raved in her mind, trying to break the hold he had on her body, but she was at his mercy, and the man had a dark agenda. The sense of helplessness was suffocating. Her spirit screamed in defiance even as her body betrayed her.

He grinned down at her, his eyes gleaming with sadistic pleasure, as he tilted her chin up. "Undo my pants." His voice rumbled in a low, menacing whisper.

A tear escaped, sending a hot trail down her cheek, stinging as it flowed into her cut. The pain was a cruel reminder of her lack of defense. Her hands shook as she fought the command, her mind screaming in defiance, but it was useless. Her fingers moved, unthreading button after button until his length was free of fabric. Each movement felt like a betrayal, her body acting against her will.

She closed her lips tightly, her jaw set in a rebellious line, and glared up at him. Her eyes burned with hatred and fear.

He grabbed her hair, his grip painfully tight, and yanked her head back. "Open your mouth," he ordered, his voice thick with cruelty.

Her mouth opened wide enough to accommodate him, but before he could capitalize on the situation, a sudden bang on the door made him pause.

"Xoltan!" a voice called from the other side of the door.

A growl formed in his chest, low and menacing. "I'm a little busy." His voice rang with irritation.

The interruption was unexpected, and the tension in the room shifted. A flicker of hope ignited within her despite the fear that still gripped her.

"There's been a breach!" The urgent shout from outside the door severed the tension.

His growl became feral, a deep, guttural sound that sent a shiver down Lanae's spine. He stepped away, tucking himself back into his pants with a frustrated snarl.

Relief washed over Lanae, a fleeting moment of respite, until Firetwill leaned close, his breath hot against her ear.

"Spread your legs out and wait for me. If by chance it's your dragon and he finds you, you are to kill him. We can't have him destroying the stone with his fire. Understand?"

"Drop dead," Lanae spat, her voice filled with insolence. But despite her words, her knees widened, her body betraying her once again. She knew the order would be executed if Draven found her. The dark magic riding her blood compelled her to obey against her will. The thought of harming Draven filled her with a wrenching anguish.

"Pleasure yourself until I return. I want you dripping wet for me."

When her hand slid down between her legs, her cheeks flushed hot with a mix of shame and anger. Firetwill's face split into a grin, the kind that made her want to vomit. The room chilled, the air filled with her humiliation. Her body moved against her will, each motion a betrayal of her own autonomy. The emotional turmoil within her was like a storm, waves of despair crashing against the walls of her mind. She fought to hold on to her sanity, praying for a way to overcome the dark magic that held her captive. The thought of Draven finding her like this, and the possibility of being forced to harm him, filled her with a soul-crushing dread. Tears welled up, threatening to spill over, but she fought to keep her composure, clinging to the hope that somehow she would find a way to resist.

DRAVEN FOLLOWED RORIK THROUGH the catastrophic remains of Solstice City and into the shifting Citadel. Nero perched on Draven's shoulder, with his claws digging into Draven's skin. The griffin's anxiety mirrored Draven's own frantic mood. Firetwill's motives for Lanae left him more desperate than he had ever felt before.

Rorik raced past the council's meeting rooms and into a dimly lit back hallway. His breath came in short, ragged pants, his steps whispering on the stone floor. He slid to a stop at an ancient, arched opening, its surface inscribed with runes that shimmered in the dim light. Glancing back at Draven, his eyes were filled with uncertainty. "I don't know what we are going to find on the other side." He unsheathed his sword with a metallic hiss.

Draven nodded and did the same, the weight of his blade a comforting presence in his hand.

"Have you seen the stone?" Even though the need to free Lanae was racking every nerve, the stone's destruction had to take precedence. Otherwise, they'd all be Firetwill's slaves.

Rorik's grim expression deepened. "It's on a pedestal in his heavily guarded throne room."

Draven ran a hand over his face, feeling the rough stubble of days without rest. "I need you to find Lanae while I go destroy the damn stone before the realms merge." His words conflicted with his wants, but he had to take care of the greater threat before he rescued the woman who captured his heart.

Rorik gave him a curt nod and re-gripped his blade, as if silently talking himself into this suicide mission.

Together, they approached the portal, its surface a swirling vortex of dark energy. As they stepped through, a sensation of being pulled apart and reassembled washed over Draven. The world around them twisted and warped, the remnants of Solstice City fading away, replaced by the shimmering marble hallway.

Firetwill's stronghold pulsated with a malevolent energy. Its obsidian walls gleamed with dark magic that made the very sandwich in Draven's stomach churn with unease. The atmosphere was thick with a suffocating aura, the air prickling with an electric charge that set every nerve on edge.

"The throne room is that way." Rorik pointed his sword toward a dimly lit hallway that seemed to stretch into an endless void. Shadows danced along the walls, flickering like ghosts in the oppressive darkness.

Draven locked his gaze with Rorik. "Find Lanae and get her home." Each word was a struggle against his primal urge to follow those orders himself. His skin rippled with the stress of his decision, muscles taut with the strain of keeping his emotions in check.

Rorik's firm nod was a lifeline, anchoring Draven in the swirling maelstrom of his own fears and doubts. It gave him the strength to turn away from the path his heart desperately wanted to take and instead march toward his destiny. With each step, the burden of his task pressed heavier on his shoulders, but his dedication remained unbroken. The fate of the realms depended on the destruction of the stone, and he would not falter now.

THE SHADOWS ENVELOPED DRAVEN, and Rorik turned in the opposite direction, his mind spinning with options. *Would Firetwill lock her in the dungeons?* He shook his head, dismissing the thought. If he used that damn machine on her like he did on Lanae's brother, she'd be sharing his bed. The thought of his friend compromised like that burned, along with the fact he had no idea where the sleeping quarters were.

He forced himself to breathe, to calm his racing heart. The surrounding air stunk of moldy stone and decay, and he glanced around the corner at another empty hall. This was an area that he wasn't familiar with, one that seemed to run parallel to the one he sent Draven down. He kept to the walls, using his ability to cloak himself in shadows as he slunk through the hallway. His heart throbbed in his chest.

Movement made him plaster himself in an alcove, crowding the air from his chest. Three doors down from where he hid, a soldier pounded on a door, the sound echoing through the empty hall.

"Xoltan!" the soldier's commanding voice rang out.

A muffled response came that Rorik couldn't make out, but the tone screamed with irritation.

"There's been a breach," the guard said, his voice tense.

A few heartbeats later, an angry Firetwill stomped out the door, his presence radiating malevolence as he followed the guard into the heart of the castle. Rorik's muscles tensed, every instinct screaming at him to run, but he held his ground, waiting until they disappeared from sight.

Once they were gone, Rorik slid to the door their enemy had vacated. His senses heightened, and he checked the hallway again before slipping into the room. He closed the door behind him and then turned to survey the bedroom. The sight before him froze his muscles and robbed him of breath.

Lanae was naked on her knees, her hand between her legs, her face a mask of mortification and despair. Heat filled his cheeks, but his embarrassment was nothing compared to the pain he saw in her eyes.

"Lanae?" he whispered.

"I can't stop." Fresh tears cascaded down her cheeks. "Blood cursed to do whatever that sadistic bastard wants." Her breath hitched, and her chin trembled. "He ordered me to do this until he came back. And to kill Draven if he found me." Her sob filled the room, a sound of pure anguish.

"Fuck." Rorik glanced around, his mind racing. A wardrobe sat to his right, and he stepped inside, grabbing a tunic off the shelf. "I need to get you out of here." He approached her, his heart breaking at the sight of her suffering, and offered the fabric for her to put on.

She cried harder, her hand still playing with her sex, her cheeks reddening further as her tortured gaze met his. He huffed, sliding the garment over her head, his hands shaking with helplessness. She threaded one hand through the sleeve and then switched hands to thread her other arm through the fabric.

She made eye contact with him. "I bet you never thought you'd see me like this." She let out a little laugh.

He smiled, thankful for her trying to infuse some humor into this moment. "Maybe one time in my dreams, but no. This isn't as sexy as I thought it would be. Now get up. We need to go."

"Unfortunately, I have no control of my body," Lanae said through clenched teeth, her body trembling.

"Draven's going to freak the fuck out." Rorik looked at the door, his mind racing with the implications.

Lanae's hand stilled. "He's here?" Her voice vibrated with fear.

Rorik nodded.

"Get me as far away from him as you can. Otherwise, I am compelled to kill him, and he's the only one who can destroy the stone." Her hand went back to masturbating, her eyes filled with desperation.

Rorik closed his eyes, scrambling for what to do. He'd have to carry her out, but he couldn't in her current condition. The thought of Firetwill's forces killing him was a distant worry compared to the image of Draven's rage at the sight of Lanae in his arms while pleasuring herself. The very idea made his stomach churn with dread.

A morbid thought surfaced, and he steeled himself for what he had to do. "This is going to hurt." He braced himself. His heart fell with a clang as he fisted his hand, the knuckles turning white with tension.

"What are you doing?" Lanae asked. Her eyes widened as she caught his clenched fist.

"Getting you out of here," he replied, his voice steady despite the turmoil within.

Rorik threw a punch, connecting with her temple, hitting hard enough to knock her into oblivion. Her eyes rolled back, and she slumped to the ground, her body finally at peace. The sight of her unconscious form filled him with a guilty relief.

He kneeled beside her, his hands trembling as he brushed a strand of hair from her face. "I'm sorry, Lanae." He unclasped the belt from around Lanae's neck. "Draven is going to skin me alive," he muttered and bound her hands behind her back with the belt. He didn't need her fingering herself while he carried her out of there, and he didn't want her free to follow through with a kill order.

With a deep breath, he gathered her limp form into his arms, careful not to jostle her too much. The warmth of her body against his was a stark contrast to the cold, unfeeling stone of the castle walls. He glanced around the room, his eyes searching for any signs of danger, before making his way toward the door.

Every step was a struggle, the weight of his burden both physical and emotional. He knew Draven would be furious, but he also knew that he had done what was necessary to protect Lanae. As he moved through the dimly lit hallways, the shadows closed in around him as he conjured his cloaking magic.

Rorik's mind raced with thoughts of what lay ahead. He had to get Lanae to safety, but he also had to ensure that Draven could destroy the stone. He glanced toward the portal and made a decision that would change his fate.

AT THE SOUND OF footsteps, Draven reached for the nearest doorknob and slid inside a room, latching the door as quietly as he opened it. The darkness surrounded him, and above the beating of his heart, the sounds of intimacy invaded his ears.

The gentle creak of bedsprings and pants increased behind him. His thoughts flew to Lanae, and he shifted to his dragon sight. Dread wrapped around him, but he made himself glance directly into the bedroom despite what he might see.

A trail of clothing led to the bed, and his mind stalled at the familiar face on the pillow. Caelum stared up at the girl riding him as if she were his universe. It took Draven a moment for recognition to set in, but as soon as it did, the girl from the ball came into focus.

He glanced around the ornate room that reminded him of his sister's room in their castle eons ago. When his gaze landed on the dressing desk on the other side of the room, his lips pulled back in a silent snarl. A thin crown suited for a princess sat on the surface.

A royal spy. One who had Caelum under a mind spell. Their enemy.

Flames flickered on his fingers, and her gaze swiveled in his direction.

She gasped, but Caelum never stopped looking at her. Rorik had said his mind had been taken, but he didn't understand the extent of it until this moment.

"You." She rolled off Caelum before pointing at Draven. "Kill him, Caelum."

Caelum's gaze moved to Draven, and within that vacant expression flared a murderous glare fueled by the girl's order. Caelum stood and started toward Draven with his hands out in claw formations, as if he intended on clawing him to death with his blunt fingernails.

Nero squawked, and a bolt of lightning shot out of his beak, hitting Caelum in the chest.

Caelum's back arched, and light encased him until dark mist shot from his mouth, eyes, and ears, as if the spell inside was fleeing from a dark death.

Then Caelum crumpled to the floor.

Fury surfaced through Draven, and he blew a targeted stream of fire at the traitorous fae princess, hot enough to kill on impact. Her death was swift. Her ashen form remained with her mouth poised in a silent scream.

"What the..." Caelum looked down at his naked form and then up at Draven as the scent of burned flesh swirled around them.

"The girl from the ball." Draven waved at the burned form on the bed.

Caelum blinked, and his expression darkened. He surveyed the room and grabbed his pants, sliding them on before he looked at Draven. Shame painted his cheeks red.

"Thank you," he said as he picked up his discarded shirt.

Draven glanced at Nero. "I didn't break the spell. Our little friend here did." He took a moment to pet Nero, who puffed up with pride.

"Well, thank you, Nero." Caelum finished buttoning his shirt. "I guess I owe you one. Maybe a nice, juicy mouse?"

Nero squawked in approval, and Draven couldn't help but chuckle despite the tension. The little griffin's enthusiasm was a small, welcome distraction from the surrounding chaos.

He glanced out into the hallway again, ensuring it was clear, and then shut the door quietly. "I need you to go right until you get to the end of the hallway. There's a portal to Solstice City." Even before he finished, Caelum was shaking his head.

"I'm not leaving until we have Lanae," Caelum insisted, his voice firm.

"Your sister would be devastated if anything happened to you. I promise I will get her out of here. But I need to destroy that stone first,"

Draven replied, his tone pleading for understanding.

"Draven, I can help. We have a mind connection, remember?" Caelum closed his eyes, his brow furrowing in concentration as he tried to reach out to Lanae.

"Caelum, please be reasonable," Draven urged.

Caelum opened his eyes and pressed his lips together, a shadow crossing his expression. "Either she's blocking me or she's sleeping. I am staying, Draven." He put his hand out, his will unwavering.

Draven cocked an eyebrow, a mix of frustration and admiration in his gaze.

"A weapon?" Caelum asked after a moment.

"She will cut my heart out with her bare hands if anything happens to you," Draven warned, his voice tinged with exasperation. But he unsheathed two knives and handed them to Caelum.

Caelum glanced back at the bed, a wry smile tugging at his lips. "Yeah, well, the enemy princess popped my cherry. So, I already had something humiliating happen." He took the offered weapons and secured them in his belt.

Draven smirked, unable to resist the humor in the situation. "It didn't look like it was so horrible when I came in."

Caelum rolled his eyes, his cheeks flushing with embarrassment. "I may have derived some physical pleasure..." The blush deepened. "But my mind wasn't mine, so does it really count?"

Draven snorted a laugh, the tension easing. "Fair point. Just stay close and don't do anything reckless." He opened the door and slipped out with Caelum on his heels.

A sudden commotion in the direction they were heading stopped Draven in his tracks. His heart clamored in his chest, each beat a painful reminder of the stakes. Among the chaos, a voice cut through the noise, clear and agonizing—the one voice that could stop his heart or make it soar. Her sobbing rant drilled home the dangers surrounding them, each word filled with pain and despair.

"Shit," Caelum said.

Draven glanced over his shoulder, meeting Caelum's troubled eyes. The worry etched on his face mirrored Draven's own fears.

"She's in there, but she's blood cursed." Caelum's voice trembled.

Draven's mind raced. Lanae was so close, yet the curse rendered her an enemy. A flame of sorrow burned in his chest upon imagining her suffering, the pain she must be enduring.

As they approached the source of the commotion, Draven's senses heightened. He could hear her sobs more clearly now, each one a dagger to his heart. The hallway seemed to stretch endlessly, the shadows closing in around them. His hand tightened around the hilt of his sword—not for the fight he faced, but for the hope that he could reach Lanae before it was too late.

CHAPTER TWENTY-FOUR
Battle of Realms

LANAE'S EYES FLUTTERED OPEN, and her breath hitched. She struggled against the binds holding her wrists together as Firetwill's last command racked her body. A need stronger than survival burned through her veins, and she glanced at the person carrying her.

"Rorik, I need..."

"Shush," he said. "I can't have you fucking yourself when I find Draven."

Heat brushed her cheeks and logically she understood, but the damn order had her body aching to obey. "You're bringing me to Draven?" she hissed as his words penetrated through the agony twisting inside her. A new pain surfaced at the thought of him. The cracks in her heart deepened.

"We need to ensure that stone is destroyed," Rorik said. "Now be quiet or we will be caught." He glared at her.

Against the will beating at her skin, Lanae shut her mouth, but her legs rubbed together in a lewd manner, trying to provoke pleasure as instructed.

Rorik rolled his eyes and moved through thick shadows toward a door hanging ajar. Somehow, Rorik and his shadows avoided the guards, and he slipped inside. The throne room was a vast chamber, its walls lined with torches that cast flickering shadows on the polished stone floor. At the far end, on a pedestal surrounded by a shimmering force field, lay the stone—a dark, pulsing entity that seemed to absorb the light around it.

The same need she felt when she first saw the gauntlet stone sang in her veins—a relentless, burning desire that consumed her every thought.

Rorik stepped farther into the room, his eyes scanning for any sign of danger. Suddenly, he gasped, tripping over an unseen obstacle and dropping her to the floor.

Pain shot through her as she hit the ground, but it was nothing compared to the horror that followed.

Rorik's hand went to his side and came away bloody, his eyes widening in shock as black magic wrapped around him, binding him in place. The dark tendrils tightened, cutting into his flesh and drawing more blood, staining the floor red.

Xoltan stepped out of the shadows, his eyes gleaming with malevolence as he glared at Rorik. "You aren't the dragon." His voice dripped with contempt.

"I came back to rescue a soldier," Rorik said, his voice strained with pain. His brow broke out in sweat, and blood dripped from his leg, pooling around him.

Xoltan grabbed Lanae by the arm and hauled her to her feet, his grip bruising. "You look good in my tunic," he practically purred as he unbound her hands. "Did you give your friend a nice show?"

Lanae gagged but said nothing. Defiance radiated through her.

Rorik's eyes blazed with disgust and anger, his body trembling with the effort to break free from the dark magic.

"Do you think she is wet enough for me?" Xoltan asked Rorik, his voice a sickening mockery of concern.

"You are a twisted bastard," Rorik spat. A venomous tone colored his voice.

Xoltan stepped behind Lanae, his hand sliding under the tunic.

"Don't." Lanae desperately tried to keep her composure, but another tear escaped as his fingers dragged across the apex of her thighs.

He pulled his glistening fingers into view, a wicked grin twisted his mouth. "I'd say she's more than ready." He slipped them into his mouth, savoring the taste, before handing her a serrated blade. "Slit his throat." He nodded toward Rorik.

"Please don't make me do this," Lanae pleaded, her voice breaking even as her hand wrapped around the hilt of the knife. "I'll do anything you ask, but please, not this."

Her sobbing plea echoed on the walls of the empty throne room, a haunting sound that seemed to reverberate through her very soul.

"You already will do anything I ask." Xoltan grinned, his eyes alight with sadistic pleasure. "Saw his head off with that knife and bring it to me." He pointed at Rorik, his voice unyielding.

Lanae wept as she stepped closer to Rorik, her heart breaking with each step. The bastard had given her a blade that would ensure her friend would suffer until he bled out. She reached up and grabbed a handful of his hair with one hand, fighting herself as the hand holding the blade rose to the soft flesh of his throat.

"I hate you, you bastard," Lanae screamed at Xoltan as she ripped through Rorik's skin. "I'm so sorry, Rorik," she blubbered as blood seeped down the front of his tunic, turning it bright red.

Rorik's eyes reflected the same terror riding through her, his body convulsing as he choked, spurting blood. Her horrified screams continued as she sawed mercilessly through his skin, the sound of the blade ripping flesh curdling her stomach.

She continued sawing even when she hit bone, her muscles quivering with the effort. Finally, the knife broke free, severing his head completely. Every muscle in her body trembled as she collapsed like a broken doll, gripping her friend's head and the weapon she had used to end his life.

The tunic she wore dripped with his blood, the crimson stains damning evidence of her actions. Her gaze landed on the knife still clutched in her hand. Murderous thoughts filled her head as she looked back up at Xoltan.

"Drop the knife." His voice held nothing but a cold and unfeeling presence.

She screamed, the sound filled with all the pain and anguish she felt, and the blade dropped to the floor with a clatter.

NERO TOOK FLIGHT, HIS tiny wings flapping furiously as he zigzagged down the hallway. Draven reached out, desperate to catch the little griffin, but Nero was too quick, sliding into the open door where Lanae's cries were coming from. The sound of her pain was a knife to his heart, each sob tearing at his soul.

Caelum gripped Draven's arm, his fingers digging into the fabric. "She told me not to let you go in there before she shut down the connection." Desperation clung to his voice.

"Search the castle for more intruders!" The order rang out through the door, and the guards surrounding the throne room jumped into action, their footsteps echoing off the stone.

The guards split up into teams of two, running down the hallways with their weapons drawn. Draven's instincts screamed at him to fight, to protect Lanae, but Caelum's quick thinking saved them from a premature confrontation. He grabbed Draven and dragged him into a small space behind a woven tapestry on the wall, putting his finger over his lips in a plea for silence.

Draven's pulse thundered in his ears as the sound of feet pounded the floor outside the hall.

Doors opened and shut with alarming speed, and he traded a tense glance with Caelum. It was only a matter of time before they found the dead princess, and then all hell would break loose.

Moving soundlessly, Draven crept toward the source of Lanae's continued sobs, his heart aching with every step. The smell of blood and death wafted into his nose, the sickening scent twisting his stomach into knots.

Feet shuffled inside the room. "That's a good girl. Make sure it's nice and secure." Firetwill's cruel voice sliced through the air, tearing at Draven's composure. "Now crawl to me."

Draven's grip on his sword tightened until his knuckles turned white. He winched his eyes shut, reining in his fury until it was a tight ball in his stomach. Operating on pure emotion would only get them killed—or worse, enslaved. No matter what he found inside that room, his first responsibility was to destroy the stone, and then he would deal with Firetwill.

He glanced at Caelum, who nodded in silent understanding. "I got her. You do what is needed to save all of us." Caelum's voice was a steady anchor in the storm of Draven's emotions.

With a nod, they slipped through the open doorway. The sight that greeted them froze Draven in place, his rational thought obliterated by a fury so complete he couldn't contain the rage. Rorik's was the only mounted head on one of the many spikes in front of the gauntlet stone. Lanae was on her hands and knees, her body shaking with sobs. Blood smeared her face and hands, and the oversized tunic dripped with it.

Xoltan sat on his dais with a smirk of satisfaction twisting his features, his focus solely on Lanae.

Firetwill's lips curled into a predatory smile as he casually flicked open a button on his trousers. He watched Lanae with a mixture of amusement and annoyance, clearly relishing the power he held over her. "Come finish what we had started in my chambers before your soldier friend decided to play the brave hero." His voice carried brutal mockery.

Unaware of the deadly audience lurking in the shadows, Firetwill's eyes remained fixed on Lanae. He unhooked another button on his breeches, confidence radiating from his every movement. The dim torchlight cast eerie shadows on his face, emphasizing the cruel gleam in his eyes.

Lanae turned her head away from the stone dais and vomited on the floor, the sound echoing through the throne room. Her movements were jerky and mechanical, as if she were a puppet on strings. She crawled upward with an eerie, detached precision.

Firetwill focused solely on the satisfaction of his twisted desires. Little did he know, his reign of terror was about to face a reckoning he had never anticipated.

Firetwill tsked at her slow approach. "After I fuck your mouth, you will clean that up."

A deep, menacing growl rumbled from Draven's chest, reverberating through the room and instantly pulling Firetwill's attention away from Lanae. The air around them seemed to thicken, charged with the raw power of Draven's fury. Firetwill turned, a cruel smile spreading across his face as he locked eyes with Draven. The look of sadistic pleasure in his gaze was unmistakable, his eyes sparkling with a dark, twisted delight.

"Ah, Draven." Firetwill's voice sliced with malice. "So eager to join the fun."

Lanae's eyes widened in horror as black tendrils of magic snaked through the air, wrapping around Draven and Caelum like living chains.

The dark energy pulsed with an unnatural malevolence, constricting around them in an unforgiving vise. Draven's muscles strained against the bonds, his face contorted with a mixture of rage and pain. The searing blast of the magic burned into his flesh, and he bellowed his rage.

Caelum, caught in the same unyielding grip, struggled to stay on his feet. His breaths came in sharp, ragged gasps as he fought against the invisible force. The room was thick with tension, every second stretching into an eternity as they battled against the dark power binding them.

Firetwill's laughter echoed through the chamber. When his gaze flickered back to Lanae, his smile widened, and the sense of impending doom settled heavy in Draven's soul.

THE IMPULSE TO KILL Draven took hold of her muscles, and she climbed to her feet.

"Later, my dear. He will keep, but my libido won't."

Her head whipped around, and she gawked at him even as her knees dropped her back into a crawling position. A small part of her sagged with relief, even if she knew it was short-lived. As soon as she finished with Xoltan, he would demand their heads, too.

He laughed as she moved up the stairs, a chilling sound that sent shivers down Lanae's spine. Triumph painted his expression, the sick satisfaction he derived from their suffering. A thunderous beat vibrated in her chest, a surge of adrenaline urging her to act, to fight, to do something—anything—to save them.

Draven roared in the bindings. His flames flared and doused under the magical tethers holding him in place.

She continued to crawl up the steps and came close to throwing up again at the sight of Xoltan stroking his wicked cock and waiting for her mouth to replace his hand.

Storm magic surged through the chamber, and Xoltan stilled.

Lanae sagged with relief as she scanned the rafters. She had seen a little of this type of magic once, just before they were taken by the dark fae. The flash of a wing caught her attention, and her heart burst with adrenaline and hope.

"While I'd like nothing more than to fuck you in front of him, it's time to rid this world of dragons for good." He buttoned himself up and swiped the serrated knife off the floor, filling her with abject horror.

Lightning struck the black magic that bound Draven and Caelum. The dark tendrils writhed and let out a high-pitched scream that made

Lanae want to cover her ears. The binds disintegrated under the assault, freeing Draven and Caelum from their sinister grasp. The air crackled with residual energy, and the smell of ozone filled the room.

Draven turned toward the stone and exhaled a plume of flame at it. The fire roared to life, engulfing everything in its path, including the empty spikes and Rorik's head. Its heat seared even from a distance. The stone pulsed with light, absorbing the assault, and a low hum resonated through the chamber.

Firetwill laughed, a chilling sound that echoed off the stone walls. "Thank you, dragon. You've now given the stone enough power to speed up the merge."

Fuck. The thought leaped forward in her mind, an icy dread settling in her chest. Everything they had been told about the gauntlet stone was a lie. And now their fates were moments away from being sealed.

Draven roared, the sound reverberating through the room, and stepped toward Firetwill with his sword brandished in front of him. A spark of fury ignited in his eyes, and his muscles tensed, ready for the fight.

"Kill him," Xoltan ordered, his voice crisp and unyielding as he handed Lanae the serrated knife. "Kill them both and bring me their heads."

"No!" Her cry echoed through the room even as she took the weapon in her hand. Her heart pounded with the impossible choice before her. Draven's eyes met hers with a silent plea to remember who she truly was beneath the dark magic's control. Her grip on the knife tightened, her knuckles turning white.

Caelum stepped forward, his expression resolute. "Draven, I'll hold her off. Figure out how to destroy that fucking stone!"

Nero's storm intensified, sealing the room in a vortex of power. The wind howled, and debris swirled around them. The guards outside pounded on the doors, but they couldn't breach the barrier Nero had created.

Xoltan's eyes narrowed.

As Draven advanced toward the stone, Lanae's internal struggle reached its breaking point. Her mind was a whirlwind of conflicting emotions, and with a desperate scream, she lunged at Caelum. Their blades clashed in a fierce battle, the sound of metal ringing through the chamber. Caelum fought valiantly. His eyes filled with determination, but Lanae's strength, fueled by dark magic, overwhelmed him. Her movements were swift and brutal, each strike more powerful than the last. She had a moment of clarity, enough to at least give her brother a few more minutes to live and escape. With a swift strike to his temple, she knocked him out, sending him crashing to the ground, his body limp and motionless.

She turned to the greater threat. Draven had gotten close enough to the stone while Caelum had stalled her. His bold roar rose above the storm surrounding them, a primal sound that echoed through the chamber. As he brought his weapon down on the stone, a blast of lightning hit the edge of his blade, fueling it with bright power. The moment it connected, the stone shattered into a thousand pieces, along with his sword. The explosion sent shards flying in all directions, and the dark magic permeating the room wavered, its hold weakening.

"Kill him!"

Firetwill's command rooted in her muscles, and she launched at Draven with a feral intensity.

Draven pulled a knife out of his belt and raised it just in time to block her wild strike. The force of their collision sent a shock wave through his arm, but he pushed her away, his eyes pleading. "Fight it, Lanae."

Tears blurred her vision as she swung the blade again, her heart breaking with each strike. "I can't." A sob escaped her lips as his blade blocked hers again. "I love you." Her voice trembled with emotion, and she launched another set of strikes. This time, the blade found its mark, drawing blood from Draven's side.

Draven winced, the pain clear in his eyes, but he shoved her away with fierce resolve. "I love you too. Remember that if this all goes to shit."

Each clash of their blades echoed with the intensity of their struggle, the lines between friend and foe blurred by the malevolent force controlling her. The metallic ring of their weapons filled the air, a haunting symphony of conflict.

She swung again, and he caught her hand, twisting her wrist. Pain flared, white-hot, and she dropped the blade with a shrill cry. She screamed as her hand balled into a fist and she struck him, sending him back a step. Her heart pounded in her chest, every beat a desperate plea for control.

Before she could launch at him again, Nero's storm swirled around her, its energy seeking to purify the corruption within her. She dropped to the ground, her body convulsing as the storm's magic surged through her. Lanae bellowed, her voice raw and agonized, as the dark magic within her fought to maintain its hold. Black smoke billowed from her pores, reducing her to a screaming pile of writhing agony.

With a haze of pain keeping her from following his orders, Firetwill seized the moment. He unsheathed his sword and placed the tip on her throat. His eyes gleamed with cruel satisfaction as he pressed the cold steel against her skin. "Surrender," his voice dripped with malice, "and I'll spare her."

DRAVEN SWALLOWED HARD, HIS throat dry as the seer's vision swarmed before his eyes. The gauntlet stone was no longer a threat, but Firetwill still loomed. If he dropped his blade now, Lanae would be lost to this madman's whims. If he didn't, she'd be free of the madman, but lost to Draven until the gods saw fit to end his misery. The stress of the decision crushed him just as completely as a boulder.

A quick no jerked Draven's head, and he cursed the relief he saw flash through the agony gripping Lanae. Her eyes, wide with fear and desperation, locked onto his. She mouthed the words, "I love you," as Firetwill raised the sword, his lips curling into a sadistic smile.

A flash of wings appeared and Nero landed on Firetwill's face, his talons clawing at the dark lord's eyes. Firetwill let out a howl of pain, staggering back. Nero released his hold a second before Caelum's shoulder collided with Firetwill, sending him sprawling on the steps. The impact was brutal, knocking the wind out of him and leaving him vulnerable. He tumbled far enough from Lanae to give Draven an opening.

And he took it. Blinding fury fueled his fire, and he bellowed as it blasted from him, a torrent of flames that engulfed Firetwill. The dark lord's screams were cut short, and his body reduced to a hunk of ash. The room fell silent, the only sound the crackling of the fading flames.

Caelum glanced up at Draven from his protective position over Lanae as she whimpered below him. Her body shook with the aftershocks of pain, her face pale and drenched in sweat.

A bolt of lightning struck the ash figure, exploding dust throughout the throne room. The shock wave knocked Draven off-balance, the rush of adrenaline fueling him faltered, and he fell to his hands and knees. Both the cuts she had landed, and the fear born of his choice, lanced his ability to function properly.

She still writhed; her body contorted with pain as Nero's storm continued its cleansing. Her screams echoed in the cavernous room, a haunting melody of suffering.

The griffin landed next to her and covered her face with its wing. A flare of light encompassed her, along with a blood-curdling scream, as more black smoke filtered from her skin. When he removed his wing, the cut on her face bled black smoke. She coughed it out, each heave racking her body, and when all that seeped from the wound was blood, it knitted back together at a snail's pace, leaving only a faint scar.

Her eyes found his, filled with a mixture of pain and gratitude, and then rolled up into her head as if the expulsion of magic had taken her soul with it.

Draven crawled toward her, his wounds and exhaustion taking their toll. Every movement was agony, but he forced himself forward. He reached out, his hand trembling as he touched her cheek, his skin cool against her fevered flesh.

"Lanae." His whisper held the desperation clutching his chest, a plea for her to come back to him.

Lanae's eyes fluttered open and met his. "You didn't surrender." Her weak voice was filled with awe.

His lips twitched into what he hoped was a smile. "You would rather meet the gods in heaven than be his plaything for the rest of your days."

"I thought you loved her." Caelum sat up next to Lanae, rubbing the bump on his head with a wince.

"I love her enough to let her go." Draven swallowed hard, keeping eye contact with Lanae. "At least, that's what I figured you would want."

She let out a soft laugh, a sound filled with relief and understanding. "You figured right."

He dropped his cheek to the cold stone and closed his eyes. His strength waned as the storm's energy dissipated around them, leaving them in a fragile, temporary peace.

CHAPTER TWENTY-FIVE
Uncertain Futures

A SHUFFLING NOISE FROM beyond the dais yanked Draven's eyes open. Nero had done his magic on the cut on his side while he had fallen into an exhausted stupor. Lanae hadn't moved either, but her wide gaze met his.

"Can't we catch a fucking break?"

Caelum's exhaled words almost pulled a smile to Draven's lips, but the fact they were still in Firetwill's realm bunched his nerves into action. Draven climbed to his feet, every muscle protesting as he swiped the sword from the ashes, pointing it toward the noise. The blade trembled in his grip. "Show yourself," he growled, his voice a deep rumble.

Lanae slowly sat up with Caelum's help, her movements pained and deliberate, as more shuffling sounded. Each step echoed through the silent chamber, adding to the tension that hung thick in the air.

Varkir limped into view, the yôkai looking even paler than Lanae, his skin an eerie shade of gray. Dark circles surrounded his eyes, reflecting the torment he had endured.

Draven didn't lower the sword. Anger and mistrust clouded his eyes. "You bastard," he spat, the words filled with venom.

Varkir lifted his hand in a placating gesture. "I was under a blood curse. But I did my best to work around the orders I had been given." His eyes pinged to the griffin perched on Lanae's shoulder. "Without that little creature finding its powers, we were all well and truly fucked."

Draven lowered the sword, his grip still tight. Suspicion lingered in his eyes.

"What do you mean, work around?" Lanae spit out, her voice full of accusation.

Varkir sighed and wiped his face, the weariness clear in his movements. "I followed his orders. But he didn't say that I couldn't do anything else. The one drawback of a blood curse...if the instructions are not explicit, it gives you the opportunity to act on your own accord for a brief period." He waved at Nero. "Both the seer and your little friend there were messages I was able to get through on my own before being imprisoned again."

"Oh." Lanae studied her hands.

Varkir met Draven's gaze, his expression serious. "Xoltan's death released those of us who were blood cursed by him. But the balance of the castle and his surrounding forces that went through the mind control machine seem to be in suspended animation." He nodded toward the corridor outside, where the guards had been trying to breach Nero's storm.

Draven turned and stared at the bodies frozen in whatever position they had been when Firetwill met his maker. The sight was both eerie and unsettling.

"Can we snap them out of it?" Draven focused back on Varkir.

"No. They wait for a new master to arrive."

Varkir's words sent a chill down Draven's spine, producing gooseflesh on his arms.

"Nero broke the curse in me," Caelum said.

Varkir sighed. "Perhaps if your griffin was fully grown, he might have the power to release the legions of victims, but even then, I have my doubts. Some of these poor souls have been under Xoltan's control for years. As for you, Caelum, the curse hadn't had a chance to take root. That's why Nero had the ability at his young age."

"What will wake them?" Lanae climbed to her feet with Caelum's help, her voice trembling.

Varkir stared at them, his expression grave. "The extinction of the Firetwill line." His gaze moved from Lanae to Draven; his words hung heavy in the air. "They will bend to Alestain's will just as they did to Xoltan."

Lanae and Caelum exchanged a devastated look.

"What is it?" Draven asked.

"Our parents are under the thrall of the mind machine," Lanae said, her eyes filled with the kind of pain that took him back to when he crawled out of the ash to a changed world. The anguish in her voice twisted a knife in his heart.

Draven licked his lips, his stomach dropping to the floor. The enormity of their predicament crashed over him like a tidal wave.

"And Alestain will want vengeance for his brother's death." Varkir stared at Draven. The implication was clear. The threat hung over them like a dark cloud.

His hope for a peaceful existence with Lanae just burned up in smoke. Alestain Firetwill had a mindless army at his disposal and the Dragon's Heart to wreak havoc at will.

LANAE LOOKED AT THE remains of Rorik, her eyes fixating on his headless body. The sight ripped at her insides, a wave of despair crashing over her. The metallic tang of blood and the acrid stench of burned flesh filled the air, making her stomach churn. She fought to keep the bile from rising, her hand trembling as she reached out to touch his lifeless form. "Can you please get Rorik so we can take him home for a proper burial?" Her voice wavered, and a shudder shook her form. "If you had come in earlier, that could have been you." She suppressed a sob, her chest tightening with the effort.

His death had been brutal, the kind of brutality that nearly shattered Lanae's mind. The memory of it played on a relentless loop in her head, each detail more horrifying than the last. If Nero hadn't come into the throne room and disrupted the dark magic accosting her, her brother's head and Draven's would have accompanied the macabre sight. The thought of losing them both twisted the knife in her heart.

"How about we bring back his ashes?" Caelum suggested, his gaze fixed on Rorik's headless body with a mix of revulsion and sorrow.

Lanae licked her lips, feeling the dryness of them, and glanced at Draven. She moved away from the body, and her silent plea was met with understanding. Without her asking, he blew a bright stream of fire at their friend's remains. The heat of the flames brushed against her skin, turning Rorik into an ash figure before her eyes.

Caelum crossed to a table on the far side of the room, his steps heavy with grief. He grabbed an empty goblet and returned to the ash form, carefully scooping up a cupful. "Will this be enough?" His voice thickened with emotion.

"It will have to be," Draven replied, his tone grim. "We need to get back and see how much of Solstice City is left."

"Before we go, we need to destroy that mind machine." Caelum's eyes hardened with purpose.

Lanae nodded, her mind already moving to the next task. "And find our parents. I don't want to leave them here."

With Varkir guiding the way, they navigated the castle's labyrinthine passages, the oppressive atmosphere weighing heavily on them. The room where Lanae and Caelum had materialized was directly below the throne room, and as they entered, they were met with the haunting sight of mindless drones standing with vacant eyes and frozen forms. The eerie silence was punctuated only by the distant hum of the mind machine.

"We can kill them all." Draven's gaze swept over the room. "Then he won't have an army at his disposal."

Both Lanae and Caelum shook their heads. "They are innocent. He's been using them for ages. I'd like to free them from this nightmare, not execute them," Lanae said, her voice firm despite the turmoil inside her.

"And what if they ultimately attack Solstice City?" Draven propped his hands on his waist, challenging her mercy.

"Then we do what we have to, but I cannot stand by and watch you kill innocent people who have been brainwashed. Channel your anger on that thing." She pointed at the mind machine that had robbed Caelum of his will.

Draven did not hesitate. He drew in a deep breath and blew a stream of fire that was white and blue. On contact, the glass in the contraption shattered, turning to a fine mist before it hit the ground. The metal melted into a pile of useless material, the oppressive hum silenced forever.

WITH THE MIND MACHINE destroyed, Draven gathered Lanae's and Caelum's parents over his shoulder. The weight of their unconscious forms was a stark reminder of the cost of their fight. The surrounding air was thick with the acrid scent of burned machinery and the faint metallic tang of blood. Their footsteps echoed dully on the stone floor, each step reverberating with foreboding that seemed to cling to them like a second skin. Shadows danced on the walls, cast by the flickering remnants of magical flames, and Draven couldn't shake the feeling that he had made a grave mistake by leaving a sleeping army just waiting for Firetwill to come and wake them for battle.

As they approached the portal back to Solstice City, the hum of its energy filled the air—a low, thrumming sound that set Draven's teeth on edge. The portal itself shimmered like a mirage, its surface rippling with an iridescent sheen that distorted the world beyond it. The otherworldly light it emitted cast an eerie glow on their faces, making their expressions appear ghostly and surreal.

Once they crossed through the portal, Draven turned and placed his hand on the runes etched into the archway. The stone was cool and rough under his fingertips, and he could feel the faint pulse of ancient magic coursing through it. Taking a deep breath, he uttered words in old draconian, a spell to destroy portals he had learned as a child. The words felt heavy on his tongue, resonating with a power that seemed to vibrate in his very bones.

Magic gathered around them, a palpable force that made the air crackle with energy. The portal solidified, its surface morphing into a mirror where Draven could see Lanae, Varkir, and Caelum's open-mouthed expressions, their faces etched with confusion. He threw a punch into the center of the mirror, his knuckles meeting the cool, smooth surface with a resounding crash. The portal shattered into a thousand glittering shards, disappearing into hissing smoke trails as they hit the floor, leaving behind a faint, acrid smell of ozone.

"What was that?" Lanae's voice trembled.

"I know an old spell or two on manipulating portals. After all, how do you think I got into the city?" Draven cocked an eyebrow and smirked, the corners of his mouth curling up in a way that was both reassuring and mischievous.

LANAE NURSED A TEA as she stared out over Solstice City. The streets below were a hive of activity as they began the arduous task of reconstruction. The streets buzzed with fresh energy as magical beings of all kinds worked together to transform the cityscape.

"Heroine of Solstice City," someone called, and Lanae turned to see a group of fae children waving excitedly up at her.

She smiled and waved back. But she was not a heroine. Draven was the hero. He had eliminated the threat, but he didn't want to be a spectacle.

And the council was in complete disarray since the conflict. Two of the members were in a state of catatonic suspension. Faide had begged her to step into one of the compromised seats, but she had declined the offer. She was a warrior at heart and now, more than ever, the city needed protection.

"Lanae, the council needs you," Caelum said. "You have the strength and vision to lead us into a new era."

Lanae felt the burden of his words. She had always been a warrior, but now she was being asked to become a leader—a role that carried its own burdens and responsibilities. "I'll consider it once the danger is behind us, Caelum," she replied, her mind a whirlwind of thoughts. "But for now, let's focus on rebuilding."

DRAVEN SAT IN A quiet alcove in the garden behind Lanae's house, his body still recuperating from the intense battle. The warm sunlight filtered through the leaves, casting a dappled pattern on the ground. His eyelids tipped closed and he let the peaceful sounds of the city soothe his restless mind.

Despite the momentary tranquility, an unsettling presence gnawed at the edges of his consciousness. He couldn't shake the feeling that something—or someone—was watching him. His senses, honed by decades of vigilance, told him that this was not a mere figment of his imagination.

Nero perched beside him, the little griffin's eyes attentive.

Draven reached out, stroking Nero's feathers. "Do you feel it too, Nero?" he said. "Alestain is coming."

Nero chirped in agreement with his gaze fixed on a distant point in the forest.

Draven's unease grew. The shadows of his past threatened to engulf his fleeting peace.

LANAE APPROACHED DRAVEN, HER chest tight with their recent battles. She dropped to her knees next to him, resting her hand on his arm. "How are you feeling?" Her voice was laced with concern.

Draven's gaze met hers, his eyes weary but filled with a flicker of hope. He gave her a shrug, attempting to lighten the mood. "Figures the moment I find my heart, the world turns to shit," he replied, letting a small smile play on his lips. The corners of his mouth twitched as he tried to hide the exhaustion that tugged at him. "But I guess I'll just have to make the best of our time until my sources come back with information."

He pulled her into his lap, the warmth of his embrace offering a fleeting sense of comfort. He caught her lips in a soft kiss. The taste of their shared struggle lingered between them.

She pushed away from his chest, her brow furrowing. "You mean Varkir?"

"Yes. He's searching for anything related to the Dragon's Heart for me. If I can get that from Firetwill, then we have a fighting chance to rid the world of this threat." His words were determined, a promise to her and to himself.

Lanae's expression grew serious as she glanced at the house. They had brought her parents back, and Nero had tried his storm magic to unlock them from their catatonic state. But they had been in the thralls of mind control for too long. They secured the windows and locked them in their bedroom and prayed they could find the secret to break the spell over them before Firetwill called them into action.

The guilt of her actions gnawed at her. "I don't know what to do with them," she admitted, her voice breaking.

Draven sighed and gently brushed her hair back. "I don't have any wisdom to share with you."

He kissed her again, a tender gesture meant to reassure her. Her blood heated under his touch. The connection between them sizzled.

"All I can do is make the most of the time we have before we face another battle." His words whispered across her lips, a vow of support and love.

She grabbed onto him, taking the solace he offered. The world outside was chaotic and uncertain, but in his arms, she found a moment of peace. In the heart of Solstice City, amidst the ruins and the rebuilding, a new dawn was breaking. And with it, the promise of a brighter future—one they would fight to protect, no matter the cost.

The End

FIRE & FAE BONUS SCENE

T HE MOON HUNG LOW, an argent sentinel casting a silvery veil over the secluded glade at the base of a mountain lake. Lanae's eyes lingered on the faint glisten of Solstice City in the distance, its golden lights like phantom beacons of the life she was leaving behind. The forbidden nature of this sacred event weighed on her chest, sharp and exhilarating, as though her heart itself were defying gravity. The air hummed with the whisper of a breeze, cool against her skin, carrying the mingling scents of wildflowers, crisp pine, and the faint minerality of the lake's edge. Above, the stars glittered like shards of ice, their cold light softening the shadows that pooled beneath the ancient oaks and clung to the forest floor.

This was the perfect night for a wedding, a night that seemed to hold its breath alongside her. The council's edict—rigid, unjust, and steeped in fear—tried to shackle her fate, but they had no right. They could never dictate whom she could or could not love. Draven was her fate bound, her soul's mirror, the fire in her veins, and she loved him with every fragment of her being.

Instead of the grandiose spectacle of a fae union—a celebration marked by glowing processions and musical harmonies that carried through the night sky—she and Draven had chosen this intimate rebellion. This moment belonged to them alone. Here, there were no prying eyes or disdainful whispers, just her brother, her griffin, and the profound weight of what they were about to vow.

Lanae stood in the shadows with her brother at her arm. Her fingers tightened on his as she sought steadiness in his presence. The crushed pine needles beneath her feet added a grounding texture to her nervous energy, their subtle aroma mixing with the night's earthy symphony.

"Are you certain about this, Lanae?" Caelum's voice broke the fragile stillness, the low timbre resonating with a mix of brotherly concern and reverence for what she was about to risk. He stood at her side, dressed in the same elegant suit he'd worn to the ill-fated ball before the nightmare of the gauntlet stone. He looked dashing, as always, but his sapphire eyes were veiled with unspoken worry rather than the familiar quirk of mischief.

She turned to him, her lips curving into a soft smile. The affection she felt for her younger brother swelled, a quiet tide of gratitude and love. "I have never been more certain of anything in my life, Caelum. The council's fear will not dictate whom I love. Not now. Not ever."

His slow grin broke through the concern, warming her like sunlight after rain. "Okay."

Through their telepathic link, his unrestrained joy for her washed over her like a cloak of comfort. It was his silent way of saying he would stand by her, come what may. *Thank you, Caelum. Your blessing means the world to both of us,* she whispered across their connection.

He gave her hand a gentle pat. "You make a beautiful bride, Lanae."

In the distance, a faint roll of thunder murmured across the mountains, accompanied by a sliver of lightning that streaked the horizon. Nero's ethereal signal that the time had come.

Caelum stepped out from behind the tree, guiding her onto a narrow path that had been strewn with crushed rose petals. Their vibrant red hues created a stark contrast against the moonlit silver of the glade. The petals' delicate scent mingled with the sharper aroma of pine, wrapping Lanae in a moment of sensory wonder.

And then she saw him. Draven. He stood at the center of a gorgeous floral dais, its intricate arch laced with firefly light that shimmered like captured stars. For a moment, her breath caught—he seemed unreal, a dream conjured by the night itself. His fiery hair, neatly styled, glinted under the glow of the fireflies, and the dark leathers he wore were newly fitted, every detail pristine. The family crest carved into his breastplate glinted faintly, a symbol of pride and defiance. But it was the twinkle in his emerald eyes, that familiar spark of love and mischief, that sent her heart racing.

The world narrowed to just him as his lips spread into the smile that always unraveled her. Her knees weakened under its power, but she pressed forward, driven by the need to reach him, to make the promise that would bind them forever.

At the center of it all, their newest ally stood—a figure of shadows and substance. Varkir's form shimmered between corporeal and smoke, his energy ancient and imposing, a being that transcended mortal concerns. His presence lent the ceremony a gravity that no council decree could tarnish. This glen had been his suggestion, and as she stepped into the sacred space, she couldn't imagine a more perfect haven for the vows they were about to exchange.

AS LANAE STEPPED FROM the shadows, Draven's heart faltered, his breath catching like a gasp frozen in time. The moment struck him with an intensity that bordered on pain—an ache that began in his chest and spread outward, leaving his senses raw. She was radiant, a vision draped in twilight. The folds of her midnight-blue gown shimmered faintly, catching the silver sheen of moonlight as if the stars themselves had graced her with their essence. The fabric moved with her, whispering softly against the forest floor, and he wondered whether her gown had been spun from starlight or dreams.

Her white and pink curls tumbled over her shoulders like a cascade of moon-kissed silk, each strand luminous in its hue. His gaze lingered on the delicate circlet of silver that adorned her brow. It gleamed faintly, catching the light as though it were an extension of the moon above, but what truly arrested him were her eyes. Those infinite pools of blue shimmered with a depth of devotion that pierced him to his very core. They were windows into her soul, and in them, he found himself reflected—every flaw, every triumph, every piece of his being laid bare.

A sharp exhale from Caelum's approach jolted his lungs back into motion, breaking the trance that had momentarily ensnared him. Heat surged across his face and neck, a flush ignited by oxygen rushing into his starved chest. Pride swelled within him, fierce and unrelenting. He could feel it thrumming in his very bones as Lanae's brother brought her closer.

Caelum's grin softened his angular features, easing some of the tension that hung in the air. His voice was steady, yet laced with the weight of familial tradition, as he kissed Lanae's hand. "As the head of our household, I give this union my blessing." His words rang out like a final declaration of defiance against a council that had dared to deny this moment.

When Caelum passed Lanae's hand into his, Draven's fingers closed around hers instinctively. Her skin was warm, softer than he remembered, and the delicate press of her fingers against his felt like a tether to his sanity. For a breathless moment, he couldn't speak, the magnitude of her touch filling every corner of his mind.

As they turned to face each other beneath the sprawling arms of the ancient oak, he was dimly aware of Nero's silent arrival. The griffin landed soundlessly beside Lanae, the faint ruffle of feathers the only indication of his presence. Draven's eyes flicked toward the creature briefly, marveling at the ethereal glow of its pastel feathers. They shimmered like molten sunlight, casting faint hues onto Lanae's gown. Nero's luminous eyes, filled with an unnerving wisdom, seemed to promise protection and strength as the beast spread its wings in a motion both majestic and reverent.

Varkir, their enigmatic ally, stood between them. His shadowed form flickered like smoke caught in an unseen current, his half-corporeal presence lending the ceremony an otherworldly gravity. When he nodded, the simple motion sent a surge of resolve through Draven's chest.

He took a step closer, his pulse hammering like a war drum, echoing in his ears. Lanae's face was closer now, every detail etched into his memory—the subtle freckle just above her cheekbone, the curve of her lips trembling with restrained emotion. He spoke, his voice steady despite the torrent of feelings coursing through him. "Lanae, in the eyes of the stars and the forest, I vow my life to you. I will raze the universe for you, in this life and the next if that is your wish. Not even the council's decrees can sever the bond we share. You are my wings that allow me to soar, my compass that will always guide me back to you, and my home where my heart forever belongs."

Her hand tightened in his, anchoring him to this moment. Her tears shimmered in the firefly-lit glow, and when she spoke, her voice trembled like the first delicate notes of a song. "Draven, in the face of every storm, I will stand with you. Your light burns in the darkest corners of my soul. Today, I choose you, despite the world's disapproval, for my heart will always be yours."

Varkir raised his arms, his murmured incantations threading through the fabric of the night. The ancient words wove a tapestry of magic around them, filling the air with a faint golden luminescence. It enveloped them like a blessing, a force that transcended law and mortal understanding.

Nero's low, resonant cry seemed to echo the magic, harmonizing with the forest's quiet hum. Draven's gaze never wavered from Lanae's, even as the light faded, leaving only their joined hands and the immutable truth of their union.

In the moonlit glade, they became more than lovers, more than rebels defying a council's decree—they became bound. Not by authority, but by a love that was infinite, untouchable, and undeniably their own.

328

FIRE & FAE DUET
BOOK 2
KINGDOM OF FIRE AND FAE

Welcome to Solstice City—a realm where floating markets dazzle beneath the luminescent glow of rune-powered streetlights. And destiny's threads entangle Lanae and Draven in a perilous weave.

In a world teetering on the brink of chaos, Lanae and her brother confront their gravest challenge yet. Alestain Firetwill has resurfaced, commanding an army ensnared by his sinister mind control, turning allies into adversaries and family into fierce foes. Racing against time, the siblings must break their parents free from Firetwill's grip before they're forced into a heart-wrenching battle against their own flesh and blood.

Meanwhile, Draven embarks on a treacherous journey to reclaim the fabled Dragon's Heart. With Solstice City freshly risen from its ashes, the city's fate now hangs by a thread. Should Draven falter, the city will be reduced to cinders once more.

As fire clashes with fae, and magic intertwines with love, the power of family, courage, and loyalty is put to the ultimate test. Can these bonds withstand the overwhelming darkness? The fate of Solstice City—and the world—rests in their hands.

Dive into this electrifying conclusion where every whisper hides a secret, and every shadow might conceal an ally—or a foe.

CHAPTER ONE
Solstice City Reborn

AS DAWN BROKE OVER the rejuvenated Solstice City, its cobblestone streets glistened with the first light of day, thrumming with newfound energy. Lanae Nightshade wandered through the bustling markets with her brother Caelum, their footsteps resonating against the stone paths. The aroma of freshly baked bread and exotic spices filled the air, mingling with the distant sound of merchants hawking their wares. Vibrant banners and colorful awnings fluttered in the gentle morning breeze while the sunlight danced off the polished marble of the surrounding buildings. The crowd was a kaleidoscope of cultures, with vendors showcasing their handmade crafts and produce.

Lanae's eyes sparkled as they stopped at a blacksmith's table, eyeing some of the newly crafted swords on display. The sun gleamed off the polished blades, casting a dazzling array of reflections. She admired the intricate engravings on the hilts and the craftsmanship of each piece.

"Don't you think you have enough swords?" Caelum asked as he fiddled with the pommel of his new Solstice City guard sword, the fresh leather strap of his sheath creaking with each movement. His newly minted uniform, crisp and immaculate, made him stand out among the crowd.

Lanae side-eyed him, and pride filled her. Today was his first day out of training. She just hoped it would be much less eventful than her first day during the height of the war with the dark fae.

"You can never have enough swords." Her lips turned up in a grin.

Since they had defeated Xoltan Firetwill, there had been no more attacks from the dark fae. They had sent a missive to the council that they would like to start the peace process. The parchment had arrived sealed with an unfamiliar sigil, and she had been given the honor of delivering it straight to the council.

Draven had scoffed when she told him, but he still carried a monstrous chip on his shoulder against all fae. Well, all besides her and Caelum. At least he came to a truce with Faide and the council after Caelum had recounted what Draven had done to the gauntlet stone and his participation in defeating the dark lord.

A shadow crossed over the table, and she looked up into those intense green eyes that held her heart. Draven Emberwing was a force of nature all on his own. His commanding presence sent a shiver of excitement through Lanae. His crimson hair, tousled by the morning breeze, framed his chiseled features.

"Another sword?" He echoed her brother's words, his deep voice reverberating through the air.

Caelum snickered beside her, the sound almost swallowed by the bustling market around them. He reached out to inspect one of the knives, its blade gleaming under the morning sun, and he paused, drawing a sharp breath.

Dread filled Lanae, and she shot her gaze to her brother's face. That vacant look she remembered from the mind-control machine graced his expression, but the assault of his emotions in her mind confirmed her brother was still inside his head. Unlike what had happened in Xoltan's court, where his expression had been truly empty.

His gaze cleared, but the unfiltered terror in his eyes as he looked at her squeezed her chest like a vise. His knuckles turned white around the knife handle before he released it with a clatter.

He blinked and swallowed hard, glancing between her and Draven. "I think our reprieve is over." Even his words shook, a tremor that echoed the fear pulsing through the telepathic connection he had with Lanae.

Caelum hadn't had a vision in years. With him coming of age, his unique powers were coming into their own, and as a little kid, he had been prone to random spells, as their parents called them. But seeing his vacant look brought those memories back with a vengeance.

"What did you see?" She faced him, her heart thumping in a wild timpani beat.

"Mom and Dad reanimating." He glanced toward their house, where they had imprisoned their catatonic parents after the war with Xoltan. All Xoltan's mind-controlled minions had fallen into a catatonic state, waiting for another Firetwill to take control of them again. The house, once a sanctuary, now loomed like a prison.

Draven pulled him away from the vendor stall. "You have visions?"

"I used to get them a lot when I was little, but they stopped when I hit puberty." Caelum ran his fingers through his hair, the motion quick and agitated, a clear divergence from his usual calm demeanor.

Lanae put her hand on his forearm and squeezed, but her stomach knotted. "Do you know how long we have?"

Caelum shook his head, his eyes unfocused. "Weeks. Days. Hours. I don't know." He turned toward the Citadel, the one building that wasn't structurally destroyed by the attempt at merging realms. It still stood stoically in the center of the city as a symbol of their resilience. "I need to warn the council."

"I'll check that the safeguards are still in place at home," Draven said, his jaw set. "Go with your brother."

Lanae leaned up and pressed her lips to Draven's. That familiar tingling of their fate bond rolled through her body, a momentary comfort to the turmoil roiling her abdomen. "Thank you."

She headed away from the shiny swords with Caelum by her side. Her mind raced with worry. Perhaps Caelum's first day might be even more daunting than hers was, after all.

CHAPTER TWO
Guard Duty

CAELUM FIDGETED BY LANAE'S side as the Fae Council flowed into the ornate room, their robes trailing behind them like the tails of comets. Golden light filtered through the stained-glass windows, casting colorful patterns on the polished wood floor. This was the first time Caelum had been before the entire council, and nerves bit at the edges of his palms, making them itch.

Faide Frostvale, the head of the Fae Council, settled into his seat, his presence commanding attention even among the esteemed assembly. His violet eyes, sharp and knowing, locked onto

Caelum with an intensity that made him shift uncomfortably.

"You have news?" Faide's voice was calm, but the underlying authority in his tone was unmistakable.

"Not news exactly." Caelum glanced to Lanae for support, his sister's presence a comfort amidst the storm of his anxiety. Lanae's expression was serene, betraying none of the turmoil radiating through their bond.

"My brother had a vision." Lanae's voice rang out clear and strong, the acoustics of the grand hall magnifying her words so they bounced from wall to wall, echoing in the ears of every council member.

Faide's eyebrow rose, and he leaned forward, the movement almost predatory in its focus. "Well, spill it, boy."

Caelum chewed his lip, trying to formulate a more politically correct way of delivering the message, but the urgency of the situation made him abandon decorum. In the end, he just blurted it out. "Alestain Firetwill is awakening his forces."

Six words.

And every council member paled, their stares turning to the empty seats. The once-vibrant council now had positions still vacant, haunting reminders of those who had succumbed to Xoltan Firetwill's mind-control machine. The silence that followed was thick with dread, each member's face a reflection of the collective fear that gripped them.

Faide's fingers drummed on the table, breaking the heavy silence. "We have prepared for this moment for the past three years." His words dripped off his tongue in a measured calm that belied the magnitude of the situation. "Please notify the senior guards and have them meet us in the situation chamber."

Caelum swallowed hard, the reality of his vision's implications settling like a lead weight in his stomach. He glanced at Lanae, who gave him a reassuring nod. They had a battle ahead, and every second counted.

"Yes, sir." He turned with Lanae at his side and headed out of the council chamber. Caelum's mind raced as he and Lanae descended the winding staircase, the echoes of their footsteps a rhythmic token of the urgency of their mission. The grand corridors of the council building bustled with activity, unlike the last time Caelum had graced these halls. Council assistants hurried past, their robes a blur of colors, while guards stood at attention by every doorway, their presence a constant indicator of the ever-present need for vigilance.

A shudder throttled his spine at the memory that surfaced, the stark contrast between now and then making him uneasy. Lanae gave him a questioning side-eye, her brows knitting together in concern.

"Just remembering the last time I was in this part of the building." Caelum's voice was just a whisper as the memories threatened to overwhelm him.

"After the battle with Xoltan?" Lanae's tone was soft, but there was an edge to her words, a shared understanding of the pain they had both endured.

He shook his head, a rueful smile tugging at the corners of his lips. "No. When you were tried for treason." His words were heavy with the weight of the past.

Lanae's eyes softened, and she reached out, briefly squeezing his hand in silent support.

He surveyed the number of people moving through the corridors, noting the determined expressions and the sense of purpose that permeated the air. "It's a lot busier now."

"Well, they moved all the city offices here. It isn't just the council anymore," Lanae explained, her gaze sweeping across the bustling scene. "The administration, logistics, and even the intelligence units are all centralized here now. It's become the heart of Solstice City's governance."

Caelum nodded, taking in the transformation. The once solemn and almost deserted halls were now alive with activity. As they continued their journey through the corridors, the memories of the past faded, replaced by a dread that made each footstep heavy.

As they crossed the threshold into the bustling streets of Solstice City, the vibrant energy of the metropolis enveloped them. Children laughed and played in the squares, and street performers entertained clusters of onlookers with their skills.

Caelum's thoughts, however, were far from the lively scene around them. His brow furrowed as worry gnawed at him. "What if we aren't completely free of their influence?"

Lanae let out a breath, her gaze warming as she looked at him. "We are," she reassured, though her tone carried a hint of exhaustion.

"But what if we aren't?" He stopped abruptly, grabbing her arm and making her meet his intense gaze.

"Caelum, we both were freed by Nero's magic. It severed the hold that bastard had on us." Her firm voice rang through the air and she placed a hand on his shoulder, a placating gesture that set him on edge.

"I haven't had a vision for years. So why now?" His voice wavered, carrying hints of fear and confusion. He glanced around, taking in the thriving city that had once been on the brink of despair.

Lanae sighed, and her eyes reflected her empathy as much as their telepathic bond. "Maybe it's because the need is greater now than ever. Visions come when they're most needed, Caelum. Perhaps Nero's magic awoke something within you that lay dormant until now."

Caelum's grip on her arm loosened, and he nodded slowly; the worry clutching his belly eased. He looked at the city around them, the people who depended on them, and a renewed sense of resolve to keep all he held dear safe flared. They had overcome so much already, and with Lanae by his side, he knew they could face whatever challenges lay ahead.

LANAE SCANNED THE CITY as they made their way to the guard barracks to inform the generals that they were needed at the Citadel. Her mind turned over Caelum's question. Even though she had told him Nero had broken Firetwill's hold over them, his query had burrowed under her skin. The bustling streets below, filled with the clamor of preparation, seemed a world apart from her inner turmoil.

At the barracks, they relayed their orders to the gathered generals. The air was thick with urgency as the leaders nodded in understanding, their expressions grave. The looming threat was tangible, and there was no room for hesitation.

Once the messages were delivered, she and Caelum exchanged a brief but significant nod. "Stay sharp," he murmured before they parted ways, each heading to their respective stations.

Lanae made her way to the training grounds. The rhythmic rattle of weapons and the shouts of warriors greeted her as she arrived. She scanned the area, her eyes landing on a familiar figure, who she had closely trained with over the last couple of years.

Jenna, one of the formidable women warriors, was in the middle of an intense training session. Her movements were almost as precise and powerful as Lanae's, which made for a good sparring partner. The clash of their swords echoed through the training grounds, drawing the attention of nearby warriors who paused to watch the impressive display. As the bout ended, Jenna removed her helmet, revealing a crop of blonde hair with purple highlights and a smile of accomplishment.

Lanae approached, ready for an outlet to work out the anxiety still stiffening her muscles. "Are you ready for a real sparring session?"

Jenna rolled her eyes playfully. "Give me a second to get a drink and then I'll kick your ass."

Lanae let out a bark of a laugh, the sound carrying across the training grounds. "When have you ever kicked my ass?"

"You never know. Today may be that day." Jenna grinned and sidled up to the cooler for a drink of fresh spring water. She took a long sip, seeming to savor the refreshing flavor before wiping her mouth with the back of her hand. "Besides, I've been working on some new moves. You might be in for a surprise."

Lanae raised an eyebrow, intrigued. "New moves, huh? Well, I'm always up for a challenge."

Jenna's smile widened as she set her drink aside and picked up her sword. "Good. Let's see if you can keep up."

Lanae squared off, waiting for Jenna to make the first move. When it came, she parried, striking the sword away with little effort. The rest of the guard gathered closer, eager to witness the friendly yet fierce competition between two of the Citadel's finest warriors.

DRAVEN SLID INTO THE house and stopped in the entry, tilting his head to listen. At first, only silence reached his ear, then a scratching sound came from the back of the house. His brow furrowed in suspicion.

"Nero, you better not scratch up that door again!" he called out, his voice echoing through the quiet house. With a resigned sigh, he closed the front door and strode through the hallway toward the kitchen.

Upon entering the kitchen, Draven found Nero perched on his bed, the picture of innocence. The griffin's large, soulful eyes blinked up at him, as if to say, "Who, me?" But the wood shavings scattered across the floor told a different story.

Draven crossed his arms and tapped his foot, raising an eyebrow at the griffin. "Seriously, Nero? We've talked about this."

Nero cocked his head to the side, letting out a small, pitiful squawk. Draven couldn't help but smirk at the theatrics.

"You're not fooling anyone with that look." Draven bent to gather the shavings. "You know, if you wanted attention, you could just ask. Instead, you turn our doors into toothpicks."

As Draven swept up the mess, Nero shuffled closer, nudging his head against Draven's arm. The affectionate gesture made Draven chuckle despite himself.

"All right, all right. You're forgiven." He gave Nero a scratch behind the ears. "But seriously, buddy, if you keep this up, we're going to run out of doors."

Nero let out a rumbling purr, clearly pleased with himself.

Draven shook his head, unable to stay mad at his mischievous companion for long. As he finished cleaning up, he glanced toward the main suite in the house where they had locked up Lanae's parents.

"Any noise from the bedroom?" Draven nodded toward the door, his expression turning serious.

Nero shook his head, a low growl rumbling in his throat as if to confirm that all was quiet.

"Good," Draven said, and the knot in his stomach released. "The last thing we need is more trouble."

Nero's wings fluttered and his tail thumped against the floor, agreeing with Draven's sentiment.

Draven gave Nero one last affectionate pat before heading toward the bedroom to check on Lanae's parents. As he moved, he muttered under his breath, "You know, for a griffin, you sure know how to make a mess."

Nero chirped in response, his eyes twinkling with mischief.

Draven couldn't help but laugh. "Yeah, yeah, I love you, too, you big troublemaker."

His skin itched with anxiety as he stopped in front of the door. He wiped his sweaty palms on his trousers and shook his hands to loosen his muscles before reaching up to the top of the doorframe to retrieve the key. It was hidden among the cobwebs and dust, a seldom-used relic. With a deep breath, and a twist of the key, he unlocked the door, hearing the faint click that seemed louder than it should be in the silent hallway. He opened the door; the hinges creaked in protest, and he peered in.

The room was dimly lit by a single candle. Lanae's parents still lay prone on the bed, their breaths shallow and rhythmic, untouched by the passage of time. The air brimmed with the fragrance of aged linens and a faint trace of lavender, a remnant of happier times. He stood there for a moment, watching them with a pang of helplessness.

He shut the door gently and locked it again, returning the key to its dusty perch. He walked back to the kitchen, his footsteps echoing in the narrow hallway. "I need to go let Lanae know that her parents have not woken. Did you want to come?"

Nero, who had been lounging in the corner, nearly pounced on him. The griffin was no longer the tiny creature Lanae had found years ago. Now, he was the size of a pony, his powerful body rippling with muscle. His head reached just shy of Draven's, and his wingspan was almost as wide as the kitchen itself. Soon, they would have to figure out an alternative nest outside rather than the oversized bed that took up the entire corner of the kitchen. Nero's golden eyes gleamed with excitement, his beak clicking softly in anticipation.

The people of Solstice City had become used to seeing Draven walking with Nero. The two enigmas in a city of varying species were a familiar sight, yet they never ceased to draw curious glances: Draven, the last dragon, with his unsettling presence and piercing green eyes, and Nero, the majestic griffin, an ancestor of the first griffin, and a symbol of strength and mystery.

Draven gave Nero a stern look, his brow furrowing as he took in his walking companion. "Don't even think about showing off today. It's already been a trying morning, and I don't think Lanae would be pleased if you set your storm loose." His voice carried a weight of authority, but also a touch of weariness.

Nero squawked in response, his feathers puffing up as he rolled his eyes. The griffin's expressive face illustrated his defiance, but also a hint of playful mischief. He shifted his weight from one taloned foot to the other, a clear sign he was brimming with restless energy.

Draven side-eyed him and exhaled, the sound filled with resignation. He knew Nero too well; the griffin would likely test all their patience before the day was done.

CHAPTER THREE
Rebellion and Revelation

THE MOMENT JENNA FAILED to block her sword, Lanae's eyes sparkled with determination as she pulled back just before the blade touched the skin of Jenna's neck. Her grin widened at her sparring partner. "It looks like I won again." Her voice carried a teasing lilt.

"Damn it," Jenna muttered under her breath, dropping her sword with a clatter that echoed through the training grounds. She trudged over to the cooler, her steps heavy with frustration, and grabbed another drink. The sound of the ice shifting in the cooler contrasted their earlier tension.

"You're getting better." Lanae stepped beside her, her fingers brushing against the cool metal of the cooler before she grabbed a drink for herself. The cold liquid was a welcome relief, soothing her dry mouth and tired muscles. This time, it took her longer to defeat Jenna. "That spin away move was impressive," she added, the compliment genuine.

Jenna met her gaze, a flicker of pride in her eyes. "Thanks." She finished her drink in one long gulp and crumpled the paper cup, tossing it into a barrel under the cooler. "So, how are things with your dragon?" She waggled her brows with a playful grin.

"Good as always." Lanae's smile was brief, a mere shadow of her usual warmth. Caelum's vision had soured her mood, and the sparring session hadn't dispelled the dark cloud hanging over her. If anything, it had compounded the pressure. They all had to be ready for the next attack, and she wasn't sure all the guards would make it out of this next war alive. She started to step away, but Jenna's hand on her arm stopped her.

"What's wrong?"

Lanae glanced down at Jenna's hand, the warmth of the touch contrasting with the cool air, and then met her gaze. "The peace we've had might not be for much longer." As if to punctuate her words, a shadow passed over the sun, casting a fleeting darkness over the training grounds.

"What happened?" Jenna asked, concern etched on her face.

But Lanae was no longer listening. Her lips pressed together in a thin line as she spotted Nero doing rolls in the air above the training grounds. As he came out of the last one, a web of lightning cracked through the air, the sharp sound startling the nearby guards.

The soldiers on the training field ducked and covered their heads, their armor clinking softly.

"Lanae!" one of the elite guards overseeing the training in the absence of the generals yelled with annoyed authority.

"Nero!" Lanae called, her voice cutting through the noise. The griffin swooped down, soaring close enough to her head for the rush of air from his wings to ruffle her hair. She caught the mischievous glint in Nero's eyes as he passed over her, the griffin's laughter almost audible in his gaze.

Draven jogged across the field, his boots thudding against the ground, and stopped by her side. "Sorry. He needed to get out of the house before he ruined the door again," he said, slightly out of breath but with a rueful smile.

Lanae palmed her face, the tips of her fingers pressing into her temples as she peered through her fingers at him. "Really?" Her voice was a mix of exasperation and disbelief, her eyes narrowing.

Draven smirked, the corner of his lips curling up in that familiar, nonchalant way. "Your parents are fine, by the way. No indication of motion at all." His tone was casual, almost as if discussing the weather.

Relief sagged her shoulders, the tension draining away. "Thank you for checking." Her tone took on a soft hush.

She sent the information to Caelum through their mind link, the sensation like a gentle brush of feathers in her consciousness. Just as she finished, Nero dive-bombed the group again. The echo of his wings sliced through the air like a whispering storm. This time, he clasped a soldier by the arm with his talons, lifting him a few feet off the ground before releasing him. The soldier yelped in surprise, his armor clinking as he landed.

"You had to let him out?" She waved a hand toward the rebellious creature, her frustration bubbling to the surface.

"I told you long ago that griffins are notoriously unstable," Draven replied, his smirk never fading.

"He's not unstable. He's just acting out." She stabbed her gaze in Nero's direction.

The griffin hovered in the air, his eyes gleaming with mischief. His feathers rustling in the wind were almost a challenge, daring her to say otherwise. The sun glinted off his pastel plumage, creating an almost ethereal glow around him as he circled back for another pass.

This time, when Nero swooped down, Lanae extended her arm and shot vines from the soil. The thick, green tendrils coiled around his talon with a serpentine grace, pulling him to the ground. Nero squawked loudly, the sound echoing off the nearby trees, and he narrowed his eyes at her, a mix of surprise and irritation flashing in his golden gaze.

She approached him, her boots crunching on the dry leaves and twigs scattered across the training ground. Wagging her finger, she fixed him with a stern look. "This is not a time for fun and games. We need to train without you terrorizing us. Wait for Firetwill's forces to get here, and then you can let your full powers strike."

Nero's beak snapped shut with an audible click, and the feathers on his head ruffled, standing on end. A low rumble emanated from his chest, resonating through the air. The sound was almost like a distant thunderstorm, echoing his raw power. The mention of Firetwill's name had triggered his protective instincts. The griffin's memory of the man who nearly destroyed his newfound family burned fiercely in his mind.

Nero's eyes reflected his fierce protectiveness, mixed with a desire to release his pent-up energy. She sighed softly, reaching out to pat his feathered neck, running her fingers over the warm, soft down. "Soon, Nero," she whispered, her voice gentle. "But for now, we need to stay focused."

"I NEED TO GO. I'm supposed to be meeting Varkir at the bar." Draven stepped beside Nero and glanced at Lanae. "Did you want me to take him back home?" He hooked his thumb at the griffin.

"He really needs to exercise." Lanae glanced at the troublemaker, her furrowed brows threaded with touches of irritation and concern. "Are you going to behave and go hunting?" Her voice was firm, but there was a softness underlying it, a plea for cooperation.

Nero nodded his head and chirped, the sound a high-pitched melody that filled the air.

"No livestock." Draven pointed at him, his finger stern and unyielding. "Understand?" The memory of the previous debacle flashed in his mind, the chaos and cost of smoothing over the outrage regarding the mystical teenage predator.

Both he and Lanae had laid into the beast, their voices raised in frustration as they yelled at him about his piss-poor actions. The echo of their words still seemed to linger until the creature had taken to the skies. Nero had come back a while later with talons full of gold, the glint of the coins catching the sunlight. If Draven had to guess, he would have bet Nero had gone back to the Isle of Dreams, where he got the medallion that had awakened his powers, and cleared the place of coin.

The griffin's wings fluttered, the feathers rustling like a whisper in the wind, but he inclined his head, agreeing to Draven's terms. The vines Lanae had bound him with released, slithering back into the soil. Nero took flight, the powerful beats of his wings creating a gust of wind that rustled the surrounding leaves. He banked over the outer walls, heading to the woods where deer and wild boar were plentiful.

Draven leaned down, his eyes softening as he stole a kiss from Lanae. That tingle that flared any time they touched cascaded through him like a balmy shower, heating him from the inside. Her lips were warm and familiar, and although he wished to linger there, she was on the training field and unless he picked up a sword to spar, he was intruding on her practice. "I'll see you at home later. If anything changes..." His eyes scanned the walls, their gaze sharp and attentive, and then returned to hers, filled with an unspoken promise. "Send Nero to get me."

The sound of Nero's wings beating faded into the distance, leaving a sense of relief from the guards hanging in the air.

He turned and strode off the field, the burning of the eyes of every guard drilling into his back like hot coals. Over the last few years, he had sparred with Lanae on occasion and impressed even the seasoned veterans on the guard. The clang of swords and the grunts of exertion still echoed in his ears. But even if they wanted him on the force, he wouldn't agree because mistrust of the fae still lingered in his heart like a shadow that refused to fade.

When he entered the newly built tavern, the scent of fresh wood and spilled ale greeted him. He crossed to the bar, where Nicoli, the sexy djinn bartender, was mixing cocktails for a rowdy group. The clinking of glasses and the hum of conversation filled the air. As he slid into his seat, the leather creaked under his weight. She looked up at him and grinned, giving him a head nod of acknowledgment. Her eyes sparkled with mischief, but she had learned over the past couple of years not to push him for wishes. Despite her and Lanae being longtime friends, it still took Lanae's serious threat to slit her throat to stop her from flirting with him.

The tavern was alive with energy, the laughter and chatter of patrons creating a lively atmosphere even at this early hour. The flickering candlelight painted shifting patterns on the walls, enveloping the room in a cozy glow. Draven drew a lungful of air. The scent of roasted meat and spices mingling with the faint hint of Nicoli's exotic perfume and alcohol permeated the place.

It didn't take long for a trail of smoke to sail through the door, curling and twisting through the air before materializing in the seat next to him. The smoke coalesced into a humanoid form, and Varkir's smile settled on his face as he went from ethereal to corporeal in a matter of seconds. His arrival was accompanied by a faint scent of sulfur and a whisper of warmth.

At least this time, his clothing wasn't a tattered mess like the first time they met. He wore a neatly pressed dark tunic and trousers, the fabric clean and free of any rips or stains. Since freeing him from Firetwill's clutches, the yôkai had cleaned up enough that even his natural gray pallor didn't look so sickly. His hair, once matted and unkempt, now fell in smooth, sleek strands around his angular face.

"What news do you have for me?" Draven asked, his voice low but filled with curiosity and a hint of urgency.

Nicoli slid a drink in front of each of them, the glasses clinking softly on the wooden bar top before she dashed off to address another patron. The amber liquid inside caught the light, casting a warm glow between them.

Varkir took a moment to savor his drink. He swirled the liquid thoughtfully before taking a sip, his eyes meeting Draven's with a twinkle. "I've managed to gather some information about the Dragon's Heart."

His voice still had that ultra-smooth quality that made Draven second-guess whether or not to trust him. It was the kind of voice that could either soothe or deceive, and the uncertainty gnawed at him. But the man knew how to dig up information, and he had been loyal to Solstice City and Lanae ever since his return from imprisonment. The sound of clinking glasses and murmured conversations filled the space around them, a backdrop of noise that ratcheted Draven's tension. The low hum of the tavern, mixed with the occasional burst of laughter, created an almost claustrophobic atmosphere.

"And?" he asked when Varkir didn't continue. His ire rose enough to produce smoke from his nostrils. The faint tendrils curled into the air, dissipating quickly.

"And you are not going to like it." Varkir fidgeted in the seat, toying with his drink before chancing a glance at Draven. His normally confident demeanor was replaced with unease, his fingers tapping nervously against the glass.

Draven took a breath, cooling down the aggravation that simmered just below the surface. "I won't kill the messenger." He smiled, though it was tight-lipped and strained. "Out with it."

"Well, it seems the Dragon's Heart no longer carries any magic or power. It's just another defunct talisman that Alestain wears like a badge of honor." Varkir's words came out in a rush, as if getting them out quickly would lessen the blow. He took a gulp of his drink, nearly draining the cup.

Icy dread filled Draven's chest, the sensation like a heavy boulder settling in his stomach. He had been counting on that damn stone to help him fully shift like he could as a child. Losing that hope was a crushing weight. "How is that possible?" he asked, the words laced with disbelief and desperation. The room closed in around him, the noise fading to a dull roar in his ears as the reality of Varkir's news sank in.

"I also found information relating to ancient documents about the Dragon's Heart that might give you some glimpse into what drove the power in that relic," Varkir said, his voice tinged with cautious optimism.

Draven stiffened and turned fully toward Varkir, his eyes narrowing as he processed the words. "You could have started with that," he retorted, his voice edged with irritation.

Varkir chuckled, the sound a low rumble that seemed to vibrate through the air. He shrugged, a nonchalant gesture that belied the seriousness of the situation. "I'd rather leave you with hope than deal with your moody devastation," he replied, his eyes twinkling with mischief.

Draven didn't know whether to throttle the man or pat him on the back. The stress in his body eased, and a mix of frustration and gratitude swirled within him. The noise of the tavern seemed to recede, leaving a bubble of focused conversation between them.

Varkir's expression softened, his gaze earnest and unwavering. "My sources mentioned these documents are in a language that no one can decipher, so their ideas of what it might or might not contain are just hearsay," he explained, his tone serious now, each word measured and deliberate.

Draven's mind raced, the possibilities and risks flickering through his thoughts like a whirlwind. The revelation settled heavily on his shoulders. "Where is it?"

The flickering candlelight cast dancing shadows on Varkir's face, highlighting the uncertainty etched into his features, the play of light and dark emphasizing the somber reality of their conversation.

"It's not in this realm. But I've asked my people to bring it to me," Varkir replied, his voice steady but laced with the tension of the unknown.

"Thank you." Draven raised his glass to his friend, the liquid inside catching the light and shimmering like molten gold. He downed the drink in one smooth motion, the fiery liquid burning a path down his throat and lighting a fire in his stomach. The sensation was a strong juxtaposition to the cold dread that had filled his chest moments before. The warmth spread through him, igniting a resolve that had been smoldering within.

Hope—no matter how tenuous—was a beacon he couldn't afford to ignore.

CHAPTER FOUR
Magical Breech

LANAE AND JENNA HEADED toward the mess hall to grab a bite before they went to their respective stations throughout the city. The midday sun cast long shadows, and the air was infused with the aroma of grilled meats and fresh bread wafting from the army kitchen. Their footsteps echoed in the cobblestone streets, accompanied by the distant clamor of the bustling city.

A lone elite guard approached them, his armor gleaming in the sunlight with every powerful stride. His gaze locked onto Lanae, a penetrating look that made her skin prickle. His physique came close to that of Draven's: wide shoulders, a broad chest, arms built to break, and powerful legs that seemed capable of snapping necks if he so chose. His crop of golden hair glistened like a halo, but his eyes were as dark and foreboding as Xoltan Firetwill's.

"Mmm." Jenna licked her lips audibly as she scanned the elite guard. The sound broke the silence like a whip crack, making Lanae's heart jump.

"Lanae Nightshade?" His deep voice rumbled as he stopped before them.

"Aww, you always get the sexy ones," Jenna muttered, her voice laced with amusement.

Lanae threw her a look, annoyance flickering in her eyes, and then nodded at the guard. She thought she knew all the guards, elite or otherwise, in Solstice City, but she had never laid eyes on this one before. There was something unsettlingly familiar about him, yet alien at the same time.

"Granger Spiritwalker." He moved his hand in a crisp salute, the motion sharp and practiced. "You are needed in the situation room."

Lanae returned the salute, her eyes narrowing with suspicion. "I don't believe I've met you before."

"I've been traveling the realms for some time on council business," he replied, his gaze shifting to take in the city around them, "and came back to Solstice City recently." He glanced around at the city with a strange mixture of nostalgia and wariness. "It has changed a great deal since the last time I graced these streets."

"When was the last time you were here?" Jenna asked, still standing by Lanae's side, her tone curious but cautious.

His brow furrowed, and a shadow crossed his face. "It's been eleven or twelve years."

"So, before the peace talks fell through." Lanae's intuition prickled as he nodded. There was a heavy silence, broken only by the distant cries of hawkers in the market and the rustle of leaves in the breeze. "What type of business does the council have in other realms?"

He smiled, but it didn't reach his eyes. "Collecting allies."

"And the realm you were in was not impacted by the near merge three years ago?" Lanae pressed. She had seen the damage that caused to the fae realm and that of the seer, and couldn't imagine what other realms looked like after they stopped the destruction.

He let out a laugh, the sound harsh and grating. "That's when I attempted to get back to Solstice City, but that proved difficult and communications between realms were nearly destroyed."

"Oh." His answer appeased some of the anxiety making her skin itch, but it didn't completely dispel the unease. "Well, shall we?" She waved for him to lead the way. "See you in a bit," she said to Jenna.

Jenna gave her a wink and walked away. "Have fun!" she called over her shoulder, her voice echoing through the narrow streets.

I doubt the council situation room will be anything close to fun. Lanae's thought bounced into her mind, and then she focused on the presence next to her. His footsteps fell in rhythm with hers.

He glanced at her, his expression unreadable. "I heard you were the one who ended the siege."

"I was there." She didn't want the credit for overcoming that evil. Draven had insisted to the council that Lanae be awarded the accolades and not him. He wanted to remain in the shadows because of the danger of the Dragon's Heart.

"Your humbleness is unexpected." He raised an eyebrow, his gaze piercing. "Taking down a tyrant is something to brag fiercely about." A smile toyed on his lips, but there was an edge to it.

"Yes, well, all the death and destruction that Firetwill caused..." She stopped speaking and shook her head, the memories weighing heavily on her mind. "It's not something I enjoy reliving," she finally said.

"I guess you never get over taking a life, even if it is in the midst of war."

"Exactly."

Once they were out of view from the guards, Granger led her onto a side street that headed toward the Citadel. The narrow alley was shrouded in shadows, and the distant murmur of the city seemed to fade away. Before they stepped onto the main thoroughfare, Granger grabbed Lanae's arm, his grip firm and unyielding, and tossed a vial on the street before them. A sharp, hissing sound filled the air, and a portal opened, sucking them through the ether.

DRAVEN RETURNED TO THE house to find Nero in the backyard with a small deer carcass. The coppery tang of blood mingled with the earthy aroma of the forest surrounding them. Nero glanced up when Draven cracked the back door to check on him, the sound of the creaking hinges cutting through the quiet afternoon.

"Nice catch," Draven said, his voice strained but attempting to sound casual. He was glad Nero wouldn't be eating them out of their meat supply for a day or two. The glimpse of the fresh kill was a grim indicator of the harsh reality they lived in.

He inspected their food supply, the cool air from the storage pantry hitting his face as he opened the door. Pulling out ingredients for dinner, his mind raced with all that Varkir had told him. A weight settled on his chest, heavy and suffocating at the thought of never being able to shift into his full dragon form again. The kitchen seemed too small. The walls closed in on him as the enormity of the situation sank in.

Caelum strolled in as Draven set the roast he was making in the oven. "Lanae's not here?" He looked around, his voice a sudden intrusion in the tense atmosphere. "Huh." He closed his eyes, and a crease of concentration appeared, deepening with each passing second. The silence was thick, punctuated only by the crackling fire in the hearth.

When Caelum's eyes opened, Draven's heart fell with a bang into his stomach. "What?" Dread coiled around his insides.

"It's like she's not here. I can't reach her." Caelum's voice was tight with worry, his normally calm demeanor cracking.

If Lanae was shutting her brother out, that meant she was in trouble. Draven shut off the oven with a sharp click and grabbed his sword, the cold weight of the weapon grounding him. He cracked the back door and stared at Nero, who was still working on his meal. "Lanae's missing."

Nero dropped the meat immediately and took to the skies, his powerful wings beating against the air with urgency. Draven closed the back door, the finality of the sound echoing in the empty kitchen, and stalked to the front of the house where Caelum waited at the open front door, tension radiating from him in waves.

"Last I saw her, she was on the sparring field with Jenna." Draven crossed the threshold, with Caelum by his side. He closed the door behind them, locking the house up tight as if to keep the looming dread at bay.

"I think Jenna might be at Mystic Spirits with a few of the guards," Caelum said, his voice tight, the concern mirrored in Draven's own heart. The tension between them was deep, a silent agreement that finding Lanae was their top priority.

They headed toward the bar, each step filled with mounting anxiety. The streets were alive with the sounds of the city winding down for the evening, but Draven's mind was consumed with thoughts of Lanae. Caelum's inability to reach his sister tied knots in Draven's stomach. Every instinct in Draven screamed at him to find Lanae, to protect her from whatever shadows lurked in the corners of their world.

Mystic Spirits was hopping with guards and fae looking for a refreshment at the end of a busy workday. The raucous laughter and clinking of glasses filled the air, creating a marked disparity to the unease gnawing at Draven's insides.

Draven scanned the bar, his eyes darting from table to table until his gaze landed on Jenna sitting with a half dozen other guards. The candlelight played across their features, shadows darting and shifting, yet there was no mistaking Jenna. She was laughing at something one of the guards had said, her smile bright and carefree.

"Jenna!" Draven called out, his voice cutting through the din of the bar. The conversation at their table halted, and Jenna's head snapped up, her wide eyes locking onto Draven's.

Draven and Caelum made their way over to the table, the urgency in their stride unmistakable. "Jenna, we need to talk," Draven said, his tone leaving no room for an argument.

Jenna's smile faded as she took in their serious expressions. "What's going on?" she asked, concern creeping into her voice.

"Lanae's missing," Caelum said bluntly, his eyes scanning the room as if hoping to catch a glimpse of his sister.

Jenna's eyes widened, and she stood up abruptly, the chair scraping loudly against the floor. "She was with me on the sparring field earlier, but then she got called away by an elite guard." Her voice was tinged with worry.

Draven's jaw tightened. "We need to find her now."

Jenna's brows furrowed. "The guard's name was Granger Spiritwalker. He said she was needed in the situation room. He seemed familiar, but I couldn't place him."

Caelum's eyes narrowed. "Spiritwalker... I don't like the sound of this. We need to check the situation room."

Jenna nodded, determination replacing the worry in her eyes. "Let me know if she isn't there." She reached out and squeezed Caelum's hand.

Caelum nodded. "I will."

As they left Mystic Spirits, Draven's heart spurred into a gallop, and he prayed they would find Lanae safe and unharmed.

THE MOMENT THEIR FEET hit the ground, Lanae's heart rampaged in a feral beat in her chest as she struggled to reach her sword. Granger's grip was like iron, and he easily stripped the steel from her grasp. With a forceful shove, he sent her stumbling backward. Her foot caught on a bump in the floor, and she crashed to the ground, the cold, hard surface jarring her bones. Bars slammed shut with a deafening clang, caging her in a cell.

"What the hell?" she spat, scrambling to her feet. She launched herself at the cell door, her fingers clawing through the opening between the bars. An icy fear scraped across her skin, sending a jagged tremor down her spine.

Granger's hand shot out, grabbing her wrist and yanking her arm against the bars. His feral smile sent a chill of fear through her. Pain seared through her skin where her skin touched the cage, and the acrid stench of burning flesh filled her nostrils. Her skin sizzled, and she yanked back, cradling her arm to her abdomen. Her eyes widened in horror as she took in her surroundings. The room was hauntingly familiar, the unanimated forms frozen in time around her like macabre statues. Every breath was laden with the stink of decay, and a cold sweat broke out on her forehead.

"A fitting iron prison for a murderess," he sneered, his voice dripping with contempt.

Lanae's chest throbbed violently, each beat echoing in her ears like a war drum.

Granger walked around the cage as he inspected his palm with a casual indifference that sent a rake of shivers crawling down her spine.

"I must be going, but when I return, your punishment will begin," he continued, his voice a chilling promise. "Before the war is through, you'll be begging me for death."

His cold, piercing eyes flicked up to meet hers, and for a moment, it appeared he could see straight into her soul. The air around her grew colder, and she wrapped her arms around herself, trying to ward off the chill.

As Granger walked away, his footsteps echoed in the silent room, each step punctuating her impending doom. She was left alone with the fae statues, their lifeless eyes staring at her, their expressions frozen in time. The oppressive air swirled, steeped in the scent of decay and fear. Lanae's breath came in shallow gasps, her mind racing as she tried to escape this nightmare.

CAELUM LED THE WAY to the Citadel, the air thick with tension. As they ventured closer to the situation chamber, the cold, stone walls seemed to close in on them, amplifying their footsteps. The guards in front of the door straightened, their eyes narrowing in suspicion as they pinned Caelum and his companions with a look that usually would have had him turning around and avoiding the confrontation. But this was his sister's well-being, and he needed to know whether she was in that room or not.

The sharp bite of metal armor and the musty odor of the ancient building filled his nostrils, and Draven's anxiety rolled off him in waves, sparking his own unease into a frenzy. The cold air bit at his skin, and his breath came in short, sharp bursts. Nero stalked next to them, his movements predatory, as if hunting for his next meal. The silence was deafening.

"Have you seen my sister?" Caelum asked with desperation.

The guards glanced at each other, their expressions unreadable. "Our shift just started a half hour ago, and no one has come in or out of the room," one of them replied, his voice flat and emotionless.

"We were told Granger Spiritwalker escorted her here earlier today," Caelum insisted, his throat tightening with fear.

Their eyes blinked in unison. "Granger never showed up for his shift," the guard on the right mumbled.

Caelum's throat tightened further, a lump forming as panic threatened to overwhelm him. "Can we please see if she is in there?" he pleaded, his voice trembling.

The guards hesitated, their eyes darting back and forth.

The air grew colder as the situation pressed down on Caelum's shoulders. The shadows in the hallway seemed to stretch and lengthen, creating an oppressive atmosphere that made it difficult to breathe. His heart worked itself up, each beat echoing in his ears as he waited for their response. The world around him seemed to fade away, leaving the unbearable tension and the desperate need to find his sister.

Draven's growl rumbled through the air, a guttural sound that made the hairs on the guards' arms stand on end. The metallic rasp of swords being drawn echoed in the corridor, but it was Nero who snapped first. With a flash of electrifying blue, he surged forward, his lightning crackling and causing the guards to dive aside, their faces contorting in fear. The scent of ozone and burned hair drifted in the air as Nero reared up, his talons gleaming menacingly. When he slammed his front talons into the door, the wood splintered and the hinges screamed in protest before the door flew open, crashing into the wall with a thunderous boom.

Inside the room, conversations ceased mid-sentence, and every head swiveled toward the source of the commotion. Faide's eyes narrowed as he straightened, his fingers twitching toward his own sword. He glared at the massive griffin and Draven standing defiantly in the doorway. The room's occupants were a sea of wide eyes and slack jaws, and Caelum's heart thrummed wildly as he scanned the crowd, frantically looking for

Lanae. His breath hitched when he couldn't spot her.

"Where is my wife!" Draven's snarl was more than a question—it was a promise of chaos. His eyes darted around the room, every muscle in his body coiled tight like a spring ready to unleash fury.

Caelum's heart when haywire. He knew Draven's secret nuptials had been a bombshell waiting to drop. Lanae had kept it from the council and the guard, not wanting to rock the boat. The council's disapproval was the least of their worries now.

"What did you say?" Faide's voice was a low, dangerous growl as he stepped closer, his eyes flashing with barely contained anger.

The tension in the room was thick enough to cut with a knife. A door at the back of the room creaked open, and all eyes snapped to it. Lanae stepped out, and her eyebrows rose at the collective attention. Before Draven could utter a word, Faide's fury was directed at her.

"You married him without the council's blessing?" Faide's voice was sharp, his finger jabbing at Draven as if his very presence was an affront.

Lanae's eyes widened, her mouth falling open in surprise. She blinked rapidly, like a deer caught in the headlights, before she gathered herself and squared her shoulders. She might have been startled, but Lanae was not one to be easily cowed.

Caelum reached out to Lanae telepathically, desperate to connect, but found only silence. His heart flailed. She had blocked him, just as she did on the battlefield. His mind flashed to another setting where she kept him out: the bedroom. He could still remember the mortifying moment he had heard her moan in his mind—he had practically begged her to block him then. The battlefield he could handle. But her intimate moments? No, thank you.

The room buzzed with nervous energy, the silence heavy with unspoken threats and simmering anger. This was far from over.

"Perhaps you should head home with your husband, Lanae." Faide's tone left no room for debate, his voice as cold and unyielding as a glacier.

Lanae opened her mouth, the faintest breath of protest escaping her lips, but Faide's icy glare silenced her immediately.

"Go home. Now. We will discuss your situation as soon as we have a solid plan of attack." His words struck with the finality of a judge's gavel.

Lanae's shoulders sagged for a moment, but she quickly composed herself and strode to the door, her footsteps echoing in the tense silence. As she passed by the trio, her eyes flicked to Caelum, fury reflected in her irises, and Caelum felt sorry for Draven and the fireworks that were sure to go off the moment they entered the house. Nero squawked loudly, his keen eyes daring anyone to challenge them further, his feathers puffing up in agitation.

"Come on," Caelum muttered, grabbing Draven by the arm and steering him away from the hostile stares that bore into their backs like daggers. "Before you get me in trouble, too."

Draven's jaw was clenched so tightly that his teeth might have cracked under the pressure, but he allowed himself to be led away. An unmistakable tension charged the air, thick enough to choke on, and the magnitude of every unspoken word pressed down on them.

Nero gave one last indignant squawk, as if to say, "This isn't over," before following Lanae, his claws clicking ominously against the floor.

Lanae remained silent, the tension simmering just below the surface, a powder keg waiting for a spark.

A BONE-WRINGING CHILL ran through Lanae as the room grew darker, the shadows creeping across the polished marble floor like grasping fingers. She sat in the middle of the cage, her knees drawn to her chest, utterly exposed and on display. The chill in the air seeped into her bones, making her tremble uncontrollably. Her gaze flicked to the empty bucket in the corner, a stark reminder of her humiliating predicament.

As the day wore on, the growing pressure in her lower abdomen became impossible to ignore. She glanced around the room, her eyes lingering on the motionless figures. None of them moved a muscle, all still trapped in the mind-control coma, just like her parents. The eerie stillness was both a curse and a relief; at least no one was watching her every move.

With a resigned sigh, Lanae gave in to the inevitable. She slid her pants down to her ankles and squatted over the bucket, closing her eyes as her urine emptied from her bladder. The sound of the liquid hitting the metal echoed in the silent room. She bit her lip, fighting back tears of frustration and humiliation.

As she buttoned her pants back up, her stomach let out a loud, rumbling protest. The hunger gnawed at her insides, a relentless ache that refused to be ignored. She wondered how long she would be subjected to this silent torture, deprived of food and water, with only a bucket to relieve herself in. Each passing minute crawled like an eternity, the gnawing fear and uncertainty growing stronger with every second.

Desperation clawed at her as she tried to summon her magic. She focused her thoughts, willing the vines to burst through the marble floor to give her some semblance of control in this nightmare. But just like the last time she was in this hellish place, nothing stirred. Her magic lay dormant, unresponsive to her pleas.

The cold, unyielding marble beneath her seemed to mock her efforts, its smooth surface a vivid contrast to the wild, untamed power she sought to unleash. The room remained deathly silent, save for the faint rustling of her clothes and the distant drip of water. The oppressive darkness pressed in on her, magnifying her sense of dread.

Hours passed, and the gnawing sensation of hunger took hold. Her stomach growled incessantly, the sound echoing in the silence like a beast demanding to be fed. She pressed her hand to her belly, trying to quell the growing discomfort. Her throat was parched, each swallow painful as if she were trying to gulp down shards of glass. The metallic tang of the stale air hung heavy in the cell.

Deep-seated dread crept over her, curling around her thoughts like a dark, suffocating fog. Her mind raced with questions and fears, each one more terrifying than the last. *What was happening outside these walls? What plans were being made?* The uncertainty was maddening, and a knot of anxiety tightened in her chest.

She tried to reach out to Caelum telepathically, but there was nothing but an empty void. The lack of connection was disorienting, rendering her more isolated and vulnerable. She closed her eyes, trying to center herself, but the darkness only seemed to magnify her fears. Every creak and rustle in the cell clanged like a harbinger of doom, making her heart launch into high gear.

Draven's image floated into her mind. His determined eyes and fierce love made her hope flare. But even that hope was tinged with fear. *What would he do to get her out? What would he sacrifice?* The questions swirled around her mind, each one adding to the growing sense of dread.

She hugged her knees to her chest, trying to find some warmth and comfort in the small gesture. Her breaths came in shallow, ragged gasps, and she fought to keep her emotions in check. The cell closed in on her. The walls pressed tighter and tighter until she couldn't breathe.

Lanae had faced countless battles and dangers, but this—this waiting and uncertainty— was a different kind of torture. The physical discomfort was nothing compared to the mental and emotional agony of not knowing what lay ahead. And as the hours ticked by, her situation pounded down, threatening to crush her spirit.

The hours dragged on, each one more torturous than the last. Hunger, thirst, and fear gnawed at her, wearing down her resolve. The silence was maddening, every sound amplified in the suffocating darkness. Lanae closed her eyes and tried to block it all out, clinging to the hope that somehow, some way, she would find a way to break free.

CHAPTER FIVE
The Encroaching Darkness

DRAVEN FOLLOWED LANAE'S POUNDING footsteps, each step echoing through the dark corridors like a drumbeat of impending doom. He kept a safe distance, not daring to approach her while the anger radiated from her like a lethal poison.

Caelum and Nero stepped in line with Draven. The griffin's golden eyes, usually filled with mischief, were now narrow slits of suspicion. "She's still blocking me," Caelum whispered, his voice audible over the echoing footsteps.

"She's pissed." Draven glanced at Caelum, his brow furrowing. "I guess I can't blame her. I acted on impulse and emotion and spilled our secret."

Draven's gaze shifted to the griffin next to him. Nero's gaze was locked on Lanae as she walked a half a block ahead of them. Normally, when they were out, his preference was to walk with Lanae, not him and Caelum. His usual open and mischievous eyes were narrowed, his ears pinned back against his head. His nails clicked on the cobblestone, a sharp, rhythmic sound that added to the tension.

"That wasn't your finest moment, but at least they know," Caelum said.

Draven sighed, his irrational actions pressing down on him. "The last time she didn't heed the council's directives, she was tried for treason." He slashed his gaze to Caelum, the memory of that debacle still fresh and painful.

Caelum nodded, his expression grim. "The last time, there were some members controlled by Xoltan Firetwill."

Draven grunted an acknowledgment as they rounded the corner to their street. The familiar sight of their house should have been comforting, but Lanae walked right past it, her mind clearly elsewhere.

"Where are you going?" Draven called as he stopped at the walkway leading to their place. Caelum and Nero headed inside, their footsteps fading into the background.

Lanae turned, her eyes darting around before she backtracked to the house. She bypassed Draven without a word, her face a mask of frustration and distraction. The minute he closed the door, she spoke, her voice sharp and accusatory.

"You interrupted the meeting before we could settle on a plan." Her gaze bore into him, hard and unyielding.

He cocked his head, studying her. "That's why you are mad?"

"Yes. Why else would I be?" she snapped, her tone defensive.

Draven glanced over her head at Caelum and then met her gaze. Something unsettling gnawed at him. "No reason." His skin prickled with unease.

Nero squawked from the kitchen, pulling her attention away. "What is that thing doing inside?" she demanded, her voice tinged with disdain.

Draven couldn't believe those words tumbled out of his wife's mouth. Hell, he no longer believed this was his wife. There was only one sure way to find out. He reached for her and wrapped his fingers around her wrist. The expected tingling sensation of their bond was absent. No electric connection sparked between them. He narrowed his gaze, suspicion turning to certainty. "You are not Lanae," he growled.

She twisted her wrist and moved her arm down, breaking free of his grip with a fluid motion. Then she spun around him and delivered a swift kick to his lower back, sending him off-balance. He stumbled, catching himself on the couch, but by the time he reached the front door, she was gone, with only the echo of her footsteps and the lingering sense of alarm in her wake.

MOVEMENT OUTSIDE HER CAGE jerked Lanae from her stupor, and she lifted her gaze. The cold iron bars prevented her from leaning closer. Shadows danced under the dusky haze outside her cage. Her heart stuttered at the green eyes studying her from the other side of the bars. A flicker of hope ignited within her, pushing back the despair that had settled in her chest. She shot to her feet. "Draven."

"Hello, love. It's time we get you out of there. Don't you think?"

His voice soothed her frazzled nerves, and for a moment, the damp, musty air of the cage seemed to lift.

Lanae's heart soared and she stepped forward, reaching through the bars for him, but he moved away. The lack of contact left her fingers tingling with a desperate longing.

A key turning in the lock caught her attention, the metallic click echoing through the stone chamber. She glanced at the metal positioned in the lock, blinking in surprise. "How did you get the key?"

"I found Granger and beat it out of him." His eyes glinted with a hint of satisfaction. He opened the door, using it as a barrier between them before he spun on his heels and headed toward the hallway. "This way."

A gnawing itch surfaced in Lanae's mind, but she was not about to complain about his no-nonsense attitude. She followed him down the stairwell and into the dungeons without question.

The air grew colder, the stink of mold intensifying with each step. When he stepped into an open cell, she hesitated, her instincts screaming at her to be cautious.

"Draven?" she called. Her voice held the slightest of trembles.

He glanced over his shoulder at her and smiled, though it lacked its usual warmth. "The exit is hidden somewhere over here." He ran his hand over the rough stone wall. "Come help me find the lever to open it."

Alarms sounded in her head, but she stepped to the wall next to him, running her hands over the cold, uneven surface. As her fingers got close to his, he snapped an iron cuff around her wrist. The metal bit into her skin, and she cried out, blinking at the iron singeing her wrist and then up into those familiar green eyes.

His hand grasped her throat with a vise-like grip, pressing her against the wall.

The cold stone sent racking quakes down her spine, and she blinked at his feral sneer, her brain clearing enough to note that there was no tingling from his touch. "You aren't Draven."

"Funny, your husband said the same thing earlier." His voice dripped with malice as he pressed his body against hers, pinning her to the wall.

The stench of sweat and decay filled her nostrils, making her gag.

She swung with her free hand, but as swift as a lightning bolt, that wrist was bound in iron as well. The cuffs burned against her skin, leaving angry red welts.

When her captor stepped back, his form altered, shifting from Draven to her own image, to Granger, and then to eyes that were frighteningly familiar. His nearly black eyes stared at her with the same contempt as Xoltan had. Although this fae's form was more muscular and powerful than Xoltan's. His hair shone bright with a weave of silver and white threaded with midnight, and his complexion was a pleasant golden tan, as if he spent days in the tropics. If she had been single and this was a bar, this fiend would have caught her attention.

His lips twerked into a grin, and he glanced around the dungeon with an air of disdain. "This is a much better place for you than on display in the main hall."

Rage flared within her, and she kicked out, her foot connecting with his shin. The impact sent a jolt of satisfaction through her, but it was short-lived.

He struck as quickly as a snake, his palm leaving a sting so hot on her cheek that her vision blurred with bright lights from the impact. The force of the blow made her ears ring, and she fought to stay conscious, her heart gunned into overdrive as she faced the twisted fae before her.

"Who the fuck are you?" she demanded, her voice trembling as adrenaline pumped her muscles full of fury. The dank air of the dungeon closed in around her, amplifying her sense of urgency.

"Allow me to introduce myself. Spric Firetwill. Shapeshifter extraordinaire." He bowed with a flourish, his movement fluid and almost graceful, close enough to tempt her. The dim light glinted off his hair, casting an eerie glow on his features.

She kicked out again, her foot slicing through the air, nearly connecting with his face.

He jerked back just in time. His sudden motion sent a surge of satisfaction through her. His hands balled into fists, and his gaze darkened, becoming a storm of malevolent intent.

She braced herself; her heart jackhammered in her chest, and she parried the incoming swing with a desperate burst of strength.

She deflected his first hit, but the second landed squarely in her abdomen. The impact was like a sledgehammer, yanking all the air from her lungs and doubling her over. Pain radiated through her torso, and she gasped, fighting to stay upright.

He stepped out of reach, his breath coming in heavy huffs, his anger drilling into her as hard as his fist had. The air crackled with tension. He grabbed her face with a rough hand, his grip bruising, and tilted it up, forcing her to meet his gaze. "While I would love to spar with you and see what type of damage you could do, this is my domain, and you will show me some respect. Especially since your life is in my hands." His low, dangerous growl crusted ice over her backbone.

She spit at him, her defiance unfiltered, and received a backhand to the same cheek. The force of the blow sent her reeling, knocking her to the ground. Her cheek throbbed with pain, and her vision blurred with tears. The cold, hard stone bit into her skin as she lay there, struggling to regain her bearings. The tang of blood filled her mouth, reminding her of her vulnerability.

The dungeon's oppressive silence closed in around her, broken only by the rasp of his heavy breathing and her own ragged gasps. She forced herself to look up at him, her eyes blazing with defiance. She knew she couldn't afford to show any weakness, not now, not in front of him.

"Respect?" She spit a wad of blood on the floor, the metallic taste lingering on her tongue. "You'll never have my respect." Her voice was insolent, though her body trembled from the pain and exhaustion. The stone floor beneath her seemed like ice against her skin, and the dim light cast eerie shadows on the damp, moss-covered walls.

He smiled with a calculated expression that jellied her spine. "Then I'll have your life." His words dripped with menace, and the surrounding air seemed to grow colder, amplifying the dread settling in her chest.

An artic chill started in her stomach and spiraled outward, sending goose bumps up her arms and down her spine. She tried to mask her fear, willing her muscles to stay steady, but the way his smile widened, she knew he saw the brief flash of terror in her eyes. The air suddenly thickened, and her heart beat against her sternum like a drum.

"After some much deserved torture, of course." His words dripped with sinister delight, echoing off the stone walls.

He turned and left her lying on the cold, damp floor, the pain of his fists still fresh and throbbing in her body. Mold and decay filled her nostrils, and his receding footsteps reverberated in the eerie silence, leaving her alone in the darkness with her fear.

CHAPTER SIX
Ties of Blood

DRAVEN RAN BOTH HANDS into his hair as he paced their living room. The soft glow of the lanterns cast long shadows on the walls, adding to the oppressive atmosphere. "What in the ever-loving afterlife was that?" he exclaimed, his desperation and confusion ringing through the room.

Caelum blinked incessantly, his eyes narrowing in concentration as he tried to telepathically reach his sister. The strain caused his temples to pound, and the silence in his mind was maddening. Not a damn thing was coming through, and he was just as frantic as Draven. A sudden thought jerked his head up, and his eyes widened with realization. "Granger."

Draven spun toward him, his movements abrupt. "What?"

"We need to speak to Granger. They said he never showed for work. Maybe he saw that thing's actual face." Caelum's voice was filled with urgency as he headed for the door, still dressed in his uniform.

Draven followed without hesitation, his steps echoing loudly in the quiet room. He put his hand up at Nero, who was watching with anxious eyes. "If she comes back, have her let you out and find us. Okay?"

Nero nodded, his feathers rustling softly.

Caelum waited impatiently for Draven to lock the door before he headed to the neighborhood of upscale homes near the Citadel where the elite officers lived. The frosty night air bit into their exposed skin, and the cobblestones beneath their feet seemed to reflect the tension in the air.

The minute they stepped into the neighborhood, the sound of a commotion drew their attention. A gaggle of guards were milling about, their voices raised in anger. A hulking figure threw a punch at another guard, the impact resonating with a sickening thud. His rambling curses reached Caelum's ears, and even under the shadowy glow, he could see the bruise on the fighting man's temple.

Granger yelled he did not desert his post, his voice a mix of anger and desperation. The surrounding guards were clearly trying to arrest the poor bastard, their grips tight on their weapons.

Caelum jumped into a sprint, his heart pumping a ragged breath. He had to intercept before they arrested Granger. The cool night air whipped against his face, and the uneven cobblestones threatened to trip him, but he pushed on, determined to reach Granger in time.

"Wait!" His call distracted the guards and Granger, halting their struggles. The chilly night air seemed to grow still as all eyes locked on Caelum, and Draven trailing him. The distant sounds of the city were a faint murmur, overshadowed by the tension crackling in the air.

As Caelum approached with his palms out in supplication, one of the arresting guards snarled at him, his face contorted with irritation. "This is none of your concern, newbie." The guard's breath was visible in the chilly air, adding to the harshness of his words.

Beating other officers was highly frowned upon by the guard, even during an arrest. Caelum pointed at the blue and purple bruise marring Granger's face. "Clearly Granger was knocked unconscious, unless you caused that fucking bruise." He expected the guards to recoil.

And recoil they did. It was as if Caelum's words had knocked some sense into these men. The tension in their stances eased. "No. He had that when we arrived," the lead guard said, his tone defensive.

The man's name embroidered on his uniform was faded, but Caelum squinted at it until he could make it out—Kale.

"Look, Kale," Caelum continued, his voice urgent, "Jenna said Granger came to escort my sister to the situation room."

Granger growled, his eyes dark with frustration. "I did no such thing."

Caelum put his hand up to calm him. "I know. But someone wearing your face did. Just like someone wearing my sister's face infiltrated the situation room meeting that we interrupted. The person who came back to our house was not my sister."

Skepticism blanketed the group. The guards exchanged dubious glances, and even Granger crossed his arms, his brow furrowed in doubt.

"How do you know?" Kale asked, his gaze piercing.

"Because I know my wife. And that was not her," Draven growled, his conviction clear.

Caelum let his eyes drift shut, and he huffed a breath. "You all know I have a telepathic connection with Lanae." When he opened his eyes, everyone was nodding. "I could not telepathically reach her, even when she was in our home and in front of me. I didn't even feel her blocking me out. That's how I knew it wasn't her."

"And Nero wouldn't go near her," Draven added.

At the mention of the griffin, the guards straightened and dropped their tight-armed stance. They had seen the bond between Nero and Lanae out on the training fields over the last three years. "Nero doesn't leave her side," one of the other soldiers said, his voice laced with respect.

"No. He doesn't unless she forces him to," Caelum replied, his eyes meeting each guard in turn.

"Maybe he was upset with her for stopping his storm antics this morning," one officer suggested, trying to rationalize the situation.

"Have you ever seen that griffin turn a cold shoulder on Lanae?" Caelum challenged.

They all grumbled and shook their heads, acknowledging the truth in his words.

Caelum met Granger's gaze, his expression earnest. "I am hoping you can tell me what the person who did that to you looked like." He pointed at the bruise on Granger's face.

Granger's eyes darkened with the memory. "I was blindsided. The only thing I saw was a pair of upscale steel-toe boots and a black duster coat before darkness claimed me. And then I woke up in my own bed and I couldn't find my uniform." He looked at the officers surrounding him with his frustration on full display. "And then these buffoons showed up."

The cold air blanketed them, the reality of their situation sinking in. They had a shape-shifting enemy among them, and the stakes had never been higher.

DRAVEN'S PULSE POUNDED IN his temples like a roar of an avalanche, echoing with relentless intensity. The arguments still raged between the guards, creating a whirlwind of frantic energy, the air thick with the metallic tang of tension. His one relief was that the council and generals had not settled on a course of action before his and Caelum's interruption.

Whoever had been impersonating Granger and Lanae hadn't gotten the vital information on the pending battle tactics. Their deception was foiled in the chaos.

He grabbed Caelum's arm, his fingers gripping with urgency, pulling him away from the guards who were now bickering heatedly, their voices a commotion of discord over what to do with the newfound information and Granger's orchestrated desertion. "Caelum, I need to go find Lanae," Draven said, his voice low but vibrating with intensity.

"I'm going with you," Caelum replied, his eyes dark with determination.

"No. You need to stay here and make sure the shit doesn't hit the fan. If my hunch is right..." Draven's voice trailed off as he mopped the sweat from his face, the salt stinging his eyes.

"You needed me last time," Caelum insisted, his gaze unwavering.

"If she is there, she's not there for breeding." The word hissed from between Draven's lips like a curse. "She's there because they think she killed Xoltan."

Caelum blinked, the reality of Draven's words sinking in, then closed his eyes. The heavy truth hung between them, thick as the fog that shrouded Solstice City. Few knew Draven had been the true savior. Outside of Faide and Varkir, no one else knew besides Caelum. Lanae had been revered as their liberator. "Fuck."

"That's usually my line," Draven muttered, a sardonic edge to his voice.

Caelum's lips twitched into a wry smile. "I am going with you," he repeated, his voice firmer.

"No. You are not. You are going to make sure your parents stay safe. If Alestain is there, he will reanimate his brother's minions. He needs an army before he attacks."

"How are you even going to get there? You destroyed the only portal to that realm."

Draven met his gaze, his eyes burning with resolve. "With another ancient draconian spell."

Caelum lifted an eyebrow, skepticism mingling with curiosity. He crossed his arms, the leather of his tunic creaking. "You mean you not only know how to destroy portals, you know how to open them?"

Draven smirked, the expression a fleeting glimpse of his confidence. "How do you think I got inside these walls to begin with?" He glanced around, ensuring no one was eavesdropping on their tense exchange.

Caelum wiped the perspiration from his face, conscious of the grit from the day's battles.

"You also have to go tell the council that the person in the war room was not Lanae. That is just as important as making sure your parents stay put." Draven tapped Caelum's chest, the gesture both reassuring and commanding.

"Fine. But I'll need more than my word after the shitshow earlier." Caelum glanced at the group of soldiers still arguing, then crossed to Granger.

Draven didn't wait to see what Caelum said to the elite guard. He slipped through the shadows, his steps quick and silent as he went in search of a secluded alley where he could perform his spell.

LANAE BANGED THE BACK of her head against the cold, unforgiving stone wall in frustration, the dull thud reverberating in the dank, confined space. The cell walls seemed to shrink, the oppressive darkness highlighting her inability to break free from the heavy chains around her wrists. Her abdomen still ached where Spric had punched her...a deep, throbbing pain that wouldn't let her forget the assault. Her stomach growled its gnawing emptiness, and she wondered just how long she would be deprived of food.

The iron door to the dungeons creaked open, the sound echoing through the narrow corridors. She held her breath, her pulse quickening. When Draven stepped in front of the cage, her heart stuttered, a moment of hope flaring before being crushed. The lack of weapons hanging on his belt and the keys in his hand told her this wasn't her sweet dragon. This was an imposter, a cruel mimicry.

He grinned a twisted smile that made her nerves jitter through her muscles in a flight response. He slid the key in the lock and turned it before he swung the door open; the hinges groaned in protest. He stepped inside, the dim light casting ominous shadows across his face.

"Stop with the mind fuck." Her voice remained steady despite the terror clawing at her insides. She scrambled to her feet, the chains rattling with her movement.

His laughter bounced off the rock walls, a chilling sound that seemed to mock her defiance. He stepped closer, the air swirling heavy with menace.

She shifted into ready form, muscles tensing, and waited. Her reach wasn't far, but if he came into her sphere, she'd try her damnedest to land a hit. He moved to the outer edge of where the chains halted her punch, a deliberate taunt. The wicked gleam in his eyes was enough to send a bolt of fear through her, icy and paralyzing.

"It's time to face my father." His voice crawled in a low, menacing growl. He inched closer, the dim light casting a sinister shadow across his face.

Lanae swung with all her might, her fist slicing through the musty air.

The bastard's reflexes were lightning-fast. He caught her fist with a sharp, audible snap, his grip like iron. In one swift motion, he twisted her arm behind her back. Her joints protested with a sickening crack. With a brutal force, he slammed her into the back wall face-first. The impact reverberated through her skull, a dull thud echoing in the confined space. The cold, rough stone scraped against her cheek, and blood filled her mouth as she bit down on her lip.

He pressed against her, the weight of his body pinning her to the cold, unyielding wall. The clinging dampness of the cell enveloped them. "Besides, I enjoy messing with murderers," he sneered, his breath hot against her ear.

With a surge of defiance, Lanae slammed her head back. The satisfying crunch of bone meeting bone echoed through the confined space as she connected with his face. He grunted, a guttural sound of pain and surprise, and cursed under his breath, his grip momentarily loosening.

He moved his free hand to grip her throat hard enough to cut off her air. "If you keep this up, you will be more than just bloodied and bruised."

"Fuck you." She hissed out the curse from what little air she could get.

"Is that what you want?" He pressed his pelvis against her, and she stilled at the feel of his hard length pressing into the small of her back. "Because I think I have time to oblige."

He tightened the chain on her shackles, forcing her hands to pin to the wall.

The minute his hand removed from her throat, she gasped for breath, the precious air filling her lungs. Desperation clawed at her insides, and she screamed, "No!" Her voice echoed through the cold stone walls, a haunting cry of defiance.

He released the chains, the metallic clinking sound reverberating in the silence. "Then be a good girl and put both hands behind your back," he commanded, his voice dripping with sinister intent.

Lanae inched her trembling hands behind her back, the cold shackles biting into her skin. She hated the fear lashing her form, the icy tendrils wrapping around her heart. She could deal with the physical pain, the bruises and blood, but the thought of something more vile sent waves of dread crashing over her.

Another set of manacles clamped around her wrists before the ones connected to the walls clattered to the ground. He spun her around with a rough jerk, forcing her to face him. The bastard still wore Draven's form, a twisted mockery of her beloved. Anger surged within her, and she kicked his shin with all her might. The illusion of Draven wavered like a mirage.

He snarled and grabbed a handful of her hair, yanking her head back painfully. His cloying scent, a sickening blend of sweat and decay, filled her nose, making her stomach churn. "I will cut off your foot if you kick me again," he threatened, his voice a venomous hiss.

"Drop the façade," she commanded, her voice steady despite the turmoil roiling inside her.

He chuckled, a dark, sinister sound that reverberated through the cold, damp air. "I don't think so. What better way to screw with your mind than having the image of your husband beat you to within an inch of your life?" His eyes glittered with cruel amusement as he spoke.

She swallowed hard, her throat dry and constricted. The metallic tingle of fear lingered on her tongue as he yanked her forward with a vicious tug. The rough stone floor slid against her feet, and the cold, oppressive air pressed in around her, heightening her sense of helplessness.

He gripped her arm with an ironclad hold, his fingers digging painfully into her flesh as he dragged her up the winding staircase. Each step echoed ominously in the narrow corridor, the sound amplifying her sense of dread. The air grew colder the higher they ascended, and Lanae's heart hammered in her chest like a steady pulse of thunder.

When they crossed into the throne room, the sudden shift in atmosphere was almost suffocating. Lanae shivered involuntarily at the view of the immaculate marble floor and the gleaming dais. The room was eerily pristine, every surface polished to perfection, erasing any trace of the carnage that had unfolded here three years prior. The contrast was jarring, a cruel mockery of the memories that haunted her.

Yet no amount of cleanliness could wipe away the horrors embedded in her mind. Rorik's dying screams echoed hauntingly in her ears, a ghostly chorus that resonated with her deepest fears. She could almost see the blood that had pooled on the floor, feel the oppressive weight of despair that had filled the room. The raw anguish of that moment crashed over her like a tidal wave, threatening to drown her in sorrow.

A man with hair as white as Rorik's stood with his back to them, his posture rigid and alert. The dim light of the chamber cast long shadows across his form. When he turned, the faint glint of light illuminated his face. A face that, if he had black hair, would have mirrored that of his brother. The one Draven had shown her in his memory. But what struck her more than the face from Draven's past was the heart-shaped crystal that was sewn into his chest plate. The Dragon's Heart. Except now it did not hold that vibrant red color she had seen in Draven's memories, as if all the power in the stone had been used and all that was left was an empty shell.

His gaze fell on the form Spric wore. His face blanched, the color draining away as though he had seen a ghost. He took an involuntary step back, his heel hitting the cold, unforgiving glass behind him with a sharp, echoing clink. Fear flashed over his features, contorting them momentarily into a mask of terror. "Viserion?" he asked in a whisper, his voice quivering with dread.

The illusion of Draven faltered before dissolving completely, leaving Spric standing in his true form. He cocked his head at his father, a curious glint in his eyes. "Who is Viserion?" His voice carried a note of genuine confusion.

Alestain's face twisted with anger, his eyes narrowing into slits. His voice rose, echoing off the marble walls. "Why the hell would you wear the illusion of the dragon king in front of me?" he demanded, the words laced with a mixture of fury and incredulity. The tension in the air was palpable, a charged silence settling between them.

"I wore the illusion of her husband, not the dragon king." With a brutal shove, he pushed Lanae forward, the force sending her sprawling to her knees.

The rough stone floor scraped against her skin, tearing at her clothing. She winced at the pain, but kept her eyes fixed on the man in front of her.

Alestain's face twisted with rage, his eyes burning with a fierce intensity. "You dare mock me with such trickery?" His thunderous roar echoed through the chamber. He took a step forward, his presence menacing, but Spric remained unperturbed, a smirk playing on his lips.

Lanae's heart ricocheted in her ribs, each beat a painful sign of her vulnerability. The memories of her captivity and the torment she endured flooded her mind, but she forced herself to focus, to find a way out of this hellhole.

Spric's eyes gleamed with malice as he turned to Alestain. "You misunderstand, Father. It's not mockery. It's a lesson." He reached down, grabbing Lanae's chin and forcing her to look up at him. "A lesson in justice."

Alestain's expression shifted, a flicker of uncertainty crossing his features. He glanced at Lanae. "What lesson?"

Spric's grip tightened, his fingers digging into her skin like iron claws. "The lesson that no one is beyond the law," he snarled at her before meeting his father's gaze.

A tremor ran down Lanae's spine at his words, a shiver of dread that she couldn't suppress. She could see the twisted satisfaction in Spric's eyes, the malevolent gleam that revealed how much he enjoyed her suffering. The room shrank around her, the air saturated with the scent of damp stone and fear. But she refused to break. Gritting her teeth, she summoned her strength, preparing for whatever came next. Her heart went on a spree, drumming a rapid beat in her ears.

"What fucking law?" she spat, the words slipping out in a fiery outburst of defiance. Her voice echoed sharply in the confined space.

"You killed a king," Alestain snapped, his tone harsh and accusatory, reverberating off the cold stone walls. A damning indictment that only deepened the oppressive atmosphere.

"A king who exiled you for killing all the dragons." Every syllable was tinged with quiet defiance. She didn't deny killing Xoltan because that would implicate Draven, and her protective instincts were far stronger than her sense of self-preservation. Her eyes, intense and unyielding, bore into Alestain's with a fierceness that mirrored the storm brewing outside. "Which clearly wasn't the case."

Alestain blinked several times, the flickering torchlight casting shifting shadows across his face, before his eyes narrowed into sharp, probing slits. "You are the wife of the new dragon king?" His voice was low, almost a growl, filled with distrust.

"There is no dragon king. Solstice City is run by the Fae Council. We are not a monarchy like we once were centuries ago." Her voice held a quiet strength, unwavering despite the tension crackling in the room like a taut bowstring.

"Well, that will certainly change once I am through with it." He speared his son with a glare as cold and unrelenting as a winter's night. "Her pretty head on a pike will make a gory statement at the head of our army, don't you think?"

Spric's face drained of color, the blood visibly retreating, leaving him pale and wide-eyed. "Uh, sure?" His grip on her face loosened with a minor tremble.

It seemed like her captor might love to use his fists, but the idea of killing didn't seem to sit well with the young shapeshifter. The scent of sweat and fear permeated the room, mingling with the aroma of the stone walls.

"Once I awaken the army, we will deal with the murderess. Let her rot in the dungeon until it's time for her to meet her maker." The words were accompanied by a dismissive wave, his back already turned to them as he gazed out of the window at the twilight sky, lost in his own grim thoughts. The distant laments and howls of the wind outside seemed to echo the cold finality of his decree.

LANAE'S FOOTSTEPS ECHOED SOFTLY in the narrow stone stairwell, the air thick with the indication of earth. The flickering torchlight cast long shadows on the ancient walls, creating an eerie atmosphere. The silence stretched between them until they descended.

"You're not a killer, are you?" Her voice was audible over the creak of each wooden step.

"Shut up," he snarled, his tone dark and cutting like the blade he always kept by his side.

"Have you ever fought in a war?" She pressed on, her eyes narrowing as she sought the chinks in his armor. She could sense his unease, his reluctance to relive those memories. The scent of sweat and leather mingled with the cold air surrounding them.

"If you don't shut up, I will throw you down the staircase," he threatened, his eyes burning with a fierce determination, though his hands trembled just the slightest bit.

She fell silent, allowing the tension to build. The only sound was the rhythmic thud of their boots on the wooden steps. "Taking a life is not easy," she finally said in the confined space.

He halted, his breath hot and ragged against her face as he slammed her back into the rough stone wall, the impact resonating through her bones. He loomed over her, his body a wall of seething anger and muscle.

"I have never been a soldier during wartime. I've never had to kill," he growled, his voice a low, dangerous rumble that reverberated in the pit of her stomach, but his words confirmed her suspicion.

She met his gaze with a calm, soft understanding instead of defiance. "I never took it lightly." Her voice was soft and steady despite the closeness of his threatening presence. The sincerity in her eyes seemed to reach him, and he hesitated, the hard lines of his face softening for a fleeting moment.

"Then you will understand why I will have to do what I am ordered to when the time comes," he muttered, the fire in his eyes dimming into a smoldering ember.

"I've only killed when my life was on the line. I never sought to deliver death. And I've chosen not to kill someone I viewed as an enemy." Her words hung in the cold, damp air between them, filled with the sincerity of her conviction. The chill nipped at her skin, a pronounced difference to the heat of the confrontation.

He stared at her, his gaze piercing, as if her words were chipping away at his will. His breath was a mix of frustration and uncertainty swirling in the limited space they shared. He stepped back, giving her a few inches of breathing room, but the tension remained intense. "How was your life on the line with my uncle?"

"He had a sword to my throat," she replied, the memory causing a slight tremor in her voice.

His gaze dropped to her throat, inspecting it for any signs of injury. The torchlight flickered, throwing shadows that danced across her skin. He scoffed and crossed his arms, his skepticism clear. The aroma of leather and iron saturated the air, blending with a subtle hint of fear.

Lanae gulped down a steadying breath, her chest rising and falling in a measured rhythm. She closed her eyes and summoned an illusion of her bolting down the stairs, the echoes of phantom footsteps and the imagined swish of her hair trailing behind her. The sound was convincing, reverberating through the stairwell.

Spric's eyes widened, and he immediately ran after the illusion, his heavy boots pounding on the wooden steps.

Lanae opened her eyes and took another breath, creeping up the stairs to the landing they had passed moments before. Each step was deliberate, the wood creaking softly under her weight. Her heart clanged in her chest, but she maintained her calm.

She turned the knob with a slow, careful twist and cringed at the slight creak it made. The illusion below held strong. The echoes of Spric's ranting about what he would do if he caught her filled the air, masking her movements. The door opened, revealing a dark hallway. She stepped into the shadows, her movements as silent as the night itself, and shut the door with the same stealth.

Leaning against the cold stone wall, she allowed herself a moment of respite, her breathing shallow and controlled. She then squatted as low to the ground as she could, her muscles tensing and protesting the position. Slowly, she threaded one ankle through her bound wrists and then the other. The iron cuffs bit into her skin, but she ignored the pain.

She stood and let out a breath, her hands now in front of her. She flexed her fingers and the warmth of returning circulation tingled through each appendage. With her hands freed, a surge of confidence filled her. She was ready to defend herself if needed. She silently thanked the gods above for twilight, this near to a full moon, knowing this was the time her powers were close to their strongest. Even these iron cuffs couldn't douse her power of illusion. If he had gotten her back in that cell, it would have been another story entirely.

Her eyes slowly adjusted to the murky shadows that cloaked the hallway. The air was cool and musty, carrying the scent of aged wood and long-forgotten secrets. She crept toward the first door, her heartbeat echoing in her ears. Testing the knob, the smooth, cold metal pressed against her skin. It turned easily, and she slid into the room, her breath shallow with anticipation. She hoped to find a weapon or something to pick the lock on her shackles.

The candles flickered, casting jittery, elongated shadows that danced on the walls. She paused, her eyes widening at the expansive laboratory before her. The space was eerily still, the silence almost deafening. Figures stood motionless at each workstation, lifeless yet ominously poised for reanimation. The flickering candlelight gave them a ghostly appearance, their shadows stretching grotesquely across the room.

Lanae moved cautiously through the labyrinth of tables, her footsteps a whisper on the cold stone floor. The air filled with burning wax and faint chemical scents. She glanced at the carvings etched into the side of each table, deciphering the intricate inscriptions that explained each workstation. Her eyes flitted from one word to another until they landed on "portals."

Her gaze shifted to the capped vials lining the table. There had to be a hundred neat green vials, arranged meticulously in rows of ten. The glass gleamed faintly, the liquid inside shimmering with a mysterious allure.

She reached for them, her fingers brushing against the cool glass. The room suddenly came alive with the sound of rustling fabric and the creak of ancient joints. As if on cue, the figures in the room started to move all at once.

CHAPTER SEVEN
Parental Struggles

TWILIGHT PAINTED THE SKY the color of the pink highlights in Lanae's hair, the hues blending with the soft lavender and deepening indigo of the evening. Draven took a breath, calming his jumbled nerves, the crisp night air filling his lungs and grounding him in the present.

"Focus," he whispered, his breath forming a misty cloud in the cooling air. The key to opening portals was homing in on where you wanted it to drop you before you cast the spell. He did not want to be dropped right in the middle of the throne room. If Alestain was there and had reanimated the army, that would be a dangerous place to appear. Same with showing up where they destroyed the mind machine.

His thoughts jumped to the room where he found Caelum in a compromising position. The memory brought a slight flush to his cheeks, but it was a safer place to materialize than either of the other rooms that held disturbing memories.

He uttered the spell in the guttural language of his kin, the ancient words rumbling through his chest, and the air churned like a rising storm. The draconian words took no time to open a vortex between worlds before him. He stepped through it without the usual tug and tumble of a normal portal. This was more like stepping from one room to another, or over a threshold of a house, the transition smooth and seamless.

The minute both his feet touched down on the cool obsidian floor, the portal hissed out of existence behind him. He stared at the ashes at the foot of the bed, the remnants of what once was a figure now a scattered, fragile dust. Time had knocked the ash-formed figure into a delicate pile. Nothing in the room had changed, not even the discarded clothing on the floor. The air was stale, carrying a faint scent of decay and old fabric.

He picked up the shirt and the skirt, the fabric rough and brittle in his hands, and tossed them over the conspicuous pile, covering it from view. He chewed on his lip, the motion mingling with his thoughts, and glanced at the bedroom door, wondering whether the halls were safe.

He stepped toward the door, his boots barely making a sound on the hard floor. The sudden noise in the hall had him backing up quickly. His heart whirred in pace with a galloping horse's hoofbeats. He scanned the room, his eyes darting to every shadow. When his gaze landed on the wardrobe, he moved, slipping inside as stealthy as a ghost, the wood creaking under his weight. The bedroom door opened, and then someone yelled, "Clear!" before slamming it shut again.

Draven let out a breath he didn't realize he was holding, the tension draining from his body. He sagged on the back wall, which shifted with a soft click, revealing a hidden path through the walls. He nearly laughed, remembering the secret passages in their castle long ago. The memory brought a brief smile to his lips.

He slid inside the narrow passage, the walls pressing close against his shoulders. He sucked in his stomach and shuffled through the tight space, the stone walls cool and rough against his skin.

A familiar voice boomed, stopping him in his tracks. The sound reverberated through the cold stone walls, sending a quiver tripping up his back.

"I am Alestain Firetwill. You now bow to me." The voice was deep and authoritative, filling the cavernous space with its oppressive weight.

Cold fury gripped Draven, his muscles tensing like coiled springs. He squeezed his eyes shut and fisted his hands, the rough texture of the worn leather gloves biting into his palms. He couldn't light this place on fire with the possibility of Lanae being here. As much as he wanted to raze this castle and reclaim the Dragon's Heart, he had to find her first.

After a moment, a chorus of voices replied, "Yes, master." Their unified response echoed eerily, like a dissonant symphony in the vast chamber.

"I want this castle cleaned and polished until it shines."

"Yes, master."

"Find my son and bring the prisoner up from the dungeon. It's time to enact justice for my brother's death." The command was filled with icy determination, each word cutting and precise.

The patter of running feet leaving the throne room echoed through the tight space, bouncing off the ancient stone walls. Draven moved with purpose, his footsteps light and swift. A cool draft filtered through the narrow corridor, carrying with it a bouquet of mildew and decay.

He moved until he found a staircase, the worn steps descending into darkness. The flickering torchlight cast elongated shadows that danced eerily on the walls. The air grew colder as he descended; the chill seeped through his clothes and bit at his skin. He had to get to Lanae before the minions did.

LANAE'S FINGERS TREMBLED AS she grabbed a handful of the green vials, their glass surfaces cool and smooth against her skin. With a sweeping motion, she knocked the remaining vials to the floor. The sound of shattering glass echoed around the room, a chaotic symphony as dozens of portals tore open, distorting the air with a shimmering iridescence.

She staggered back, her vision momentarily obscured by the swirling vortexes that blocked her view of the people reanimating in the room. Her heart pounded wildly in her chest, each beat a drum of urgency as she darted toward a door at the back. The vials clinked together as she slid them into her shirt, keeping one gripped tightly in her hand.

The hallway buzzed around her, the faint hum of arcane energy vibrating through the walls. She thought of home, the image of safety and warmth flickering in her mind as she tossed the vial to the ground. A brilliant flash of light erupted as the portal opened.

Spric's thunderous footsteps echoed as he barreled down the hall after her.

She dove through the gateway, tasting the sweetness of freedom as the sensation of space bending gripped her. She plopped on the hardwood floor of her home's entryway in Solstice City. Her relief was cut short as Spric crashed down on top of her, his eyes wild with fury.

"Oh, no you don't." His breath hissed in her ear.

One vial freed from her shirt and rolled on the hardwood as she scrambled to get away, her breath coming in ragged gasps.

Nero's squawking roar tore through the air, jerking both their heads up. A bolt of lightning split the room, its bright light momentarily blinding.

Spric threw himself off her, narrowly avoiding the electrifying strike. He swiped the vial off the ground and bolted out of the house, leaving Lanae heaving on the floor, her limbs trembling with adrenaline.

Nero turned and disappeared into the open door of her parents' bedroom with the same urgency as he had chased Spric with.

Lanae's chest cramped with the triple overdrive her heart jumped into. *Alestain had reanimated his minions.* Which meant her parents were awake. She jumped to her feet and slid into the room, her breath hitching at the scene before her.

Her father had his hands around Caelum's throat, his grip merciless. Her mother, frantic, was throwing belongings into a bag as if packing for a long trip.

"Let him go!" Lanae's cry rang through the room, mingling with the sharp, crackling sounds of lightning from Nero.

One bolt connected with her mother, causing her to stiffen; a small wisp of black smoke escaped her lips. Desperation surged through Lanae as she grabbed her father, trying to wrench him off Caelum. Caelum's face was turning an alarming shade of blue from lack of oxygen.

"Lanae?" Her mother met her gaze, a plea etched into her features.

"Tell Dad to stop choking Caelum!" Lanae cried, her voice breaking.

Her mother moved quickly, snatching a vase from the table and smashing it against her father's head. He crumpled to the floor, unconscious.

The vacant look of those under mind control returned to her mother's eyes. But before she could retaliate against them, Lanae grabbed

Caelum, his limp body heavy against her, and with Nero by her side, she dragged him into the hall and locked the door behind them.

Caelum gasped for breath, his chest heaving as he curled into a ball, tears streaming down his face.

I'm here. Lanae sent the thought, her heart aching with a deep, resonating pain. He moved closer, hugging her with a tight grip, his form trembling violently with sobs that racked his entire body. She brought her chained hands over his head, the cold metal links pressing against the back of his tunic, and held him close as the severity of the chaos that had just unfolded settled heavily on her shoulders.

"They didn't even recognize me," he sobbed, his voice breaking, each word a dagger to her heart.

"You were seven when they were taken. You've grown quite a bit since then." Her voice was gentle yet tinged with an underlying sorrow.

He nodded, but kept his arms around her, his grip tightening as if she were the only thing anchoring him to reality, keeping him from shattering into pieces.

"Where's Draven?" she asked when her breathing returned to normal and Caelum's sobs had subsided into soft, hiccupping breaths. The warmth of his tears soaked into her shirt.

Caelum pulled away slowly, and she moved her arms from around him, the chains clinking softly. He stared at the iron bindings on her wrists, his brow furrowing in concern, and wiped his face free of tear tracks. "He went to find you."

Caelum lifted his hand and touched her face, his fingers gentle and warm against her bruised skin. She winced at the contact and instinctively recoiled, the pain flaring sharply. She could only imagine what she looked like after the brutal beating Spric had given her—the swelling, the darkening bruises, the cuts that still oozed blood.

His words were slow to register, her mind foggy now that the last remnants of adrenaline had been exhausted. But when they finally sank in, her stomach plummeted, a heavy, nauseating drop. "What do you mean he went to find me?" she asked with a voice tinged with dread.

AS CAELUM STUDIED HIS SISTER, his eyes tracing over her bruised and weary features, an immense gratitude filled him...Lanae had come back in time to save his ass. The rumblings in the bedroom had been impossible to ignore, and the desperate need to see their parents had overridden every logical reason for not opening that door. He closed his eyes, seeking solace, and pressed his forehead to hers. Her skin was cool, a stark contrast to his own heated flesh.

"Draven went to Xoltan's castle to find you." His whisper was heavy with worry.

She let out a squeak of despair, her breath catching in her throat, and reached inside her shirt.

When she pulled out the green vials, recognition of the portal magic he had seen before registered. He swiped them from her hands with a swift motion, transforming from the devastated younger brother into the protector he had always been. The vials were cold and fragile in his grip, reminding him of the danger they represented.

"You cannot go in your current condition." His voice was firm, yet laced with concern. He climbed to his feet on shaky limbs, every muscle protesting the movement. He nodded toward her wrists, the bindings chafing against her skin. "At least let me get those off, and then we can arm up before we go on another suicide mission."

"I need to get him out of there." Her voice shook as she climbed to her feet, the strain of the situation evident in every syllable.

"And we will, but you need some patching up before we go." His voice was rough, each word scraping his throat now that his own adrenaline had faded. He worked a forceful swallow down his throat and flinched at the pain.

Nero squawked, his voice a piercing cry that echoed in the quiet room. Now that they were both on their feet, the griffin strode up to Lanae, his movements graceful despite his size. He nuzzled her gently, his feathers soft against her skin, before brushing a wing against Caelum. The touch was comforting, almost like a warm embrace, before Nero wrapped Lanae completely in his wings.

Caelum's throat tingled, and he reached up, scraping his fingers over the spot where his father had gripped him. The prickle of pain was fading, the magic of Nero's touch soothing the ache. He swallowed, this time without discomfort. "Thanks, Nero." His voice was filled with gratitude as he ran his hand over the griffin's head.

Nero unfurled from Lanae, tucking his wings neatly against his body before leaving the two of them to stare at each other's unblemished skin. The transformation was almost miraculous, their injuries healed by the griffin's magic.

"I love that griffin." Caelum forced a smile, the expression stretching the muscles of his face in an unfamiliar way after all the stress and pain. He nodded for Lanae to follow him to the kitchen, the promise of a momentary respite giving them both a flicker of hope.

A ROAR OF ANGER had Draven freezing in place. The stone walls, coarse against his back, protected him from being found, but that didn't stop his heart from drumming a staccato beat in his chest.

"She escaped. Find her!"

A wisp of a smile found his lips as he backtracked up the rickety stairs to the last offshoot. He could almost smell her—her familiar lavender scent—as he slid down another secret passage. The damp, musty air clung to his skin, chilling him.

Thundering footsteps shook the walls, causing dust to rain down, and then silence enveloped him.

He shuffled a few feet, the faint lavender scent guiding him like a beacon. The passage narrowed, and he had to hunch over, the stone brushing against his shoulders.

A thud echoed in the hallway, followed by a metallic clang.

"God damned griffin." The angry mutter echoed as if the person was right beyond where Draven stood. He pressed closer to the wall and the vibrations of the voice.

A door creaked open. "Fuck." The curse rippled the surrounding air, sharp and raw. "Are there any left?"

"No, sir. She broke them all."

"I'm going to hunt her down and torture her until her last damned breath." A beat passed. "Start making more."

"But sir..."

A choked sound reverberated through the wall, a strangled gasp.

"You. Start making more of the portal potion."

"Yes, sir." The door slammed shut with a resounding thud.

Draven stayed still and held his breath until the footsteps faded into obscurity. *Portal potion.* He nearly laughed, the sound muffled by the stone surrounding him. His wife had destroyed their ability to move freely from realm to realm. A grin stretched his lips. Her lavender perfume still wafted in the air.

Draven searched for a larger area in the secret passageway that would give him the space to conjure a portal. The narrow, damp corridor was lined with jagged stones that scraped his arms as he moved. He turned a corner and halted, his eyes widening. The dead end before him was the perfect space, a small alcove with just enough room.

He tilted his head to listen. The only sound was the faint brush of footsteps echoing in the distance. The musty scent of mildew clung to the air.

As quietly as possible, he uttered the draconian spell, his voice a hushed whisper that reverberated off the walls. A smile spread across his lips as the gateway opened, shimmering with a soft, iridescent light that revealed the comforting sight of his home. He crossed the threshold, and the portal snapped closed behind him with a soft hiss.

In an instant, a cold, sharp blade pressed against his chest, stopping him in his tracks. The cold, steely scent of the sword mingled with the familiar aroma of lavender.

He lifted his hands at Lanae's narrowed gaze, her eyes filled with suspicion. Her nostrils flared, drawing in a deep breath.

"Lanae, it's me."

"I will not be fooled by your trickery again," she replied, her voice as sharp as the sword she held.

CHAPTER EIGHT
Ally in the Shadows

*D*ID THE BASTARD REALLY *think she'd fall for this ruse?* She growled, a low, guttural sound, and pushed the tip of her blade through his leathers, smiling when he hissed. The cold steel met resistance, sending a shudder up her arm.

"Um. Lanae?" Caelum stepped into the room, the clinking sound of his lock-pick kit breaking the tension.

"It's the fucking shapeshifter son of that Firetwill asshole," she spat, her voice dripping with venom.

The man's green eyes, so much like Draven's, searched Caelum out in a silent plea for help, a flicker of fear evident in their depths.

"Are you sure that's him?" Caelum's voice held a wariness that made her itch to finish this dick off.

"He liked to screw with my head and use that form when he used his fists." She nodded toward the redheaded giant in their living room, her expression hardening.

"Nero!" Caelum called, his voice firm and commanding.

Lanae swore she saw a fleeting look of relief pass over the shapeshifter's face. It was a far cry from the horror he had displayed when Nero emerged from the bedroom, lightning crackling at his feather tips.

When Nero bolted across the room and nuzzled against Draven, Lanae gasped, her lungs robbed of breath. "You even fooled Nero."

"How did you know the image wasn't me?" Draven's hands remained in the air in surrender, his voice steady.

"I'm not disclosing that to you." Her voice trembled with uncertainty.

His lips tilted into a smile. "There was no electric tingle when we touched. Which was the same way I knew it wasn't you here in our home earlier."

She blinked, his words short-circuiting her brain. Then her gaze dropped to where she pierced his leathers and probably his chest with her sword. If she pushed hard enough, she'd spear his heart. She pulled the blade out, the sound of tearing leather echoing in the room, but she stood her ground. "On your knees."

He dropped slowly to his knees with his palms still facing her, the movement deliberate. He slid one hand behind his head and reached out to her with his other hand. "See for yourself."

"It's a trick." Her insecurity flared, and her heart jumped.

The image of Draven closed his eyes, his breath steady. "Caelum, hold a knife to my throat to make sure I don't move."

Caelum put the lock-pick kit on the table and crossed to Draven, unsheathing the knife on Draven's hip. He held it against the soft flesh of Draven's throat and nodded for Lanae to confirm this was indeed her husband. "If it isn't him, I'll gladly spill his blood."

Fear almost kept Lanae in place, but that small ember of hope ultimately had her moving forward. She lowered the sword and separated her hands as far as the chain would allow before she wiped her free hand against his.

That blessed tingling spark zinged through her, igniting heat in her chest. She dropped the sword.

The metal clattered on the floor. Caelum moved the blade from Draven's neck and stepped away, busying himself with the lock-pick set.

Lanae threw her arms around Draven's head, slamming into his body with the full force of her relief. Her tears dampened his shoulder as she released a sob.

He wrapped his arms around her, pulling her against him so every point on her body was in contact with his. The tender heat from his embrace enveloped her, his heartbeat steady and reassuring against her chest. The tingle of contact chased the fear and doubt from her mind, sending a gentle warmth through her veins. She sagged against him; her legs could no longer support her weight.

"I could have killed you," she whispered, her voice trembling with a mix of relief and guilt.

He kissed her temple; the gentle press of his lips soothed her frayed nerves. "It's only a flesh wound. I'll heal." His breath tickled her skin, carrying a hint of the familiar scent that always calmed her.

She closed her eyes, pressing her cheek against his shoulder. The rough texture of his leather tunic brushed beneath her fingers. The essence of smoke and herbs clung to him, a comforting reminder of home. His arms tightened around her, his hand gently stroking her back in slow, soothing circles.

The room was silent except for their breathing, the tension slowly ebbing away with each shared heartbeat. The rhythm of each steady rise and fall of his chest lulled her into a sense of safety she hadn't felt in days.

"I thought I'd lost you," she said against his skin.

"You'll never lose me," he replied softly, his words a promise that resonated deep within her.

She nodded, her tears soaking into his tunic, but she didn't care. She was home, in his arms, and nothing else mattered.

DRAVEN MET CAELUM'S GAZE. His eyes filled with a silent plea of appreciation, hoping his gratitude would be understood without words. The flickering torchlight cast shadows across Caelum's face, highlighting the concern in his eyes.

Caelum's cleared throat rasped in the quiet room. "We need to get those cuffs off." He rattled the set in his hands, the clinking of metal echoing sharply.

Lanae sniffled, her breath hitching as she released her hold around Draven's neck. The warmth of her body left him, replaced by a sudden chill.

Draven glanced at the iron cuffs, the cold, unforgiving metal pressing into her wrists. A burn ring, raw and angry, marred her skin underneath, the sight igniting a protective anger within him.

He grabbed her hands, the rough pads of his fingers brushing against her cold, clammy skin as smoke rolled from his nostrils. The bitter fumes of burning filled the air. "What exactly did that bastard do to you?" he growled, his voice rumbling like distant thunder. Iron didn't affect dragons the way it burned the fae. To him, it was only cold metal.

With a furrowed brow and narrowed eyes, he slid his index finger between her wrist and the iron shackle, the metal biting into her flesh. Focusing his fire to a point on the tip of his pad, the heat intensified. The iron glowed a vivid red just before his finger burst through. He sliced through the metal in seconds and tore it away from her tender skin. The stench of scorched iron lingered in the air.

He repeated the process with the second cuff, his actions swift and precise, then crossed to the kitchen. The iron cuffs clattered into a bucket of soapy water with a sharp hiss, steam rising as the water boiled on contact, cooling the searing metal.

Lanae followed, her wrists raw and bloody from the damn iron, the scent of copper mingling with the lingering smoke.

Draven took a drag of a breath, his aura shimmering with residual heat, then turned to meet her gaze. His eyes, a stormy green, softened as they locked onto hers. "You never answered," he murmured, concern threading through his voice.

"You distracted me with your fire." Her lips tilted into a wry smile, her voice a soft whisper. "They did nothing beyond what Nero healed. Just bruises and cuts."

"I should have razed that castle while I had the chance." He locked his gaze with hers. "But I needed to see that you were okay before I rendered it and everyone inside to dust."

CAELUM WIPED THE SWEAT and grime from his face, his brow furrowing as he leaned heavily against the doorway. "Maybe you should have," he muttered, his voice thick with regret and exhaustion.

Both Lanae and Draven turned to look at him, their eyes locking onto his disheveled figure. The air in the tense room charged with unspoken fears and unhealed wounds.

"Look, I was just as uncomfortable leaving that castle standing when we left three years ago," Caelum continued, his voice a low, angry growl. "And now that all those people are reanimated and under another Firetwill's rule, I'm not discounting the opportunity to turn it to ashes."

Lanae's eyes flashed with defiance. "Those people are not responsible for their actions." Her hands trembled despite the evenness of her voice.

"Just like Dad?" Caelum's anger flared, his face contorting with pain and bitterness. "If we unleash Draven from our moral binds, Mom and Dad will be free." He pointed toward the bedroom, where the relentless banging on the door echoed through the hall.

"And we will be no better than the tyrant we are trying to stop."

Lanae's quick volley back ruffled his nerves, her sharp words cutting through the haze of his fury.

Caelum's jaw clenched, the muscles twitching in frustration. Iron and sweat clung to the air, circulating with his recent near-death experience at his father's hands. His heart was a drumbeat of conflicted emotions. He looked at Lanae, her resolve unbroken despite the haunted look in her eyes.

Draven looked beyond him toward the dimly lit hallway, the flickering torchlight casting eerie shadows on the brightly painted walls. "Your parents reanimated?" His voice held a mix of disbelief and concern.

"Yes," Caelum replied, his tone laden with bitterness. "And my father tried to kill me. If Lanae hadn't come back when she did, I would be dead." His words dripped with the acrid bite of betrayal, the memory still raw and painful.

Draven crossed to the heavy wooden bedroom door, his footsteps nearly silent under the babel of bangs. He let out a frustrated roar, a primal sound that reverberated through the space and silenced the relentless pounding. The door shook under his fury, the vibrations resonating through the entire house.

Caelum raised an eyebrow, a flicker of disbelief crossing his features. He had only heard that type of roar from Draven once before—when Xoltan had bound them in the castle, demanding that Lanae provide humiliating favors in front of them. The memory sent a tingle down his back, the echoes of their captor's cruel laughter still fresh in his mind.

When the dragon turned back, his eyes, glowing like molten gold, swept over Caelum, visually inspecting him for any signs of injury. A burning wood scent hovered in the stillness, a signal of his brother-in-law's fiery temper.

Caelum's shoulders tensed under the scrutiny. His recent ordeal played havoc in the weary burn of his muscles. "Nero healed me, too."

"Good," Draven grunted, his voice a low, rumbling growl. But the aggravation remained carved in his features, like cracks in a stone facade.

LANAE WAS JUST AS mystified by Draven's outburst as her brother, her thoughts swirling with confusion and unease. But Nero's approach sidetracked her from them. The griffin closed the distance with a graceful glide, his wings rustling softly as they moved through the air. He gently brushed her wrists with his soft, downy wings, the feathers cool against her skin. The iron burns faded, albeit slower than her bruises and cuts. The tingle of healing took hold, a maddening itch spreading across her skin, and she had to fist her hands to keep from scratching.

"I need some air," Caelum said and left her alone with Draven and her now silent parents.

Draven sauntered back into the living room, his movements heavy with exhaustion. He unclasped his leather armor, the worn straps creaking as they were released, revealing a growing bloody spot on his shirt where her sword had pierced. The faint whiff of blood reached Lanae, tightening her muscles with alarm. She rushed to his side, her heart spasming in a frenzy in her chest. When she reached for his shirt, his hand shot out and grabbed hers, his grip firm but gentle.

"I am all right." His dragon eyes met hers. They gleamed with an inner fire before he blinked, the transformation complete, and his eyes shifted back to the emerald irises that made her knees weak.

"You are bleeding. At least let me clean the wound I caused." Her voice dripped with concern.

"Fine." He stripped his shirt, revealing a deep gouge seeping blood. His muscle-bound chest and tight abs would have made her smile had it not been for the severity of the injury. The coppery scent of blood filled the air, sharp and metallic.

"Fucking hell," she muttered and turned to Nero. "Please fix that cut." She pointed at Draven.

Nero strolled over to Draven, his feathers rustling softly as he moved. He brushed his wing over Draven's chest, the cool touch of his feathers smearing blood on his pristine wings. The griffin's magical healing touch worked, but the process was slow and agonizing.

Draven shifted in the seat, his muscles tensing and his face contorting in pain. He grit his teeth, the pressure building in his jaw. "I swear the itch is sometimes worse than the injury," he growled, his voice strained.

Lanae snorted a laugh, the sound tinged with relief, and left him to deal with the stitching of skin. She grabbed a few wet rags to clean off the blood, the cool water soothing her own raw nerves.

As she returned to Draven's side, she couldn't help but question the outburst. "Draven, what was all that at my parents' door about? It's not like you."

Draven's eyes flickered with unease as memories clawed at his mind. "My worst nightmares, Lanae. Every night, I see what could have happened and when you went missing, I thought the worst."

He took a cleansing breath, the sound shaky and uneven. "I dreamed of you being tortured, hurt, used, and broken. The thought of those nightmares becoming reality..." His voice broke, the vulnerability seeping through his tough exterior.

Lanae's heart clenched at his words, understanding the depth of his fear. The raw emotion in his voice pulled at her soul, and she reached out, her hand gently resting on his arm. The soothing warmth of his skin grounded her from her icy turmoil. "I'm safe now, Draven. They didn't break me."

Draven's eyes softened, the fierce determination in them burning bright. "I told you once that I would burn the universe down for you. I meant it," he whispered, his voice rough with sincerity.

She leaned forward, her breath mingling with his as she pressed her lips to his. The world around them faded away, leaving only the warmth of their embrace. Draven's hand slid into her hair, his fingers tangling in the soft strands as he held her in place. The kiss deepened, a surge of emotions passing between them—love, relief, and a promise of passionate protection.

CAELUM STALKED TOWARD THE barracks, all the frustration and aggression building up in his bones like a coiled snake ready to strike. His breaths were shallow and rapid, the uptick of his heart pounding a relentless rhythm against his ribs. He needed a release, and he knew just where to get it. The echoes of his boots on the cobblestones reverberated through the alleys, each step a resounding declaration of his simmering anger. The damp evening air clung to his skin, mingling with the aroma of rain and earth, grounding him in the present moment.

Granger stepped out of an entrance to a side street, his face shadowed by the dim, flickering rune lights above. The soft hum of the runes mingled with the distant murmur of the barracks, creating an eerie, almost otherworldly ambiance. Granger's presence was a sharp distinction from Caelum's stormy demeanor—an island of calm amidst the turmoil. The cool night breeze ruffled his hair as he took a tentative step forward. His eyes locked onto Caelum's, containing a fusion of respect and apprehension. A light aroma of leather and steel from Granger's armor permeated the air between them.

"Caelum." Granger's voice was steady; a quiet strength behind his words cut through the tension like a blade through fog. "I was hoping you'd come to the barracks. I want to thank you for coming to my aid today. If you hadn't shown up, I'd likely be in the dungeon awaiting a morbid sentence. They take desertion seriously." He cleared his windpipe, the sound echoing softly in the narrow alley. "I owe you a debt of gratitude."

Caelum paused, the strain in his muscles momentarily easing as he regarded Granger. "You don't owe me anything, Granger," he replied, though the roughness in his tone was softened by an undercurrent of sincerity. The flickering light cast fleeting shadows across his face, highlighting the tired lines etched into his skin.

Granger shook his head, taking another step closer, the gravel crunching softly beneath his boots. "No, I do. You saved my position, my life, and that of my family. I do not take things like this for granted." He straightened his posture, the determined resolve reflected in his eyes catching the light. "From this moment on, I swear my loyalty to you. Whatever you need, whenever you need it—you have my word."

A brief silence enveloped them. Granger's oath hung between them like an unspoken promise. The distant sounds of soldiers preparing for the night shift drifted to their ears, reminding them that there was a world beyond their conversation. Caelum could see the earnestness in Granger's gaze, the unwavering commitment behind his words. Plus, having an elite guard on his side could be a good thing, especially with his entire soldier career shadowed by his sister's accolades.

"Your loyalty is appreciated, Granger," Caelum finally said, a hint of a smile breaking through the hardness of his expression. "And I will hold you to it."

Granger nodded, the sincerity of his vow sealing their bond. As they stood there in the dimly lit alley, a newfound alliance was forged—one that would shape their future friendship in ways neither of them could yet foresee.

CHAPTER NINE
Love and Loyalty

DRAVEN LEANED HIS FOREHEAD against Lanae's. Her breath mingled with his in the quiet of their living room. The atmosphere was heavy with the lingering scent of lavender and the faint metallic tang of blood. She gently cleaned his chest with a cloth dipped in warm, soapy water, the soft fabric pressing against his skin in soothing strokes. With the banging from outside silenced and Caelum off doing God knew what to relieve his stress, Draven veiled his gaze and savored the sensation of the warm cloth gliding over his chest. He would have continued kissing her, relishing the taste of her lips, but she

433

insisted on cleaning the mess up before they revisited the heat building between them.

"How did your meeting with Varkir go?" Her soft murmur vibrated against his chest.

Her question pulled a weary sigh from his lungs. "Varkir said the Dragon's Heart no longer has any magic or power. But Alestain still wears it on his breastplate." He leaned back and met her gaze, the gravity of his words pulling his lips into a frown.

She nodded, the movement causing her hair to brush lightly against his cheek. "Makes sense," she replied, her tone carrying a note of resigned understanding.

"What do you mean?" He cocked his head, studying her unwavering gaze, the flicker of candlelight casting shadows that danced across her features.

"I saw it. But it wasn't the same as what I saw in your memory. It's just a clear crystal that he has sewn into his leathers over his chest," she explained, her eyes reflecting the dim light.

Draven dropped his head onto the back of the chair, the soft fabric pressing against his scalp as he stared up at the ceiling. "If it had any power left, I would have known while I was in Firetwill's castle." His voice reverberated with frustration and exhaustion.

She put aside the bowl and cloth, the clink of porcelain against wood echoing in the stillness. Climbing into his lap, she wrapped her arms around him, her embrace warm and comforting, banishing the chill that had settled in his bones.

He let out a small, quiet laugh, the sound a rough, dry chuckle that mingled with the crackling of the fireplace. "Varkir also said there was an ancient document somewhere that has the history of the Dragon's Heart, but his network was still looking for it." His voice rumbled low, like distant thunder, as he relayed the information.

She perked up, her eyes widening with a spark of hope. "Oh. That sounds like good news." Her voice was soft, almost musical, cutting through the heavy silence of the room.

"Eh. He wasn't convinced that it would have much insight." He lifted a shoulder in a halfhearted shrug, the movement causing a ripple of pain to spread across his chest. "Either way, I don't know that I'll ever shift again, never mind fly."

"You've had just as bad a day as I've had." She nestled into his shoulder; her hair brushed against his cheek, her scent making him think of a bouquet of roses and wildflowers.

"Yeah, well, I also made the mistake of asking the council and generals in the war room where my wife was." His words were laced with bitterness, the memory of their reactions still fresh in his mind.

Her form stiffened in his arms, and she shot a glare at him, her eyes narrowing with the bite of disbelief. "You what?"

Draven swallowed hard, the column of his throat rippling into a lump, making it difficult to speak. "I was not thinking. Plus, I was frantic to find you, and it was hard enough to get past the guards. I wasn't in the mood to be dicked around by the council." His voice was rough, like sandpaper, as he tried to convey his frustration.

"What happened afterward?" Her pouty lips formed a perfectly kissable scowl as she stared him down with narrowed eyes.

"You came out of the bathroom," he replied, the memory vividly clear in his mind; her eyebrows shot up and her eyes widened in surprise. "And Faide told you to go home. He'd deal with you later."

She blinked wildly, her lashes fluttering like the wings of a butterfly, and then hung her head. "Alestain's son is a shapeshifter."

"I figured someone was, because it certainly wasn't you. Nero wanted nothing to do with you, and your reaction to him being in the house was comical." He chuckled softly, the sound mingling with the crackling of the fireplace.

"How did you know for sure?" Her voice was just a whisper, as if she feared the truth.

He brought his hand up to her cheek, the warmth of her skin against his palm soothing him. "I touched her arm and there was no buzzing electricity between us. And with you, there always is. My nerves hum when we touch." He grinned at her, his eyes crinkling at the corners.

She nodded again, her expression softening like a wilting flower in the evening light. "He nearly fooled me as well." She turned and kissed his palm, her lips warm and soft against his roughened skin, like velvet brushing against stone. The magnetic pull of her gaze never left him.

His smile faltered, the corners of his mouth tugging downward as dark thoughts of what the shapeshifter could have done to his wife clouded his mind. "And?" His unease bloomed, and he tried to anchor himself to her words and not drift into a sea of dreadful possibilities.

"And nothing. But your image freaked Alestain out." She chewed on her lower lip for a moment, her teeth grazing the tender flesh. "Who is Viserion?"

The name of his father, spoken after so many years, brought a bloom of warmth in his chest, like a hearth fire suddenly roaring to life. "My father."

"Your father was the king?"

Her question, filled with innocent curiosity, amused him, as did her wide, imploring eyes, shimmering like moonlit ponds. "Yes. What did you think I meant when I said I was dragon royalty?"

"Royalty covers an awful lot of people." Her eyebrows slowly rose, drawing her forehead into gentle furrows. "That means you are a king."

He shook his head, a soft chuckle escaping his lips. "King of what? There is no monarchy left here. Besides, the council is doing a decent job of running things."

"King of the dragons," she said, as if that meant anything significant.

"Sweetheart, I am the only dragon left." His gaze dropped to her belly. A pang of tenderness and hope flickered in his soul. "Unless you aren't telling me something."

She blanched, the color draining from her face like ink from a washed parchment.

He pulled back, his brows knitting together as he studied her with concern. "You don't want children?"

"I do. Just not now." Her voice was a whisper, heavy with unspoken fears and desires.

His chest tightened, a vise grip of worry squeezing his heart, and he cocked his head, trying to decode her words.

"Not until this business with the Firetwills is over. Besides, you'd be an overprotective ass if I was pregnant during wartime."

Her clarified statement loosened the noose around his chest, a rush of relief flooding him, and he let a smile surface, a light breaking through the storm clouds. "I get it." He would be overbearing and unbearable if she were pregnant, and he knew it. Despite how adept she was with a sword, he would have a great deal of issues with her going out to fight for Solstice City.

The idea of her charging into battle with a baby bump under her armor tickled him in a grim sort of way. He could almost see it—her fierce determination undeterred, belly leading the charge. "Imagine that: you, sword in hand, shield on one arm, and a little warrior in the making on the other." He chuckled softly. "I'd be an anxious wreck."

She arched an eyebrow, a smirk playing at the corners of her lips. "You'd be more than an anxious wreck—you'd be a hawk hovering over the battlefield, and I don't think even the Firetwills would stand a chance against your overprotectiveness."

He barked a laugh, loud and hearty, the sound reverberating through the room and easing the burden from his heart. With a swift, confident motion, he pulled her to his mouth and kissed her deeply, his lips pressing firmly against hers. His arm slid under her knees, cradling her effortlessly as he picked her up without breaking the passionate kiss.

He craved some alone time with her, yearning for the intimacy of their connection. The thought of Caelum walking in on such an intensely private moment sent a wave of unease down his spine. He needed the assurance of their solitude, a sanctuary where he could spoil her undisturbed until she cried out his name.

Draven paced down the hallway to their bedroom, each step echoing in the quiet corridor. His heart danced with anticipation. As he reached the bedroom, he turned the brass knob and entered, closing the door firmly behind him and locking it with a decisive click.

The room enveloped them in a cocoon of warmth and familiarity. A hint of lavender drifted in the air, mixing with the subtle fragrance of her perfume. He gently set her down on the plush bed, the soft fabric yielding to their weight.

His eyes locked onto hers, the intense passion burning between them as strong as the hum of their connection. He reached out, gently brushing a strand of hair away from her face. "It's just us for the next couple of hours," he murmured, his voice low and filled with longing. "No interruptions."

She smiled, a slow, knowing smile that sent a thrill through him. This was their moment, a stolen piece of time just for them.

LANAE CAUGHT THE HEATED spark in his eyes and grinned. It had been a while since they had the time to explore each other. After the hellish time of being captive, she longed for the warmth and comfort of his touch. But she needed to wash away the filth of the dungeon first.

"Can we move this to the bath?" She cocked an eyebrow at him, her voice laced with sultriness, the suggestion hanging in the air like a tantalizing promise.

His smirk widened into an all-out grin, eyes twinkling with anticipation. "I've never had you in the bathtub." His voice hinted at a playful challenge, and he waved for her to lead the way.

A thrill raced down Lanae's spine as she turned and headed toward the bathroom, the cool tiles underfoot contrasting with the warmth radiating from her skin. The soft glow of candlelight flickered in the corners of the room. The scent of lavender and eucalyptus filled the air, a calming yet invigorating blend that seemed to heighten her senses.

She reached the clawfoot tub, its porcelain surface gleaming under the warm light. She started the bath and added her favorite soap powder. The rush of water filled the room like a soothing symphony. The sweet citrus steam curled in the air and created a cocoon of warmth around them.

He approached her from behind, his presence a comforting, solid force. His hands rested on her shoulders, the touch sending a quiver of anticipation through her. He gently turned her to face him, his gaze locking onto hers, embodying a mix of desire and tenderness.

"Let me take care of you," he murmured, his voice a low, velvety promise.

His fingers trail down her arms, igniting a path of sensation. As the tub filled, he helped her in, the warm water enveloping her like a comforting embrace. He followed, settling in behind her, his chest pressed against her back, his arms wrapping around her in a protective hold.

The water lapped gently around them, and they sank into the tranquility of the moment, their connection deepening in the quiet refuge of the bath. His hands roamed her body, not in urgency but in reverence, as if rediscovering every curve and line.

"I love you, Lanae Emberwing."

His soft whisper sent a wave of gooseflesh over her arms, and her nipples hardened under the soft, kneading stroke of his fingers. When his lips brushed her neck, she tilted her head back to give his mouth more access. The tickle of his tongue glided from the base of her throat to her ear, creating a molten heat in her core.

She moaned softly as his fingers danced over the bud at the apex of her thighs, heightening every nerve in her body. He played her like a fine instrument until a tidal wave of passion crashed through her. Her pants echoed on the marble walls, and he covered her mouth with his, tangling his tongue with hers in a sensuous war for dominance.

Lanae twisted in his grip and straddled his lap, lowering herself onto his hard member in slow sweetness. Her head tilted back in ecstasy as she slowly rode him. The water sloshed around them, cresting and ebbing in the same rhythm as their bodies.

She pressed her mouth to his, swallowing their keening desire. The kiss transcended time and space, launching them into a blissful orbit as they surfed the wave of passion beyond the flash point.

CAELUM STORMED DIRECTLY TO the sparring room, his jaw clenched and his heartbeat thundering in his ears. He needed to punch, hit, or swing a wooden sword until the searing hurt ripping through his muscles drowned out the anguish gnawing at his core. The last hour at home had been an unrelenting nightmare. The memory of his parents' blank stares, void of recognition, twisted like a knife in his chest. It wasn't until Lanae entered that any semblance of familiarity flickered in their eyes. And it was all because of her.

Jealousy was a venomous thing, he knew, but he couldn't help the bitterness that rose in his throat whenever the relentless comparisons to his sister shadowed him like an oppressive fog.

He stepped into the training hall, the warm glow of candlelight flickering against the stone walls. He stalled at the door, his breath catching in his throat. Only one soldier was inside, and her presence stole the air from his lungs. Jenna moved with a fluid grace, her maneuvers a dance of precision and power that left him in silent awe.

Caelum watched Jenna's every move, his own body tense and still as her elegance mesmerized him. The rhythmic sounds of her practiced motions filled the hall, echoing softly against the ancient stone. Her intensity and focus radiated from her, the way her muscles coiled and released with every swing of her sword.

He took a rapid pull of wind into his lungs, the cool air of the training hall mingling with the warmth of the candlelight, creating a strange, calming contrast. For a moment, the troubles of the past hour seemed to lift, replaced by the serenity of Jenna's fluidity and strength.

Finally, Jenna paused, as if sensing his presence. She turned, her eyes locking onto his, and a small, knowing smile curved her lips. "Caelum," she greeted, her voice smooth and steady. "You look like you could use some sparring."

He managed a nod, his voice caught in his throat. "I... I need to clear my head."

Jenna's expression softened, understanding flickering in her gaze. "Then let's begin." She handed him a wooden sword. "Sometimes, the best way to silence the chaos inside is through movement."

As they squared off, the tension in Caelum's body dissolved. With each clash of their swords, his frustration and jealousy channeled into something productive, something he could control. The physical exertion was a welcome distraction from the emotional turmoil, and for the first time in hours, a semblance of peace settled in his soul.

Through the sparring, Jenna's encouragement and guidance were like a balm to his troubled soul. Her presence, her strength, and her quiet understanding made all the difference, helping him find his balance amidst the storm.

As they finished the final round, both breathing heavily, Jenna lowered her sword and stepped closer. Caelum's heart swelled, a different tension rising within him. He hesitated for a moment, searching her eyes for any sign of uncertainty, but found only warmth and an unspoken understanding.

With a tentative step forward, he closed the distance between them. Jenna tilted her head, her gaze unwavering. Tentatively, Caelum leaned in, capturing her lips in a soft, tender kiss. The world melted away, giving him a brief respite from the chaos and pain that had consumed him.

A throat cleared, shattering the delicate intimacy of the moment, and Caelum stepped away from Jenna as if she were on fire. His skin prickled with sudden, icy awareness.

"You know that's not allowed." Granger's fierce scowl and crossed arms filled the doorway to the training room, his voice a growl of reprimand. The flickering candlelight cast harsh shadows on his stern features, emphasizing the disapproval etched into every line of his face.

Caelum's heart froze mid-beat and then launched into a tirade, anger and frustration bubbling to the surface. "I didn't think I'd be calling in that favor so soon," he snapped back, his voice tight with barely restrained fury. The air cracked with unresolved tension, their unsaid words pressing down like a heavy storm cloud.

Granger's eyes narrowed, a spark of recognition flickering in their depths. "You're playing a dangerous game, Caelum," he warned, his tone icy. "One misstep, and you'll lose more than just your privileges here."

Caelum's jaw clenched, the bitterness of the last hour resurfacing with a vengeance. "I've already lost my parents, Granger," he retorted, his voice raw. "What's a little more risk compared to that?"

Granger's gaze softened, a rare glimpse of empathy breaking through his hardened exterior. He sighed, the tightness in his shoulders easing. "Just be careful," he muttered, stepping aside to let Caelum and Jenna pass. "Don't let your emotions cloud your judgment."

Caelum nodded curtly, his mind a whirlwind of conflicting thoughts. He glanced at Jenna, her eyes filled with unspoken concern and support. Despite the prevailing chaos, her presence grounded him, providing a fleeting sense of stability.

As they left the training hall, Caelum couldn't shake the impression that this was just the beginning of something predestined. With Jenna by his side, a glimmer of hope sparked his determination into a flame that refused to be extinguished.

CHAPTER TEN
A Plea for Mercy

MORNING CAME FASTER THAN either of them wanted, and Lanae groaned as she rolled into her pillow, its linen surface cool against her cheek. Draven grumbled, his deep voice vibrating through his chest as he pulled her tighter, cocooning her in his warmth. She sighed, savoring the moment, the mingling scents of pine and leather from his skin enveloping her.

"I need to get up and get ready to go to the training grounds." Her voice was a murmur, reluctant to break the spell of their shared stillness. She rubbed his arms, kneading the taut muscles beneath her fingers, before peeling them off her and climbing out of bed. The cold air hit her skin like a wake-up call, and she shivered, glancing back at Draven, who now lay sprawled across the bed, his auburn hair fanning out on the pillow.

A sharp knock on the door interrupted her thoughts, echoing through the quiet room. She pulled on her robe, the soft, worn fabric brushing against her skin, and hurried to the door. The cold stone floor sent a chill up her spine with each step. As she opened the door, the scent of his honey tea wafted in, circulating with the faint aroma of candles burning low.

Caelum stood outside her bedroom, his posture rigid, a sealed scroll bearing the Council crest clutched in his hand. His eyes were shadowed with fatigue, matching the lines of exhaustion etched on his face. The golden crest shimmered, highlighting the dark circles under his eyes. He looked just as exhausted as she was. A silent understanding passed between them as she reached for the scroll, its weight heavier than the parchment itself.

Lanae took the missive, breaking the seal with trembling fingers. The parchment crinkled as she unrolled it, her eyes scanning the formal script.

Captain Nightshade,

You are hereby summoned to appear before the Council immediately to discuss matters of grave importance. Your presence is not only requested, but demanded.

By the authority of the Fae Council

Lanae's heart thundered as she read the words, each line of the summons etching an icy dread into her chest. She met Caelum's gaze, his tired eyes reflecting her own unease; the Council's demands draped on her shoulders like an invisible burden. The echo of Draven's confession from yesterday still lingered in her mind, sharp and troubling.

"I guess I should head to the training yard without you?" Caelum cocked an eyebrow, his voice a tentative bridge between their shared worries.

Lanae nodded, the motion causing a strand of her hair to fall across her face. She brushed it away absently, her mind already racing with the implications of Draven's slip-up. The scent of burning wood from the fireplace mingled with the crisp morning air, grounding her in the present moment.

She looked back at Draven, who had propped himself up on one elbow, his expression now serious. The playfulness of their earlier moments had vanished, replaced by a steely resolve in his eyes. His hair, tousled and dark, framed his face, shadowing his determined gaze. The atmosphere grew colder, the profound implications settling over them like a winter frost.

"It seems I have more pressing matters than training today." She handed Draven the scroll.

He scanned the parchment, the furrow in his brow deepening with each line. His grip on the scroll tightened, the paper crinkling under the pressure. "We better get ready," Draven replied. The determination in his tone was mirrored by the way he swung his legs over the side of the bed, the mattress creaking softly in protest.

"This is for me to appear, not us," she started, her voice catching as the enormity of the situation hit her anew. The scent of parchment and ink seemed to cling to her fingers, a tangible reinforcement of the Council's authority.

"Look, I got you into this mess. I'm not letting you take the fall alone. Besides, their rationale for not approving our marriage was ludicrous." Draven's words were filled with conviction. He reached his hand out, clasping hers. The strength in his grip relayed his unspoken promise to stand by her, no matter the cost.

The day that had begun with warmth and comfort now loomed with the uncertainty of what lay ahead. The soft light of dawn filtered through the curtains, casting a golden hue over their faces, magnifying the growing tension in the room. The air seemed heavier, laden with the grim anticipation of the Council's demands. The faint aroma of morning dew mingled with the lingering scent of the night's embers, grounding them in the present moment. They shared a fleeting glance, a silent acknowledgment of the challenges they were about to face together.

"Besides, I am the king of the dragons." He flashed her a cheeky smile, his eyes twinkling with mischief. The corners of his mouth curled upward, breaking through the tension like a ray of sunshine piercing through storm clouds.

DRAVEN SLIPPED INTO THE kitchen while Lanae finished dressing, the faint clinking of utensils and soft sizzle of the stove filling the quiet morning air. The aroma of freshly cracked eggs mingled with the scent of buttered toast, creating a comforting symphony of breakfast fragrances. He whisked the eggs with practiced ease, the golden yolks swirling into a creamy mixture, before pouring them into the hot pan. The toast popped up, perfectly browned, and he spread a thin layer of butter, watching it melt and seep into the warm bread.

Nero squawked, his feathers ruffling in agitation as he tried to steal a piece of toast from the tray. The crisp, buttery aroma of the toast seemed to tempt the griffin beyond reason. Draven growled a warning, his voice a low rumble that made Nero pause. The griffin's sharp beak hovered inches from the toast before he reluctantly backed off, his golden eyes glinting with frustration.

While the eggs cooked, filling the kitchen with the savory scent of breakfast, Draven opened the back door. The cool morning air rushed in, carrying the earthy fragrance of damp soil and fresh grass. He gestured for Nero to step outside. "Go get your own food. But remember the rules."

Nero gave one last disgruntled squawk before hopping out, his wings unfurling as he prepared to take flight. The clatter of his talons clicking against the stone patio faded as he disappeared into the early light.

Draven quickly returned to the stove, the faint hiss and sizzle of the eggs reminding him to act swiftly. He retrieved the eggs just before they browned too much, their savory aroma filling the kitchen. Carefully, he set the plate of eggs and toast on a tray, the golden hue of the toast complementing the fluffy eggs. Beside them, glasses of freshly squeezed orange juice gleamed in the morning light, their citrusy tang adding a refreshing note to the meal. The tray, with its carefully arranged components, was a picture of simplicity and care, a small island of normalcy amidst the morning's tension.

Lanae came in a few minutes later, her footsteps soft against the kitchen floor. She stared at the tray, her eyebrows knitting together in confusion. "We don't have time to eat," she said with a tongue that could shear a sheep.

"I know. But your parents are awake and will need nourishment," Draven replied, his tone gentle yet firm. He reached out, handing her a glass of juice, the cool condensation dampening his fingers.

She blinked at him as if the thought hadn't even crossed her mind, the realization dawning slowly. The room was filled with the mingling scents of breakfast and the unspoken weight of their responsibilities, a quiet testament to the care and consideration Draven had taken amidst their chaos.

"I don't think Caelum thought to feed them either." She drank what Draven offered and then placed the empty glass in the soapy water in the sink, the bubbles clinging to the rim as it sank into the foam.

Draven headed down the dimly lit hallway to her parents' bedroom with Lanae following him. The scrape of their footsteps echoed softly against the stone walls, the faint creaking of floorboards under their feet added a rhythm to their steps.

Balancing the tray carefully, Draven reached up to the top of the door molding, his fingers brushing against the smooth wood before finding the hidden key. The cool metal was reassuring in his grasp as he brought it down, the quiet clink of the key sounding like a small but significant moment amidst the morning's unfolding events.

He swung the door open, the hinges creaking softly in the early morning quiet. The room was dimly lit, the heavy drapes drawn tight, allowing only slivers of dawn light to filter through. The air inside was thick with a musty scent, mixing with the faint aroma of the breakfast tray.

As they stepped inside, Lanae's parents, disheveled and wild-eyed, lunged toward them. Her mother's once gentle hands now clawed at the air, and her father's eyes, usually filled with wisdom, were clouded with a frantic desperation.

Draven reacted quickly, balancing the tray with one hand while raising his free arm to fend off her parents' frantic attacks. The eggs wobbled precariously on the plate, and the juice threatened to spill over the rim of the glasses.

Lanae stepped forward, her voice steady yet urgent. "Mother, Father. Please, calm down. We brought you food." Her words seemed to pierce through the haze of their minds, and for a moment, there was a flicker in their eyes.

Her father hesitated, his movements slowing as he stared at her and then at the tray Draven had balanced on his hand. Her mother's hands dropped as if she understood her body's needs, her breathing ragged as she took a step back.

Draven carefully set the tray down on a nearby table, the clinking of the glasses a small sound amidst the tension. The aroma of the warm breakfast filled the room.

Lanae moved closer to her parents, her hands raised in a gesture of peace. "We brought you breakfast. Please, sit down and eat. You need your strength." The soothing scent of the eggs and toast seemed to reach them, and slowly, they calmed, their frantic energy dissipating.

Draven's muscles tensed, his senses sharp and ready to react if needed. The room was charged with the anticipation of potential conflict, the air heavy with the scent of breakfast and lingering tension. But as the moments passed, the familiar, comforting scent of eggs and toast, along with the grumbling of Lanae's parents' stomachs, coaxed them to the table without further incident. Their hunger overpowered their agitation, and they ate in silence, the clinking of cutlery a gentle, reassuring sound in the background.

Lanae backed out of the room, the flutter of her heart visible in the throbbing vein in her neck. The cool air in the hallway contrasted with the tension-laden warmth of the room.

Draven followed closely behind, the creak of floorboards under his boots the only sound breaking the silence, unwilling to turn his back on her parents even for a second. He locked the door with a soft click; the sound echoed in the quiet. He measured the metal key's weight, a small anchor of normalcy, before he let it go and returned it to its hiding place atop the door molding.

Then he wrapped Lanae in a hug, his arms encircling her with warmth and strength. The sensation of her pressing against his solid chest offered a small measure of comfort, a buffer against the turmoil that was evident in her eyes. The tension slowly eased from her body, and he held her close, his own resolve bolstered by the simple act of being there for her.

"We need to go," he said, even though he just wanted to stay here and hold her until the sadness in her eyes disappeared. The slight tremor in her shoulders as she inhaled through her nostrils resonated deep within him.

When she pulled away, the walls closed in on them as their reckoning loomed ahead.

LANAE THREADED HER FINGERS through Draven's as they drew near the Citadel. The cool, smooth touch of his skin against hers was a small anchor in the whirlwind of her emotions. Her nerves left her jumpy, each rustle of leaves and distant murmur of the city making her heart race. But the steady hum of their connection calmed her and gave her the steel spine she would need in front of the council.

She led Draven through the grand atrium, the soft echo of their footsteps resonating in the vast space. As they ventured deeper into the belly of the building, the air grew thick with the rich aroma of ancient wood and lingering traces of magic. The enormous tree at the center of the Citadel sprouted from the ground, its majestic branches growing beyond the top of the tower, casting dappled light that danced on the stone floor.

The winding staircase, intricately carved into the tree's bark, spiraled upward, inviting them to ascend. The texture of the bark was rough under her fingers as she gripped the railing for balance. Lanae led the charge up the stairs, the ascent making her dizzy as they climbed higher and higher. Halfway up, they reached an arched doorway leading to the council court, seamlessly carved within the great tree.

The council seats were masterpieces, their intricate designs showcasing the skill of the artisans who crafted them. The wood surrounding the floor was a rich tapestry of swirling patterns and delicate carvings, where guests and dignitaries once voiced their grievances. Today, it was where Lanae and Draven would submit to the council's questions.

The guest seats were carved to match the council member seats, each one resembling woven tree limbs, down to the finely detailed leaves. But they were empty today. Only the council graced this hall, and all eyes were on Lanae and Draven as they stepped into the center. The council's scrutiny was heavy on their shoulders while they waited for the flurry of accusations to fall.

Faide Frostvale stood before them, his usually stoic features marred with barely concealed anger. His violet eyes blazed with such force that Lanae's skin prickled. The room thickened with tension as Faide pointed an accusatory finger at Draven.

"Why is he here?" Faide's voice was sharp, each word like a dagger thrown into the stillness.

Draven's chest puffed out in defiance, ready to speak, but Lanae quickly squeezed his hand, catching his attention. The fiery energy of his palm against hers was a fleeting comfort amidst the rising storm.

"Because he is my husband and whatever punishment you seek to enact, he stands with me." Her voice was firm, each word a shield against the council's impending judgment.

Smoke billowed from Draven's nose, a visible sign of his mounting anger. He released Lanae's hand, crossing his arms over his chest. The muscles in his jaw jumped with restrained fury. "You know who I am, right?" His voice carried the edge of violence, a low growl that reverberated through the room.

Faide stared at him, his gaze unyielding. "You are a dragon."

Draven inclined his head, acknowledging the truth. Lanae opened her mouth to speak, but Draven put his hand out to stop her, his gesture commanding silence.

"Lanae is a superb warrior and a passionate woman. The kind of woman who is fit to be a queen."

The bold proclamation sent murmurs rippling through the council. Many of the members leaned forward with wide-eyed stares.

Warning bells clamored in Lanae's head, an uproar of fear and apprehension. "Draven," she whispered, but he cut a glare at her, silencing her with a look.

"I know the council has Solstice City's best interest at heart, which is why I have not laid my claim on this realm. But understand this: if you move to punish her for marrying me, then I will have to rethink my position." His voice was unwavering, the words carrying an unspoken threat.

"And what position is that?" Faide snarled, his anger barely restrained.

"I am the son of Viserion Emberwing."

The declaration sent a shock wave through the council. A few of the older members recoiled, their eyes wide with disbelief.

Draven's gaze pinned them with an unwavering intensity. "And as the son of the dragon king, the throne is rightfully mine."

Lanae held her breath, her heart picking up speed. This was not what she wanted. She had not come here for a showdown that would question the council's validity.

"From the looks on a couple of your faces, it seems you remember my father. But do you recognize who nearly wiped this city off the map?" Draven's voice echoed in the tense silence of the council chamber. The air crackled with Draven's unspoken threat hanging like a storm cloud over their heads.

"Your father," one of the bolder elderly council members said, their voice wavering but holding a note of defiance.

The chamber seemed to hold its breath, the tension like a live wire cascading across the floor.

Draven's sarcastic and bitter laugh filled the room, echoing off the wooden walls. It was a sound that cut through the air like a knife, filled with years of pent-up frustration and anger. "No." His voice dripped with disdain. "Alestain Firetwill cursed my father with the same type of mind control that you witnessed three years ago in our last skirmish with the Firetwills."

A chill ran through the air.

He continued, his tone laced with bitterness. "And then he stole the Dragon's Heart and used it to rid this realm of dragons and fae enemies alike."

The silence that followed was heavy, filled with the unspoken realization of the severity of Alestain's actions. The flickering torchlight cast eerie shadows across the council members' faces, their expressions ranging from shock to disbelief. The air charged with a storm of emotions that brewed beneath the surface as Draven's revelation sank in.

"You have laid blame on the dragons when it was one of your own who brought this realm to its knees." Draven's accusation flung out like a whip. His voice launched through the air with the force of a physical blow. The room vibrated with the intensity of his words, the echoes lingering in the charged atmosphere.

His eyes burned with a fierce, indignant light, and the muscles in his jaw tightened as he spoke. "We are protectors by nature. Not the war-mongering beasts you made us out to be." The heat of his anger radiated from him, and the council members recoiled, his accusation layering over them like a heavy shroud.

"And now Alestain Firetwill has woken his brother's army and will come to enact his final revenge on this city." Draven's voice resonated through the chamber, each word a harbinger of the impending doom.

The council members exchanged anxious glances, their eyes wide with the news.

He glanced at Lanae, the intensity of his gaze a silent acknowledgment of her bravery. "But not as quickly as we assumed because Lanae destroyed his ability to travel realms before she escaped his prison."

The council members' whispers filled the room like the rustling of leaves in a storm. Some leaned forward in their seats, their brows furrowed in contemplation, while others reclined, their expressions a blend of disbelief and grudging respect.

Faide's mouth popped open, and the anger in his eyes gave way to a flicker of something akin to respect.

The reality of Alestain's threat sunk in. The soft murmurs of the council became a backdrop to the sense of urgency that now pervaded the chamber, each member grappling with the implications of the news. The enormity of what lay ahead was undeniable.

"We are aware that the mind-controlled have woken. The dungeons are active with them trying to escape, as if the call to action has severed their ability to rationalize." Faide's voice echoed through the chamber like a stiff wind. His eyes still blazed with barely contained anger. "And while we were warned of the imposter in our midst yesterday, that still does not lessen Lanae's betrayal. She went behind our backs after we explicitly denied your union."

The tension in the room thickened. The council members shifted uneasily in their seats, their expressions carved with disapproval. The soft rustling of robes and the creak of wooden seats added a sense of foreboding to the moment.

The ridiculousness of Faide's accusation stung like a physical blow. The heavy silence amplified the magnitude of his words and sparked the fight within her. Draven's presence beside her was a reassuring anchor, his steady breath and the radiant comfort of his proximity grounding her amidst the council's misplaced judgment.

"My private life has no bearing on my ability to defend this city." Lanae's voice echoed off the timber walls, reverberating through the chamber like a clarion call. "I love Draven Emberwing and will defend him just as vehemently as I do this city. I did not require your approval to join my heart to his. It was not a betrayal of my position or of my loyalty to you."

Her anger at their judgment flared bright, a fierce heat that seemed to radiate from her very being. The intensity of her emotions caused fresh growth to sprout from the ancient walls, delicate vines unfurling and creeping up the wood, their leaves glistening with a vibrant green.

The council members watched in stunned silence, their eyes wide as they witnessed the tangible manifestation of her power. The cavernous space seemed to come alive with the pulsating rhythm of her determination, the recent growth serving as a testament to her power. The flickering torchlight danced across the fresh foliage, casting intricate shadows that mirrored the complex emotions swirling within the chamber.

Faide waved at the ivy vines crawling up the walls, their leaves rustling softly in the otherwise tense silence. "This is why we did not sanction the union. Your offspring will be the death of this city," he declared, his voice cold and unwavering. His words hung like a dark cloud overshadowing the room.

"Our offspring are none of your concern." Draven's statement carried a finality that fell like a bomb, the room recoiling from the impact. The air crackled with the dragon's silent threat, leaving everyone in the room on edge.

Lanae drew a lungful of oxygen, calming the mounting anger inside her. The cool air grounded her as she prepared to address the council. "We can have a discussion relating to your fears about our relationship later. Right now, we have a more pressing issue. Alestain wants Solstice City to be a monarchy that *he* leads. He is the threat we need to face. Not Draven."

Her voice was steady and commanding, each word resonating with conviction. The council members exchanged uneasy glances, their faces etched with combining elements of reluctance and recognition of the truth in her words. The air in the room seemed to grow thicker, the scent of the ancient tree mingling with the subtle aroma of tension and uncertainty.

Faide's eyes flickered as anger slowly gave way to contemplation. He glanced around the room, noting the pensive expressions of his fellow council members.

One of the elder council members, a fae with silver hair and a wise, contemplative gaze, leaned forward. "Alestain is the immediate threat we must address. His ambitions endanger the very foundation of our city."

Murmurs of agreement rippled through the council, the impending threat uniting them in a common cause. The room hummed with the collective resolve of the council, the ancient magic that permeated the Citadel responding to their determination.

Faide let out a heavy sigh, the stiffness in his shoulders visibly easing. "Very well," he conceded, his voice softer but still authoritative. "For now, we must focus our efforts on defending Solstice City from Alestain's forces. We will address the matter of your union at a later time."

Draven's grip on Lanae's hand tightened briefly, a silent acknowledgment of the minor victory. The air lightened as the oppressive weight of judgment lifted. The council members nodded in agreement, their expressions shifting from accusation to determination.

"What of your parents?" Faide asked, his voice softened by a hint of empathy, the usual animosity tempered by the seriousness of the situation. His eyes, though still stern, held a flicker of concern.

"They are awake, but they do not recognize Caelum or me." Lanae's voice trembled as she spoke, each word a bitter pill that she forced herself to swallow. The burden of her parents' condition brought forth her sense of helplessness and sorrow. The sting of tears bloomed in the back of her eyes, but she blinked them away, drawing strength from the power within her.

"I don't know what strategies you and the generals have planned, but I must implore you to curtail the killing if we are attacked." Her voice steadied, taking on a pleading tone as she addressed the council. "These people fighting with Alestain are not of sound mind. They do not have a will of their own." The enormity of the statement lingered, the realization of the enemy's plight adding a layer of complexity to their struggle.

"In order to free them from their prison, we have to eliminate the Firetwill line." Her words were a somber proclamation, the finality of the solution settling over the council like a shroud.

The council members exchanged glances, their faces reflecting a range of emotions, from reluctance to grim determination. The air was thick with the unspoken understanding that their actions would shape the future of Solstice City. Faide's gaze softened further, the flicker of concern now a steady flame. The shared burden bound them together in the face of the coming storm.

CHAPTER ELEVEN
The Calm Before the Storm

CAELUM BLOCKED ANOTHER BLOW from his sparring partner, the clash of wooden swords echoing through the training yard. Sweat trickled down his brow, stinging his eyes as he moved with practiced precision. The musty scent of old leather and iron filled his nostrils, mingling with the slight tang of blood from a scrape on his arm. Each strike reverberated through his bones in a testament to the physical demands of his training.

Yet his mind was miles away, replaying the memory of Jenna's kiss. He could still feel the softness of her lips and the warmth that spread through him, igniting a fire in his chest. The world had seemed to stop in that moment, the noise of the training room fading into a distant hum. Her scent—fresh like a field of wildflowers—lingered in his memory, a constant distraction from his sparring. His thoughts danced around the way her eyes sparkled with mischief, the way her laughter rang like a melody he couldn't quite get out of his head.

A sudden, forceful strike brought him back to the present, the impact jarring his arm painfully. He winced, tightening his grip on the sword. His sparring partner's breathing was heavy, mirroring his own exhaustion. Caelum shook his head, trying to refocus on the fight, but Jenna's presence was a persistent shadow in his thoughts, making each movement both automatic and surreal.

He yielded after another blow, his muscles aching from the relentless sparring. Dropping his sword to the ground, he trudged toward the cooler, his mouth dry and parched. The anticipation of the crisp, cool water made his steps quicker. As he reached the water trough, he grabbed a metal cup, relishing the coolness against his palm. He poured himself a drink; the water cascaded in a sparkling stream that splashed gently onto the rim.

He took a long, refreshing gulp, the icy liquid soothing his dry throat and revitalizing his senses. Wiping his brow with his arm, he sighed in relief, the brief respite giving him a moment to collect his thoughts.

His gaze wandered to the neighboring fields, where the more senior soldiers practiced with a disciplined grace. Their precise movements and the clash of steel echoed through the air, a symphony of martial prowess. Among them, his eyes homed in on the object of his growing desire—Jenna. She moved with fluid elegance, her every motion exuding confidence and skill. The sunlight caught her hair, creating a halo of golden light around her, making her stand out even more vividly against the backdrop of the training ground.

Caelum's chest thrummed wildly as he watched her, the memory of their kiss lingering in his mind. His senses were heightened, every detail of the moment etched into his memory—the softness of her lips, the sweet scent of her skin, the warmth that had enveloped him. He couldn't help but be drawn to her, his thoughts consumed by her presence even as he stood on the sidelines. The desire to be near her, to experience that connection again, was a fire that burned within him, making it hard to focus on anything else.

When Jenna finished sparring, she wiped a bead of sweat from her forehead and scanned the field. Her eyes quickly found him, a warm glow spreading across her face as she caught sight of Caelum.

The hint of a smile that tilted her lips was enough to send a rush of heat through his soul, melting away the exhaustion of the day.

Before he could savor the moment, a loud commotion erupted at the far end of the yard. Caelum's heart skipped a beat as Nero bounded toward the training field. Nero's powerful wings flapped, sending gusts of wind that kicked up clouds of dust. In his sharp talons hung the carcass of a cow, and his fierce golden eyes gleamed with mischief.

The griffin's arrival was a whirlwind of chaos. Caelum hung his head, swearing under his breath as the griffin circled the sparring field, drizzling soldiers with fresh blood. The coppery scent filled the air, blending with the earthy aroma of disturbed soil and the musty scent of sweat. Nero cawed triumphantly, as if his kill represented a badge of honor. The beast knew the rules. Draven was going to roast him alive.

Soldiers scattered in all directions, trying to avoid the troublemaking creature. The sound of armor clanking and hurried footsteps echoed around the field. At least they weren't cowering in fear like the prior day when Nero exercised his storm powers, summoning dark clouds and lightning. The environment was charged with the pungent scent of death, and the occasional breeze carried the whiff of fresh blood.

With an air of dominance, Nero came to a halt just a few paces from Jenna. His feathers shimmered in the sunlight, an array of pastel blues, vibrant pinks, and rich purples that were both beautiful and terrifying. He spread his wings wide, casting an enormous shadow over the training ground, as if challenging anyone who dared come near his meal. The sunlight glinted off his sharp beak, highlighting its lethal curve.

Caelum's hands balled into fists at his sides, his knuckles whitening. He crossed the grounds with determined strides, marching right up to the griffin. His breath quickened with the fury filling him, each exhale a harsh sign of his mounting anger. The closer he got, the more the oppressive heat radiated from the beast.

"What do you think you're doing?" he snapped, his voice a strained growl.

Nero's gaze flicked to Caelum with a glint of mischief. He lowered his head, and with a quick, savage motion, took a chunk of meat out of the dead bovine in his talon, gobbling it down. The sound of tearing flesh was sickeningly audible, making Caelum grit his teeth.

Jenna's hand landed gently on Caelum's arm, urging him away from the beast. Her touch was soft, a vivid disparity to the roughness of the situation.

He covered her hand with his and squeezed, drawing strength from her presence. "Nero won't hurt me," he assured her, his voice steady but tense.

Nero's head tilted, as if mocking Caelum. The griffin's eyes sparkled with a mischievous glint, seeming to understand the trouble he was causing.

Caelum put his hands on his waist and stared at the creature, his thoughts racing. The last time Nero grabbed livestock, they had been warned by the council of the consequences if it were to happen again. The memory of that stern reprimand made his pulse pound in his ears, adrenaline sharp on his tongue. "They will demand reparations, Nero." His low voice was filled with warning.

Nero cawed loudly, a sound that echoed across the field, and then took to the skies with his meal, powerful wings stirring the air into a frenzy. The gusts of wind carried the scent of death and disrupted the peace of the training ground. But the damage had been done, and all the guards would be talking about was the damned griffin and his propensity to pillage their livestock. Caelum watched him go, a mix of frustration and resignation settling over him.

He turned to Jenna, shaking his head with a wry smile. "I'm sorry. He's in a teen phase." He shrugged, as if that explained everything.

Jenna burst out laughing, the sound a sweet, musical relief against the tension hanging in the air. Her eyes sparkled with amusement, her laughter sending ripples through the stifling atmosphere. "Griffins are dangerous, Caelum," she said between chuckles, wiping away a tear of laughter from the corner of her eye.

Caelum lifted a brow, the corners of his mouth twitching in a playful smirk. "Just like dragons?" His voice was light and teasing.

Her laughter bubbled up again, and the sound was contagious. The way her eyes crinkled and her shoulders shook made it impossible not to join in. Caelum chuckled too, the shared moment of humor breaking the tension and lightening his spirits. It was a pleasant distraction from the chaos of the last few days, a gentle prod that even in the midst of trouble, there could still be moments of levity.

Their laughter echoed across the training ground, drawing curious glances from the other soldiers. Despite the blood-streaked field and the distant figure of Nero in the sky, for a brief moment, everything seemed right in the world.

"I'm heading off to clean up. Care to join me?" Jenna hooked her thumb toward the neatly lined houses where most of the soldiers lived. The houses, though simple, stood in orderly rows, their wooden frames weathered by time but well-kept. A fragrant mix of soap and fresh laundry wafted from the direction of the barracks, promising a reprieve from the grime of the training field.

Caelum glanced around, his eyes flitting between his sparring partner, the bustling training grounds, and the houses. The clinking of swords and the shouts of soldiers practicing filled the air. He knew he should decline, but the way his soul cried out for her was more powerful than getting into trouble with his superiors. A magnetic pull toward her filled him, a warmth that called him away from the rigid structure of his training routine.

After all, what he did on his lunch break really shouldn't be monitored by the powers that be. The thought brought a smirk to his lips, a hint of rebellion sparking in his chest. He could almost hear the distant chatter of his comrades, see the knowing glances they'd exchange if they saw him leave with Jenna. Yet, the prospect of spending even a few moments in her company outweighed the potential reprimand.

He took a step toward her, the decision made. The dusty ground crunched beneath his boots, and the cool breeze caressed his flushed skin, bringing with it the mingled scents of pine and earth. "Lead the way." His steady voice trembled with anticipation. As they walked side by side, the noise of the training ground faded behind them, replaced by the quieter, more intimate sounds of their shared steps and the crunch of leaves in the wind.

Caelum's heart pounded in tune with the carnal thoughts breezing through his mind as he followed her into her small cottage. The door groaned open, and a comforting warmth greeted him. The wooden floorboards creaked underfoot, each step echoing the rhythm of his racing pulse. The soft afternoon sunlight filtered through the windows and danced on the walls, shaping shadows that swayed like ghosts in a silent waltz. The cozy space was adorned with handmade quilts and rustic furniture, evoking a sense of simplicity. As his eyes adjusted to the change from the bright sunshine outdoors, his gaze fell on a small fireplace with the remains of a fire still burning, its warmth spreading through the room like a tender embrace. The crackling embers and the gentle ticking of an old clock on the mantelpiece created a soothing symphony that seemed to calm his racing thoughts.

The gentle creak of the door closing sent his pulse pounding, and he turned to Jenna. A soft ray of sunlight highlighted her face, making her eyes sparkle like twin stars. "Cute place." He forced a smile as nerves bit at his skin like a legion of red ants.

She stepped closer, eliminating the distance between them, and her warmth mingled with his own. "You look nervous." Her voice was soft, almost teasing, as it reverberated through the quiet room.

A breathy laugh escaped, and as he lifted a shoulder, the fabric of his shirt brushed against his skin. He licked his lips, tasting the lingering sweat from the sparring match. "I'm not very experienced. So, yeah, I am just a little." His voice wavered, betraying his attempts to sound casual. He discreetly rubbed his damp palms against his leathers, trying to steady his trembling hands.

She put her hand over his heart, and her eyes melted with his honesty. "I don't have that much experience either," she admitted, her voice a gentle whisper that seemed to wrap around him like a tender embrace.

The heat of her touch sent a spine-dithering thrill down his back, and his crazed heart quickened beneath her palm. His breath caught in his throat, and he struggled to maintain eye contact, his cheeks flushing with exhilaration. Her words resonated deeply within him. A wave of relief washed over him, easing the tension that had gripped him moments before. The intimate connection between them grew stronger, and he leaned into her touch, savoring the moment as his pulse synchronized with hers.

Their restraint snapped at the same moment, and they collided in a kiss that shed the breath from his chest. Her soft lips glided over his, and her tongue tangled in a dance that had him tearing at the clasps of her armor. She pawed at him with the same urgency, guiding him toward her washroom as their armor and clothing fell in scattered heaps.

Jenna guided him into her bathroom, and Caelum broke the kiss and glanced around at her sleek, modern lavatory as he slipped his boots off. He whistled, impressed by the layout and the ceiling-mounted rain showerhead that promised an entirely unique experience from the rustic soaking tub he was accustomed to. Before he could ask her how it worked, she yanked him into the stall with her.

She turned the knob on the back wall and water cascaded down in a gentle, enveloping flow, almost like standing under a soft, warm rain. He hesitated for a moment, letting the water trickle through his fingers, marveling at the sensation, and he grinned at her. The soothing warmth had his eyelids dropping closed as he surrendered to the unfamiliar but delightful experience.

"This is heaven," he whispered, letting the water loosen his weary muscles. The warmth wrapped around him like a comforting embrace, easing every ounce of tension from his body. Steam rose around them like a gentle mist, softening the harshness of the day. "I'm never leaving your bathroom," he added with a contented sigh, a smile pulling at the edges of his lips. The aroma of lavender filled the air, merging with the sound of the water cascading down his back, creating a serene symphony that lulled him into pure bliss. His hands slipped down her shoulders, and he pulled her to his bare chest. He opened his eyes and met her amused gaze.

"You've never taken a shower before?"

Her teasing grin sparked the fire inside him. Instead of answering, he kissed her again, tasting her lips before he moved to the crook of her neck and licked a trail to her ear. "Can't say as I have."

He spied a bar of soap on a nearby shelf and grabbed it, running the sweet lavender scent over her body, the suds glistening on her skin as they rid her of all traces of dirt from the sparring field. The warm water cascaded around them, creating a soothing symphony of droplets. Her eyes fluttered closed. A soft sigh escaped her lips as she leaned into his touch, the tension melting away with each gentle stroke.

There was something undeniably sexy and intimate about washing the woman he craved, and Caelum never wanted this to end. The tingle of her skin against his fingers left him on the edge of a precipice that he could easily jump into. Each stroke fanned the flames into a burning desire.

When he reached to put the soap back on the shelf, she gently grabbed his wrist and tsked him, a playful glint in her eyes. "My turn," she purred, taking the soap from his hand.

"Oh, by all means." Her feather-light touch lingered on his skin. As she lathered the soap, the silky suds between her fingers, he couldn't help but notice the way the steam swirled around them, creating an intimate cocoon that made everything outside disappear. The sound of the water, the soft rustling of their movements, and the steady rhythm of their breathing blended in perfect harmony. He had thought the shower itself was heaven, but the gentle glide of her hands running over every inch of his skin went beyond all expectations. It nearly undid him.

When she put the soap back and dropped to her knees, he groaned at the image of his goddess sliding her mouth over the tip of his throbbing member. Caelum threaded his fingers through her wet hair, pushing it away from her face as the water rained down around them. Her delicious strokes sent a flurry of emotions through him, creating a pool of heat in his lower belly.

"Fuck, Jenna." His hoarse whisper tilted her lips in a smile as she met his gaze and nearly swallowed him whole in a deliberately slow crawl.

His fingers tightened in her hair. Hell, every muscle tightened with anticipation as she sucked her way to his tip. A purr of approval rumbled in his throat, and although he wanted to tilt his head back and close his eyes from the intensity of this moment, he kept his eyes on her and the magic her mouth was creating at a cellular level.

She twirled her tongue around his sensitive tip. "Come for me, Caelum."

Oh fuck, she didn't. The fragmented thought barreled through his head as his body trembled against the need to obey her request. He pushed his hips deep, hitting the back of her throat. The sensation shot liquid heat from his balls through his entire form, and he roared with his release. The sound echoed in the bathroom.

She pulled away with a smirk, the corners of her lips curling upward. As the water cascaded down her face in a cool, refreshing stream, she leaned back and let the droplets splash onto her skin. The rhythmic sound of the water hitting her body created a soothing symphony. With a graceful tilt of her head, she filled her mouth, the liquid swirling around like a refreshing torrent. After a moment, she rinsed and spat, the water splattering on the floor with a satisfying splash. Finally, she stood, droplets of water tracing paths down her skin, glistening under the light.

His body trembled with aftershocks, and he wrapped her in his arms, kissing her tenderly and holding her close as if she were his anchor. She reached over and hit the off button on the shower;

the water stopped abruptly, sending shivers nipping at his spine through his overheated skin. The air grew chilly, causing goose bumps to rise on their damp skin.

Her generosity would not be ignored. With determination to hear her moan his name, he swept her off her feet, cradling her against his chest, and headed out of the bathroom. She giggled, a sound that seemed to warm the very air around them, and then pointed toward her room.

Leaving a trail of wet footprints on the polished wood floor, he carried her to the bedroom, their laughter echoing softly in the hallway. The scent of her favorite lavender soap floated in the air, joining with the fresh aroma of clean linens. He gently laid her down on the bed, his gaze never leaving hers, committing every detail to memory.

The world outside seemed to pause, granting them a moment suspended in time. The soft rustling of leaves and the distant chirping of birds created a gentle symphony, wrapping them in a cocoon of stillness. But it shattered abruptly with a brisk knock at the door, echoing through the tiny cottage like a thunderclap.

Caelum stilled, his heart drumming in his chest. Meeting Jenna's gaze, her eyes widened with alarm.

"Jenna?" a familiar female voice called out, cutting through the silence like a knife.

His breath caught in his throat as the reality of the situation set in.

"Your sister," Jenna whispered.

He rolled off her, his movements hurried but silent. The urgency in his voice was clear as he whispered, "Our clothes are in the hall."

Jenna chuckled softly, the sound barely more than a breath. "Your clothes are," she teased, opening a drawer and pulling out a fresh pair of undergarments. She slipped them on with a playful grin, clearly enjoying the moment.

Caelum raked his hand through his hair and shot her a look that clearly conveyed his lack of appreciation for her humor. "I can't go out there like this," he hissed, gesturing wildly at his obvious arousal.

Jenna snorted a laugh, unable to contain her amusement. "Raincheck?" She glanced at the bed and then back at him as she grabbed a clean uniform. With a swift motion, she slid it on, the fabric making a soft, rustling sound.

Heat brushed his cheeks, and he nodded, attempting to regain his composure. "You can bet on it," he muttered, a hint of a smile playing on his lips.

The knock came again, more insistent this time, rattling the door in its frame.

"I'm coming," Jenna called out, her voice calm and steady. She crossed to him and gave him a quick peck on the lips before twirling her wet hair into a messy bun. With a mischievous finger wave, she left the bedroom, leaving him to deal with his predicament.

A moment later, the front door clicked open and closed just as quickly, and the murmurs from outside the house faded into a low hum.

LANAE GAVE JENNA A once-over as she stepped out of her cottage and closed the door in a hurry.

Jenna's face was flushed, and her hair was hastily twisted into a messy bun, damp tendrils escaping around her face. The fresh scent of soap wafted from her, mingling with the earthy aroma of the surrounding woods.

"Sorry, I was just cleaning up," Jenna said, out of breath.

Lanae raised an eyebrow, a knowing smile playing on her lips. "It's all right," she replied, her eyes twinkling with amusement. "Ready to head back to the Citadel?"

Jenna nodded, smoothing her uniform and adjusting her hair one last time. They set off down the narrow path leading away from the cottage. The path was lined with tall, ancient trees that cast long shadows over them, and the air was filled with the earthy scent of the forest, mingling with the fresh aroma of pine. The soft crunch of their footsteps on the gravel path added a rhythmic undertone to their walk.

As they strolled toward the barracks, Lanae couldn't help but notice the subtle smile playing on Jenna's lips. "What's got you so amused?" Lanae asked, her tone light and teasing.

"Just thinking about how much of a mess Nero made this morning," Jenna replied, her voice carrying a hint of laughter.

"Nero?" Lanae raised an eyebrow.

"He brought another cow to the training grounds," Jenna explained, her eyes twinkling with amusement.

Lanae sighed and wiped her forehead. "That beast is going to be the death of me."

Jenna laughed, the sound like a musical note blending with the ambient forest noises. "Caelum handled it. Although he's not exactly used to being caught off guard."

"Yeah, he doesn't like surprises," Lanae agreed, her curiosity piqued by the way Jenna grinned. "Care to explain that grin?"

Jenna blushed but managed to keep her composure. "Not really." Her attempt to sound casual failed.

Lanae raised an eyebrow, a sly smile playing on her lips. She had seen the way Jenna and Caelum looked at each other, the unspoken connection between them. "Was Caelum with you in the cottage today?" she asked, her tone dripping with playful curiosity.

Jenna's eyes darted away, her cheeks flushing an even deeper shade of red. "Why do you ask?" she replied, her voice wavering.

Lanae chuckled softly, enjoying the moment. "Oh, no reason. Just curious if he was lending a hand with the 'cleaning up,'" she teased, putting air quotes around the last two words.

Jenna bit her lip, trying to suppress a smile. "Lanae, you're impossible," she muttered, her fingers nervously fidgeting with the hem of her uniform.

Lanae wasn't about to let her off the hook that easily. "Come on, Jenna. Spill the beans. Was he there or not?" she pressed, her eyes sparkling with mischief.

Jenna shifted uncomfortably, her gaze still avoiding Lanae's. She let out a resigned sigh. "All right, fine. Yes, he was with me," she admitted.

Lanae's grin widened, a triumphant gleam in her eyes. "I knew it! So, how was it?"

Jenna couldn't help but laugh at the absurdity of the situation. "It was...nice," she replied, a shy smile curving her lips. "We just talked and...well, you know."

Lanae's expression softened as she reached out and gently squeezed Jenna's shoulder. "I'm glad to hear it." She infused her voice with as much sincerity and warmth as she could. "You two make a good team, both on and off the field." The subtle scent of pine mingled with the distant hum of activity from the Citadel, creating a peaceful backdrop to their conversation.

Jenna's smile faded, her gaze dropping to the ground. "Thanks, but you know it's forbidden, Lanae." Her voice thickened with frustration.

Lanae's lips curved into a knowing smile as she shrugged, her eyes twinkling with mischief. "So was me marrying Draven," she replied, her tone light and playful. She was genuinely happy for her brother and his choice in Jenna, despite the challenges they would face.

She studied Jenna's contemplative expression, noticing how her brows furrowed and her eyes seemed to search for answers in an invisible distance. "It's only worth it if what you have is precious enough to fight for."

Jenna glanced up at Lanae; the flicker of uncertainty in her eyes sent Lanae's heart plummeting.

Lanae paused, considering the situation. Her mind raced through memories of her little brother—the laughter, the arguments, the hurt he experienced after his first infatuation. She gulped down a steadying breath, and her heart gave a kick. "Would you fight for him?"

Jenna's lips parted, as if to speak, but no words came. She swallowed hard, the decision settling heavily on her shoulders.

The road closed in around her as though the very air around them was holding its breath along with her as she awaited Jenna's answer.

CHAPTER TWELVE
Spy Network

INSTEAD OF GOING HOME after the disastrous council meeting, Draven peeled off from Lanae once she got to Jenna's neighborhood and headed to Mystic Spirits, hoping to settle his burning aggravation with a stiff drink. The narrow streets were bustling with daytime activity, the sun's rays casting a warm glow on the wet pavement that still shimmered from an early morning dew. The scent of fresh rain mixed with the earthy aroma of blooming flowers from the nearby market, filling the air with a refreshing fragrance.

As Draven approached Mystic Spirits, the sounds of conversation and clinking glasses spilled out into the street. He pushed open the heavy wooden door, the hinges creaking as he stepped inside. The bar was filled with natural light streaming through large windows, illuminating the dark, polished wood and casting playful patterns across the room.

Draven made his way to the bar, his boots tapping softly against the worn floorboards. He nodded to the bartender, a burly man with a mane of graying hair, and ordered a stiff drink. As he waited, he scanned the room, searching for a familiar face. The indistinct murmur of voices and the occasional burst of laughter created a lively atmosphere, but his gaze remained sharp and focused.

Just as he took his first sip, savoring the burn of the alcohol as it slid down his throat, he spotted Varkir in a shadowed corner, hunched over a table. The spy's nearly clear eyes met Draven's, and with a subtle nod, Varkir beckoned him over. Draven could see the flicker of unease in Varkir's gaze, a sure sign that he had valuable information to share.

Draven approached, his curiosity piqued. Aged wood and spiced cologne filled the air. "Got something for me, Varkir?" His voice was barely audible above the ambient noise of clinking glasses and hushed conversations.

Varkir leaned in, his breath carrying a hint of mint as he spoke in a conspiratorial whisper. "Our spy network isn't the only one in Solstice City."

Draven's grip tightened around his glass, the cool surface pressing into his skin, the anticipation mingling with his lingering frustration. "I'm listening," he replied, his focus entirely on the spy's next words.

"My sources tell me that Alestain Firetwill is working on a portal potion that can rip open the realms and let an army through."

Draven's jaw clenched, the news aligning with what Lanae had said. But she had destroyed all the vials before she came back. He gave a slow nod for Varkir to continue.

"They are using the Dragon's Heart."

Draven tilted his head, his eyes narrowing as he stared at Varkir. "I thought you told me the Dragon's Heart held no power?"

Varkir shifted in his seat, the wooden chair creaking under his weight. "It doesn't, per se." He bit his lip, glancing around to ensure they weren't overheard. "It seems if they chip off pieces and turn them into liquid, it allows them to add it to the portal potion ingredients they have and it magnifies it by a thousandfold."

Draven pinched the bridge of his nose as the tension mounted. "So, they are destroying the stone?"

Varkir shrugged, his expression one of resignation. "Alestain is chipping small pieces off for their use."

A low rumble of discontent came from Draven, and he took a larger sip of the drink, relishing the way it burned going down his throat, the warmth spreading through his chest. "Anything on that document you mentioned?"

Varkir pulled a parchment out from his cloak and handed it to Draven. The texture of the aged paper was rough against Draven's fingers. "I'd wait until you are home to read that," Varkir said.

"And one other thing. There seems to be a spy within the city that is feeding Alestain information on the troops."

Draven clenched his teeth. "Do we know how they are communicating?" His voice carried the sharp edge of frustration.

Varkir shook his head, his movements slow and deliberate. "My sources don't know who it is or how they are communicating. Just that they are." His features scrunched into frustration, his brow furrowing deeply, mirroring the tightness in Draven's expression. The dim light cast shadows on Varkir's face, highlighting the lines of concern etched into his skin. The air charged thick with tension, and uncertainty hung heavy in the space they shared.

Draven attempted to piece together what Varkir was trying to relay, and something did not add up. "Who told you this?" he demanded, casting a glare at Varkir, his ire increasing at the holes in the information. His eyes burned with intensity, the frustration clear in the tense set of his shoulders.

Varkir shut his mouth and closed his eyes, taking a deep breath. "My source is questionable," he admitted.

Smoke bled from Draven's nostrils, a visual manifestation of his rising anger. "Then why did you even bother to tell me this information?" he growled, slashing a glare at Varkir. His voice cut through the ambient noise of the bar.

"Because…if I didn't and it is credible, you'll have my head," Varkir responded, his tone tinged with fear.

He wasn't wrong. Draven took a breath and calmed the rising inferno in his chest. The heat dissipated with each measured inhale. "Take me to this source," he ordered, his voice steady but firm. He had allowed Varkir to run the network since they came back from Xoltan's castle free of Firetwill's mind control.

"Draven," Varkir started in a tone that screamed impossible. The desperation in his eyes was unmistakable.

"I have given you my trust in merging our spy networks. And this is the first time you've given me unreliable information. Why?" Draven's voice was laced with disappointment, his eyes boring into Varkir.

Varkir wiped his face, the frustration evident in the furrow of his brow. "As I said..."

"Don't give me that bullshit," Draven snapped, his patience wearing thin.

Varkir dropped his lids and grumbled as he hung his head. When he glanced up at Draven, his jaw tightened with resolve. "I can feel someone reaching out to Firetwill's realm. I just can't tell you who," he admitted, his voice heavy with the revelation.

Draven's eyes narrowed. "You? You're the unreliable source?" he questioned, his tone laced with disbelief.

"Yes," Varkir replied, his voice a strained whisper, the admission hanging heavily in the air.

Draven studied him, his piercing gaze searching for any hint of deception. "Explain," he demanded as his pulse quickened.

Varkir took a deep breath, his eyes reflecting a hint of terror. "I sense the echo of the call since the mind-controlled have awakened. I was under the blood curse for a long time, Draven." His voice wavered.

The stinging reek of fear burned Draven's nose, mingling with the ambient aromas of the bar.

"The pull of Xoltan's realm has fluctuated over the last couple of days, as if a communications channel has opened or portals have opened." Varkir let out a half laugh, devoid of humor. "At least I recognize the sensation and have been able to ignore the call to arms." He stared at the bottom of his drink as if it held answers he couldn't decipher, his fingers tracing the rim of the glass.

Draven's heart calmed as he processed the information. "Portals have been opening and closing," he stated, the realization settling in.

Varkir's gaze jumped to meet his, a flicker of fright reflected in his pale irises.

"Alestain's son has been here at least twice. He had the balls to kidnap Lanae and then try to pass his shape-shifting ass off as her." Draven's jaw clenched in anger.

Varkir's eyebrows shot up, and he leaned back in his chair, the wood creaking under his weight. "Why didn't you tell me that when we last met?" he demanded, his eyes widening in surprise.

"All of this shit has gone down since we last met," Draven replied, finishing his drink with a final, decisive gulp. The burn of the alcohol lingered in his throat. "Have you felt anything since last night?"

Varkir closed his eyes, his face tightening in concentration. After a few moments, he shook his head, the movement slow and deliberate. "Not since the early evening," he murmured, the frustration evident in his voice.

Draven reached into his cloak and pulled out the only vial left of Firetwill's batch, the green liquid shimmering under the pale glimmer. "I need this analyzed. Who should I go to?" he asked, spinning the clear canister in his fingers.

"May I?" Varkir held out his hand, and Draven offered him the smooth, cool glass. "Where did you get this?" His eyebrows cocked with curiosity and concern.

"Lanae grabbed three of them before she destroyed the rest that were lined up on a table in Firetwill's lab," Draven explained with a shrug. "She used one to get back."

"And where are the others?" Varkir's gaze intensified.

"She lost one in a wrestling match with Alestain's son." Draven pointed to the vial in Varkir's hand. "That is the last one."

"The best sprite I know who dabbles in portal potions is Jairamon. He guards the Isle of Dreams between his laboratory stints," Varkir said, his voice steady and assured.

Draven's chest rumbled with a deep growl. "He sold us a portal potion when we were trying to get Lanae out of the Citadel dungeons," he recalled, the memory flooding back with vivid clarity.

"While I know you can find the Isle of Dreams on your own, I can lead you to his laboratory, since I have some business I need to discuss with the sprite."

Draven nodded, and Varkir handed the jar with the green liquid back to him.

The two rose from their seats, the bar's ambient noise fading into the background as they focused on their next move. The cool metal of the vial in his hand reflected the light, casting small, shimmering glints around the room as they crossed to the door.

Outside, the sun was high in the sky, its rays casting a warm glow over the bustling streets. The scent of fresh rain still drifted on the air, interwoven with the fragrant aroma of blooming flowers and the city's earthy odor. Draven and Varkir moved swiftly, their footsteps echoing on the cobblestones as they headed toward the edge of the city.

The journey to the Isle of Dreams required a trek through the forest outside the city walls. A trek Draven barely remembered. The last time he crossed this way was with Caelum and Nero, looking for the magic to open Nero up to his ancestral powers. That had been one of the quests Varkir had sent him on while Lanae rotted in the Citadel dungeons. One that made it possible for them to beat Xoltan.

The towering trees formed a canopy overhead, their leaves rustling softly in the breeze. Shafts of sunlight pierced through the foliage, creating a dappled pattern of light and shadow on the forest floor. The air was filled with the sweet scent of wildflowers and the distant calls of unseen creatures.

Draven scanned the surroundings for any signs of danger. The forest was alive with subtle sounds—the whisper of leaves, the chirping of birds, and the occasional snap of a twig underfoot. Varkir walked beside him, the tension between them clear in their synchronized, purposeful strides.

As they closed the distance to the cavern that led down to the Isle of Dreams, the fog he remembered rolled like a living beast. It flickered and pulsed, casting an otherworldly glow on the surrounding trees. The path down was just as harrowing as he remembered, but without Jairamon guiding them, the climb was slower and more treacherous. They took care to place their feet on the slippery mud and shifting rock, cursing as the fog thickened around them.

When they reached the bottom of the ravine, the fog cleared, revealing a clearing covered in soft moss that glowed with a gentle, ethereal light. A lazy river cut through the ground, breaking up the lush land with a vein of bright blue, as if the water came from glaciers in the far north. The stream carved a path around an island of moss, and the familiar hum pulsed with rhythmic energy through Draven. Golden coins still littered both the water and the moss. There was more than he recalled, and his dragon growled in want. The shiny objects represented wishes of those who came to request wealth, health, or myriad things from this mystical relic.

Varkir led him beyond the Isle of Dreams and into a clearing. On the other side, a serene landscape of rolling hills lay beyond, with crystalline lakes and vibrant, dreamlike flora. A small, ivy-covered stone building that exuded an air of ancient wisdom sat in the valley.

As they approached, a sprite appeared at the doorway, his iridescent wings catching the light and creating a cascade of colors around him.

"Draven, Varkir," Jairamon greeted them, his voice melodic and welcoming. "What brings you to my isle?"

Draven held up the vial, the green liquid shimmering within. "We need your expertise, Jairamon. Can you analyze this?"

Jairamon took the glass vial and stared at the green shimmer of the liquid, the sunlight catching and refracting within it. "It looks like the same portal potion that I had given you to return to Solstice City." He uncorked it and took a cautious whiff. His brow creased, and he beckoned them inside with a swift gesture.

Draven stared at the door and raised an eyebrow, his broad shoulders tensing. He would never fit through the opening, never mind be able to stand up in the building. "You go," he said to Varkir, his voice a low rumble. After all, the man could become smoke.

And that is exactly what Varkir did. His form dissolved into a wispy, smoky tendril and slithered inside the house.

Jairamon stopped in the doorway. "I'll open the window so you can hear what we say." Jairamon met Draven's hard stare with a resolute nod.

"Thank you," Draven replied, his voice edged with impatience.

Jairamon stepped inside, and a window creaked open, allowing Draven to hear the conversation within.

The air drifting from the window held the scent of herbs and potions. Jairamon moved to a wooden table cluttered with alchemical tools and carefully set down the vial. "This potion...it's not just mine," he murmured, his fingers lightly tracing the glass. "There's something else in here."

Varkir reformed into his solid state, his brows furrowing. "What do you mean, something else?" His voice rose with suspicion. "Have you ever sold your recipe?"

Jairamon's wings fluttered in agitation, the colorful light scattering around the room. "I have never sold my recipe, Varkir. It is my creation, guarded closely."

"Then how did this unknown substance get into the potion?" Varkir pressed, his frustration mounting. "Who could have had access to your ingredients?"

Jairamon's eyes flashed with annoyance, his voice growing sharper. "Are you accusing me of incompetence? I know my own potions. This substance—it's not something I would ever use."

Varkir stepped forward, his posture tense, his shadow stretching across the room. "I'm not accusing you, but we need answers. This is serious. If someone else knows your recipe, they could be dangerous. We need to find out who and how."

Jairamon breathed slowly, visibly trying to calm himself. The ambient sounds of the valley outside amplified the tension between them. "I understand the critical nature of the situation. I will help you identify this substance. But I assure you, my recipe has not been compromised."

Draven watched the exchange through the small, ivy-framed window, his eyes narrowing with intensity. "Let's focus on analyzing the potion first. We can worry about the origins later," he interjected, his voice steady and commanding, carrying authority.

Jairamon nodded, his iridescent wings settling back into a calmer rhythm. "Very well. We will sort this out."

Jairamon went to his workstation, the air filled with the scents of various herbs and potions. He opened one of the intricate contraptions, its brass gears clicking softly. Carefully, he poured a single drop of the green liquid from the vial before recapping it. He moved a scope over the contraption and stared into it, his fingers deftly adjusting the focus. As he muttered to himself, taking meticulous notes, the soft glow of the laboratory's lanterns cast a warm, golden light over the scene.

Draven stared through the tiny window as a cool breeze brushed against his face. He exchanged a glance with Varkir, who lifted a shoulder in a nonchalant shrug. They both returned their gazes to the little sprite, waiting with bated breath.

After a few minutes, Jairamon pulled away from the machine and sent a curious glance up at Draven. "This is my recipe, but modified with something I have never seen." His eyes reflected a mix of confusion and intrigue.

"How many vials have you sold?" Draven's question rumbled through the room, causing all the glass to rattle, the vibrations echoing in the small space.

"Too many to count. Selling potions is my business," Jairamon scoffed, his tone defensive. He looked into the contraption again, his brow furrowing deeper. "It looks like blood was mixed in with my portal potion. But not fae blood," he added with a hint of concern.

The rhythmic hum of the laboratory's machinery and the distant chirping of birds outside were the only sounds that broke the silence.

Dragon blood. The thought pierced Draven's mind like an icy dagger. His heart pounded in his chest, each beat echoing with the revelation. The implications were staggering, and an icy dread settled in his stomach. He needed to get home to read whatever was on the parchment tucked in his pocket. If the Dragon's Heart still had traces of dragon blood, Alestain had the power to cross realms just like Draven.

CHAPTER THIRTEEN
Desperate Measures

LANAE TRUDGED HOME FROM the Citadel after a long day of standing guard, the creak of her armor reminding her of the battles she fought, both on and off the field. The cool evening breeze brushed against her face, carrying with it the scent of blooming moonflowers. She was lost in thought when Caelum sidled up next to her at the intersection of the cobblestone roads at the edge of their neighborhood. The cobblestones were slick with evening dew, dulling the echoes of their footsteps in the stillness.

"Hey, Lanae." He kept pace with her. His presence was a comforting contrast to the chill in the air. He slowed as they edged closer to the house, his expression dropping into trepidation. "We should try to reach them again." He nodded toward the side of the house where their parents' bedroom was.

Lanae sighed and nodded, her heart heavy with uncertainty. "I'm not sure it will do any good."

"We can't give up on them." Caelum shot her a determined look as they advanced toward the house, the gravel crunching under their boots.

Caelum had always been the one with the sunnier outlook. And she smiled at the hope lit in his eyes, especially after the last harrowing encounter they had with their parents.

The blooming moonflowers climbing up the front walls of their home let off a sweet, intoxicating scent as they approached their walkway, their petals glowing softly in the moonlight.

Caelum paused outside the front door, his hand on the handle. "Oh. I almost forgot. Nero slaughtered another cow today."

Lanae tilted her head back in defeat and groaned. "Just what I needed today." She marched through the house to the back door and swung it open, the hinges creaking. Nero pecked at a partially picked carcass, the cold metallic essence of blood blending with the garden's earthy fragrance. "What did you do?"

Nero had the sense to bow his head in shame, but the way his eyes tilted up to look at her made his supplication even more mocking. He lifted a talon and dropped a handful of gold coins at her feet, the clinking sound filling the silence.

"You think that will buy you goodwill from the farmer you stole that beast from?" She swiped the coins into her hand and counted them out. Although her words had been scolding, the sum he brought back would more than make up for a lost cow. But it was the principle of the matter.

Caelum rubbed the back of his neck and sighed. "I already reamed him on the training field. I think he's restless from the stress that we've all been under lately."

"You stay put. I don't want you flying off unattended again. Understand?" Lanae pointed at the griffin with a stiff finger, her tone firm.

Nero nodded slowly and then dipped his head back to his gruesome meal, the sounds of tearing flesh filling the air.

Lanae sighed, knowing that their bond with Nero was as much a source of strength as it was a challenge. She closed the back door and looked toward their parents' bedroom. "We'll deal with Nero later. Right now, we have more pressing matters."

Caelum grumbled and went about fixing a small tray of food for their parents, the clinking of dishes breaking the stillness.

Lanae needed to lighten the dark mood that blanketed the two of them. A playful smirk pulled at her lips, and she couldn't resist commenting on his earlier escapades. "Speaking of pressing matters, did I interrupt another 'meeting' with Jenna?"

Caelum's cheeks flushed. "Maybe," he admitted as he balanced the tray on his hand. "She invited me to her house after I reprimanded Nero."

"And how did that go?" Lanae raised an eyebrow.

"Um... I think I'm in love with her, Lanae," Caelum said softly, his voice filled with a hopeful fear.

Lanae's expression softened, but she couldn't hide her concern, especially after her conversation with Jenna earlier. "Just be careful, Caelum. You know the laws. If Jenna isn't willing to fight against them, you might end up with a broken heart."

"I know," Caelum replied, his voice filled with determination. "But I have to try. She's worth it."

She turned her attention to the bedroom door and gathered her resolve. Tonight would be different. It had to be.

They moved cautiously to the bedroom where their parents were held captive. Lanae's hands trembled as she slid the key into the lock and grasped the doorknob, pushing it open with a creak. The room was dark, shadows dancing across the walls. The stale odor of confinement filled her senses.

"Mom? Dad?" Caelum called out.

In an instant, their parents lunged at them from the shadows, knocking the contents of the tray over as they ambushed both Lanae and Caelum. Their attack knocked both Lanae and Caelum on their backs as their parents held broken glass to their throats. Lanae's heart clanged in her chest, her breath quick and shallow. The glazed, empty look in her parents' eyes hit like a sword in her midsection, reflecting the control that gripped their minds and the morbid possibility of death at their hands.

"Please, fight it!" Lanae cried out, tears welling in her eyes as she stared up into her mother's blank eyes. "It's us, your children. Remember us!"

Her mother's face contorted with confusion.

Lanae's heart ached, seeing the torment they were in. "Mom, Dad, you must break free," she pleaded, her voice breaking. "We need you."

Caelum lay still with his hands out at his side, staring at their father. His terror echoed in her mind as well as carved into his features. Pain at the rejection accompanied the mind-bending fear. "Please, Dad. Don't." His voice cracked, and a tear slipped out of his eye.

For a moment, their parents' eyes flickered with recognition. They recoiled from both of them, shooting to their feet with abject horror written on their faces. The shards of glass fell from their grip, clattering to the floor. But in a fleeting blink, the mental barrier slammed down, the mind control too deeply rooted.

A shaky sob rose in Lanae's throat as her parents' faces twisted in agony. The struggle was intense, a battle fought within their minds. Lanae climbed up on shaky feet and stepped toward them, reaching out in hopes she could touch the part of them that still remembered love.

But the control tightened its grip, and their parents' eyes glazed over once more. They hesitated as their features twisted into hateful glares, and they made a sudden dash for the door.

Caelum scrambled to his feet, and they leaped for the door before it slammed shut, but their parents were faster. The scraping of the lock being engaged echoed in the dark room.

Caelum tried the doorknob, and it didn't move in his hand. "They trapped us in here." Caelum banged on the door. "Let us out, now."

The only sound that came through was the slam of the front door.

Lanae crossed to the window in time to see two figures slinking through the shadows and slipping out of sight.

"Nero!" Caelum shouted, hoping the griffin would hear them.

From outside, Nero let out a savage cry and hopped over the fence in the back. He approached the window and beat his powerful wings against the wall, the sound like thunder against the night.

"Go get Draven," Lanae ordered.

Lanae and Caelum exchanged a grim look. Their parents had escaped, but at what cost?

As the darkness enveloped them, they held onto the faint glimmer of hope that still burned within their hearts. Together, they would face whatever challenges lay ahead, united in their relentless pursuit to free their parents from the chains that bound them.

DRAVEN MOPPED THE SWEAT from his forehead. His hand trembled as the sprite continued to examine the glowing potion. The laboratory was filled with the acrid odor of burning herbs and the soft hum of arcane energy. The thick and oppressive air weighed on Draven's shoulders.

The sudden beat of wings captured Draven's attention, and he looked up to see Nero diving from the sky, his majestic feathers glinting in the dim light. The griffin landed gracefully next to Draven, his talons digging into the earth with a soft thud. Nero cawed, pawing at the ground with a sense of agitation.

The griffin grabbed the hem of Draven's sleeve with his beak and pulled, his golden eyes filled with urgency.

A flare of anxiety coursed through him, and his heart ran amok in his chest. He turned to the small, grimy window and called out, "Varkir, I need to go."

Varkir met his gaze, his expression inscrutable. "I'll find you once Jairamon is done here," he replied, his voice a whisper against the backdrop of the bubbling potions.

Draven marched away from the sprite's laboratory, the chill of the night air biting at his skin. The sky was painted in deep hues of indigo and violet, with stars scattered like diamonds. It was late enough for both Caelum and Lanae to be home, probably preparing dinner.

"Home?" Draven asked the griffin, and Nero responded with an emphatic nod, his feathers rustling.

Draven spoke the ancient draconian spell that called his portal magic to the surface. The familiar warmth spread through his veins. The air around them shimmered and shifted, distorting the world for a moment. He reached out and grabbed a handful of the griffin's soft scruff, and they stepped through the portal together, emerging in the familiar confines of the living room.

The sudden pounding from inside Lanae's parents' bedroom nearly made Draven growl in frustration. The muffled voice that followed sent a jolt of dread through him, pooling in his belly like cold lead. He crossed to the door, his pulse quickening.

The key wasn't on the doorframe, nor was it in the keyhole. The knob resisted his touch, refusing to turn. "Lanae?" he called out, just to be sure.

"Draven, help us," came the desperate reply, muffled yet unmistakable.

"Step back," he yelled, bracing himself. He counted to three in his head. His dragon strength surged to the surface. With a powerful kick near the knob, the entire frame shuddered. "Damn reinforcements," he muttered, his breath coming in quick, frustrated bursts. They had fortified the door to protect against their parents escaping, and now he was paying for their thoroughness.

Determined, he stepped back to the far side of the hall. With a deep breath, he barreled toward the door, leading with his shoulder. The impact sent a pulse of pain radiating through him, but this time, the door groaned in protest. It was giving way, inching closer to rescuing those trapped inside.

With a determined glare, Draven took a step back once more, his shoulders squared and muscles tensed. He let out a frustrated growl, channeling his dragon strength into another powerful kick. The doorframe groaned, but still held firm, mocking his efforts.

"Damn it!" Draven spat, his breath coming in sharp bursts. The urgency of the situation pushed him to the brink.

Nero stood beside him, pacing anxiously and occasionally letting out a worried caw.

Draven pounded the door with his fists, the wood echoing his frustration. The door shuddered under the barrage, but stubbornly refused to yield. "Lanae, hold on!" he yelled, his voice strained with desperation.

His nostrils burned with his lungs' drag of air, his body trembling with exertion. With one final burst of energy, Draven hurled himself at the door, shoulder first. The impact sent a jolt of pain through him, but the door finally splintered and gave way.

Draven stumbled forward, his momentum carrying him into the room. He sprawled out on the floor, the sudden give of the door leaving him momentarily disoriented.

As Draven pushed himself up, the scent of dust and aged wood filled his nostrils. His eyes locked onto Lanae and Caelum, who were huddled together at the farthest point from the door. Relief washed over their faces. The faint, musty odor of the room blended with the lingering aroma of dinner, producing a disorienting olfactory experience.

Nero filled the doorway, his majestic form casting a protective shadow over them. The griffin gave a thankful caw, his feathers ruffling in response.

"Thank you, Nero!" Lanae's voice trembled with gratitude. She crossed the room to Draven, her footsteps echoing softly on the wooden floor. "And thank you for coming so quickly." She placed a whisper of a kiss on his cheek, sending that pleasant jolt of electricity through him, a spark of warmth amidst the chaos.

Draven nodded, still trying to steady his breathing as he wrapped his arm around her. Her warmth seeped into him, providing a brief moment of solace. "What happened?" he asked.

"They attacked us when we brought dinner in," Caelum said, his voice strained. He wiped his throat, his fingers coming away with tacky, dark-red blood.

The metallic scent of it mingled with the other odors, turning Draven's stomach.

Draven lifted Lanae's chin gently, his fingers grazing her soft skin. Anger mounted at the red scratch on her neck, an unwanted reminder of the danger they faced outside the fragile sanctuary of their home.

"We thought we could get through to them." Lanae met his gaze, her eyes reflecting the hurt and devastation that mirrored her brother's. Their shared pain added to the already stifling atmosphere of the room.

Draven's heart pined with the need to protect them, his resolve hardening with each passing moment. The scent of blood and fear lingered.

And now that danger included Lanae and Caelum's parents. The very thought sent a slice of fear skittering down his spine. Icy tendrils wrapped around his heart, making each breath a struggle against the tide of dread. He clenched his fists as the tremor of uncertainty rippled through him.

He shivered at what he might have to do to protect those he loved the most and what it might mean for their future. The image of Lanae's eyes, filled with hurt and devastation, flashed in his mind. He knew he had to be strong for her, for all of them, even if it meant facing the unthinkable.

CHAPTER FOURTEEN
Bitter Truth

DRAVEN DROPPED INTO THE worn leather chair by the fire, its warmth enveloping him like a comforting embrace. The crackling flames cast flickering light dancing across the room. He pulled the parchment Varkir had given him out of his pocket, its texture rough and ancient under his fingertips. He spread the fragile paper on the cocktail table in front of him, the faint aroma of aged parchment mingling with the smoky scent of the fire. He smoothed out the creases, as if that could soften the agitation growing inside his soul.

From the kitchen, the savory scent of dinner being prepared wafted through the air. Lanae and

Caelum were busy cooking, the clatter of pots and the sizzle of ingredients providing a backdrop to the evening. His hovering after the scene in their parents' bedroom had irked Lanae enough to shoo him away, her eyes flashing with frustration. None of them mentioned the unspoken truth that now hung heavily between them—her parents, free from captivity, would likely join the enemy side once the war began.

He shook the morbid thought away and focused on the words on the parchment. It had been ages since he had seen the draconian language, and his mind struggled to form the ancient words and their meanings. The faded ink and intricate script seemed to pulse with an almost mystical energy.

"What's that?" Lanae's voice broke through his concentration as she came into the room, wiping her hands on a dish towel. The succulent scent of herbs clung to her, mingling with the odors of the kitchen.

"An ancient parchment that explains the Dragon's Heart," Draven replied, glancing up at her. "Varkir procured it for me." He flipped his eyes back to the paper, its importance pressing down on him.

"Is it authentic?" She stepped closer, her curiosity piqued as she scanned the document. The firelight highlighted the concern etched on her face.

"Yes. This is in draconian." He tapped the foreign language, the rhythmic tapping a faint echo in the room. He glanced up at her.

Lanae's lips pressed together, a frown forming. "What if it's another trick?"

Alestain's brother, Xoltan, had manipulated them before, but Draven knew better. The rich, earthy scent of the parchment filled his senses, grounding him in the moment. Even if their history books had been spared, no one outside the dragons knew draconian. "We never taught the fae our ancestral language."

"Tell me what it says." Lanae moved to the chair opposite him, the flickering firelight radiating on her determined face. She waited, her eyes fixed on Draven with an expectant gaze.

Draven's hand hovered over the parchment, his fingers tracing the ancient script. The warmth of the fire caressed his skin, but it did nothing to ease the chill of uncertainty that settled in his bones. He swallowed hard, his throat dry. "What about dinner?" He nodded toward the kitchen, where the savory aroma of cooking wafted from.

"Caelum's got it," Lanae replied, her voice steady. She cocked her head, as if studying him, her eyes reflecting concern and curiosity.

Draven's pulse quickened, a reluctant thump against his rib cage. The enormity of the parchment's contents pushed down on him. The fire crackled, filling the silence that stretched between them. Hesitation gnawed at him, the fear of what the ancient words might reveal.

His mind raced, grappling with the significance of the Dragon's Heart and the implications it held. The creases on the parchment seemed to deepen, mirroring the furrows of worry on his brow. He inhaled, the scent of old paper mingling with the smoky aroma of the hearth.

Lanae's eyes held her unwavering trust. It was both a comfort and a burden. The flicker of hope in her gaze spurred him to push past his hesitation. He exhaled slowly; the tension eased just a fraction.

"All right." His voice carried a hint of the trepidation throttling his muscles. He read the ancient text, the draconian language rolling off his tongue with a sense of reverence and caution. Each word was heavy with a piece of his destiny.

The more he read, the more sadness flushed his skin, a heavy weight settling on his shoulders. It had been nearly a century since he had heard more than just a few spells spoken in his native language. The ancient draconian words, both foreign and familiar on his tongue, stirred memories long buried. His chest squeezed at the profound sense of loss, each word like a ghost of the past.

When he finished, he stared at the parchment with a lump in his throat. The firelight cast a warm, flickering glow on the delicate script. The room was silent, save for the soft crackling of the fire and the faint clatter of dishes from the kitchen.

"That was beautiful. What does it all mean?" Lanae's voice held reverence, her eyes wide with wonder.

"It means the dragons were the ones who fueled the stone's magic, not the other way around," he replied. His voice carried the bone-deep sorrow accosting him. The parchment seemed fragile in his hands, like the delicate threads of their history. "They annually offered their blood to connect to the stone." He bit his lip.

"It was a rite that I had not joined yet. When a dragon turned thirteen, that was when they joined the annual rite." He wiped his face with a trembling hand. Fate had seen that he never experienced that sacred ritual.

Melancholy painted her expression, making her lips pull down at the edges, and her eyes shined with unshed tears. The firelight reflected in her gaze, adding a glimmer of sadness. He looked away from her, swallowing his own tears at all he had missed, the bitter splash of regret lingering in his mouth.

"Once the ritual was completed, the dragon could leverage the power of the community if they needed to. And if the stone ever got into the hands of an enemy, they could wield it against us." He sniffled, the scent of old parchment and burning wood filling his senses. He let out a bitter laugh, the sound hollow in the quiet room. "According to the parchment, if that happened, all the dragons would be killed." Heat ran down his cheeks; a mix of anger and sorrow burned with the path of his tears. "And the Dragon's Heart would never hold power again."

"You don't know that." Lanae's voice carried a fragile thread of hope.

He tapped the parchment, the sound a sharp contrast to the silence. "Yes, I do. If they stopped the annual blood ritual and the Dragon's Heart's power died, it would take centuries of annual blood rites of the entire clan to spark it back to life. That's hundreds of dragons." He let that sink in. "And there certainly isn't enough blood in a single dragon to resurrect the damned thing."

Lanae reached over and took his hands in hers, her touch warm and reassuring against his cool skin. The soft pressure of her fingers sent a wave of comfort through him, momentarily easing the turmoil in his chest. She gently squeezed in a show of support, her eyes searching his face for answers. "What does this mean for you?" she asked with a voice filled with concern.

He laughed, a hollow sound that did nothing to mask his frustration. Uncertainty pressed down on him as he pulled away from her hands, the warmth slipping away. The worn leather of the chair creaked under his weight as he leaned back. He raked his fingers through his hair. The silky strands slipped through his fingers, tangling as he tried to collect his thoughts.

He had been counting on the Dragon's Heart to give him the power to fully shift, but knowing it was a dead crystal, where did that leave him? The flickering firelight cast shifting shadows on the walls, mirroring the chaotic storm of emotions inside him. The scent of fiery wood filled his nostrils, grounding him in the moment yet reminding him of the burning question that now haunted his mind.

"I don't know." His eyes found solace in hers.

LANAE'S THROAT CLOSED AT the soul-wrenching devastation reflected in Draven's eyes. The certainty that finding the Dragon's Heart would give him the ability to shift lay shattered at their feet, like delicate glass. Her back went ramrod straight as determination to wipe that look away raged through her, a fiery resolve burning in her chest.

"When was the last time you fully shifted?" she asked with a soft edge of fortitude.

His silence unnerved her, a heavy quiet that made her question whether he had ever shifted at all. The seconds stretched on, each one amplifying her anxiety.

"It was the morning of the day our world went to shit," Draven finally replied, his voice a hollow echo of pain and loss.

Relief washed through Lanae, a soothing balm against the raw edges of her worry. He had done it before, so he could do it again—even without the magical crystal. "Tell me about it," she urged, her voice a gentle coaxing.

Pain washed over Draven's face, his features contorting with the memory. "I flew with my older siblings. I was the youngest in the family, and my sister told me I could never beat them in a race. She was quite the brat at times, but I loved her, and I never backed down from a challenge." His lips tilted into a smile, a bittersweet curve that didn't quite reach his eyes. As he spoke, his gaze grew distant, the firelight casting shifting shadows on his face.

He chuckled softly, a sound tinged with nostalgia, and glanced down at his hands, the fire's glow highlighting the creases of his palms. "I finally beat them that day. I was faster than all my older siblings." His smile faded, leaving behind a hollow ache. "My mother looked so proud, but my father just vacantly stared at me and walked away. His lack of any sort of comment hurt, and I went to my room to lick my wounds.

My brothers and sister tried to console me, but my mother shooed them outside. If they hadn't gone outside, perhaps they would have survived."

The guilt layered over every word tugged at Lanae's heartstrings. Her own eyes burned with unshed tears. "Oh, Draven."

Draven's vulnerability shut down at the empathy in her voice. He stared at the parchment with his history and loss heavy in his heart. "It was supposed to be an extinction event." His throat bobbed as he swallowed. "Why was I spared?" His question hung in the air, a haunting echo of survivor's guilt.

"Perhaps because fate knew your soulmate wasn't born yet." Lanae offered a kind smile, her eyes softening as she cocked her head to the side.

Draven blinked at her, the flickering shadows reflecting in his eyes. He crossed his arms over his chest, as if shielding himself from her words. "Fate?" he spat out, the word carrying a bitter edge. His eyes shuttered, a spark of fury igniting in their depths.

Lanae lifted her shoulder in a delicate shrug. "I like to think fate knew better than to snuff out your life." She picked at her fingernail, the faint sound just audible above the crackling fire. "If not for you, I would be Xoltan's plaything." The solemnity of her words lingered, reminding them of the dark reality they had overcome together.

Draven grumbled, the sound low and rugged, and rubbed his face with a weary hand. The rough stubble on his jaw rasped against his palm, a physical manifestation of his inner turmoil. "I know. Fate is cruel, but at least she offered you as a gift to soothe my troubled soul." His lips finally tilted into a smile, a fleeting warmth amidst the tension. "Otherwise, I would have had to hunt down that fickle bitch and torch her into ash." The fire's glow highlighted the determined glint in his eyes.

A quick burst of humor fell from Lanae's lips, the sound light and airy. She pressed them together to stifle the laughter. It would be so like Draven to go after a presence like fate. She let the image linger in her head—Draven, fierce and determined, stalking an ethereal being. The thought lit a fire inside her, a flicker of warmth and amusement that momentarily chased away the shadows of their situation.

She had to shake it away and focus on Draven yet again. His presence, solid and grounding, drew her back to reality. "After we eat, we should go down to the training grounds so you can try to shift," she suggested, her voice gentle but firm. The scent of cooking from the kitchen mingled with the scent of smoldering fire, creating a comforting backdrop.

The humorous glint in Draven's eyes faded, replaced by a shadow of worry. "You know my fire gets unstable after attempting to shift." His voice carried a sour note of caution. The fire's glow highlighted the worry lines etched on his forehead, the flickering light casting shifting shadows on his troubled expression.

"What's the worst that could happen?" She tried to keep her tone light, but the underlying concern seeped through.

DRAVEN COULD NOT BELIEVE she even suggested for him to try shifting. She had seen how volatile he was after his partial shift years ago. And for her to say what's the worst thing that could happen? Aggravation built in his core. "I could sneeze and burn this house down. Or hurt you or Caelum or Nero." Draven's voice rumbled with frustration. He rubbed his face, the rough stubble rasping against his fingers.

"Or you could finally push yourself past your mental barrier and shift." Lanae's voice carried a sharp edge, her eyes hardening with determination. She crossed her arms over her chest, the gesture both defensive and challenging.

A surge of frustration welled up inside Draven, like a coiled spring ready to snap. "Mental barrier?" he repeated, his voice low and taut with tension. He ground his teeth together, the muscles in his jaw clenching painfully. The air popped with his unspoken resentment, the flickering firelight casting sharp shadows on her face.

Just as his anger threatened to ignite, Caelum stepped into the room, cutting off the scathing remark poised on his lips.

"Dinner's ready," Caelum announced, the scent of the meal wafting through the air, uniting with the whiff of burned essence of the fire.

Draven tore his gaze away from Lanae. A mix of anger and helplessness churned within him. Her insinuation pressed down on him, a heavy burden he wasn't sure he could bear. His breast swelled with an in-breath as he tried to steady the whirlwind of emotions that threatened to overwhelm him. The warmth of the fire did little to chase away the chill that settled in his bones.

Lanae stood and headed toward the kitchen, her heels clicking sharply against the hardwood floor. The small shake of her head to her brother nearly pulled a smoky growl from Draven, the bitter scent of his frustration filling the air.

"Don't unload my shit to your brother," he snapped, his voice echoing off the walls.

Caelum glanced at him with a hardened expression, the muscles in his jaw tightening. "She wasn't." He stepped in front of Draven as Lanae passed through the kitchen door, stopping him with a palm to his chest. The contact was firm, the warmth of Caelum's hand seeping through Draven's shirt. "Do not speak to her with that tone."

The protective flare in his eyes caused Draven to pause, the intensity almost tangible. He shuttered his gaze and sighed, the tension in his shoulders easing. Caelum had become more than just a little brother-in-law. He had become one of Draven's more level-headed friends. "She wants me to try to shift."

Caelum cocked a single eyebrow, the flicker of curiosity in his eyes. "Really?" He dropped his hand from Draven's chest, the absence of warmth noticeable.

"Yeah," he said.

They walked into the kitchen, where sweet scents of freshly brewed tea and baked bread filled the air. They took their seats at the table with no other conversation, the silence punctuated only by the distant hum of the rune lights.

They ate in tense silence, the clinking of utensils against plates the only sound filling the room.

Caelum's forehead creased halfway through the meal, and he lifted his gaze to Draven. "Is there a reason you shouldn't try?"

"Because partial shifting makes my fire unstable." Draven tried to keep his irritation from his voice, but it seeped through, his jaw tightening with frustration.

Caelum sat back, trading a glance with Lanae, the subtle shift in the air indicating their silent communication. "But what if you find you can fully shift?"

Draven opened his mouth, intent on whipping a snide remark at Caelum, but thought twice and closed it. Caelum wasn't being glib with him and deserved an answer in kind. "I haven't fully shifted since before the dragons fell." The words were bitter on his tongue, a reminder of past failures.

"But—"

Lanae tried to butt in on the conversation, but Caelum held up a hand, cutting his sister off with a calm authority that Draven found both reassuring and irritating. Draven traded a glance with Lanae, then refocused on Caelum, ignoring her rising annoyance with him.

Caelum was the calmer of the two siblings, and curiosity reigned over his questions, not some ticking clock to doom like Lanae's. So, when his head cocked, and he asked, "Can I ask why?" Draven didn't have the instinct to snap. Instead, a flicker of something—respect, perhaps—braised his skin.

"I thought my shifting ability was tied to the Dragon's Heart. But it isn't." Air whizzed over his teeth, bringing a wash of coolness to his lungs, momentarily soothing his agitation. "Your sister thinks I have a mental block that's stopping me."

"Is she right?" Caelum took a sip of his tea, the steam rising in lazy tendrils, while waiting for Draven to answer.

Draven put his silverware down and pushed back his seat. He crossed to the back door and stared out at the picked bones in the yard, the stark-white remnants a grim reminder of Nero's carelessness. He bit his lip, the coppery taste of blood mingling with his thoughts as he considered the possibility of whether Lanae was right. If he had a mental block, he had no idea how to overcome such an obstacle.

His denial of being able to fully shift was ingrained over a century of failed tries. The partial shift in the battle for the gauntlet stone had been the most progress he had made, but there still was a barrier that stopped him.

A chair scraped behind him, breaking his reverie, and a warm hand landed on his shoulder, sending a buzzing calmness through him. He turned and met Lanae's questioning stare, her eyes searching his. Then he looked beyond her at Caelum.

"I don't know." His admission burned in his throat like acid. "If she is, I don't have a clue how to break whatever mental hold is stopping me."

"YOU SHOULD AT LEAST try." Lanae scanned his fearful features, noting the worry in his clenched jaw and the furrow of his brow. Waves of apprehension radiated from him. Wrapping her arms around him, her fingers brushed the tautness of his muscles. "Even if you fail today, we can try again tomorrow and the next day and keep trying until you break through whatever is holding you back."

"But the risks," he started, his voice carrying a rough edge that betrayed his inner turmoil.

She covered his mouth with her hand, and his warm breath tickled her palm. "If I recall, those effects happen when you exhausted yourself." She met his gaze, her eyes locking onto his, searching for the slightest hint of reassurance. "I'll make sure you get your rest."

He positively glowered at that, the fire in his eyes momentarily igniting before he looked away, a muscle ticcing in his jaw. But he didn't turn down the option, and she could sense a sliver of hope piercing through the layers of doubt.

CHAPTER FIFTEEN
Breaking Barriers

FOR THE THIRD NIGHT in a row, they stood on the empty training ground. Land stretched out before Draven, an expanse of flattened dirt and scattered stones that seemed to whisper both promises of grandeur and humiliation. The scent of freshly turned earth mixed with the crisp evening air, while the soft rustle of leaves created a rhythmic backdrop. Birds watched from the treetops, their curious eyes gleaming like tiny jewels in the shimmering moonlight, eagerly waiting for the comedic spectacle of the evening: Draven the Inept, attempting to shift. Again.

"Lanae," Draven whined, shifting from one foot to the other. The rough grit of dirt crunched beneath his boots. "We've been at this for hours."

Lanae rolled her eyes and traded a glance with Caelum, who leaned against a tree at the sidelines. "It's been thirty minutes, Draven. Now focus. Close your eyes and picture your dragon. Feel him within you."

Easy for her to say. She wasn't a shifter. She had no clue how this was supposed to happen. His memories of instruction from when he was little were hazy at best. Over a hundred years had pushed those memories into the recesses of his mind, shrouded in a fog he couldn't penetrate. His dragon seemed to prefer napping or mockingly snorting fire every time he tried.

But it wasn't just that. The deaths of his kin weighed heavily on him, creating a mental block he couldn't seem to break. Survivor's guilt gnawed at his resolve, leaving him in a state of helplessness and unworthiness.

Draven pressed his eyes closed and breathed in the scent of damp earth and pine. He attempted to commune with his inner beast, focusing on the last time his scales had surfaced during the fight for the gauntlet stone. His dragon had taken control, forcing a partial shift. But that had been born of fury and panic.

"Lanae, I can't." He met her gaze, eyes filled with frustration.

"You can." She stepped closer, her scent of lavender and steel enveloping him as she put her hand on his chest, sending that familiar humming spark through him. "Now imagine your dragon, Draven. Feel the shift."

He squeezed his eyes shut again, envisioning scales sprouting, wings unfurling, bones snapping into place. *Wait, was that his stomach growling?* Dinner seemed like it had been hours ago, and frankly, he'd rather shift into a sandwich right now.

Lanae clapped her hands, the sharp sound echoing in the stillness, breaking his feeble concentration. "Draven, you're not even trying!"

"Of course I am!" he protested, the heat of embarrassment flushing his face. "You think I don't want to take to the skies again? That I want to be land-bound and vulnerable?"

She sighed, crossing her arms, the light catching on the white and pink threads of her unbound hair. "You are not vulnerable. You have never been vulnerable. You are a fucking dragon king, a force to be reckoned with. Now act like it."

Her words bolstered his ego, and he took a breath, the crisp air filling his lungs. He tried again. This time, a twinge flared, a small spark of hope. His arms tingled, his chest warmed...and then nothing. Absolutely nothing. His beast roared with displeasure, its fiery breath searing the edges of his consciousness.

"You're overthinking it," Caelum called from the sidelines, his voice smooth and steady. "You need to let go of whatever is holding you back."

Easy for him to say. Letting go meant embracing the possibility of becoming a scaly cannonball mid-shift and hurting both Lanae and Caelum in a fiery blast.

Lanae took his face between her hands, her touch cool against his flushed skin, and studied his eyes. "You will not harm us. And it's time to move past your survivor's guilt. You've held onto it long enough." Her determined gaze left no room for argument.

He braced himself, grounding his feet in the loose soil, focusing on the imagined strength of his dragon form. He could almost hear the triumphant roar of success...just before he sneezed a plume of fire and stumbled backward, the heat singeing the air.

"This isn't working, Lanae. Maybe I'm just broken," he said, half-joking, half-defeated, the tinge of ash lingering on his tongue.

She shook her head. "You're not broken. You're just...complicated. Now, breathe. Feel the ground beneath your feet and let the shift come naturally."

Following her guidance, he closed his eyes once more, grounding himself. The world quieted, the ambient sounds fading to a distant hum, and the faintly familiar connection to his dragon brushed his skin. He latched onto it, willing the change.

A sudden warmth enveloped him, the heat radiating from within, and for a brief, glorious moment, he thought he'd done it. Until he opened his eyes to find he'd shifted...into a partially scaled, half-human, half-dragon mess. His dragon slammed against his mental barrier, frantic to be free of his human cage.

Lanae and Caelum burst into laughter, the sound ringing in his ears, and despite himself, Draven joined in. Because really, what else could he do? The heat of embarrassment brushed over his scaled cheeks, a deep crimson.

"Well," he said, trying to keep his balance, "at least I didn't turn into a sandwich."

Lanae wiped away tears of laughter. "Small victories, Draven. Small victories."

The training grounds echoed with their laughter, the evening air carrying the sound into the trees. And even though he hadn't fully shifted, Draven knew he was making progress. Slowly but surely, he'd get there. But he wasn't sure he'd be able to master the change before the war came to their doorstep.

LANAE WAS GIDDY AT the partial transformation. The cool night air carried the scent of pine and earth, mingling with a hint of smoke from Draven's breath. This was the first time in the last three grueling nights he had actually pulled his dragon to the surface. Albeit a partial shift like he had the last time in the throes of war. But a shift all the same.

She launched herself into his scaly arms, the rough texture of his scales cool and firm beneath her fingers. As she pressed kisses on the soft reptilian skin that covered his face, warmth radiated from him.

He jerked away, his eyes wary, the sharp lines of his newly transformed features catching the moonlight.

"Stop being self-conscious. You're a gorgeous beast," she whispered, her breath mingling with his. She kissed him again, this time on the lips. The sharp teeth that lined his mouth grazed her own.

He shuttered his eyes, a low rumble escaping his throat, and the subtle shift of his scales burrowing back under his skin sent tremors down her spine. When his lids opened again, Draven's bright-green irises gazed down at her with an intensity that made her heart race. He returned the kiss, his lips warm and inviting, igniting the familiar warmth in her belly.

"Come on, guys."

Caelum's sharp voice washed his disdain over her, reminding them of their surroundings. Lanae reluctantly pulled away, her eyes still locked with Draven's. The training grounds, once filled with the echoes of their laughter, now appeared charged with their sexual tension. The air seemed to hum with anticipation, the shadows deepening as the night wore on.

Draven's breath came in short bursts, and his eyes searched hers, reflecting the turmoil hiding under the guise of lust.

She peeled herself out of his arms. "We need to keep going," Lanae said. "You were so close, Draven. I know you can do this."

Draven nodded, determination flaring in his eyes. He glanced at Caelum, who stood with arms crossed, his expression unreadable. "All right, let's try again."

This time, the scales came out in seconds, not minutes or hours like before. Her heart leaped inside her rib cage, and she stepped back, giving him room to explore the new form that seemed to stretch the space enclosing his body. She wondered what he would look like as a full-grown dragon. *Would all his scales be the same color, or would they differ?*

A sudden gust of wind swept through the training grounds, carrying the scent of something foreign and dangerous, like the crackling of the ozone itself.

Draven's eyes flew open, and his scales retreated. His gaze scanned the surrounding area.

"Did you feel that?" Lanae asked.

Before Draven could respond, a low growl rumbled from the shadows. The night seemed to hold its breath. The once comforting sounds of the forest were now eerily silent.

"Something's coming," Caelum said.

The three of them stood tense and ready, the training grounds now a stage for an impending confrontation. Lanae's heart pounded in her chest, her body humming with the power of the full moon overhead. Whatever lurked in the darkness, it was about to force their hands in ways they hadn't anticipated.

CHAPTER SIXTEEN
Sacrificial Love

A PLUME OF BLACK smoke coiled menacingly above the city, a familiar and ominous signal that sent an icy shiver down Draven's spine. Alestain's dark magic. The acrid scent of burning filled the air, stinging Draven's nose as the significance hit him like a tidal wave. His head snapped toward Caelum, eyes wide with urgency. He had no time left to master his shift.

A piercing caw sliced through the tense atmosphere, drawing their gaze skyward. Nero, the griffin, plummeted toward them with eyes blazing like molten gold, mirroring the frantic turmoil within Draven. The surrounding air crackled with the griffin's raw, untamed energy.

"At least he came at a full moon," Lanae remarked, her voice carrying a forced nonchalance that scarcely masked her own anxiety.

Draven let out a bitter huff, his breath visible in the chilly night air. "All fae seem to be strongest at the full moon." His eyes, sharp as a blade's edge, locked onto hers. "Including Alestain."

Lanae's confident demeanor crumbled, her expression shifting to one of dawning dread. Her smug features fell into an unmistakable look of "oh shit." She and Caelum might be stronger tonight, but so were all the fae forces under Alestain's sinister command.

"We need our weapons." Lanae spun to Draven, her voice tight with urgency.

The speedy clip of Draven's heart thundered in his ears as he realized their weapons were across the city, back at their home. The thought of leaving the safety of their position to retrieve them filled him with a sense of dread. He grabbed Lanae's hand, needing her heat to fight against the cold rippling through the air. "Hold on to Nero," he instructed, waving Caelum closer.

He closed his eyes and whispered the draconian portal spell, the ancient words rolling off his tongue like molten lava. The air shimmered and rippled, a gust of wind whipping through their hair. The portal opened with a crackle of energy, revealing the familiar sight of their home, the weapons gleaming on the walls like silent sentinels.

They stepped through the portal, the sensation of being pulled through space disorienting but fleeting. The familiar scent of their home greeted them, a mixture of wood smoke and herbs that calmed Draven's racing heart for a moment. They quickly grabbed their weapons, the cool weight of the steel providing a sense of reassurance and readiness.

With their swords in hand, they stepped outside into the chaos of the city streets. The acrid stench of smoke was even stronger now, mingling with the iron tang of blood and the earthy undertone of freshly turned soil. Shadows danced along the walls as flames flickered in the distance, casting a hellish glow over the chaos that had taken hold of their home.

The sounds of battle assaulted their ears—clashing swords, the shouts of the mind-controlled fae, and the terrified cries of the citizens. Draven's chest pounded in sync with the frenzied rhythm of the conflict. He saw the glint of moonlight on armored figures advancing toward them, eyes vacant and glowing with Alestain's malevolent influence.

"Stay close!" Draven shouted over the racket, his voice a guttural growl that barely reached Lanae and Caelum. The intensity of their determination and fear layered over him as they prepared to face the oncoming wave.

Draven's sword clashed with the first of Alestain's warriors, the impact sending a jolt up his arm. He danced through the chaos with a lethal grace, his movements fueled by a fierce determination. The air around him buzzed with the magic of his enemies, each strike a clash of wills and weapons.

Lanae and Caelum fought at his side, their synchronized efforts a testament to their bond and training. Despite the odds, a sliver of hope remained. If they could hold their ground, if Draven could push past his mental barriers and fully embrace his dragon form, they just might stand a chance.

CAELUM FOUGHT WITH THE same sense of dread layering over his mind that plagued his sister. With each strike of swords, accompanied by the empty stare of the attackers, they edged closer to their worst nightmare. Magic crackled in the air from all elemental factions on both sides, an overwhelming symphony of power and chaos.

Lanae and Caelum's magic surged through the ground beneath their feet, causing the very earth to tremble with their might. With a swift motion, Lanae summoned thick, twisting vines that erupted from the cobblestones, ensnaring the legs of their enemies and dragging them down with a muted, bone-crunching thud. The rich, loamy scent of freshly turned soil and crushed leaves filled the air, a pronounced opposition to the acrid stench of burning and blood.

Caelum's hands glowed as he called forth jagged spikes of rock from the ground. They shot up with a deep, rumbling growl, impaling the attackers and forming a makeshift barricade. The surrounding ground pulsed in rhythm with their heartbeats and responded to their every command.

Around them, the city was a maelstrom of elemental magic. Fire roared and crackled, its searing heat radiating in waves that singed the vines caging their enemies. The air shimmered with the haze of heat, and the scent of charred wood and sulfur was nearly suffocating. Water magic swirled and danced, droplets hanging in the air like glistening pearls before lashing out in powerful torrents that doused the flames and swept enemies off their feet. The cool, refreshing scent of rain mingled with the harsher stench of battle, offering a momentary reprieve.

Air magic whipped through the streets, carrying whispers of wind that sliced through the combatants with razor-sharp precision. The gusts howled and whistled, lifting debris and scattering it like confetti in a storm. The sharp, metallic tang of ozone filled the air, and static electricity prickled along his skin.

Nero's lightning crackled and danced overhead, casting eerie, flickering shadows across the battlefield. Bolts of raw energy struck with deadly accuracy, their blinding light followed by the deafening boom of thunder that shook the very ground. The scent of singed air and ionized particles was sharp and tangy, adding to the discord of sensory overload.

Despite the overwhelming odds and the mayhem of magic around them, Caelum and Lanae fought with a synchronized elegance, their earth magic providing a solid foundation amidst the chaos. The ground pulsed with life beneath their feet. With each magical cast and swings of their swords, they chipped away at the enemy forces, driven by a fierce resolve to protect their home and each other.

Caelum swung his sword, the clash of steel ringing in his ears as he deflected the next mindless soldier's strike. His muscles tensed, readying for the next attack, but he hesitated as he locked eyes with his opponent. Shock flooded his veins, freezing his movements. His father's face, contorted with malice and void of recognition, stared back at him from beneath the enemy's helm. The man, once a pillar of strength and kindness, now looked at him with nothing but bitter hatred.

Above them, Nero lit up the sky, sending bolts of lightning that crackled and sizzled through the air. The griffin's fierce cries echoed like thunder, each bolt striking with unerring precision. Caelum's father took the brunt of the assault, his body convulsing as black smoke billowed from his nose and mouth, choking him. His sword slipped from his grasp, clattering to the ground with a hollow clang. When he looked up, his eyes mirrored Caelum's, filled with a flicker of recognition and despair.

Caelum gasped, the sudden realization piercing his heart like a dagger. It was a moment he had longed for, to see a glimmer of his true father behind the facade of the mindless soldier. But doubt gnawed at him—he couldn't trust it. Not here, not now.

"Caelum?" His father's voice, though weak and lilting, tore at his soul. The simple question held a world of pain and longing.

Caelum nodded, his throat tight with emotion.

But the moment of connection was brutally shattered. Movement to his right caught his father's attention, and with a sudden burst of strength, his father shoved him back. Caelum stumbled, colliding with another warrior. They both turned in time to witness a mindless minion drive a sword into his father's side. The sickening sound of metal piercing flesh was drowned out by Caelum's shocked cry.

His father's sacrifice ignited a storm of fury within him. The blade had been meant for Caelum, and his father had taken the fatal blow without hesitation. Anger surged through Caelum, raw and unyielding. The ground beneath the soldier's feet rumbled and cracked as Caelum's earth magic erupted. Rocks and debris shot up in an explosive force, shredding the attacker to pieces in a grisly display of power.

The battlefield seemed to pause for a heartbeat, the air thick with the stench of blood, smoke, and earth. Caelum's chest throbbed. His father's sacrifice pressed down on him. But amidst the chaos and pain, a resolve crystallized within him. He would honor his father's memory by fighting with everything he had, to protect those he loved and to defeat the darkness that threatened to consume them all.

He let a battle cry loose from his lungs—a raw, primal sound that echoed through the chaos of the battlefield. The cry tore through the air, reverberating off the buildings and filling the night with its fierce resonance.

The roar surged from deep within him, carrying a fire from years spent in the background, the frustration and determination igniting a fire in his chest. His voice was a powerful force, mingling with the din of clashing steel and the crackling of elemental magic.

Gone was the younger brother relegated to the shadows—in that moment, he was a warrior in his own right, ready to show the world the true extent of his abilities.

CHAPTER SEVENTEEN
Shattered Unity

THE BATTLE RAGED AROUND Draven, a chaotic symphony of clashing steel, elemental magic, and agonized cries. Frustration surged as he lost sight of Lanae and Caelum in the fray, the press of bodies and the swirl of smoke obscuring them from his view. He couldn't afford to lose focus now—his enemies were relentless, and Alestain's dark magic loomed like a shadow over the battlefield.

He had to get to Alestain. Their only hope was to cut down the man who controlled the masses.

Draven's sword cut through the air, his dragon fire thrumming just beneath the surface. Each strike was precise and powerful, driven by his determination to protect those he loved. He spun around to deflect an incoming blow, only to find himself face-to-face with Alestain.

The dark sorcerer's eyes gleamed with malevolent satisfaction. "So, you are the last Emberwing," Alestain sneered, his voice a silken threat. "Ready to see your family again?"

Draven's grip tightened on his sword. "My family is here in Solstice City."

Alestain's laugh was cold and hollow. "Ah, yes. That feisty wife of yours. I would have preferred her head on a pike at the front of my army, but I'll have to settle for yours." He raised his hands, and dark tendrils of magic coiled around them, crackling with malevolent energy.

Draven braced himself, his muscles tensing as he prepared to face the full force of Alestain's power. The very air vibrated with raw energy, and the ground beneath their feet trembled in anticipation. Heat eviscerated his insides as his fire begged to be let loose. But without the knowledge of where Lanae or Caelum were, he wouldn't resort to flame. He'd just have to use his sword and his wits until he located his family.

A PANG OF ANXIETY rushed through Lanae as she lost sight of Draven and Caelum, the press of bodies and the chaos of battle tearing them apart. The acrid stench of smoke and the metallic tang of blood filled her nostrils, while the clamor of clashing steel and agonized cries echoed in her ears. She pushed forward, her earth magic surging through the ground beneath her feet, causing the earth to tremble in response.

She spun and swung her blade, the clang of metal on metal shuddering up her arm.

Spric's sharp eyes took her in as he pushed her away, a sneer curling his lips. "Oh look, I finally found the one who got away." His eyes gleamed with malicious intent. "I'm tempted to give you the same type of beating I received for letting you get away." He swung his pristine sword in a deadly arc, the blade glinting ominously in the flickering light.

She met his steel and spun out of his reach, her movements fluid and precise. A guttural cry cracked the night, and Caelum's devastation bloomed in her mind, flipping her panic buttons. She had to find Caelum and Draven—but first, she had to deal with the immediate threat before her.

Lanae's grip on her sword tightened, her knuckles turning white. "You're not a killer, Spric. Get out of my way."

Spric laughed, a harsh, rough sound that grated on her nerves. "Oh, but I am." He raised his sword, and the space surrounding him crackled with dark energy, a tangible manifestation of his malevolence.

"Your sword doesn't have a speck of blood on it," she taunted, her voice steady despite the fear gnawing at her insides. She parried his strike, her blade deflecting his with a ringing clash. She stepped in, aiming to take advantage of his momentary imbalance, but his fist shot out with lightning speed.

Before she could dodge, his fist collided with her nose. A fountain of blood flowed out, the sting of it blurring her vision. She coughed, spurting blood from her mouth as she tried to maneuver away from him, but he spun her around and kicked the back of her knee. Pain exploded through her leg; before she hit the ground, his arm clasped around her neck, and he smashed her wrist with the pommel of his sword.

Her weapon clattered to the ground, the sound lost amidst the chaos. Lanae scratched at his arm, her nails digging into his flesh as panic surged through her. The world narrowed to the suffocating pressure on her throat and the desperate need to breathe.

A woman she would have recognized anywhere stepped in front of them, her mother's eyes sharper than they were the last time Lanae saw her. She held her blade out as if to run her through, her expression a mix of determination and sorrow. Lanae's brain fogged from the lack of oxygen, her vision tunneling. She sent a silent prayer to the gods that Draven wouldn't raze the universe when he found her.

CAELUM'S EMOTIONS NUMBED. IF he thought about his father's sacrifice too long, he would falter. Lanae's panic seared through him, and he spun, scanning the crowd for her. In the chaos, he glimpsed Jenna instead and that protective need flared.

She fought like a seasoned warrior, and his heart clenched at the sight of her. They all were fighting for their lives and he couldn't afford to be distracted. He swung his sword, deflecting an attack, but pain exploded in his side as he was struck from behind.

Caelum staggered, his vision blurring as he fell to the ground. He tried to push himself up, but the pain was overwhelming. Jenna's voice reached him through the haze of agony.

"Caelum!" she cried, her voice filled with desperation as she fought to get to his side. She rushed to him, her hands trembling as she tried to stanch the bleeding. "Don't leave me," she whispered, her voice breaking. "Please don't leave me. I love you."

Caelum's heart ached at her words. He reached up to touch her face, his fingers brushing against her tear-streaked cheek. "I love you too, and I don't plan on leaving any time soon," he said through the brutal agony accosting him.

Between being hit and Lanae's fading energy, his frantic need to get to his family surfaced, forcing him to his feet despite his wounds.

ALESTAIN'S MAGIC HIT DRAVEN in a brutal blow, knocking the wind out of him as it pounded his chest to a pulp. He was amazed he still stood against the dark sorcerer's relentless magic. His muscles strained against the onslaught, but he refused to give in. He had to find Lanae and Caelum—he couldn't lose them.

A wave of wind hit from above, and Draven glanced up.

Nero soared over the battlefield, his keen eyes taking in the chaos below. He swooped down, sending bolts of lightning into the enemy ranks, his fierce cries echoing across the battlefield.

But even the mighty griffin wasn't invincible. Alestain sent a blast of dark magic at Nero, and it struck true. Nero's wings faltered, and he plummeted toward the ground. Draven's protective flare demanded he save Nero before the griffin hit the earth, and he bellowed his anguish to the gods above.

CHAPTER EIGHTEEN
Dragon's Roar

LANAE STARED INTO THE eyes of the woman who raised her with love, the mother she cherished with all her heart. Her vision blurred behind the mist of unshed tears. One escaped out of the corner of her eye, trailing heat down her cheek and catching the faint glimmer of moonlight. The chill of Spric's relentless grip around her throat sent deep muscle shakes down her body. Her head swooned with the dizziness of not enough oxygen, the world narrowing to a pinpoint of pain and fear.

When her mother lunged forward, the sound of her blade meeting flesh was a sickening squelch that echoed through the chaos. Lanae blinked, her mind numb to the anticipated agony. Spric's hold faltered, and as Lanae glanced down, she noticed her mother's blade had sliced through the fabric of her shirt, the cool steel perilously close but miraculously sparing her flesh.

She spun out of Spric's grip, the rush of air filling her lungs with a burning clarity, as her mother withdrew her blade from the enemy's side. The pungent bite of blood mingled with the damp earth and sweat of battle.

"No one harms my daughter."

The snarling declaration, filled with primal ferocity, took Lanae by surprise. She shook the shock from her head and swiped her blade off the ground, the familiar weight in her hand reassuring as more mindless minions surrounded them. Spric stumbled out of the fray, the sound of his ragged breathing lost in the din of clashing swords and desperate cries.

A roar filled the air, a deafening guttural sound that vibrated through Lanae's chest. Her gaze shot to the sky, heart tumbling at the sight of Nero's limp body falling. Before she could scream her denial, a beast surged from the ground. Shimmering scales of green and gold reflected under the pale moonlight as a dragon raced to snatch Nero out of the sky, its wings creating a tempest of wind and dust.

The sight of the mighty beast rising above the fray brought the battlefield to a standstill, as every warrior, both mind-controlled and free, looked to the skies in awe and terror.

Caelum's awe brushed her consciousness like a whisper, laced with an undercurrent of searing pain. Lanae's heart pounded against her ribs as she bolted through the crowd, her mother a fierce shadow on her heels.

The air buzzed with the clash of metal and the shouts of soldiers. Dust and debris swirled around her as enemy soldiers were flung aside by the force of her earth magic, their cries drowned out by the roar of the battlefield. She pushed harder, every step a desperate leap toward the source of that pain.

When Jenna and Caelum, injured and struggling, came into view amidst the chaos, a surge of magic erupted from her fingertips. A path of thick, twisting vines shot forward, carving out a haven in the tumult. The scent of fresh earth and crushed leaves mixed with the acrid odor of smoke and blood, creating a space large enough for Draven to gently lay Nero down.

Lanae and her mother slid into the sanctuary just as the walls of vines closed in around them, cocooning them in a momentary peace that trembled with the violence outside.

CAELUIM TURNED TOWARD LANAE, his eyes heavy with unshed tears. As his gaze landed on their mother's clear, searching eyes, shock and devastation warred within him like twin storms. Her eyes, usually bright with warmth, were now clouded with fear and a desperate need for answers.

"Have you seen your father?" Her fragile whisper pierced through the surrounding chaos.

All fight left him, and he crumbled to the ground next to Nero's unconscious form. The cold, hard earth pressed against his knees, and the distant sounds of the battlefield became a muted roar in his ears. His breath came in shallow, ragged gasps as he fought to hold back the wave of grief threatening to engulf him.

"He saved me." The words left his lips like ice, as cold as the wound in his side that throbbed with every heartbeat. Lanae rushed to him, her presence a soothing balm that warmed the chill gnawing at his bones.

Before their mother could step any closer, Jenna's sword gleamed, its edge a sharp, unforgiving barrier. Jenna's stance was rigid, her eyes blazing with determination as she blocked their mother's advancement. To Jenna, the woman shielded by Lanae's cocoon was the enemy, a threat she was duty-bound to neutralize.

"You'll be okay." Lanae's voice was a fragile whisper as she glanced at Nero. "We'll all be okay." Her denial shone in her eyes, a desperate hope that made him grit his teeth.

"No, Lanae. Dad died saving me."

His voice cut through the air, sharp and jagged, making her recoil as if struck. The raw, unfiltered grief in his tone was a knife twisting in both their hearts.

"If you hadn't noticed, we were losing. There are more Solstice City guards on the ground than the enemy." The reality of their situation overwhelmed him, their losses suffocating.

Lanae shook her head, her wide eyes infused with a blend of fear and defiance. "Draven shifted."

"And what exactly is he going to do? Burn the city down?"

The sharpness in his retort made her eyes widen further, the stark truth of their peril hanging between them like a specter.

DRAVEN SOARED AWAY FROM the safe zone Lanae created, the wind whipping against his scales and the roar of battle echoing in his ears. With Caelum, Nero, and Lanae shielded from the fighting, he could focus on his nemesis. Below, the streets were a chaotic blur of Solstice City soldiers and mind-controlled enemies grappling in desperate combat.

A line of dark magic streaked toward him, its sinister energy crackling in the air. He banked sharply, the force of his maneuver sending a shudder through his wings. Glancing back, he saw the assault battering Lanae's barrier from all sides. A deep, guttural roar erupted from his throat as he unleashed a searing plume of flame, the heat intense enough to turn enemy soldiers to dust.

"No!" Lanae's cry cut through the din, stanching his flame.

He glanced at her, his eyes flashing with frustration as he banked again.

"They are innocent!" Her voice, filled with desperate conviction, rang out.

This again. He rolled his eyes, annoyance flaring. Pain suddenly exploded in his side as a direct hit of dark magic sent him veering uncontrollably into the line of buildings. The impact rattled his bones, and he let out a pained growl, the world spinning around him.

Draven shook off the pain as best as he could, his eyes narrowing in on Alestain. With a powerful beat of his wings, he soared toward his nemesis, talons extended. The rush of wind roared in his ears, mixing with the distant cries of battle and the crackling of fires below.

His claws closed around Alestain with a vise-like grip, lifting him off the ground with a surge of triumph. The enemy struggled in his grasp, but Draven held him firm, wings straining as he sped toward the training fields where he could unleash his fire without restraint.

The landscape blurred beneath them, a patchwork of smoke and shadows. As they neared the open expanse of the training fields, a sharp, burning pain sliced through his talon. He glanced down to see Alestain wielding a wickedly curved blade, blood already dripping from the wound he'd inflicted and Alestain's bloody hand pasted to the side of the open laceration.

The dark magic woven into the cut pulsed with a malevolent energy. Draven's vision wavered as Alestain chanted, the words of a blood spell resonating with a sinister power. The magic wrapped around his free will, binding it and making every swish of his wings a struggle.

Fury surged within him, a fire that roared louder than the pain. But the spell was already taking hold, the dark magic coiling around him like a serpent.

He would not be Alestain's might in this war. He'd sooner die than attack Solstice City. As Alestain's dark magic clawed at his very soul, Draven's resolve hardened. With a roar that echoed across the battlefield, he shook Alestain from his grip; the force sent his nemesis plummeting toward the ground. The air whipped around him as he soared higher, every beat of his wings a defiant cry against the curse trying to bind him.

But as Alestain fell, the insidious tendrils of the blood curse tightened their hold, wrapping around Draven like chains of fire. A searing, desperate need to save the falling figure burned through him, an unnatural compulsion that made his heart race with panic. He fought the order with every fiber of his being, but the curse's power was overwhelming.

His body betrayed him, turning against his will. His wings folded in, and with a sickening lurch, he spiraled toward the earth. The wind howled in his ears; the ground rushed up to meet him. The sensation of falling, of losing control, was a terrifying blur of motion and pain.

As he hurtled downward, following the same path as his new twisted master, blood and ash filled his mouth. The dark magic coiled tighter, binding him to Alestain's fate with a merciless grip.

"OH GODS!" LANAE CRIED as Draven flew away. The reflection of Alestain's blade slicing into Draven's talon left her heart blasting a path of ice through her veins, every heartbeat sending a shivering chill. Even from this distance, she recognized the choking scent of the black smoke of a blood curse, its oily tendrils curling into the air.

She turned to her unconscious griffin and then looked at her brother, the urgency in her voice like thunder. "Wake him up—otherwise, we are all dead." She plucked a feather, its soft down fluttering against her fingertips, and then, with a surge of raw magic, blasted the walls surrounding them apart, the stone crumbling and dust swirling in the air.

Fear clawed at her heart, a gnawing beast, as she raced toward the training fields. Draven plummeted headfirst for the ground, the wind howling in his ears, racing to catch his new master. Lanae sent everyone in her path flying back; their startled cries filled the air as she carved her way to her husband. The ground exploded in a flurry of rock and vines, the earth shaking and rumbling, pushing both allies and enemy beyond reach of her.

Draven's claws clamped around Alestain and then tossed him out of the way before he collided with the ground. The impact sent a shudder through the earth, as if it were cracking in two. The sound echoed like a thunderclap. The mighty beast hit with enough force for it to be a killing blow, and Lanae's chest exploded with panic, her breath lodging in her throat and her vision blurring with tears.

She skidded to a stop next to his bleeding talon, the slick mud splattering up her legs. Without conscious thought, she sliced a cut in her palm with the feather quill, the sharp sting followed by blood pooling in her hand. She shoved the feather itself in the cut on Draven's talon, cringing as his hot, sticky blood mingled with hers. Despite a thousand reservations swarming in her mind, she slammed her bloody palm over the cut; the wetness seeped between her fingers, and she uttered the spell Xoltan had whispered in her ear years ago—the one that made her body his to manipulate. His voice, still haunting and cold, echoed in her mind.

Magic lit up Draven's body, an incandescent glow that spread like wildfire across his scales. Sparks traveled over his body, crackling and hissing, and the scrape of bones realigning whispered in the air, a chilling symphony of clicks and clacks. A rumbling groan echoed across the field, a deep, guttural sound that vibrated through the ground.

"Get up, beast." Alestain's voice echoed from near Draven's head, authoritative and cold, cutting through the chaos.

Lanae stiffened, the breath catching in her throat. When she pulled her hand away from Draven's scales, the cut that had been there was fully healed, the flesh knit together seamlessly. She stared at her palm, blinking in disbelief. A neat little row of golden scales slashed across her palm where she had sliced it open, shimmering with an otherworldly glow.

DRAVEN'S EYES OPENED AS another annoying kick hit his skull, the jolt sending a sharp pain through his head. Alestain was ordering him to get up, his voice grating and relentless. But the compulsion to do as he demanded was not fully there. In its place was a warm glow, like Lanae had wrapped him in her magic, a comforting embrace that soothed his aching body. Her lavender scent draped around him, delicate and sweet, as if she stood right next to him, the fragrance enveloping him in a cocoon of reassurance.

He lifted his head, grumbling as he scrambled to get to his feet, the ground beneath him rough and uneven. His body hurt from the impact of the fall; every muscle protested, but not nearly as much as it should have. He had known that kind of fall was deadly, the kind that could shatter bones and crush organs, but somehow, he was alive and not just a broken heap of flesh. The breeze brushing past him was filled with the sounds of the battlefield, the clash of steel and the cries of warriors, a cacophony of chaos that seemed distant and muted compared to the warmth of Lanae's magic.

Movement near his feet pulled his attention, and his heart stalled at the sight of Lanae staring up at him in awe, her eyes wide and shimmering. *She could not be here. Not with Alestain controlling his body.* The memories of Xoltan controlling Lanae flashed in his mind, sharp and painful.

Lanae had no defense against a dragon like he had against her blades.

"Kill her!" Alestain's order rang out, a harsh, grating sound, followed by a blast of his dark magic toward Lanae. The air crackled with the malevolent energy, the shadows deepening.

Draven's body coiled with his protective instinct, muscles tensing; a wall of ivy erupted in front of her, the leaves rustling and the vines creaking as they protected her from the blast of Alestain's dark magic.

Did you do that?

Lanae's voice filled his head, and he blinked, the warmth of her presence washing over him. *Lanae?*

Her laughter rang out, both in his mind and on the field...a bright, joyous sound. The wall of ivy surrounding her burst into ashes, the embers dancing in the air. Lanae stood with her sword in her hand and a triumphant smile on her gorgeous lips, her confidence radiating.

I guess I own all of you now. She opened her palm. The bright line of golden scales down her palm made him tremble, the sight mesmerizing.

"You stupid dragon. I order you to kill my brother's murderer!" Alestain pointed at Lanae, his voice filled with rage and desperation.

Draven turned to Alestain, his eyes narrowing and falling to the clear Dragon's Heart crystal embedded in Alestain's chest plate. Righteous anger filled every cell, and he met Alestain's pompous glare. "I killed Xoltan." His dragon voice rumbled over the field, a low, powerful growl.

Alestain's eyes widened as the ramifications of the order he had just issued crossed over his features. The loss of his mighty weapon before him rang clear in every nuance of his grimace.

"Before you execute that order, kill her and then raze this city to the ground," he bellowed, his voice cracking. The order rippled over the armies, and the mind-controlled soldiers turned from their battles and ran toward the training field with murder in their eyes.

Lanae swept her arm at the edge of the field, and a flaming wall of ivy raised, the heat radiating and the flames crackling, blocking the armies from the training grounds. She glanced up at Draven with that incredible smile, her eyes sparkling.

You have my permission to enact the vengeance you've carried for the last century. Do with Alestain as you see fit.

Her words released him from waiting for orders. And Draven turned his fiery glare on Alestain. Fire built in his chest, the heat intensifying, and Alestain grinned, thinking he was going to end Lanae.

"Did you know a new blood spell could nullify all others?" Lanae called out, her voice strong and clear as she raised her palm, showing him the shiny new dragon scales that reflected iridescent under the moon's rays.

Alestain's gaze snapped to hers, his eyes widening at the meaning.

Fear, as pungent as the piss spreading over the front of his pants, hit Draven's senses just before he blasted Alestain with the full force of his dragon fire, the flames roaring and consuming both the fae and the Dragon's Heart.

A pang of guilt slashed through him at the loss of the relic his family had safeguarded, but without the power of the dragons fueling the thing, it was just a sentimental jewel. When he closed his mouth, nothing was left but scalded ground where Alestain stood. The harsh stench of burned earth filled his nostrils.

Draven turned toward his beautiful wife, his heart swelling with relief and love. "Did you know?"

Lanae raised a shoulder, her expression a mix of pride and nonchalance. "I took a chance." She crossed to stand in front of him, her footsteps light on the scorched ground, and he lowered his snout. Her embrace was warm, her touch gentle, and the wash of kisses over his nose pulled a content grumble from him, the softness of her lips like a balm to his weary soul.

"I'm not sure I like not having free will," he grumbled, his voice a deep rumble. "But you've always commanded me since we first met, so I guess nothing really has changed, except I seem to be able to wield your power and you seem to be able to cast my flames."

"Huh?" She leaned back and stared at him, her eyes wide with surprise.

"You put up that flaming wall of ivy." He nodded to the barrier still in place, the flames flickering and casting a warm glow.

She stared at it, her gaze thoughtful, and then a light, musical giggle escaped her lips. The sound of it was enough to warm his soul. Joy radiated through him. She rubbed his snout, her touch tender and reassuring. "You know, I've always wanted to ride a dragon."

"Your wish is my command." He chuckled, a deep, resonant sound, and lowered himself to the ground so she could climb onto him, the earth cool against his scales. "But you've ridden me many times already."

"Shush." A playful note filled her voice at his innuendo before she climbed onto his shoulders, her hands steady as she settled into place.

The heat of her legs wrapping around his neck sent a thrill through him, a quiver of exhilaration that rippled down his spine. He had never in all his existence seen a fae riding a dragon while they soared through the sky. Her strong and steady heartbeat against his scales made for a powerful vision in his mind, and he hoped it gave Lanae the same sense of invincibility.

As soon as she was settled in place, he stood to full height, his powerful muscles coiling and bunching beneath his scales, and launched into the air. The wind rushed past them, a fierce, exhilarating gale that whipped around them. Her laugh filled him with glee, a joyful melody that echoed in his heart and resonated through his very being.

But the minute they turned toward the city, all their joy fizzled. The sight of flames licking at the sky and smoke billowing was a wake-up call to the battle still ahead. The noxious smell of smoke filled his nostrils, and the sounds of distant cries reached his ears, a somber symphony of war.

THE JOY OF FLYING on Draven's back sent a thrilling jolt through her. The wind whipped her hair out of her face and the softness of his scales beneath her hands spread a delicious heat to her core. But dread clawed at her heart, wiping out all sensations of warmth as she caught sight of Alestain's frozen army, their unmoving forms like a nightmare tableau. The periodic clash of swords drew her attention to the few who fought without Alestain's mind control, the metallic ring hacking through the air. Her gaze zeroed in on Spric, his movements determined and fierce as he fought to get to the field.

Darkness threatened to take her into a downward spiral. Grief clenched her chest. Losing her father echoed in her soul, a deep, abiding ache that refused to be soothed. The knowledge that Spric would soon experience the same crushing blow filled her with profound sorrow, her heart aching for him. The taste of salt lingered in her throat from unshed tears, and the scent of smoke and blood filled her nostrils, the grim realities of war all too present.

Lanae used her earth magic to push soldiers away from Spric, the ground shifting and trembling beneath her command. The soldiers stumbled and cried out; the earth rippled like waves under their feet, creating a space for Draven to land without harming anyone. The scent of freshly turned soil filled the air, mixed with the acrid tang of smoke.

"Please land there," she called out, her voice steady and clear, pointing to the spot she wanted Draven to land. The surrounding air seemed to hum with energy, the magic coursing through her veins.

Draven banked in a slow circle, his wings slicing through the air with powerful strokes. The wind rustled through his scales, and the cadence of his wings beating was a deep, rhythmic thrum. He descended gracefully and landed in front of Spric with a heavy thud, the impact sending a rumbling tremor through the earth.

Spric drew back, his eyes narrowing with rage. When his gaze landed on her, his fury blasted clear in his eyes, the intensity of his anger like a physical force. "You." He aimed his sword at her, the blade gleaming menacingly in the sunlight.

Draven growled, a deep, rumbling sound that vibrated, shifting the surrounding rubble. Smoke billowed from his nostrils, the acrid scent filling the air.

"Yield!" Lanae commanded, her voice strong and unwavering, and pointed her sword at Spric. The gleam of her blade reflected the moonlight, a sharp contrast to the darkness threatening to engulf them.

Caelum stepped into view, his steps steady despite the burden he carried. One arm was draped over Jenna's shoulder, the other over their mother's. Behind him limped Nero, his movements slow and pained. Covering the three of them was a warrior Lanae recognized from the day Spric took her captive, his stance protective and alert.

Granger, Caelum's voice announced in her head, the name resonating. They formed a solid line in the event Spric made a run for it. The tension in the air was thick, a silent promise of the battle that could erupt at any moment.

"Let me down," Lanae whispered to Draven.

His discontented growl rumbled through his chest...a low, resonant sound that belied his actions. He lowered himself, the ground trembling under his weight, and she climbed off, the cool night air brushing against her skin. She gave him a kiss on his jowls, her lips warm against the rough texture of his scales, before she stepped in front of him. Draven stood, his massive form casting a shadow in the moonlight, a dark silhouette that paused the rest of the fighting, the eerie quiet punctuated only by the distant sounds of battle.

"Do you yield?" she asked Spric again as she faced him, her voice steady and commanding. The moonlight glinted off her sword, casting a silver sheen over the blade, and her gaze locked onto Spric's.

"Where is my father?" His voice quivered, laden with fear and uncertainty. His eyes darted around, searching for a glimpse of the man who had once loomed so large in his life.

"Answering for his sins in the halls of the gods," Draven said before Lanae could answer, his voice a deep, resonant growl that reverberated through the air.

The words hung heavily, echoing in the silence that followed. The tension was palpable, a sharp, cutting presence, and Draven's statement settled like a heavy shroud over everyone present.

Spric's expression crumbled, the hardness in his eyes melting away to reveal a vulnerable, anguished soul. His glare sharpened through a veil of tears, the salty droplets clinging to his lashes, reflecting the moonlight.

"Yield and release the people from their mind-controlled haze, and we will let you live." Lanae's voice held firm but carried an undertone of compassion. She waved at the figures frozen throughout the city, their lifeless stares a persistent token of the power the Firetwills held over them.

Silence stretched between them, a heavy, suffocating silence that seemed to amplify the distant sounds of the battle, the occasional clash of steel and the muffled cries of the wounded. The night air was cool, carrying the scent of burning wood and the earthy aroma of freshly turned soil.

Draven's imposing form loomed behind Lanae, a silent sentinel, his scales catching the glint of the moonlight. The dragon's eyes, fierce and unyielding, were locked onto Spric, a notice of the unstoppable force that awaited should he refuse.

CHAPTER NINETEEN
A Morbid Conundrum

SPRIC'S SHOULDERS SAGGED, HIS resolve crumbling like a fragile facade. The situation bore down on him, visible in the tremble of his hands and the way his gaze wavered, unable to meet Lanae's steady stare. The heavy atmosphere crackled with tension as thick as the smoke hanging in the air, suffocating and oppressive. Spric's chest heaved with heavy breaths, each exhale a mix of defeat and bitter acceptance, the sound like a slow, mournful sigh.

Finally, with a shuddering breath, Spric's sword clattered to the ground, the metal ringing out in the stillness—a sharp, lonely sound that echoed in the night. His knees buckled, and he fell to the ground, his head bowed in submission.

The sight of him broken and defeated stirred a complex mix of emotions in Lanae, all of which swirled inside Draven's mind like a tornado.

"I yield," Spric whispered, the words almost carried away by the night breeze.

Lanae nodded, her expression softening as she stepped forward, her sword lowering. "Release them," she commanded, her voice steady yet gentle.

Spric's face tilted up to hers with an expression filled with agony, his eyes wet with unshed tears. "I can't."

The raw honesty in his voice struck Draven, reminding him of Varkir's words after they had beaten Xoltan. *The entire Firetwill line must die to release the masses from their hold.*

Lanae must have remembered the same thing because she glanced back, meeting the dragon's gaze. Her eyes filled with regret, reflecting the injustice of what she might have to do now that Spric surrendered.

Draven's chest squeezed in response to her inner turmoil and the decision bearing down on her.

"Explain," Draven snapped, his voice a deep, commanding rumble that reverberated through the night air.

"I am a shapeshifter like my mother. I did not inherit any of my father's magic." His voice trembled as he glanced around at his father's army, suspended in frozen animation.

Lanae pressed her lips together, her sorrow suffocating, blanketing Draven with a deep sense of melancholy. "Do you have any siblings?" she asked.

He shook his head. "No," he replied, the single word filled with resignation.

Draven grumbled, the sound a low, guttural growl, and traded a glance with Caelum as he shifted back into human form. The transformation was swift, his powerful dragon form morphing into a tall, imposing figure. He reached around and took Lanae's sword from her and stepped forward, sparing her from making this heart-wrenching decision.

"Stand down."

Her sharp command gripped his muscles, freezing them in place. The intensity of her voice was like a physical force, holding him immobile.

He turned his head slowly, his movements stiff, and leveled a knowing stare at her, his eyes dark and piercing. *You know as well as I do what must be done,* he conveyed silently, his gaze unwavering.

She shook her head. "I won't condemn him for his father's actions." Her voice was steady, but the undercurrent of sorrow was unmistakable. The moonlight cast a pale glow over her features, highlighting the firm set of her jaw and the fire in her eyes.

"The council's war tribunal will determine his fate." Lanae's voice was steady and resolute, each word sharp and clear.

"And what of all these people trapped by Firetwill's dark magic?" Draven waved to the masses, his powerful arm carving a path through the air. The spectacle of the countless frozen figures, their eyes vacant and their bodies motionless, stirred a deep sense of urgency within him. The biting odor of lingering dark magic tainted the air.

"He was going to kill you," Lanae's mother said from behind Spric, her voice filled with anger.

A surge of protective instinct flared within Draven at the thought of Lanae being in danger.

Spric tensed, his muscles coiling with latent energy, and his hand moved closer to his sword, the blade glinting in the pale light as if his instincts were screaming at him to fight instead of yield.

One life for the many. Draven shot the thought to her, his mind racing. The notion echoed in his thoughts, a pragmatic solution to the dire situation.

"No." Lanae's voice was firm and her stance unyielding. She stood tall, her resolve like a beacon in the darkness.

Although Draven adored her for her principles and compassion, the mental lockdown she had placed on him kept him from taking matters into his own hands. The curse acted like invisible chains, his every instinct demanding action, yet he remained bound by her command. The moment bore down on him, the cool night air doing little to soothe the simmering frustration within.

CAELUM BLINKED AT THE sound of Draven's voice in Lanae's head, the mental link between his sister and the dragon carrying a strange sensation that reverberated through his own mind. The man's frustration blared through the link, a heated surge that made Caelum grit his teeth. He agreed with the dragon. If this asshat's death would awaken the masses, he'd put the bastard down himself.

He shook off Jenna and his mother, their worried hands falling away, and slid his sword out of its scabbard with a sharp, metallic hiss. The mass of the steel in his hand was familiar and comforting. "If you won't kill him, I will," he declared, his voice resolute and edged with anger.

"No, Caelum." Fire sputtered on Lanae's fingertips, tiny flames licking at the air as she put her hand out in a stop signal.

The fire on her fingers wasn't what stalled his breathing. It was the line of scales down her palm that made his eyes just about bug out of his head.

Lanae closed her hand, dousing the unusual flames as she traded a look with Draven.

Told you. Draven's voice filtered into her mind, and through the bond Caelum had with her. The sensation was peculiar, a whisper that seemed to brush against the edges of his thoughts.

"What in the..." Caelum started, his confusion evident.

Spric moved, and Draven shot out a plume of fire, the heat intense and scorching, melting the weapon he was reaching for. Burning metal and smoke filled the air.

"Draven," Lanae scolded, her voice sharp.

"I still have some will of my own," he grumbled, glaring at her. "Protecting you overrides the blood curse."

Caelum stared at them, his eyes moving from Lanae to Draven and back. "What blood curse?"

Instead of answering, Lanae's gaze dropped to the weeping wound on Caelum's side. Her brow knit together with concern, and her eyes darted to Nero. The pain from the wound throbbed dully, a reminder of his vulnerability.

"Why haven't you healed him?" she barked at the griffin, her voice sharp and urgent.

Nero squawked at her, the sound a mix of frustration and concern, and he stepped to Caelum's side. The griffin's feathers brushed against the wound, but Caelum did not experience the tingling relief he was used to with the griffin's healing power. Only a minor itch gripped the deepest part of his wound, then nothing.

Nero's gaze landed on Draven in a pointed gesture before returning to Lanae's.

She blinked, her eyes widening with realization. "I used it all on Draven?" she murmured, the words heavy with disbelief.

Nero nodded his head slowly, the seriousness of the situation reflected in his solemn gaze.

"The feather you took?" Caelum asked, then shook his head. "We can worry about that later. What we are going to do with this bastard, that's another story." He pointed his sword at the trembling man, the blade gleaming in the moonlight.

"Caelum," Lanae warned, her voice tense.

"He's the one responsible for beating you. Isn't he?" Caelum's anger flared, the thought of his sister's suffering fueling his rage.

Draven's murderous growl echoed in the air, stilling the remaining fighters. All eyes focused in their direction.

The fact the man at their feet wasn't ashes dug under Caelum's skin. He stared at his brother-in-law, his grip on the sword tightening. "She was black and blue and bloody when she got back. You didn't see the condition he left her in. I did." His voice was thick with emotion, the memory of Lanae's injuries cutting deep.

Draven's gaze shot to Lanae in a pleading way that sunk into Caelum, the silent communication between them a testament to their bond. And the conversation solidified into a horrible thought.

You're controlling him? He lobbed the accusation right into her head, the mental link allowing his anger and disbelief to resonate.

She winced and met his gaze in a fleeting look before she glanced at the ground. Shame colored her cheeks, a flush of pink against her pale skin. After witnessing a blood curse and seeing his parents in a catatonic state for years and then having them attempt to kill him with their own hands, Caelum could not abide by his sister's wishes.

"This is war, Lanae. And there will always be casualties." He swung his blade. It whistled through the air, but before it could connect, a lightning bolt hit the sword, shattering it.

Nero let out an ear-splitting cry, the sound piercing the night. Blinding light ripped from him, rolling over the entire city with blasts of lightning. Thunder rumbled overhead—a deep, resonant roar. Bodies dropped to the ground in awe and fear, their eyes wide with terror. The mind-controlled screamed as they held their heads, black smoke billowing from them. Dark magic fled from the white light of the righteous griffin's power.

LANAE GASPED WITH A sharp intake of breath, and she shielded her eyes from the blinding light. When the blast of brightness dissipated, her gaze fell on Nero. He swayed on his feet, his powerful legs trembling, and then his eyes rolled up into his head and he keeled over on his side. The thud of his body hitting the ground reverberated through the air.

"Nero!" Her scream shattered the night, a piercing cry of desperation and fear, and she raced to the griffin's side, her heart rapid-firing in her chest. Draven and Caelum followed close behind, their footsteps heavy and urgent.

With the bulk of everyone's attention on Nero, Spric sprinted toward freedom, his movements quick and desperate. The sight of him fleeing sent a jolt of panic through her, but she was too concerned with Nero to catch him.

Granger stepped into her line of sight and pulled his bow from his shoulder, nocking an arrow with swift precision.

Before she could intervene, Granger let the arrow fly, the twang of the bowstring and the whistle of the arrow slashing through the breeze. A split second before she could get a wall up to protect Spric, the arrow hit true, slicing through the enemy's heart. Even with the wails of the mind-controlled echoing around them, she heard the sickening sound of the arrow piercing Spric's skin, a dull thud that resonated in the silence.

Spric fell to the ground, his body crumpling lifelessly, as her fiery hedges surrounded him, the flames flickering and casting eerie shadows. The scent of burning foliage filled her nostrils, mingling with the metallic tang of blood.

CHAPTER TWENTY
Binding Flames

THE MOMENT SPRIC DIED, the cries over the city faded as the black magic coating their skin died with him. Draven cast a weary glance around the city, his eyes taking in the sight of people awakening from their suspended animation, their faces etched with confusion and relief. Burned magic permeated the air, lingering over the battle-ridden streets.

Draven reached down and placed his hand on Nero's chest, but only the cool, lifeless feathers radiated under his palm. There was no flutter of a heartbeat, no rise and fall of the beast's chest. The silence was deafening. He pressed his lips together, a tight line of grief, and stepped away, turning his back on Lanae and Caelum as they pleaded with the griffin to wake up. Their desperate voices cut through the night, but he couldn't bear to listen.

His bones tingled with the knowledge of their friend's death, a cold sensation that settled deep within him. The realization that it had been unnecessary, as unnecessary as wasting the griffin's precious healing powers on him, gnawed at him. He glanced toward the field, the memory of his fall vivid in his mind, and a strange noise escaped him, a mix of sorrow and frustration.

The speed of his descent, along with the height he had been falling from, was catastrophic. He should not be standing, much less breathing. That he was alive felt like an anomaly, and his faithful companion had paid the price. The weight of that knowledge was heavy on his heart.

Lanae's hand landed on his arm, her touch warm and grounding. There were too many ifs forming on his lips, too many questions and regrets, and he forced them all down with a swallow. He met her tear-filled gaze, the sadness in her eyes mirroring his own.

"I was dead in that field." The statement crackled with as much fire as the surrounding infernos...a raw, burning truth.

She looked at the field and then back at him. "Your wound was still bleeding." She ran her thumb along his arm in the spot where Alestain's blade had pierced his talon, the touch sending a shock through him. Her chin trembled, and she shrugged. "The bond still tingled when I touched you."

He looked away, unable to bear the confusion and pain in her gaze. "You should have let me end him."

She swung him back around to face her, her grip firm. "Nero did not want the stain of murder on any of our souls." Her whisper caressed him, a gentle balm to his aching heart. "This was not like Alestain or Xoltan. If we had executed Spric, it would have destroyed something good in us."

He closed his eyes, knowing she was right, but losing Nero hurt like a blade to the belly—a deep, twisting pain. "How's your brother?"

She glanced beyond him. "I think he'll be okay. Jenna's doting on him, and she has some experience with healing salves."

Lanae's mother stepped in front of him, her presence commanding. Her imposing figure seemed to cast a shadow over him, and the air grew cooler. The faint scent of lavender lingered in the space between them. Lanae got most of her looks from her mother, but there was a steel resolve in his wife that didn't seem to be in the woman before him.

"You're the dragon that the seer told us of?" her mother asked, her voice filled with awe and curiosity, her eyes piercing through him like daggers.

He gave a curt nod, not trusting his voice while his throat was plugged with emotion, making it difficult to speak. His heart battered his chest, the sound echoing in his ears like the drums of war.

"Mom, this is Draven, my husband." Lanae's voice carried a warm lilt meant to drive away the chill of the surrounding night.

Her mother's eyebrows shot up in surprise. "Your father just said you were fate bound to a dragon," she stammered, and her lips pulled back in a sneer. "Not that you would end up together. I knew we should have agreed to the deal with Xoltan Firetwill."

Lanae's features hardened and Draven's teeth bared at the sentiment. When he opened his mouth, Lanae hissed, "Don't."

His mouth shut in an audible snap and a low growl formed in his throat. He slashed a glare at Lanae.

Her eyes blazed with intensity, a fierce protectiveness that enveloped Draven. "How dare you even insinuate that Xoltan Firetwill would have made a better choice. Draven is my husband. And you, along with this entire city, can go straight to the underworld if you can't accept it."

The way her mother stumbled over words made his lips tilt up at the corners despite the sorrow laced through his form. "I'm not only her husband, but I am also the king of the dragons." He stared her down, tempted to make her bow to him.

CAELUM GOT TO HIS feet with Jenna's help and wiped the sorrow from his cheeks. The salt of his tears lingered on his skin, a bitter reminder of the grief that still churned in his chest. He crossed to where they stood, each step heavy with fury, and he glared at his mother, his vision tinged red.

"You really shouldn't have dropped that name here." He turned his fiery gaze to his sister. "And you should have let us take care of that thing," he growled, his voice rough like gravel as he pointed to Spric's body sprawled out on the ground with an arrow sticking out of his back.

"Your sister was right," Draven said, his tone calm and measured, a marked divergence to the storm raging inside Caelum. "That would have weighed on you and blackened a piece of your soul."

"Are you making him say that?" he shot at Lanae. His words sliced through the air like a blade.

"Caelum—" Lanae started, but Draven put up his hand, slicing her with a look that shut her up. The tension crackled in the air, palpable and suffocating.

"I still have a mind and a mouth of my own, despite the blood curse. So no, she didn't make me say that. As a matter of fact, I said the same damn thing to her a few minutes ago. But she pointed out that our surly griffin protected us in the only way he knew how. So, for us to not honor that sacrifice is blasphemy." Draven's words were like a hammer, each one pounding against Caelum's resolve, forcing him to confront the painful truth.

Caelum's chin quivered, and he clenched his jaw to stop the emotions from slamming into him like a tossed grenade. Grief threatened to consume him, each breath heavy and labored as he struggled to keep it at bay. He turned to his mother, who watched the interaction with a skeptical expression he remembered from his youth; her eyes narrowed, a flicker of disbelief in their depths.

"I'm sorry about Dad." The words tasted bitter on his tongue.

Draven shot a glance at Lanae, and his whispered question filled Caelum's head, the echo of it reverberating in his mind.

"He recognized me." Caelum's voice cracked, the sound raw and broken. The air thickened, each word catching in his throat. "And then pushed me out of the way of a killing blow." The memory of his father's sacrifice seared into his thoughts, a haunting image that lingered like a ghost, its presence chilling his spine.

He worked his throat through a sandy swallow and turned to Jenna. "This is Jenna, the girl I'm going to marry someday." His eyes met hers, seeing the flicker of surprise and hope dance in her gaze.

Jenna's hand fluttered over her mouth, her breath hitching. The subtle floral scent she carried wafted toward him, grounding him in the present.

"Jenna, this is my mother." Even though his voice carried disdain at the woman who slighted Draven, the introduction seemed to warm the chill that surrounded his mother, melting the icy demeanor as she smiled, greeting the fae with much more warmth and charm than she had Draven. The transformation in her demeanor was as more of a slight to Lanae than acceptance of the girl who made his heart ache.

Lanae took Draven's hand, leading him away as the rest of the Solstice City guards took control of the situation. Caelum hoped that whatever his sister had done to save her dragon wouldn't drive a wedge between her and Draven because he was rather fond of his brother-in-law.

Healing fae swarmed the grounds, offering their potions and patches to the wounded, Caelum included. And as his side knit with the help of magic, Jenna held his hand, unwilling to let go until long after the sun rose and most of the dead had been cleared away.

WHEN THE LAST OF the wounded were tended to and the only task left was removing the dead from the streets, Lanae turned to Draven. "Take me to the last place you truly felt at peace." Lanae's voice drifted over the silence between them, like a gentle caress in the cool night air.

His family home, before the disaster, was where he last found tranquility. The memory brought a pang of loss that tightened his chest. Draven turned to her, his gaze heavy with the past. "It no longer exists." He glanced around at the city that had been built on his family's ashes, the scent of smoke and charred wood still lingering in his mind. He muttered an incantation; the ancient words rolled out of his mouth in a whisper, and a portal opened. He pulled her through, the air crackling with residual magic.

They stepped into their bathroom, the warmth and familiarity of the space replacing the turmoil outside.

"But I can take you to the last place I truly experienced every ounce of your love." He pulled her to his lips and sampled her sweetness, the softness of her mouth against his filling him with a profound sense of belonging. "I am at your command until the day we die, and then I will serve you in the afterlife through eternity," he murmured, his voice a vow as he held her close.

Lanae pulled away, her eyes searching his. "As enticing as it sounds to have you at my beck and call, I like the side of you that challenges me and argues with me, and growls at me in aggravation. And even the one who goes against my wishes. I free you of this blood curse to obey."

A ripple of pure magic zipped through him, his skin tingling. He shook as the warm sensation left him, the bond's release like a weight lifting from his soul.

"Now strip," she commanded in a sultry tone that pumped all the blood to his nether regions.

"You first, my queen." He grinned even as the compulsion to tear his clothes off gripped him. But it had nothing to do with her command, and everything to do with wanting her skin against his.

Unfortunately, the universe wasn't ready for them to be free of strife just yet. A pounding at the front door reverberated through the entire house, each thud sending an irritated itch down Draven's spine. He dropped his head to Lanae's, their foreheads touching, and closed his eyes with a sigh. Her scent, a delicate blend of lavender and earth, mingled with the damp air around them.

"Maybe if we're quiet, they'll go away," Lanae whispered, her breath warm against his ear.

A sudden splintering sound echoed through the house, like a gunshot in the stillness, followed by the heavy thud of multiple footsteps in the hall. Draven's muscles tensed, and a growl ripped from his throat, raw and primal. The bathroom door creaked open, the harsh light from the hallway spilling in, and he locked eyes with the elite guard standing there, his glare cold and unyielding.

"You broke my front door?" Lanae snapped, crossing her arms with haughty defiance.

"You two are requested to appear in front of the council. Now." The guard's tone left no room for argument.

Draven ran his hand over his face. The rough stubble scraped against his palm as his mind balked at the order. The cool air of the bathroom contrasted with the warmth of Lanae's presence beside him. He just wanted to soak in a bath with his wife with no interruptions, letting the soothing water envelop them both.

"I just want a bath," Lanae whined, her voice carrying a note of desperation. "Can you at least give us that?"

Draven's lips tilted in a smirk. It was as if she were in his mind, sharing his exact thoughts.

But the guard was not moved by her plea at all. "Now." The guard's voice was cold and unyielding as he stepped inside the room, his heavy boots thudding against the tiled floor. He reached for Lanae's arm, his fingers nearly reaching her skin.

"If you lay a hand on my wife, I will turn you to dust." Draven's voice was low and menacing, each word dripping with a promise of retribution.

The guard's stern expression morphed into fear, his eyes widening as he pulled his hand back to rest on the pommel of his sword. His entire demeanor changed as he sensed the dangerous path he was walking, Draven's threat hanging heavily in the air.

"There will be time for a bath later," he said in a more conciliatory tone. "But the council said this was an urgent matter that could not wait."

"Fine." Lanae's frustration pulled her lips down into a scowl. She threaded her fingers through Draven's, the touch grounding him as they followed the guards out of the house. "Since you broke our door, can one of you stay to make sure we aren't robbed?" Lanae waved at the splintered front door, her glare sharp and unyielding as she cast it at the guards surrounding them.

They got a nod in return, the guard's helmet glinting in the morning light as one of them peeled off and stood at their doorstep, his posture rigid, guarding the house as Lanae requested. With the city in a state of chaos from the attack, it was a necessary precaution. Smoke clung to the air, blending with the distant cries of the wounded.

They marched in formation, with two in front of them and three behind. Their footsteps echoed off the cobblestone streets. The rhythm of the march seemed more oppressive than liberating. It reminded him of being led to a death sentence as opposed to an inquisition.

Especially after the last time he had appeared before the council, their chambers filled with the icy tension of judgment. Their prejudice of him as a dragon was as tangible as the smoke still settling on the streets. The scent of charred wood and ash clung to his clothes in a bitter testament to the recent destruction. Destruction he had a hand in rendering.

His view of the cityscape from street level was far different than it had been from the skies. From above, the city had looked like a sprawling network of lights and shadows, but down here, the harsh reality of destruction was impossible to ignore. A bank of buildings crumbling sent a shock wave through him, the ground beneath his feet trembling with the force of the collapse.

Those were the same ones that Alestain's magic had slammed him into, and the memory of impact flashed through his mind—the searing pain, the explosion of debris, and the sour tang of smoke filling his nostrils. His jaw dropped at the extent of damage his dragon form had caused, the jagged remains of once-proud structures now lying in ruins.

The Citadel stood unharmed in the center of the city, its imposing structure a stark contrast to the surrounding destruction. As they entered the building, the cool air within washed over them, and a symphony of voices rose in the distance, echoing off the high, vaulted ceilings. The higher they climbed, the more noise greeted them, a blend of anxious whispers and authoritative commands.

Draven's heart hammered against his ribs, each beat a relentless drum in his chest. Lanae's hand tightened around his, her grip grounding him as they stepped into the ornate council chambers. The room was filled to the brim with fae and other beings, their eyes glittering with curiosity and judgment.

Granger, the guard who had killed Spric and whom both he and Caelum had saved, stood in the center of the council room, his armor covered in battle gore. Silence settled around them like a heavy shroud, making Draven's ears ring from the abrupt absence of noise.

Granger cleared his throat, the sound resonating in the quiet space. "I haven't been back in Solstice City for more than a couple of weeks. I had been sent on a secret mission, one requested by Thalorian Nightshade, many years ago."

Draven's gaze landed on Lanae's, and he lifted his eyebrow in a silent question. She shrugged and looked back at Granger.

A rumble of whispering voices filled the room, and even Lanae's mother looked stunned.

"He sent me to find the last dragon. The one being capable of saving his daughter from the grips of pure evil." He glanced over his shoulder at Draven and Lanae. "Unfortunately, I couldn't find the dragon, but he certainly found Thalorian's daughter without my intervention."

"Thalorian never told me this," Lanae's mother snapped.

Granger stared her down. "Considering you were the one who begged him to make the original deal with Firetwill, he didn't think you'd condone my orders."

Her lips thinned as her dagger-like gaze moved to Draven's.

"If it pleases the court, I would like to introduce King Draven Emberwing." He waved at Draven and then dropped to his knee in a formal bow that Draven hadn't seen since his childhood.

The rustle of clothing filled the room as all the people at the floor level and in the stands surrounding the council followed Granger's lead.

Draven glanced at Lanae in stunned silence for a beat before he spoke, his voice steady despite the whirlwind of emotions. "And I would like to introduce my queen. Lanae Nightshade Emberwing." He nodded at her and brought her hand to his lips. Although he was still unsure what to think of the display, especially considering none of the council members took a knee, their gazes unwavering and filled with an air of superiority.

"Step forward," Faide demanded, his voice sharp and commanding, cutting through the tension-filled air.

Granger gave them a warm smile that should have calmed his racing heart, but it was not shared with the council running this city. Their gazes were sharp and condescending as they stared down their noses at him.

Draven and Lanae complied, their footsteps echoing against the polished marble floor as they moved toward the middle of the room. The cool, smooth surface beneath their feet contrasted with the heat of the countless eyes fixed upon them. The scrutiny of each council member's gaze scratched like a physical pressure against their skin, assessing and judging.

As they walked, the murmur of whispers from the onlookers filled the room, a low hum of curiosity and speculation. The ornate decorations of the council chamber, with its rich stories carved into the very walls, pressed in around them, giving them an acute sense of solemnity and foreboding. Draven's heart clanged in his chest, each beat resonating in his ears, while Lanae's grip on his hand tightened, her presence both a comfort and a reminder of their shared fate.

Movement to the side caught his attention as Lanae's mother took an empty council seat. Her gaze was unwavering and solemn, her eyes cold and distant, as if the council's judgment did not coincide with the crowd surrounding them. The shuffle of cloth filled the room as people rose, their robes rustling like whispers in the tense silence.

Granger moved behind Draven and Lanae, his presence a steady reassurance. Then the guard did the same, the clink of armor echoing in the quiet chamber. Draven caught sight of Caelum and Jenna joining the ranks behind them, their faces set with determination. The silent show made him wonder whether his time was up and this was an execution and not a coronation. A cold sweat broke out on the back of his neck.

Until he saw Varkir and Jairamon join the pack behind him, their familiar faces bringing a surge of hope. Then a few of the bartenders he regularly saw at Mystic Spirits stepped forward, their expressions resolute. And the girls from Lanae's women's group gave him an encouraging nod.

A shock wave ran through his body, the realization dawning on him. This was a show of solidarity. He blinked back at the scowling council, a newfound strength rising within him.

"Since the skirmish seems to be over, it is time to address your forbidden union." Faide's voice rose over the room, each word dripping with disdain and echoing off the high walls of the council chamber.

Draven unthreaded his hand from Lanae's and crossed his arms, the movement deliberate and defiant. "Your rules on what is allowed and not allowed are archaic." His voice resonated with strength.

"Nevertheless, they are our rules," Faide replied, his tone cold and unyielding.

"And yet you let the Undercity thrive?" Draven threw out the only other thing about the council rule that had burned in him, his eyes blazing with fury. "When dragons oversaw Solstice City, there was a fleeting black market presence. And now it's a haven for the perverse. Where are your rules in that scenario?" His words cut through the air, each syllable sharp and accusatory.

A few of the council members had the sense to look ashamed, their eyes dropping to the floor, their faces flushed with guilt.

"Yet you choose to enforce silly rules on the heart versus those that actually do harm," he continued, his voice rising with passion.

The crowd mumbled with approval, their voices a low rumble of agreement. The scent of sweat and anticipation filled the air, the room charged with the electricity of the moment.

"I do not condone this union with my daughter," Lanae's mother said, her voice cold and unyielding.

"You have no say in this union," Lanae retorted, her tone matching her mother's feral intensity. "You don't get to almost sell me off to a beast like Firetwill and then have a say at who truly holds my heart."

Draven's heart rocked at Lanae's words, a surge of protective anger rising within him. His dragon form simmered just beneath the surface, his muscles tensing as he fought to keep his composure.

Her mother recoiled, the shock evident in her eyes.

"You do not get to force my brother into that mind-control machine and then force me into chains in the bastard's bedroom and get to tell me who I can and cannot love," Lanae continued, her voice trembling with righteous fury.

Draven's jaw tightened, his gaze fixed on Lanae's mother. The memories of Lanae's suffering and the injustices she had endured flooded his mind, fueling his resolve. The council's glaring eyes bore into him, but all he cared about was standing by Lanae's side, supporting her in this moment of defiance.

A few of the council members shifted in their seats, the rustle of fabric and creak of wood filling the tense silence.

"We cannot condone this union," Faide repeated, his voice rising to the rafters, echoing off the high ceilings and reverberating through the chamber.

Caelum stepped forward with narrowed eyes, his gaze piercing. "Why not?"

"Because it is against our laws," Faide replied, his tone cold and authoritative.

"Fae laws, you mean," Draven snapped, his voice piercing through the air with razor-sharp precision. He looked around the building at the different species present in the room. Dwarves with their sturdy forms, their beards bristling with indignation. Elves with their ethereal light casting a soft glow around them. Gnomes with their small statures, their eyes glinting with curiosity. Goblins with their grotesque features contrasting with the elegance of the chamber. Trolls with deep-creased faces looked on with their ever-present scowls, while kobolds' magical potions clinked on their belts. Centaurs stood tall with their proud equine stature, and djinn displayed their intricate markings. Dream-traders, shifters, and even the ogres towering over all of them stood in the ranks. Their varied features and expressions were a testament to the city's diversity. The flickering light from the chandeliers cast shadows across their faces, highlighting the tension crackling in the room.

"Tell me, Faide and dear council members, since when did the fae dictate rules for all the species present in this room?" Draven's challenge was obvious. The murmur of the crowd grew louder as Draven's question resonated with those who had experienced the fae's authority. "Especially since no one other than fae has a seat on the very council that makes these arbitrary laws."

The murmuring of the crowd rose in a low rumble of discontent.

Faide's face turned bright red, his eyes blazing with fury. "I will not tolerate—" he began, his voice trembling with anger.

"Silence!" Draven's growling command shattered the room, the force of it sending racking quakes down everyone's spine. His eyes glowed with righteous flames, the heat of his anger intense. "I once told you I thought this council was doing okay by this city, and I had no intention of stepping in and declaring this a monarchy."

Hushed whispers filled the room, the tension dense enough to cut with a knife.

"However, my view of the council has changed drastically. Where were you when the masses had to defend this city from Firetwill's army?"

"We were here monitoring the battle," Faide said, his voice lacking conviction.

"Monitoring from the safety of your sacred halls?" Draven raised an eyebrow, his gaze piercing. "A good leader heads the charge. A good leader does not hide in wait for the results."

"And you think you are such a leader?" Lanae's mother snapped, her voice dripping with contempt.

"Oh hell no," Draven replied, his tone unwavering and his eyes blazing with conviction. "But your daughter fits that description. She fought for this city even when the council had turned on her. Me, I fought for Lanae, and I always will. I should not lead because I would raze the universe for her and for her alone."

He scanned the room, his gaze intense, before it landed on Lanae's mother. The emotions swirling within him were a turbulent storm— anger, love, and fierce determination. "I've bled for your daughter, and I would do it again in a heartbeat. I would lie down my life for her," he declared, his voice cracking with the sentiment. "But I will not relinquish my claim on her because of this council's asinine rules or your personal prejudices." His words reverberated through the chamber.

LANAE STARED AT DRAVEN as awe filled her, her eyes wide and shimmering with admiration. Her heart launched into the stratosphere at his adoring words, each one resonating deeply within her soul. The surrounding room seemed to fade into the background. The only thing grounding her was the fierce love she saw in Draven's eyes.

"Lanae once told me her dream was to see this society work together to rule. Where every species has a say in the laws created and enforced in this realm." Draven's words rang through the hall, prompting nods from the gathered crowd. "And if I have to claim this is a monarchy to allow that to happen, so be it," Draven continued, his voice unwavering.

"You do not have the authority—" Faide began, his tone dripping with disdain.

"I beg to differ." Varkir stepped forward and produced an ancient tome from his pocket. He slammed it down on the table next to Draven, the sound echoing like a thunderclap. "Many of you on the council recognize this book, yes?"

A few nodded in answer to his question, their faces pale. Faide was not one of them, his expression dark and unyielding.

"This is the original decree of Solstice City scribed by ancient seers," Varkir declared, his voice filled with reverence. "It states the line of authority in Solstice City. According to the decree, the authority of rule shall be bestowed upon the peacekeepers. They are as follows: the line of the first griffin, the line of the first druid, and lastly, the line of the first dragon."

Hushed whispers erupted around Lanae, the sound like leaves rustling in the wind. Validation swelled her heart with pride as she glanced at Draven.

"If fate has been unkind enough to eliminate these peacekeepers, then Solstice City must be ruled by a council representative of the species living under their protection." Varkir glanced at Draven and then at Lanae before looking back at the council, his gaze as judgmental as theirs.

"I don't see any other species sitting on the council. Do you?" Varkir asked Draven.

Draven smirked, the corners of his mouth lifting in a way that made Lanae's heart flutter. "No. I do not."

"And if I recall correctly, Emberwing is the line of the first dragon, is it not?" Varkir continued.

Draven slowly nodded, his eyes never leaving Lanae's. "Yes, it is."

"So, according to the original decree, this council has been operating against the laws of this realm?" Lanae raised an eyebrow, her voice steady despite the storm of emotions raging within her. Satisfaction surged as the council members squirmed, their authority crumbling in the face of the undeniable truth.

Draven cleared his throat, the sound echoing through the chamber. "It seems I have the ultimate authority, according to the original decree. As such, I dismantle the laws that define barriers around relationships. And I dismantle the council as it stands before us."

The room broke out in a roar of discourse, voices clashing like a storm.

Draven lifted his hand, the motion commanding attention, and silence settled after a minute, the air heavy with anticipation. "I was not finished. By this time next week, I expect to see a representative from each of your groups sitting in this chamber with us."

The council stared at the two of them as if they had sprouted multiple heads, their expressions a mix of shock and disbelief. "Wait just a minute," Faide started, his voice high and indignant.

"For what?" Draven's tone was sharp, the challenge clear.

"Arrest them." Faide waved at Draven and Lanae, his face contorted with rage.

Granger raised an eyebrow, his gaze steady. "I studied history, sir. Even I knew the council was skirting the very laws this city was built on." He pointedly gazed at each member, including Lanae's mother. "If you knew, shame on you. And if you didn't, then your unfamiliarity with our founding rules is worrisome. The only people the guard will be arresting are the ousted members sitting in the revered council seats."

"I think we're just about done here." Draven took Lanae's hand, the ember-like heat of his touch grounding her.

"I still did not give my permission for your marriage," Lanae's mother interjected, her voice tight with disapproval, slicing through the air like an icy blade.

Caelum stepped to Lanae's side, his presence a comforting warmth against her own chilled resolve. "I gave permission for them to marry." His voice rang through the chamber, echoing off the oak walls as his gaze pierced his mother's. The intensity of his words seemed to vibrate in her bones. "And according to the law, as the sole surviving male head of the household, my blessing stands." He glanced at Draven, a hint of a smile playing across his lips. "Besides, I couldn't ask for a better brother-in-law."

They left with the confrontation still thick in the room, but Lanae paused at the door. The scent of old parchment and the woodsy aroma of the Citadel filled her nostrils. "And if you ever wish to be welcomed back into my home, Mother, you'd better fix that attitude."

"It's my home," she stated with her chin jutted out, her eyes narrowing like a predator's.

"Not according to the paid-off deed. It's in our name and has been since the year after you disappeared," Caelum answered, his voice a mixture of finality and disdain. "But you're welcome to visit," he called out over his shoulder, the words hanging in the still air.

Silence fell over the room, thick and oppressive, broken only by the sounds of shuffling feet. As the entourage of support disbanded, Lanae's knotted stomach finally released, the tension draining away like sand through an hourglass.

The moment they stepped out of the Citadel, the cool breeze kissed Lanae's flushed cheeks, and the scent of earth and smoke filled her lungs.

Caelum turned to them, his expression softening. "I'm sorry about how our mother treated you, Draven."

"I'll get over it," he replied, but Lanae sensed his disappointment as acutely as her own, a shared ache in her chest.

"Since we are no longer just soldiers, I guess we should go visit the wounded and start planning what to do with the dead." Lanae scanned the battle-ridden streets surrounding them, the sights of scorched earth and fallen comrades searing into her memory.

Draven grumbled and gave her a burning look that told her exactly where he wanted to be, but he nodded anyway. "What did they do with Nero's body?" he asked Caelum.

"He's with the rest of the dead. They used the cavern you created on the training field for the bodies of our soldiers," Caelum said, his voice heavy with sorrow.

"And what of the enemy soldiers?" Lanae asked. Her heart beat like a rabbit's in her chest.

Both Caelum and Jenna grimaced. "The council ordered their heads put on spikes outside the city gates."

"Absolutely not," Draven growled, his eyes blazing with fury. His gaze moved to Granger. "If there are posts being erected, take them down and bring the bodies to the training field."

Warmth filled her at Draven's words. If he hadn't made the request, she would have. Most of the enemy soldiers were not fighting of their own volition. They should not be treated like true enemies of Solstice City. Spric was another matter, but even he did not deserve to be dismembered and displayed as a warning. "They will have their own burial plot in the fields, separate from our people, but honored nonetheless," Lanae added.

"Yes, Your Majesties." Granger bowed and instructed half a dozen soldiers to follow through on the request, their armor clinking as they moved.

Lanae blinked and watched as the guards marched away. "I don't know if I'll ever get used to being called Your Majesty."

Draven chuckled. "Likewise." He threaded her arm through his and leaned close. "I would have rather gone back to a bath." His eyes glimmered with the promise of what might have been before shuttering down with their current duty.

AS THEY DREW CLOSER to the field, a wave of scents and sights hit Draven with a force he had not prepared for. Instead of funeral pyres, they had a funeral pit full of dead bodies, lined with freshly cut flowers. The stench of death mingled with the cloying aromas of roses, lilacs, and lilies, along with an undertone of spiced oils. Each breath was a mix of sweetness and decay, a haunting signal of both life and death.

Family and friends of the dead gathered, their faces etched with grief and solemnity. The air, thick with mourning and sorrow, pressed its unrelenting burden on Draven's shoulders. As he and Lanae stopped near the head of the trench where Nero lay apart from the rest, the people surrounding them dropped to their knees in respect. Their armor scraping against the earth was like a collective sigh of reverence.

"Please. No kneeling. Not here where we should give the dead our respect rather than me." Draven's voice wavered as he spoke, the raw emotion thickening his throat. He dropped to his knee by Nero's form, his hand trembling as he ran it over the griffin's soft feathers. He plucked a handful of feathers and handed them to Lanae as keepsakes. A familiar and final connection to their loyal companion. "Thank you, my friend. I wish you well in the halls of the afterlife. We will see you again someday."

Draven's heart ached as he stepped back, allowing Lanae and Caelum to say their teary goodbyes. He watched as their faces contorted with grief, their tears mixing with the earth beneath them. The sight tore at his soul, the collective loss enveloping him.

He then moved the griffin into the funeral pit, the weight of Nero's body a physical manifestation of his own emotional burden. As he lowered the griffin into the grave, the mingling scents of flowers and death seemed to fill every part of him, a poignant token of the sacrifices made and the lives lost.

"May you all celebrate victory in the afterlife." Draven's voice rang out over the crowd.

The people responded with a roar, a cacophony of grief and pride that resonated deep within him. A pile of unlit torches sat to the side of a golden bowl of burning oil, their wooden handles rough against the fingers of those who reached for them. One by one, family members grabbed a piece of wood, lit it in the burning oil, and tossed it onto the bodies. The smell of burning wood mixed with the sweet and pungent aromas of flowers and spiced oils, creating a funeral blend that burdened the area.

As soon as the procession ended, Draven stepped close to the burning pit. The heat from the flames warmed his face, contrasting with the chill in his heart. He drowned his lungs with air, filling them with the bitter fumes of smoke and decay. With a powerful exhale, he blew a stream of white-hot flame from one side of the pit to the other, the intensity of the fire rendering the dead to ash almost instantly. The image of flames dancing in the night sky was both a tribute and a farewell, a final act of respect for the fallen.

He turned to Lanae, his eyes meeting hers in a moment of shared sorrow. "Fill it with earth." Emotion flooded his firm voice.

She opened her hands, and the piles of dirt at the edges of the pit responded to her command, rolling onto the ashes in a steady, purposeful motion. The sound of earth covering the remains was a quiet, somber accompaniment to the flames' crackling. The soil, freshly turned and now flat once again, signified not just an end, but a new beginning.

The poignancy of the moment weighed heavily on Draven's heart, signifying the start of a new era. One that he prayed would deliver every single one of Lanae's dreams.

EPILOGUE
The Promise of the Future

"I CAN'T BELIEVE YOU bought out Caelum." Lanae crossed her arms over her chest as she stood in the doorway of her brother's empty room. The air seemed different without Caelum's presence, a mixture of nostalgia and anticipation.

Draven was inside, the scent of freshly polished wood filling his nostrils as he situated a new desk in the space. He looked up at her with a lopsided grin, the light from the window catching the mischief in his eyes. "He said he and Jenna had their own place now, and we would need the space." He gave her a halfhearted shrug, his shoulders relaxing. "And I need a place to work here if you insist on staying in the guard."

Lanae's hand dropped to her protruding belly, the warmth of her growing child spreading a bloom of sweetness in her heart. "Are you sure that's the reason?" Her voice was soft, but the tease was evident.

His laugh echoed off the walls, a rich, comforting sound that filled the empty room. "Okay, maybe I was tired of having to be quiet any time things got heated with us." The room buzzed with their shared laughter, the echoes a promise of the joy and challenges to come.

"I saw my mother today."

The temperature dropped with Lanae's words. His smile faded, the memory of their last encounter still fresh and painful. They hadn't spoken more than a few harsh words since the battle, the tension between them as sharp as a blade. He wondered what vitriol she spewed this time; the thought filled him with dread.

"It seems she's reconsidered and would like to be a part of her grandchild's life." Lanae's voice was soft, almost tentative, the vulnerability in her tone tugging at his heart.

The room closed in around him as he processed her words. The scent of herbs from the garden wafted through the open window. Shadows wavered on the walls, cast by the unsteady light of the fireplace, mirroring the growing unease building in his chest.

Draven's jaw tightened, the muscles in his face working to contain the storm of emotions within. He glanced at Lanae, her eyes reflecting a mix of hope and trepidation. The sight of her, the gentle curve of her belly where their child grew, brought a warmth to his heart even as the news left him conflicted.

"What do you want?" he asked, but he already knew the answer. The hope flickering in her eyes was enough for him to put aside his reservations. Her gaze was soft, filled with a delicate blend of longing and determination that tugged at his heartstrings.

"I would like my mother to be a part of our family," Lanae said, her voice steady yet carrying an undercurrent of vulnerability. The air surrounding them pulsed with the implications of her words. "But I told her I would not tolerate any snideness toward you." She paused, the sincerity in her eyes making his resolve waver. "She agreed. It surprised me, but maybe after observing us on the council and heading up the restoration efforts, she thawed to the reality of us."

Draven's heart softened, the pressure in his chest easing as he looked into Lanae's hopeful eyes. "Then that is what we will do." He crossed the room, the wooden floor creaking softly under his weight, and took her in his arms. The heat of her body against his brought a sense of peace and determination.

"I want you to have every one of your dreams," he murmured, his breath warm against her ear. "And I once told you I'd turn the universe to ash for you. That includes torching my own reservations." Each word represented a promise etched in the space between them.

He sealed his statement with a kiss, his lips meeting hers in a tender, lingering embrace. The taste of her, sweet and familiar, filled him with a renewed sense of purpose that vibrated through him along with their electrical connection. The world outside faded away, leaving the two of them in a shared moment of tenderness and everlasting love.

The End

About J.E. Taylor

Reading books never felt so dangerous!

Explore a world of chilling suspense and fantasy with books that come alive as you read.

J.E. Taylor is a USA Today Bestselling Author, a publisher, an editor, a manuscript formatter, a mother, a wife, a grandmother, a retired business analyst, and a Supernatural fangirl. Not necessarily in that order.

She sat down to write her first book in February of 2007 after her daughter asked:

"Mom, if you could do anything, what would you do?"

From that moment on, she hasn't looked back.

She publishes supernatural suspense, urban fantasy, paranormal romance, and fantasy romance that isn't for the faint of heart.

You can find J.E. Taylor at the following places:

Website:

https://JETaylor75.com

Facebook reader group:
https://www.facebook.com/groups/jetcryptkeepers

LinkedIn:
https://www.linkedin.com/in/JTaylor8

Bookbub:
https://www.bookbub.com/authors/J-E-Taylor

Instagram:
https://www.instagram.com/JETaylor75/

TikTok:

https://www.tiktok.com/@JETaylor75

Twitter/X:

https://twitter.com/JETaylor75

Other stories by J.E. Taylor that have Dragons or Fae:

**A fallen Valkyrie. A Fae-Wraith hybrid.
Enemies become allies to survive a god's wrath.**

Odin's Order to reap an innocent soul from Earth makes me question everything I have ever known as a Valkyrie. Protecting the innocent is our basis for existing, and now I must decide. Do I blindly follow his order?

If I don't, I will be just another casualty in Odin and Thor's destruction of the realms. Anyone who challenges their rule dies a very public death, regardless of their origins. And now they have enslaved Earth.

Reyfyre, a fae-wraith hybrid, and one of Asgard's enemies, has been hiding in this realm his entire life. When he finds me, he offers asylum as long as I help him kill Odin and Thor.

With everything they have done, how can I refuse?

When a bounty is placed on my head, we make the decision to leave Reyfyre's mountain sanctuary and head to New York to get lost in the city of millions. But the trek across the Canadian wilderness brings us face to face with hidden refugees, predators, and thieves.

There's no other option but to survive.

If we die, then there will be no one left to stop the callous gods before they destroy the only realm left.

But are we strong enough to take down a god?

If you like dark twists on Norse Mythology, you will love the Fallen Valkyrie duet.

Monsters, trust issues, and a near death experience.
What else could go wrong?

The end of life as we knew it didn't come with a nuclear blast. It didn't come with the deadly impact of a hurdling asteroid. No. It came in a wave of illness that swept the world with fear, and in our quarantined silence, the monsters awoke.

Leviathans, serpent kings, and dragons came forth from the bowels of the Earth. The season of the dragon began with fire and fury and ended with a new world order. One in which these giant terrorists held all the power.

When Mikhail St. Clare betrays the monsters by saving me from death at their claws, I cannot trust the last remaining dragon shifter. Not when humankinds' survival is at stake, and he had a hand in our near extinction.

The only thing we seem to agree on is our desire to annihilate the leviathans and unseat the Serpent King. Our personal futures depend on ridding the earth of these murderous overlords.

We thought crossing the leviathan-patrolled city where every corner hides a hideous death was our most lethal hurdle. But building a bomb large enough to wipe out an entire species carries its own insane levels of danger.

One wrong move and we could destroy everyone living in New York instead.

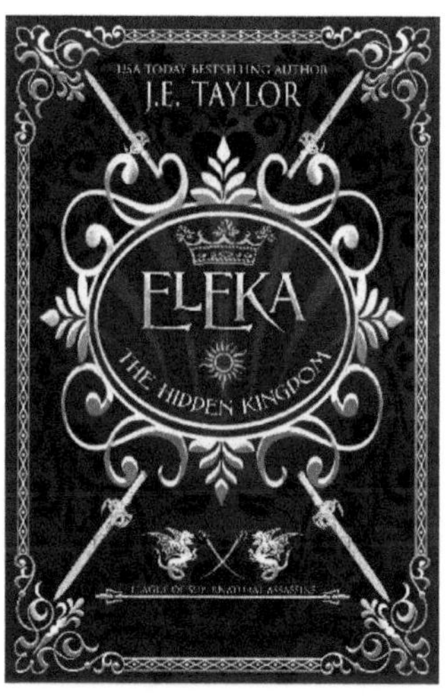

An assassin tasked with taking out a mythical fae king...
In a realm that doesn't exist...

Mya's mission is to get in, obtain the fae king's DNA, and get out.

It should be easy with her gifts, except when does anything ever go as planned?

When Mya doesn't return, the Director of the League of Supernatural Assassins sends an army of fae hybrid assassins to bring her back, alive or dead.

Avery's mission is to find Mya. If she fails, she faces certain death.

But confronting Mya may prove just as lethal.

ELEKA THE HIDDEN KINGDOM includes the following League of Supernatural Assassins titles: THE WITCH ASSASSIN and THE ELVREN ASSASSIN.

Will dragon's blood be enough to save the kingdom?

Long, long ago, a princess was born into the Kingdom of Light. She was said to be the most beautiful baby in all the world, and her tears turned into the morning dew. The king named her Aurora after the goddess of sunrise.

Royals came from far and wide to honor her birth, but one guest was not there to celebrate. When it was her turn to present a gift, the dragon queen offered something much darker. A curse that would claim Aurora on her twentieth birthday with the prick of a spinning wheel. Everyone in the kingdom, except King Henrick, would plummet into eternal darkness. Thus, the king would know the true meaning of loss.

Only three fae were left to bestow their gifts to the princess Aurora, and although they could not erase the dragon queen's curse, they could offer the kingdom a gift of hope.

Darkness would be banished with true love's kiss.

King Henrick hid Aurora with the fae in the middle of the kingdom's enchanted woodlands to keep her safe. But dragons are born of magic, too, and Aurora's hiding place was not far from the dragon's lair.

A Sleeping Beauty retelling with a little bite.

www.ingramcontent.com/pod-product-compliance
Lightning Source LLC
Chambersburg PA
CBHW040849010826
48978CB00013BA/944